# OPERATION
# CAVOLO

The Silent Codename Series Book Two

First Published by Mushroom Millie May Publishing

Copyright © 2024 by E.S.Benton

Cover Design and Typesetting by SpiffingCovers

First Published 2024
Paperback ISBN: 978-1-7392516-5-9
Hardback ISBN: 978-1-7392516-7-3
eBook ISBN 13: 978-1-7392516-6-6

# OPERATION

## The Silent Codename Series Book Two

# E.S.BENTON

# Also by E. S. Benton

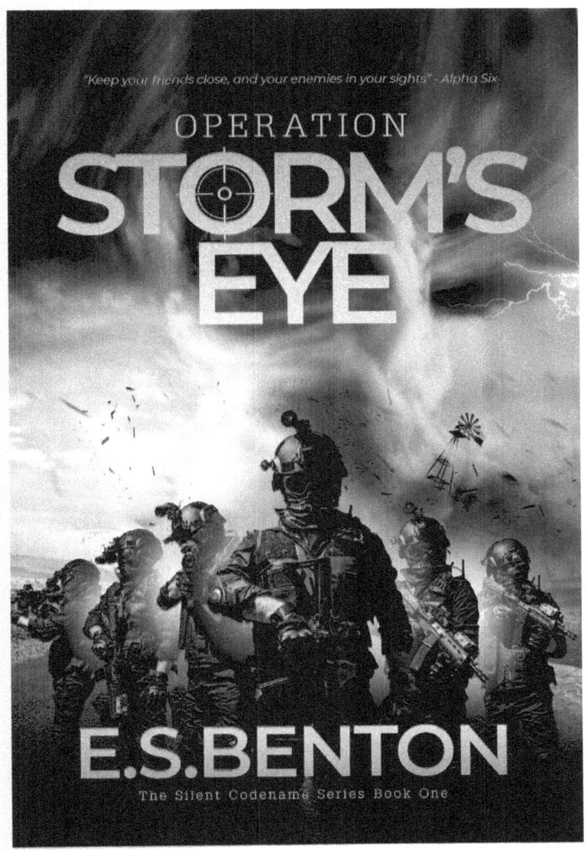

Operation Storm's Eye

**'Pulse-pounding sequences'**
*Independent Book Review*

# Acknowledgements

The acknowledgements page, the one most of you have probably already skipped past. But you're here, so I'm guessing you're hoping for a mention or if you're like me, you just like reading every page in book. And as with my first book, I'm not going to name names because the page count would probably double.

If you worked on making the story as close to word perfect as possible, if you helped to refine the story, if you gave me the guidance and knowledge to make every aspect better, if you created the incredible cover, or helped to promote and sell the book, I want to say the biggest thank you. I know many of you were paid, but even that isn't enough gratitude for what you deserve.

I also want to say thank you to you, even if you fall into the categories above, because you're taking the time to read this book, and let's be honest, that's why I do this, for people to read. I don't know whether you're in the tens, or the hundreds of people who brought this and are going to read it, but if just one of you likes this story, then I think I've been successful, so from the bottom of my heart, thank you for giving me a chance.

And now for the part that you've actually opened the book to read. So please settle down comfortably, turn the lights up high, and let this story take you on a journey...

# Contents


Prologue – The Start of the Feud ........................................... 11

Chapter 1 – The Cover of the Night ........................................ 19

Chapter 2 – The Memory of the Past ........................................ 32

Chapter 3 – The Hand of the Beast ........................................ 44

Chapter 4 – The Pit of the Viper ........................................ 57

Chapter 5 – The Tale of the Shadows ........................................ 75

Chapter 6 – The Life of the Lie ........................................ 87

Chapter 7 – The Enemy of the Enemy ........................................ 107

Chapter 8 – The Clouding of the Truth ........................................ 117

Chapter 9 – The Vault of the Vault ........................................ 129

Chapter 10 – The Price of the Deed ........................................ 171

Chapter 11 – The Conflict of the Lies ........................................ 199

Chapter 12 – The Test of the Elite ........................................ 224

Chapter 13 – The Biting of the Past ........................................ 253

Chapter 14 – The Deceit of the Deceptive ........................................ 278

Chapter 15 – The Cost of the Cure ........................................ 290

Epilogue – The Echo of the Beginning ........................................ 323

# Prologue – The Start of the Feud



In the back of an old, rusty van, Captain Frederick 'Kale' Bridge addressed his men.

"Our employer has given us the target. He wants maximum destruction, no witnesses. Anything that moves is considered hostile. Let's keep the villagers alive until we've found our target. They can all witness just how helpless he is against us. The intel given to me puts our target's location at the very centre of the village. We'll exit the van on the outskirts and move in. Expect light resistance. Any questions?"

His English accent somehow demanded respect itself. The only noise that followed was the checking of their rifles' magazines and the tightening of their bulletproof vests. The van ground to a halt, its worn brakes working twice as hard. The rear doors swung open, crashing against either side of the van, and eight operatives climbed out.

All eight of them, and the driver, slowly approached the village in a casual manner, expecting no contact. Their boots squelched in the wet mud, as they saw villagers scrambling ahead. Once at the first of the houses, made from a combination of materials found in the surrounding woods, Kale's men started to break away from the group. Only one operative entered a building, that was all that was needed. They each entered and cleared the buildings, firing their rifles wherever necessary. If any screams were to be heard, they didn't last long. Kale strolled down the middle of the muddy path, stroking his thick, brown beard, as he watched the villagers frantically run into their homes. His tactical gear covered most of his body, including his head, but his emerald green eyes and young, wrinkle-free face was exposed to the clean air. His sleeves were also pulled up to his elbows, showing a tattoo of lion on his right wrist. The rest of his men preferred to keep their masks on to conceal their faces, but Kale knew there was no need for that.

Out of the corner of his eye, he saw an approaching villager. With a long, raised stick, the villager charged forwards. With a single motion, Kale dodged to the right and raised the stock of his rifle. The stock dug itself into the villager's ribs, disarming him and throwing him to the floor. Kale stared down at the villager. His stare was met, not with fear, but with blind hatred. Kale stomped his black, leather boot down on the villager's left hand. The pain wasn't softened by the mud but was heightened by the rough grips under Kale's boot. The villager groaned, as it felt like the blood in his hand had turned to molten lava.

"Where is he!" shouted Kale, as he aimed his rifle at the villager's head. "Where is he!" he persisted even louder.

The villager continued to groan but made it clear he wasn't going to talk. Kale temporarily shifted all his weight to his right foot, before placing his left on the villager's chest, precisely where the rifle's stock had made contact.

"I've been told that you understand me. So, for the final time, where is he?" The villager mustered all his strength to spit on Kale's left boot. With a smile, Kale took his knife from his tactical vest and said, "Your silence is admirable, but unfortunately, it isn't smart. I will ensure this knife finds your chest after you watch your entire village burn to the ground."

Kale made the threat clear, before releasing his grip on the villager. He ran away, clutching his hand, and disappeared amongst the trees. He'd be back, Kale was sure of that much, and when he was, Kale would show him what it truly meant to be loyal.

Kale continued through the centre of the village with a sense of arrogance, as he continued to watch the villagers run and hide.

"Captain! I've got someone who says he knows where the target is," said one of his men in a bright red scarf, escorting a villager by his hair.

The villager seemed quite young, with only a thin beard and moustache. He was tall and skinny, and clearly in pain where he'd been escorted by his hair. Kale signalled for him to be released and took the villager a few paces away. With his arm around the villager's shoulder, Kale acted almost compassionately.

"Now, tell me. Where is the man I'm after?" asked Kale in a calm voice.

"Tell your men to stop," replied the villager, trying to bargain.

With an exaggerated smile, Kale said, "That's not how this works. Give me a location and no physical harm will come to you." Kale squeezed the villager's shoulders a little tighter. Moments of silence followed, until Kale lost all patience. He pushed the villager to the ground and trained his rifle on him. "Last chance."

"In the blue building on the far side," said the villager, as he closed his eyes and covered his face.

"Good..." started Kale, as he picked the villager up off the floor and started brushing him down, "Now, why didn't you say that to start with?" Kale held his hand up and gestured for the man to go. "As per our agreement, you are free to leave."

The villager ran for an opening in the trees and didn't stop until he was out of sight.

"Listen up, men. We've got our location. Blue building, far end. There will be time to clear up later, so for now leave the villagers. It's not like they're going anywhere. Once we have him, then you can round the rest up," announced Kale over their comms, as he headed to the other side of the village, regrouping with his men as he went.

It didn't take long for them to walk the short distance to the lonely, blue building, not in the centre but on the far side of the village. The nine operatives surrounded the building.

"You know why we've come. The bloodshed can still be avoided," said Kale, loud enough to be heard easily in the building.

A breaching charge was placed on the front door. With a single nod from Kale, several flash-bangs were thrown into the building, through the windows, and the door was blown off its thin, wooden surrounds. All eight of his men entered, whilst he waited outside.

"Clear!" shouted one of his men.

"Clear!" echoed another.

"Clear!" repeated a third.

"No sign of the target. The building's empty," said a fourth.

His men exited the building, empty-handed, and regrouped with Kale. His fists were tightly clenched, and the muscles in his cheeks stuck out further than before. He was ready to turn his wrath on the village, when he heard a twig snap from his right. The others heard it as well, putting them all on edge. Seconds later, the trees and bushes rustled violently, as tens of armed assailants emerged from the forest. Kale instantly knew there were too many to take on, and so did his men. Kale would rather die than be captured, but he knew no prison could hold him, and it would be nothing more than a temporary setback. With even more of them approaching from behind, they all laid their weapons down, confident there was no evidence to their crimes. Unfortunately for them, it wasn't a law-abiding group of operatives.

*** 

*Sixteen Months Later*

Kale was pleased with his men. Pleased with how strong they were, facing a certain, painful death. Every day, the same person would be taken away. Their screams would echo throughout the underground chamber. If he'd had his wits about him, Kale would realise it was always the same scream, like a recording playing on repeat, but he didn't. He didn't know how long he'd been there. The guards changed over at irregular times, the sun was nowhere to be seen, and the food was served only once a day, usually when he was most tired. He was allowed an hour's exercise each day, the only thing he was sure of, which was strange for someone who would surely never make it out again. A fabric bag remained over his head, as it did every minute of every day. Kale wasn't even sure his eyes still worked properly, given all this time looking through the thin fabric, but he didn't need to use his eyes. There was a dripping noise about seven metres to his left. It dripped at different intervals on different days, making it likely connected to the rain. If that was the case, it rained most days. The temperature and humidity were intense. Kale heard no sign of rats, which was unusual for a place that was surely full of half-dead corpses. Directly above him was a light, one of the few things visible through the bag. Its power supply was weak and cut out every time one of his men was taken to be electrocuted, seemingly putting him somewhere with a limited power supply. Although he couldn't be sure, Kale had to go on the assumption they were amongst a rainforest, meaning it would be futile to escape, sealing his fate. If he was going to survive, he would have to take down every guard there, which is what he wanted to do but was in no fit state to do so.

There was a soaking wet piece of fabric, somehow strung to the ceiling. It hung so it was always in contact with his face, separated only by the bag. It didn't matter where he moved his head, the wet cloth was always able to follow him, always resting against his face. He wasn't sure whether his men had the same, but what he did know was no matter how many days it sat against his face, it was still as frustrating as the first. It almost felt like the cloth had more power than he did, touching his face and keeping him subdued.

The plastic cable ties had slowly eaten away at his wrists, being too tight to move in. Although, what he found the worst wasn't his lack of vision, or his wrists that felt like they'd been stung by a thousand hornets. It was the smell, the smell of death. However long he'd been there, the smell of rotten flesh went unchanged. Even after all this time, when he'd become immune to most of the horrors down there, the smell remained as sickening as the first time he'd been forced to enter. It always seemed too strong to be real. Kale hadn't detected any signs of other prisoners, but that same smell had lingered for all the months he'd been there. Every day, when the same member of his team was dragged away, the others could do nothing but listen, and when they stopped screaming, the next one was taken. During their torture, he heard the same question asked over and over again, always by the same person. "What do you know of Fellscient?" Rarely did the torturer wait for an answer. Yesterday, Captain Frederick 'Kale' Bridge's final man failed to return. Now, it was his turn.

Two sets of footsteps approached. His hands were unbound with a single cut from a blade, a sound Kale remembered all too well. To his surprise, and anguish, the bag was torn away from his head. His eyes instinctively closed, as the burning light shone in. Although the dungeon had a dingy light to it, to him it was like looking at the sun. He was dragged along the damp, concrete floor, his legs unable to keep up with their pace. Even with his eyes still clamped shut, he counted the paces. Two paces forwards, right turn, fifteen paces forwards, left turn, and then three paces forwards. He was thrown into another chair, where his wrists were fastened with giant, steel restraints built into the chair. Kale's eyes started to open, trying to adjust to the new light. It was even brighter where he now was and he could just about make out the long cables, one end out of sight and the other connected to the metal chair.

"What do you know about Fellscient?" asked one of the two guards.

For the first time, it was a different person asking the question. Before Kale could think about it anymore, the ground began to shake. The guards shared an uneasy glance at one another, before swiftly heading further down the corridor. An explosion followed shortly after, and then two bullets were fired. Slowly, four armed figures emerged from the left, their attention quickly drawn to Kale. Two of them approached, whilst the others stood guard. They were all dressed in black with full face masks. If he could have, he would've fought them off.

"Are you Captain Frederick Bridge?" asked one of them.

Kale wasn't sure whether he was actually nodding his head or not, but speech seemed impossible. They released the restraints and helped him to his feet.

"Can you walk?" asked the same one.

Again, he nodded as much as he could. They escorted him out, supporting his weight as they went. Before long, he saw daylight. They had come to rescue him.

***

*Ten Years Later*

Kale was standing on a small, metal mezzanine clutching a photograph. He looked down to the photo; it was a picture of him and his team.

"I will make this right," he said, before slowly placing the photo into his back pocket.

He was dressed in a white coat and wore a blue hairnet. It helped him blend in perfectly with the other factory staff. His white coat helped to obscure the scars which painted his body. His once young face, now full of creases and wrinkles, held a tired expression. The thick, brown beard had turned grey and wiry. He was stood next to a large container, full of a cream-coloured liquid. After checking his surroundings for a final time, Kale removed a large vial, sealed with a bung, from under his white factory coat. He pulled the bung out, so it separated from the vial, and tipped its contents into the container. A small amount of red liquid sat on top of the cream-coloured one for a moment, before slowly disappearing under the surface and dispersing itself throughout. Kale put the bung back in the vial, placed it back under his coat, and left the factory. His revenge was in motion.

# Chapter 1 – The Cover of the Night
9th September
21:38 BST

The air was warm and thick, making it hard to take a deep breath, in the midst of the night. A dark blue van came around the corner to an almost sudden stop, as it bounced up the steep kerb, before the side door flung open. Alpha One stepped out, immediately swinging the door closed again, before walking towards an unlit alleyway. He was smartly dressed in a bright red suit, with polished black shoes, and a crisp black shirt. He walked with purpose into the shadows, allowing the van to pull away and move to its next destination. Less than a minute later, Alpha One emerged from the darkness and approached a well-lit building which stretched fourteen stories into the sky. He filled his lungs as best he could with the thick, gloopy air, unfastened the button on his jacket, and leapt up the small set of steps outside.

He could see the entrance had five guards, all oblivious to his presence, a mistake they wouldn't make again. Alpha One removed a suppressed handgun from his inside jacket pocket and pushed the heavy, glass door blocking his path. The guard sat behind the pale oak desk was the first to look towards the door. All he had time to see was a silencer pointing at his head before he slumped forwards on to the desk. The next four were all huddled in a group next to a water machine. They slowly turned to see nothing more than a flash of red, before everything went black.

Without breaking stride, Alpha One continued through the reception area and towards the lifts, at the back of a twenty-metre-long and five-metre-wide corridor.

Alpha One strode through the metal detector, setting off the piercing alarm, alerting everyone in the corridor to his presence. He raised his handgun and opened fire. Each bullet left the chamber of his gun and found its mark. Once the following six bullets were ejected from the gun, he moved behind the closest concrete pillar and replaced the clip as if it was second nature, ensuring one bullet remained in the chamber throughout, just in case.

He stayed low and swung his body around the pillar, taking out more and more of the guards. As Alpha One continued to push forwards, the guards continued to fall back. Some got cut off from the rest and resorted to leaping out from cover, trying to gain the element of surprise, but it never worked. Alpha One fired first, aware of his surroundings and where they had all hidden. Soon, the guards had nowhere left to run, as their backs were pressed firmly against the lifts at the back of the corridor. They were desperate, which is when Alpha One was most cautious. He counted nine guards left, before moving behind another concrete pillar. He knew there were still ten bullets in his handgun and, thanks to his photographic memory, remembered where each one stood. After removing one of only two flash grenades from under his jacket, he pulled the pin out and threw it towards the remaining guards. A couple of seconds later, a loud bang echoed throughout the corridor. Alpha One moved out to see all nine guards staggering around, holding their ears, with their eyes clamped shut. After firing the next nine bullets, Alpha One reloaded and headed into one of the six lifts.

Inside was clean and bright, almost sterile, with all-white walls. Everything inside was polished and glistened under the glare of the square light above. Alpha One pressed the circular metal button labelled '12', the highest button available. After gently pushing one of the guards' heads out of the way with his foot, the doors slid closed, hiding the line of bodies covering the floor.

***

*One Minute Earlier*

The dark blue van screeched around the corner of the tiny car park and stopped in front of a side door. This time, the driver's door opened, allowing Alpha Five to climb out and enter the same building from the side door. He was dressed in an all-black tactical suit, with harnesses, straps, and pockets covering most of the outside, and a rucksack on his back. He was short, skinny, and walked with an upright posture. Every part of his face seemed perfect and unbroken, and he constantly had a smug smile, as if he knew how he looked. With one forceful kick, the door came free of its hinges and tiny bolt lock. One guard was stood to the side of the door, who hopelessly threw their fist towards Alpha Five. With little force behind it, he had no difficulty stopping the guard's arm and returning a right hook. The guard stumbled back on to an old metal chair, flattening it as they collapsed to the floor. Alpha Five drew his handgun and fired a single shot at the guard's head, leaving a thick, green smudge on impact. Another guard started to climb out from under the door, but as Alpha Five walked over it, they were pinned down, unable to move. Before they could get out, Alpha Five fired another bullet, hitting the next guard in the same place, rendering them both motionless with the same green gel.

Without a single glance at the guards, Alpha Five started moving up the staircase, next to the now open doorway. He began leaping up four steps at a time, as he started his journey to the twelfth floor. The further up he got, the less steps he took at once. By the time he got to the eighth floor, he was hoping for some contact to give his legs a little rest, as no amount of training could stop the burning blood course through his veins. On the tenth floor, his hopes were met, as two guards came bursting out of the tenth-floor door. The first one crashed into Alpha Five, who immediately lowered his centre of mass to allow the guard to flip over him. As the guard tumbled over his body, he also headed over the railings of the stairs. Without a thought, Alpha Five grabbed the guard's trousers and braced himself against the railings as he tightened his grip.

"Drop him!" shouted the other guard, looking as if it was the first time he'd pulled his gun in defence, with trembling, sweaty hands.

"Seriously?" replied Alpha Five, straining to hold the weight of the guard, dangling ten floors above a concrete demise.

"No! No, don't drop me!" shouted the first guard, panic-stricken.

"Alright, don't drop him. Lift him back up!" shouted the armed guard at full volume, adrenaline coursing through his body.

"I can't, I'll need some help," said Alpha Five, as his face started to go red. The guard didn't know what to do, as he remained standing, clutching his handgun.

"Just do as he says!" bellowed the other guard, prompted by Alpha Five suddenly lowering his grip, moving him inches closer to death. The trembling guard did as he was told and grabbed the other leg.

"Okay, now brace yourself," said Alpha Five, as he slowly relieved himself of the weight.

After just a couple of seconds, he was free of the guard's weight and started moving around, stretching his arms and legs.

"That feels better," he added.

The inexperienced guard continued to hold the other one's trouser leg, whilst Alpha Five removed his sidearm and radio and let them drop to the bottom of the staircase, panicking the guard even more.

"Alright, I'll see you both later," he said, as he continued to move up the stairs, leaving them both, almost motionless.

On reaching the twelfth floor, without further distractions, he slowly opened the heavy fire door and headed through into an empty room on his right. With the lights turned off, and the tallest building opposite blocking most of the light from the city which surrounded them, the room was dark, which Alpha Five was keen to maintain. He removed his rucksack and emptied its contents. One of the items now in front of him was a laser cutter, which he immediately used to cut a hole in one of the windows. As he cut through, all he could hear outside his room was a lot of crashing, banging, and commotion, but that meant the guards would leave him alone.

***

*Four Minutes Earlier*

As the lift started its ascent to the twelfth floor, there was no jolt, and no force trying to push him down. It was only the lights of the floor buttons and the ominous 'BONG' sound which indicated movement, as each button lit up, while the sound echoed throughout the lift as it reached each corresponding floor.

"Okay, now remember floor twelve has a 'no guns' policy because of the gas pipes running parallel and adjacent to the floor. Your bullets should not be an issue, but because they have no guns, they will be in very close quarters, and you might find it hard to aim your handgun before being overrun," said VOICE.

He was in the back of the blue van, outside the building. He was rarely this close to them on a mission in the six months he'd worked with them, but for him to shut down the surveillance systems, all except those he was using, he had to be within metres of the building. Alpha One returned his handgun back inside his jacket.

"Don't worry, I'll give them a fighting chance. Anyway, I've always been one to follow the rules," said Alpha One.

He watched as the light slowly crept up the button numbers. Ten, *'BONG'*… Eleven, *'BONG'*… Twelve, *'BONG'*… After a couple of tense, and silent, seconds of waiting, after the twelve 'BONGs' had rung out, the doors opened. Before Alpha One could brace himself, four guards charged into the lift, forcing him against the back wall. Prior to any more getting in, the doors closed. His main focus, however, was to stay on his feet.

***

From outside the lift, the next group of guards waited for their turn. The noise coming from the lift was more like that of a caged animal, fighting to break out. There were groans of pain and moans of exhaustion, as the ruckus went on for well over a minute. Then, something banged against the door, again and again, as it started to bend and buckle under whatever pounding force was being used. Eventually, the cries of pain started to subside, as the guards outside became more cautious of the approaching silence. With an innocent *'ping'*, the doors opened and a figure in a red suit and bloodstained black shirt strolled out, leaving a pile of bodies on the floor behind him.

***

As Alpha One stepped out of the lift, he straightened his jacket, adjusted his tie, and watched as the guards stood ready for someone to make the first move. There were a dozen of them poised to attack, and if they attacked together, they probably could've got the upper hand, but they didn't. All it took was for one guard to lunge forwards to get them all moving. Alpha One grabbed the closest guard around the neck and swung them into the pristine white wall to his right. He then tightened his fist and threw it towards the next guard, their momentum causing them to do a backflip before landing, face down, on the floor. As the guards continued to approach, he used everything at his disposal. His arms and legs blocked multiple failed blows, allowing his fists and feet to provide their own counter-attacks. With more and more guards blocking his path, Alpha One's approach was slow, but as he came round the corner, a familiar cleaner was just ahead.

***

Alpha Three had entered the building a few hours prior. His cover was that of the cleaner, and after changing into the uniform, he had to maintain his cover until Alpha One made entry. His big, muscular arms were bursting out of the uniform, and, although only 6' tall, it was a surprise he passed as the cleaner and wasn't reassigned to security. He was left-handed, but given the number of weapons favouring right-handed people, he'd trained to use both left and right-handed weapons freely. With earphones in, playing loud music, he was getting slightly carried away with his cover, as he remained oblivious to the brawl behind him. There were batons, caps, fire extinguishers, and guards flying in all directions, but as Alpha Three swung his mop from side to side on the floor, he seemed focussed on nothing but humming to the only thing in his ear.

***

"What is he doing!" shouted Alpha One, as he continued to fend off the guards.

"Well, I don't think he can hear you," replied VOICE.

"You think!" grunted Alpha One, cracking his head into one of the guards'. As the number of guards approaching Alpha One started to reduce, he was able to edge closer to Alpha Three. With a few more right hooks and a couple of kicks capable of breaching doors, he eventually closed the gap to his oblivious teammate. Alpha One grabbed the final guard by his collar, lifted him up, and threw him on the floor. In the guard's daze, Alpha One was able to wrap his hands around his throat and squeeze until the guard had stopped wriggling. He stood up, straightened his jacket again, pulled the bottom of his trouser legs down, where they had risen above his ankles, and touched Alpha Three on the shoulder. Immediately, Alpha Three swung his mop around at shoulder height. With equally quick reactions, Alpha One ducked down, allowing the mop to pass overhead, as he made eye contact with Alpha Three, showing him that he wasn't a threat.

"You're early?" questioned a confused Alpha Three, as he looked at the trail of bodies down the corridor.

"We had to bring the breach forwards half an hour because a helicopter is arriving to pick the target up in around fifteen minutes. I know you weren't able to enter with your comms device turned on, but I had hoped you would turn it on after you entered."

"I might have forgotten that bit," replied Alpha Three, innocently, in his mixture of a New York and South London accent.

"I also thought you would be a little more observant," said Alpha One, as he leant against the nearest wall, catching his breath with deep, heavy gasps of air.

"You had better keep moving. We do not want to miss him," said VOICE.

"How about next time, I'll sit in the van and pass useless comments to you," Alpha One replied, as he headed towards the staircase at the end of the corridor. Alpha Three shrugged off his mistake, as he stepped between the bodies and proceeded to the stairs.

Two floors up, Alpha One drew his handgun, and retrieved a second, which was fastened down the back of his red trousers, and passed it to Alpha Three. With a shared single nod, Alpha One kicked the door in with a single blow, and Alpha Three flowed through first, with his gun held up. The room was dark and appeared to span the entire floor, like an office with a glass wall separating each working space. Reflections bounced from glass panel to glass panel, but they weren't fazed, as they continued to move through, the two handguns covering all directions. Their plan was simple, they needed to make it to the central zone, where they had cover from the collection of desks, machinery, and other appliances, each one capable of redirecting a bullet or two. As they moved towards the centre, they counted the guards hiding in the shadows. They were clearly waiting until they could surround the two intruders, but unfortunately, this was precisely what Alpha One was relying on. The clothes they were wearing were made from Kevlar, and whilst they would protect them, it wouldn't stop the pain, so as soon as they reached the central zone, they ensured they made the first move.

Remembering where the guards had positioned themselves, Alpha One and Three opened fire. Glass shattered and bodies dropped, as they took out as many guards as possible before they could move. Only a few moments passed until they had return fire to deal with. As they sat in the centre, bullets flew from all directions, embedding themselves in everything around. Bullets punctured water dispensers, causing water to spew out of the many holes. Coffee percolators were shattered, sending cold coffee all over Alpha Three, with large shards of glass raining down. They continued firing, taking cover, reloading, and then repeating. They had taken a few bullets, but nothing that could affect their ability to clear the room. After minutes of raging gunfire, there was finally a noticeable decline in the noise. Alpha One and Three continued to keep the pressure on, ensuring the time spent in cover was as low as possible. Alpha One spent a quarter of his time throwing fresh magazines to Alpha Three when he'd expended all his bullets. Eventually, the final guard dropped, rendering the room silent. Glass covered the floor, along with coffee, water, pieces of paper, and computers, covered in bullet holes. Alpha One finally broke the silence, as he moved forwards, with glass crunching and cracking under his shoes. They maintained a sense of caution, as they proceeded to the end of the aisle.

***

Around the corner, John Broady cowered behind the few guards he had left. As the crunching of the glass got closer and closer, the guards held their ground and gripped their handguns even tighter in their sweaty palms. Suddenly, a small metal canister rolled around the corner and down the short stretch of remaining corridor. Before John could even recognise it as a flash-bang, it exploded. He wasn't sure how long had passed, but he couldn't see and had a piercing ringing in his ears. As his vision slowly cleared, he could see his guards fall one by one. As he looked down the corridor, he could see a cleaner and a menacing figure in red approaching. Without hesitation, John turned and ran up the metal staircase behind him, his feet clanging with each step. He pushed the fire door open and took a final glance behind, seeing all his guards lying on the floor.

"Seal the door!" he screamed, as he passed another two guards.

John was on the roof, cornered, with only a few guards left to protect him. He caught sight of his helicopter approaching from the horizon, and a sense of hope rushed over him, but that hope was to be short-lived. A lot closer than the helicopter were two people approaching the roof by parachute.

As John shouted, "Kill them!" in desperation, one of his guards fell, followed by another, and then another. While he spun round, he watched his clueless guards drop to the floor, as the fire door burst open. With no one left to protect him, he started to lower his head and curl up towards the red figure. As the two with parachutes landed behind, the red figure grabbed him by his jumper and heaved him over to the side of the roof.

"Confess!" yelled the figure, before shaking John. "Confess to your crimes!" the figure growled.

John couldn't speak, as he lost the feeling in his legs. Suddenly, he was thrown forwards and found himself hanging over the edge, held up by the figure alone.

"Last chance!" he bellowed.

John just about managed to form some words, as he replied, "I did it, I did it all!" in a timid and shaken voice. "I stole the money and hid it in an offshore account under my daughter's name. You can have, you can it all if you just let me go!"

"Okay." Then, without warning, the figure released his grip and John started to fall. He swung his arms in all directions, but he was already too far away to grab anything. The last thing he remembered was heading towards the concrete floor, fifteen stories down.

****

The others watched as their target fell out of sight. A nervous moment passed, before they were all reassured by a familiar voice.

"I have the target," said Alpha Five, three floors down, in his well-spoken, but not posh, voice, as he hung out of the cut-out in the window he'd made earlier.

"Is the target okay?" asked Alpha One, as Alpha Two and Four deterred the incoming helicopter with a few well-placed, standard bullets.

"Yeah, the target's fine. He's fainted, but he's alive… and he's urinated a little… No, scratch that, he's completely wet through," answered Alpha Five.

"Well, that's going to make the van smell," added Alpha Three.

"Were the bullets any better?" asked Alpha Four.

He had a muscular face, big, bushy hair, and surprisingly bright, green eyes. His Southampton accent mostly hid his past of having one Belgian parent, and despite his average build and 6' height, he was the one who carried all their equipment, acting more as the backpack guy.

"The bullets were definitely an improvement, and glass doesn't stop them any more," replied Alpha One.

Last year, they'd been using real bullets, but Suzy had developed a new kind, one capable of rendering anyone it hit unconscious, by releasing a green gel. The gel was formed from the strongest sedative, still unknown to society, and could keep a victim unconscious for over a day, but their biggest problem had come from trying to shoot through objects, as they tended to release the soporific drug on contact. Whilst most bullets could now shoot through minimal armour, their handguns still couldn't quite pack enough punch to get through.

Leaning over the side, Alpha One saw a flurry of blue flashing lights down on the ground.

"The police have arrived," said VOICE, who'd moved the van a few minutes earlier.

"Thanks, and good job on sealing me in the lift. It gave me a fighting chance."

"Er… I did no such thing. It must have been a coincidence," replied VOICE.

"If you say so," said Alpha One. "Alright, Alpha Five, bring the target to the roof, we'll strap him to Alpha Three for the jump."

Wanting to object, Alpha Three was about to speak up but was immediately silenced by one single glare from Alpha One.

"We're even for me not helping you on floor twelve then," agreed Alpha Three, as they both started to put parachutes on, brought by Alpha Four.

Just one minute later, the target was secured to Alpha Three, and they were all ready to jump.

"Blindspot, we'll meet you at exfil site A," concluded Alpha One, as they started leaping from the building.

"A?" questioned Alpha Three.

"Yes, A."

"No, it was a joke. I was saying it like, 'Aye'," replied Alpha Three.

"Oh, I see," said Alpha One.

"You could've laughed."

"No, I'm really not sure I could have, actually," concluded Alpha One.

"Copy," said the sniper on the opposite building, ignoring the joke altogether.

Alpha One was the last to jump. He took a couple of steps' run-up and pushed off from his right foot, propelling himself away from the building. Almost instantly, he pulled the cord, and his parachute deployed. Whilst the building they had just left wasn't particularly tall, it was still the second tallest in the city. So, as they floated through the air, the view in front and below was that of a city packed into the smallest possible space, with nothing left empty. The lights shone in all directions, from vehicle headlights, to illuminated rooms, keeping them hidden against the dark sky above. On the outskirts of the city, they all landed in the same place, on the roof of a building identical to those around it. They wrapped their parachutes up and stayed prone on the roof. Whilst time wasn't on their side, they had to be patient and wait until they'd regrouped before they could complete their extraction plan, no matter how long it took.

# Chapter 2 – The Memory of the Past

10<sup>th</sup> September
01:27 BST

It might've taken another three hours of staying entirely focussed and vigilant, but eventually, they were at their exfil site. It was a small, unused runway with a single hangar. A large business jet had already parked on the runway, waiting for them to arrive. The runway itself looked overgrown and out of condition, with lumps of tarmac either loose or completely missing. Hard to see, there was a light coating of coarse, golden sand covering much of the tarmac. The jet was black and polished, its pristine paintwork glistening against the city's lights in the distance. It looked out of place on the run-down runway, but as few people knew of its existence, it made for the perfect hiding place. Two 4x4s pulled up close to the plane, one grey and the other a dark red. All six members of Alpha team jumped out, dragging their still unconscious target with them. The two drivers, who were local enforcement officers, and who weren't impartial when the odd bribe was offered, swiftly left the runway to return to their normal lives.

As Alpha One approached the jet's steps, he turned to see the hangar. It looked in a similar state to the runway, as it leant to one side, with a couple of roof panels missing and half-rotten, wooden beams holding what was left of it up. It would take nothing more than a strong gust of wind for it to be like the hangar never even existed. He noticed the runway was short. It was fine landing, and with nothing but dead grass surrounding the area, it didn't seem too dangerous, but thinking about taking off, or more specifically, crashing, was something he'd only recently taken more thought over. To say he panicked about flying was an exaggeration; it was more that he no longer took the safety for granted. Alpha One headed inside and took his seat next to the left wing. Inside, the jet screamed luxury and style, with a white interior, only single, cushioned seats, and plenty of room to both stand and walk past each other. The comfortable, padded seats reclined but were so far apart that there was no concern about anyone lying back on your lap. Each chair had a privacy screen built into it, allowing it to be completely separated from everyone else. Each one also had a vast array of additional, and rarely used, features, including heating and cooling elements, retractable tables, a freezer compartment with an ice bucket, and even speakers built into the headrests. Whilst their jet looked like a standard business model, it was far more advanced. It could fly at a much higher altitude, much faster, and completely unseen to even the best radar systems.

The door sealed shut and they made their way to the very end of the runway, feeling none of the imperfections in the tarmac.

The engines roared as the jet reached take-off speed before the grass, lifting itself up to glide into the sky. Alpha One fixed his gaze out of the window as they continued to climb, making the once enormous building they were on, look tiny and insignificant in the distance. Before long, they were away from the city and amongst the clouds. The jet rocked and shook, as the pilots plotted a course through the thinnest parts of the dense layer of clouds. It felt like they were driving down an unmade road in an old sedan, with no suspension and a racing driver at the wheel.

Eventually, they emerged from the clouds, where the sight was both beautiful and boring. Nothing could be seen, except the tranquil, dark blue sandwiched between the grey clouds and the endless sight of the universe. He continued to stare out of the window, as few things changed on the infinite horizon. Eventually, Alpha One, Scott, tried to sleep, but as he watched the thin stream of water vapour pour over the jet's left wing, he found it hard to think of anything other than what had got them to that moment. He thought about his life working as a spy with Daniel, Alpha Two. They'd worked on different floors but still knew each other. When Bosse, their new boss, had approached him about starting up a secret organisation, secret even to the other secret agencies, which is some secret, and when Daniel's family was killed in a car crash, Bosse had made sure the world thought Daniel had gone with his parents, making him the perfect candidate to join the organisation. The others joined shortly after and, before long, they'd trained enough people, all from non-military lives, to make every other agency look insignificant. Each member came from a perfectly normal and standard life, to an extent, but when it became convenient, they were all extracted, in some way or another, and, to the rest of the world, they disappeared. With new lives and extensive training, they'd become part of a highly skilled organisation.

Their only goal was to protect people, keep them safe, but then things changed. A group called M.N.G.W.A. were their new targets. They'd had a lead and sent Echo team in to put a stop to them, but after hitting a dead end, a storm struck and took down their plane as they returned home.

Alpha One lowered his head, as he gave things more thought. He wished that was where it had ended. A group called Fellscient had hired M.N.G.W.A. and an elite security team, the Night Vipers, to do their dirty work, whilst they worked towards their true endgame: a weapon capable of creating any natural disaster. Alpha team succeeded in taking down the weapon, but at a great cost. Many lives were lost, and their one chance of finding the head of

Fellscient was decapitated by Blindspot, whose call sign was still Alpha Six. He had no orders to do so and even less reason. 'I made a promise,' were the only words to leave Blindspot's lips after the event. He'd spent months, going through various tests, both mental and physical, and they gave no indication of Blindspot being a risk to the team, but what the promise was, and who he made it to, remained unanswered. Blindspot, Anthony, had never opened up about that moment, nor had he dwelled on his actions, but the thin, 6'3" Londoner had never shown anything but loyalty in the past.

That wasn't Alpha One's only concern, however. He'd also found out that Alpha Five had hidden his hitman past, with the help of Bosse.

It had been a tough six months for all of them, but with no leads on M.N.G.W.A. or Fellscient, they were glad to get back to just stopping one-off criminals that no government could touch.

***

Alpha One wasn't sure when he fell asleep, nor whether he'd recapped the past half a year in his dreams or consciously, but as the plane touched down at their own secret airfield, he was suddenly awoken.

"Nice of you to actually wake up. I was talking to you for about half an hour before Daniel told me you were asleep," said Samuel, Alpha Three, as he stood up.

Samuel was in his late twenties and, despite being born in the UK, had grown up in New York. He had blond, curly hair, and a very big build, but his most distinctive feature was his pair of amber eyes.

"Really? Now, I am surprised," replied Scott, in the most sarcastic tone he could muster.

He caught Daniel with a smirk out of the corner of his eye. It was likely the Londoner, who'd recently turned forty, had known Scott was asleep long before letting on. Whilst he had a London accent, he was able to put on a whole host of different accents, and could speak many different languages, much like Scott. Daniel was 5'11", with black hair, big, thick eyebrows, a round head, and brown eyes; he really did look just like someone capable of fitting in anywhere.

The jet was manoeuvred into the largest hangar on the runway and the doors sealed shut behind it. Their jet was scanned by hundreds of tiny cameras, capable of providing standard, thermal, and infrared images, used to create a 3D scan of the hangar and its contents, ensuring nothing was inside that shouldn't be. Once clear, the floor was lowered by thirty metres and opened into a giant, underground compound. It contained every vehicle, for land, water, and sky, that was deemed to be of 'any good' by their engineer, Suzy, as well as vehicles they'd designed and built themselves. The hangar was the size of an international airport, with the ceiling stretching out of reach of even the tallest vehicles. There was an orange glow and a strong smell of both petrol and diesel fumes, despite being well ventilated. The concrete covering every wall was mainly hidden by the vast array of vehicles, detracting from the fact they were thirty metres underground. Their jet was towed into its parking bay, and they all left to go to their separate stations.

As Scott jogged down the steps, he was met by Bosse. It was unusual for the sixty-year-old to be in the hangar at all, so Scott knew it must be serious. Bosse made eye contact with Scott, before turning and walking in the opposite direction, not saying a word. Scott didn't need to be told, as he followed the smartly dressed man, in his dark blue pinstriped suit. Due to his shorter legs, Bosse could only take tiny strides, so Scott always tended to walk at a slower pace when around him. Bosse approached a set of large double doors and raised his arms to push them. He slightly concertinaed up, as the weight of the door seemed a little bit of a struggle for him to shift. His somewhat chunky arms and pot belly eventually pushed the door open. Behind the blast-proof doors, the atmosphere completely changed. The flooring turned from cold concrete to a warm and slightly spongy, light grey floor. There were natural-coloured lights along the ceiling, and plants around every corner, creating a comfortable light and fresh air, giving the impression they weren't under metres of reinforced concrete and tungsten. Bosse led the way through turn after turn of their hidden base, the Molehill, until they finally reached his office.

Once inside, Bosse took his seat, whilst Scott shut the door.

"How did the mission go?" asked Bosse with his husky, French accent.

"Well, we got the target, so I'd say it was a success. The police had arrived before the clean-up crew got in, but that's what we expected. The guards will wake from the sedative in our bullets by this evening… probably. Alpha Four and Blindspot are escorting the target to the holding cells as we speak," replied Scott, as he poured himself a large, neat whisky from one of the numerous spirits in Bosse's private drinks cabinet.

"Please, help yourself to a drink. And I do wish you wouldn't all call him Blindspot, he is Alpha Six, that is all," added Bosse, as he frowned at the large measure Scott had poured, who merely smiled and raised his glass.

"Well, you'd better get used to it. We'll all have a name like that one day…" He took a large gulp of the drink, doing nothing to stay quiet, just to irritate Bosse further. "Anyway, I take it we didn't come all this way just to discuss our last mission, that's not really your style."

"You are quite correct. In fact, there are two reasons you are here. We have a new mission to be getting on with…" started Bosse, as he began typing on his slim laptop in front of him.

"Who's this one for? Another rich person? Or someone that actually needs our help?" asked Scott, aware he was interrupting.

"This is one of our own..." started Bosse, clearly gaining Scott's attention as he turned away from the fake window displaying a very realistic image of London's business district. Although the people in the image were small, they moved, creating a full, twenty-four hour time-lapse taken from one of the many office blocks. "In recent weeks, people have been suddenly admitted to hospital with the same poison found in their system. All of them have just one thing in common..." He then turned his laptop around to display an image of a factory. "They have all consumed food which originated from this factory. All food lines have since been recalled but the poison in the victims' systems seems incurable."

"I heard about it on the news, but where do we come in?" asked Scott, slightly confused.

"Well, we received this message yesterday," answered Bosse, as he handed over a letter. Scott unfolded it and read it to himself.

*Dear Alpha Team, as I'm sure you're aware, I have poisoned various food products which have been ingested by various, unfortunate people. I'm sure you're also aware that no cure exists. However, I am pleased to say, that is not the case; an antidote does indeed exist. All you have to do is find it... before those poor victims die. By my, accurate calculations, the first person will die on the 13th of September at 20:13, so you best not waste any time. Assuming I am correct, which I know I am, you have exactly eighty-four hours from the time you are reading this. I look forward to meeting you, face to face this time.*

*Yours sincerely, Kale.*

"And you decided to engage me in small talk," exclaimed Scott, as he finished his drink and grabbed the file on Bosse's desk, titled *Operation Cavolo*. With a quick glance at the clock on the wall, displaying 08:13, Scott began to flick through the file.

"I felt I'd break the ice a little. All the information I have given you is in that file. I did, however, notice the name of the sender was Kale, and I recalled you mentioning Crabble talking about a Kale within Fellscient, before Alpha Six blew Crabble's head off that is. So, I decided to approach Heartfell in the hope he could help… I assume you recall Heartfell was the engineer who aided us in destroying that ghastly machine capable of creating natural disasters?"

Scott knew the question was rhetorical but humoured him nevertheless with a small head nod.

"And he did help. Whilst Heartfell worked on Operation Storm, and Kale had nothing to do with it, he does remember there being a gentleman they worked with, who just so happens to own the factory in question. Apparently, he supplied the food to some of their bases and hideouts. May I suggest Delta team tails him, as I believe that will be your only lead," concluded Bosse. He turned his laptop back to face him and looked down at his screen, making it perfectly clear he had nothing more to say.

"I thought there were two reasons you brought me here?" questioned Scott, as he started to review the file.

"Oh yes, I almost forgot…" began Bosse, raising his head with a smile. "Your newest recruit is ready."

"She passed the tests?" enquired Scott, with a little excitement in his voice.

"With flying colours. Head down to your offices and you can meet Alpha Seven," he said, again planting his head in his laptop.

Hastily, Scott headed down to their offices. He moved as quickly as walking would take him, with a slight jog breaking out every few paces. Inside their office space was much like the rest of the compound, with natural-coloured lights in the ceiling and plants dotted around the room. The walls were painted a cream colour and the floor remained the spongy, grey material. There were six desks in the room, all with three computer screens, a keyboard, a separate laptop, and various pieces of paper, neatly stacked on some desks and randomly thrown on others. Opposite, there was a separate, smaller room with an all-glass wall which was Scott's office. He turned to his right to see the twenty-seven-year-old stand up from the black, office-style swivel chair. She had chestnut brown hair, tied back in a ponytail, and matching soft, brown eyes.

"Sorry about getting straight to the point, but welcome to Alpha team, Mia," said Scott.

There was no need to introduce themselves, or to the rest of the team, as they'd met many times before. Mia was the latest candidate to join Alpha team, and after unofficially recruiting her, she'd spent the past few months in high-intensity training, ensuring she was the best she could be, part of which was training with Alpha team themselves.

"I haven't exactly had a typical job interview," she replied with her calm, concise voice. Mia had a friendly personality but wasn't one to push herself into anyone's conversations, as she stood with her hands clasped in front of her, waiting for instructions.

"Usually, we don't go straight in with an active mission, but I'm afraid we'll have to make an exception. There'll be a meeting in the... meeting room, but as you know, you won't have a seat until a few... conditions, have been met. It'll make some of the others jealous if you get a seat on your first day, but I see no reason why you can't attend," said Scott, as he directed her out of their offices.

"May I ask just one question?" enquired Mia. Scott nodded, giving clear permission to continue. "Well, I just wondered if everyone had joined the same way as me."

Scott smiled, answering, "No, actually. You see, Bosse and I found you and felt you would make the perfect seventh member of Alpha team. Once we approached you, and you obviously accepted our proposal, we merely made it look like you vanished from the face of the planet. The same was true of many of our members, but some joined after slightly more…" Scott paused for a moment, trying to find the perfect word, "final occurrences. It isn't really my place to tell you their stories, but let's just say it was convenient to recruit them when we did."

They walked the rest of the way in silence, Mia a couple of paces behind Scott.

They entered the meeting room to find everyone already in their seats. There was a very large, oval table in the centre of the room, with the whole of Alpha team, four of the twelve members of Bravo team, two members of Charlie team, and all six of Delta team. There were three empty chairs, once occupied by three quarters of Echo team, as well as Bosse and VOICE in the centre.

"Sorry to have kept you…" began Scott, as he moved around and stood behind his seat. "As you all know, this is Mia. I'm pleased to say she has passed all the tests and will be in the field as Alpha Seven with immediate effect. I know you're also aware of the reason behind her appointment. Mia will act as a medic, as well as an agent. That's mainly why she had to train with all four teams because if any of us head out for a mission where a medic would be useful, Mia will accompany you. Obviously aside from that, she'll fulfil her role as Alpha Seven…"

"We have not actually been formally introduced…" interrupted VOICE. Scott merely held his hand towards Mia and gestured for VOICE to continue. "My name is VOICE. I was not given that name at birth but chose it later because I am the 'Very Overly Intelligent Computer Expert'. The voice in your ear, if you will," he continued, breaking out into laughter. He was 5'10", although he would say he was 6' tall, and always wore an oversized T-shirt, which was loose and baggy against his extremely skinny build. He had unkempt, brown hair hanging to his shoulders and always smelt of mint.

"It's very nice to meet you, VOICE..." said Mia politely. "I'm Mia and... well, Alpha One has already filled you in on my place in the team."

"You don't have to call me Alpha One outside of missions. Scott is fine," whispered Scott with a smile, as they waited for VOICE's solitary laugh to subside.

As VOICE's laughter died down slowly, Mia took in her surroundings. There were several enormous computer screens on the wall behind Bosse. They were all powered off, with reflective black screens. Over in one corner was a water machine, which stood alone. The rest of the concrete room was mainly filled with plain walls and empty spaces, being the only room with no indoor plants; it was built for practicality, not pleasure. Mia didn't realise it straight away, but VOICE had finally finished, hiding his yellowing teeth, allowing Scott to continue.

"Whilst it was nice for you all to hear Mia is now one of us, that wasn't why you were brought here..." Scott started, as everyone's gaze started to shift towards Charlie Two.

She'd been shot only six months prior, during a fight with one of the Night Viper's officers, Gold Viper. Carol was lucky to be alive, and she knew it. She was in her mid thirties, around 5'9", and had long, straight, browny blond-coloured hair.

"Carol has decided to take a few deserved months away from the Molehill. Charles will be going with her to ensure she doesn't get into any trouble..." After only a few moments thought, he corrected himself, "Actually, I think it'll be Carol keeping Charles out of trouble..."

A little laughter filled the room, as Charles and Carol shared a surprisingly intimate glance at one another. Her smile had certainly got the attention of the enormously built Charles. Everything about him was big and muscular. Even his deep, gruff voice was strong and imposing.

"This does mean Charlie team will be without either of their leaders and, as such, will be temporarily stepping back into their 'ordinary' lives until they are assigned to Operation Smash and Grab. So, Carol and Charles, I think everyone will join me in wishing you a relaxing break," continued Scott. The room broke out in applause and cheers, as if the best man had just finished his speech.

Charles raised himself from his seat and grabbed a stick, propped up against the wall, to hand to Carol.

"Are you sure you don't mind?" asked Carol, as she took hold of the stick to stand up.

"Of course not. Doc says you've fully healed, physically, so you might as well take some time now. You just need to make sure everything is healed, yeah?" said Scott, double-checking Carol knew why she was taking time off.

"Yeah, I'll be right as rain. I might even break it to Charles that I don't need this stick any more, but he thinks he's helping."

"You should be back by the end of the year, and we haven't got much more than admin to do here, so I see no issues, just break the stick thing to him gently," concluded Scott, causing Carol to give a little smirk. Both Charles and Carol left the room. As the doors sealed shut, once again making the inside soundproof, Alpha One readdressed the room, saying, "So... admin might not be the only thing we have."

# Chapter 3 – The Hand of the Beast
10<sup>th</sup> September
12:03 BST
80 hrs 10 min. Until Deadline

Sat on an oak brown bench, to the side of a path which snaked through an enormous park, Delta One was reading a newspaper. She sat there, with her blue contact lenses and long, blond wig obscured by that day's paper. She was relatively short, at 5'2" and was in her early thirties, but beyond that, no part of her disguise was truly 'her'. The park was warm that time of year and most of the people making use of it were either trying to find the faint traces of a breeze or were making the most of a beautifully sunny day. The rare rustling of the fading, greeny-brown leaves gave hope to those hiding in the shade. The grass was brown in a few patches but was still thoroughly enjoyed by the children rolling on it, laughing as they went about without a worry in the world. There were a couple of people strolling past without tops on, trying to allow their bright, white bodies to catch up to their tanned arms.

To Delta One's left was a couple pushing a child around in a pushchair. They couldn't have been much older than their mid twenties and were smiling at each other as they walked, their hands clasped together. By one of the many trees, which lined the park's footpath, a couple of men had started to shout at one another. It had attracted attention from most of those in the park and had become a potential problem.

"This is Delta One. There's a disturbance eleven o'clock of my position. It could complicate things," said Delta One, barely moving her lips. Some of her words had missing letters, such as the 'm' in 'my', resulting in an 'eye' sound, ensuring her lips moved as little as possible.

"Copy, this is Delta Four, I have eyes on the disturbance eleven o'clock of your position," he said, watching through his scope from the top of a nearby building.

The argument quickly escalated as one of the men turned violent, throwing weak punches towards the other. Light hit after light hit, the other man eventually got tired of the fight and threw one single punch, making contact with the other's jaw. He went down instantly, falling to the floor.

"Well, that's embarrassing," muttered Delta Four.

"Eyes on the prize. The cat has entered the park," said Delta Five.

Their radio went silent, as they all waited for their target to approach. It didn't take long before he passed Delta One. He was dressed in a tailored, black suit with a hard briefcase tightly clenched in his right hand. He was walking with purpose as he passed the bench, with Delta Five shortly behind. Suddenly, the target turned and pointed his long face and short black hair in Delta Five's direction. Without a second thought, Delta Five continued on his path as if he was just walking by; dressed in a plain white T-shirt and blue jeans, he blended in with the other passers-by. He got to within a couple of metres of the target and stopped. He removed his phone from inside his jeans' right pocket. Swiping his phone's screen, he put it to his ear, still under heavy surveillance from their motionless target.

"Hello… What do you mean? No, I know that… Yeah, I'm sure… No, it's n… No… Alright, I'll be there in five minutes… Well, that's as quick as I can arrive… Yeah. Yeah, I'll see you there," said Delta Five before pretending to end the fake call.

With his head shaking in annoyance, Delta Five sent a quick, fake text message, turned around, and left the park. The target seemed to buy the act and continued on his way.

"Sorry about that, but I couldn't be sure he hadn't made me. I'll get changed and head to point eleven," said Delta Five, as Delta One rose to her feet to continue tailing the target.

She tucked the newspaper under her arm and walked behind him, at a slightly quicker pace. Holding her coffee cup in front and taking the occasional sip of the lukewarm drink, it didn't take long before she'd overtaken their target. He seemed very on edge, turning around every few paces, so Delta team knew they couldn't push their luck. Making eye contact was never something they did, unless approached by the target themselves. Delta One continued with her pace. The target might have been observant, but someone that he was following was above suspicion. As soon as Delta One built a lead of around ten paces, she retrieved a pair of sunglasses from inside her handbag, opened the temples, and placed the temple handles over her ears. The glass changed direction about a quarter of the way in, so it showed the reflection from a different direction. At the right angle, Delta One was able to see behind her and could observe the target, almost as if her sunglasses had wing mirrors. She had to be careful when walking, especially at her pace, because it was unsurprisingly difficult to see behind and in front at the same time. With Delta One watching the target with her sunglasses and Delta Four watching from the top of a building, the target was under ample surveillance.

Before long, they reached the end of the park. Unsure whether the target would turn left or right when outside the park, Delta One walked through the open gateway and turned left. Immediately after turning, Delta Two walked past in her black, leather jacket with matching trousers and long, jet-black hair, covering the right-hand turn.

"Target is heading… Right, I repeat target has gone right," said Delta Four before leaving the top of the building with the target now out of sight.

Delta Two's leather jacket was covered in metal studs, some of which on the back of her jacket had built-in, hidden cameras. She stared down at her phone, much like most of the surrounding people, following each other along the thin pavement, like ants following a trail of sugar. Her phone had already accessed the cameras and locked on to their target the moment he left the park. Without a second set of eyes, it was imperative that Delta Two kept him in sight. He followed her, unbeknownst to him, down the full stretch of pavement which ran in front of the tallest buildings around.

"Where is he going?" asked Delta Three, who was watching from the next potential direction change. She was in gym wear, given the location she waited at was outside the gym. As soon as Delta Two walked past, still on her phone, Delta Three emerged from around the corner and pressed the only button at the Toucan Crossing. The cars were stopped, a buzzer sound, and a small, friendly, green man waved her across. However, it was when the buzzer went silent, and the green man turned to an angry, red one that the target quickly hopped into the road and crossed, following Delta Three. She didn't have anything to watch the target with, so slowed down and allowed him to pass. Maintaining her pace, the target slowly stretched his lead but was not at all suspicious of Delta Three. Before long, they were at the next potential direction change. Delta Six was walking in the opposite direction to the other two and turned to her left, going down a road on the target's right. The target didn't follow, he merely continued on his way.

"That makes you the only one he hasn't followed. I'm sure it's nothing personal," said Delta Five.

"Coming from the only person who got made," replied Delta Six dryly.

"I'm coming up behind you, ready to take over," said Delta Four, silencing the conversation as he approached Delta Three. She peeled off down a narrow alley, so the same face wasn't always following. Delta Four followed him a little further, until the target entered a café. Some of its seats were on the pavement, but the target went straight inside.

Delta Four walked past, informing the others.

"He's stopped at a café. He's inside sitting on the table third from the back, far left-hand side. The café's called… *The Café*. How inventive."

Once Delta Four moved away, Delta Six returned. She was dressed as if she was on her way to Ascot, with a white dress and an oversized hat. She took a seat on one of the street-side tables, removed her sunglasses, and sat in an upright posture, waiting to be served.

A waiter approached. "What can I get for you?"

"A double espresso," replied Delta Six with a half-hearted smile. Whilst she was facing the road, as most of the tables and chairs were, and couldn't see the target, she was nearby to react to any sudden emergency. She then removed her phone and placed it on the table, with the bottom roughly facing the target.

"Clockwise about half an hour," said Delta Two who was now in a car opposite the café. Her car was facing away from the café, but both the side mirrors and the rear-view mirror gave a clear picture of the target. Delta Six slowly twisted the phone clockwise by about fifteen degrees.

"Anticlockwise a touch," added Delta Two.

"As specific as ever," mumbled Delta Six, barely making a sound or moving her lips. She slowly twisted the phone anticlockwise.

"Stop!" said Delta Two eagerly. With the bottom of the phone now pointing towards the target perfectly and acting as a listening device, they were able to listen to everything he said.

Two espressos down, Delta One, who had lined her own phone up to act as a listening device, traded places with Delta Six. They hadn't received any useful information on their target in the fifty-three minutes they'd observed him for. He'd been on his laptop the entire time but seemed just as on edge as when they'd tailed him. By the time he'd finished his third pot of Earl Grey tea, their target received a phone call. Delta One, now in a white, flowery top and beige, rolled-up shorts, was unable to hear the phone call so instead continued to eat her slice of coffee and walnut cake, letting Delta Two, still in the car, obtain the intel.

"Hello... No, of course I haven't. I'd tell you if they'd come knocking... No, I can't talk freely... When...? Okay, I can be there in twenty minutes... Yeah, alright," said the target to the other person on the call.

He spent the next twelve minutes on his laptop before closing the lid and tucking it back in his briefcase. Delta One was experienced enough to know standing up and leaving the café at the same time as the target would look suspicious, so instead she stayed and finished her slice of cake. Delta Three, now in similar attire to Delta One, passed the café and followed the target.

She tailed him for the next eight minutes, without the need to be switched, until he finally entered a narrow alleyway. Delta Three knew there was no way she could just follow him down there, so passed the alleyway. There was nowhere to hide and nowhere to approach the target. Thinking quickly, Delta Three turned down the next alleyway, vaulted a locked, wire gate and climbed the nearby ladder. Before long, she was on top of the two-storey building and had the target back in sight. She pointed the bottom of her phone, so it faced the target, just before he had company. Delta Three placed one earphone in her ear, to listen to their conversation, and stayed as low as possible to observe. The unknown guest looked to be in his late forties, early fifties, with a thick, but short, grey, wiry beard and mid-length, brown hair hiding under the flat cap he was wearing. He had black trousers, a light blue shirt, and a tweed jacket, with just one button done up. For the temperatures they were experiencing, it didn't look particularly comfortable to Delta Three, but the target didn't seem fazed by it, giving the impression it was his usual choice of clothing.

Delta Three took out a small camera and started taking pictures.

"Where are you storing our information?" asked the stranger.

The target looked a little confused, asking, "What information?"

"Don't take me for a fool. A man like you stores information on someone like me, usually as either insurance or blackmail. I'm not interested in the reason. I just want to know where it is," continued the stranger.

The target swallowed hard and answered, "In my defence, I didn't know who you were. I only stored the information as insurance, just in case you tried to double-cross me. It was nothing personal."

"I don't care. Where is it?" persisted the stranger, becoming more and more infuriated.

"In my office. But there's no worry, I've got friends who'll tell me if the police issue a warrant to search my office and I'll move it if that's the case," assured the target.

"Delta Three, keep observing. I'm heading to his office with Delta Four," said Delta One who had been listening to the conversation through Delta Three's phone.

"It isn't the police that I'm concerned about. Thank you for your cooperation, but I'm afraid your services are no longer required. Our arms will be moved out of your factory within the next three hours," said the stranger.

"You can't do that…" insisted the target. The stranger looked void of any concern as he turned and headed back the way he came in. "We'll see if your boss is so happy with the arrangement," continued the target.

There were a couple of moments of complete silence, as the stranger considered the comment. He then turned back to face the target and strolled towards him, smiling.

"And we were getting on so well…" he started, moving to within a foot of the target, "but you really shouldn't have threatened me. My boss is a fool, and he will never hear of our conversation."

With a knife sliding down his sleeve and being clutched in his right hand, the stranger inflicted one decisive stab to the target. He retrieved his knife, cleaned it, grabbed the target's briefcase, climbed into his car, and left the alleyway.

As quickly as she could, Delta Three grabbed her phone, climbed off the building and headed to the target.

"Target down. I repeat, the target is down," she whispered, trying to draw as little attention from passers-by to the situation as possible. The target was lying on the floor, blood soaking his suit. Delta Three rushed over and bent down on one knee. She applied pressure to his wound but knew too much blood was gushing out.

"Code…" said the target, clearly finding it hard to talk through the pain. "Code is one-six-six-five."

"Code to what?" asked Delta Three, aware their time was short.

"I saw you… on the building," he said.

"The code to what?" repeated Delta Three, ignoring his last comment.

"The code… is… safe," he muttered.

"Yes, the code is safe now, but what is it for?"

"One-six-six-five."

"What does that mean? I don't understand. What is it for?"

"Safe."

A few seconds later, the pain disappeared and he lay, with his eyes still open, motionless. Delta Two and Five rushed up, too late. Delta Three had already moved away from his corpse.

"Alright, we need to clean up here," said Delta Two, conscious of anything that could lead back to them. "We'll meet with a clean-up crew, they'll spin his death some way," she concluded before immediately getting to work.

"This is Delta One. We've gained entry and are heading up to his office now."

"Copy, Delta One. Whoever killed our target is likely heading your way. Be advised, I saw no guards with him, which could easily mean he's skilled enough to not need them," started Delta Three, helping in the clean-up. "Also, if you find something that needs a code, try sixteen sixty-five. He said it was a code that we've got to keep safe."

***

In a tall commercial building, full of offices, Delta One and Four were stood alone in one of its many lifts. They were both now dressed in blue two-piece suits. Neither had had that long to get dressed so they both took the short lift ride to fasten their top buttons and straighten their ties. The lift doors opened, and they were greeted by a friendly secretary.

"I understand you're here for a meeting with Mr Marshall. He isn't available right now, but I'll show you to our waiting room in the meantime," she said, before leading the way.

The floor was spilt up with half-height dividers, separating the small workspaces of those inside. Once in the waiting room, which was out of sight from everything else on that floor, they immediately took a seat on one of the four comfortable-looking sofas. The secretary left them alone.

"The office we want is two floors down," said Delta Four, as they both moved over to the window.

Without wasting time, Delta One opened the window, whilst Delta Four attached a grappling hook, smuggled in under his jacket, around one of the building's exposed concrete supports. Delta One threw the other end of the line out of the window and attached herself to the cable using a harness built into her jacket. Delta Four steadied the line, whilst Delta One lowered herself two floors. Everyone in the offices below seemed far more concerned with keeping cool in front of the fans, or talking to one another, than they did watching someone pass their window, over twenty floors up. Once outside the target's office, Delta One retrieved a small laser cutter from her suit pocket and started cutting a perfect hole in the glass. With her legs braced against the window, and little wind blowing, she made light work of the glass. She returned the laser cutter to her jacket pocket and looked up to Delta Four. He'd constructed a small contraption, from even smaller components concealed inside his suit. He dropped the device down to Delta One, who caught it with ease. It had two hypersuction discs, one of which was stuck to the cut circle whilst the other was stuck to the surrounding glass. The discs weren't big but were connected to each other by a small hinge. She swung the circle cut-out on the hinge as if opening a circular window. Delta One then lifted herself in and detached the cable from her harness.

The office had frosted glass, which meant no one could see her inside. It seemed large but was an almost entirely empty space. She moved straight over to his desk, positioned in the back corner. There were numerous pieces of paper covering it. There were blueprints, maps, files, pictures, and so much more. It looked like he was in the middle of an investigation and had left in a hurry.

"Delta One, someone has just entered the building with a lot of purpose. They didn't check in, just walked straight past. They're dressed in a tweed jacket, with a flat cap," said Delta Six, who was sat in reception.

"That's the one who killed the target," added Delta Three.

With time running short, Delta One picked up the pace and took pictures of everything. One piece of paper caught her interest more than the rest.

"Alpha One, do you read me?" she asked.

"Loud and clear," he replied. With little else to do, Alpha One had been keeping up to date with Delta team's mission.

"I've got information on the target's second factory," she said.

"Second factory?" replied Alpha One, confused.

Whilst continuing to take pictures, she added, "Officially, he only has one. But he does have a second one, according to this. However, what it's used for is far more interesting. It appears to be another safe house for the Night Vipers, just like the nightclub you hit earlier this year. I'm sending you the details now, but you'll have to act quickly because, whoever this mystery figure is, they said they'd have the factory cleared within three hours." Delta One finished taking pictures and sent the one in question straight to Alpha One.

It didn't take Alpha One long to review the information.

"Thank you. Get yourselves back as soon as possible. The factory is nearby, so we'll move in straight away. Get back safe and we'll go through the evidence on our return," he concluded, immediately leaving the conversation, knowing time was of the essence.

Also against the clock, Delta One reattached the cable and lifted herself out of the window. After swinging the circular piece of cut glass back in place, she removed the device and held on to it.

"Delta Four, when you're ready, steady the line," she said, whilst watching the office door slowly open.

Just in time, Delta One activated her ascender, built into the harness, and flew two floors up. Once there, Delta Four pulled her through the window. Just before she moved in, a face popped out of a window two floors down and five windows to her left. The face was wearing a flat cap and looked straight at Delta One.

"We've been made," she announced before checking outside the waiting room for a clear route. "Delta Six, extraction plan B," she concluded.

The bottom of the cable was hovering a few metres above a maintenance lorry with an open back. From the outside, the cable looked a little like part of a pulley system for a window cleaning ledge. Anyone who was able to avert their eyes from their phones and laptops wouldn't have thought much of it. Delta Four released the cable and let it fly out of the window. Because the inside of the cable was made of a stiff, and very long, spring, the bottom of the cable moved very little, until the top came crashing down. Within a few seconds, the cable went from being upright, to being in the back of the lorry. Thanks to the stiff, sponge-like material in the back of the lorry, little sound was made, and no attention was drawn to it.

***

Back in reception, Delta Six casually moved over to the nearest wall and leant against it. After a quick glance, ensuring no one was watching, she broke the fire alarm glass call point right behind her. The alarms sounded throughout the building, telling everyone to evacuate immediately. Delta Six did the same as everyone in reception, as she headed out of the revolving glass doors. She moved towards the maintenance lorry, climbed up, and sat behind the wheel, with the engine running, waiting for the other two to return.

***

Delta One and Four had joined the other office workers leaving the building.

The secretary who had shown them to the waiting room approached, saying, "I'm very sorry about this. If we just follow everyone else out of the building, where we'll wait until it has been cleared."

"Thank you," replied Delta One, as they entered the staircase.

They moved past each floor with no sign of the nameless figure. Every step they took, they became more vigilant, but even when leaving the staircase and walking through reception, the figure was still nowhere to be seen. They both left the building and managed to break away from the secretary's line of sight before climbing into the cab of the maintenance lorry. Delta Six drove away, with all three sat in the cab, watching for the figure. They left the scene without seeing him. However, the figure did observe them. He watched from amongst the crowd, as they drove down the street. The figure made a mental note of the lorry's number plate, aware it would yield no results.

# Chapter 4 – The Pit of the Viper

10<sup>th</sup> September

15:58 BST

76 hrs 15 min. Until Deadline

Deep in the forest, just a couple of hours from the Molehill, Alpha team were stood around a thin, plastic table with Bravo One and Two. The other ten members of Bravo team stood in a circle a little further out. On top of the table was a blueprint of a factory, located a quarter of a mile east of their position.

"Alright, listen up," started Alpha One. "The factory borders this forest, so we'll have ample cover to move in. Both Alpha and Bravo will split into two teams. Alpha Four and Blindspot will stay at the edge of the forest. Blindspot will provide cover fire where necessary and pick off any stragglers, whilst Alpha Four will observe the factory through thermal cameras which have already been placed around its perimeter. Our communications will be on a local connection, so we'll be able to talk to each other but no one back at base."

"May I ask why?" enquired Bravo Two.

"It's because they're scanning for frequencies within a certain range," answered Bravo One in his deep, throaty voice, before clarifying. "Our local comms work through our CAT devices and are of a much higher frequency, far higher than they're scanning for."

Alpha One nodded at the 6'2" muscular figure of Bravo One, scary being one way to describe him, adding,

"And unfortunately, when our CAT runs the comms at that frequency it picks up a lot of interference, so a clear message would never make it back to the Molehill." He paused for a moment before continuing to explain the plan, "Bravo Two, Three, Four, and Five will enter the grounds with Alpha team through the car park. You will then gain entry to the upper floor through the external staircase, located on the north side of the building. Whilst Alpha team holds position at the side door on the west side, the rest of Bravo team will enter through the front gates on the east side. Once at the building, you will breach through both shutters simultaneously with Bravo Two's team. Once their attention is fully diverted, Alpha team will enter through the side door and strike from behind. We'll enter exactly fifteen seconds after you make entry, so ensure you take cover whilst waiting. Remember, when we arrive and breach, Alpha Four will be keeping us informed of enemy positions. Any questions?" Only silence followed. After just a few seconds, Alpha One concluded, "Good. We're expecting heavy resistance, so keep your focus. I know they're still in their infancy, but we're to use the sedative rounds on this one. Bosse has, however, allowed two magazines each of live rounds to be used in emergencies only. This is the Night Vipers' second hideout we've located and the first had a high presence of armed personnel, but that isn't our main goal here. We want to obtain any information on the antidote, that's the priority. Let's move out!"

Bravo One left immediately, accompanied by the other seven members he would be breaching with. Alpha team stayed back, folded up the blueprints and the table and placed them in a hole in the ground. They covered it with a collection of branches and moss-lined rocks before moving out after Bravo One, with Bravo Two's team right behind. They moved through the entire quarter-mile stretch of woods as if they were expecting to come face to face with the Night Vipers. They covered every direction as their feet felt for a clear path ahead. Twigs snapped and leaves rustled as they continued on their way. The ground was bone dry, with cracks appearing in the parched mud. But it was the huge roots which posed the greatest threat, lurking above the ground, waiting to catch an unsuspecting victim. It would've been easy to get lost in the twisting and constantly changing labyrinth, but their CAT devices kept them on track, acting like satnav for those on foot. The computerised arm terminals were small computers built into their tactical clothes. Before long, they were all clear of the woods and were holding their position on the muddy bank, high above the factory.

The factory was in a sunken area of land, the forest wrapped itself around most of the factory and the busy motorway covered the final side. Apart from the blue, rectangular factory itself, situated in the centre of the land, there was a car park, an outdoor storage depot and a one-way road which ran the entire perimeter.

"Bravo One in position."

"Copy, holding for complete surveillance," replied Alpha One, whilst Alpha Four continued to scan the entire area.

"Outside is clear of hostiles. I count fifty-seven heat signatures inside. I'm also getting minimal heat readings from machinery, so I'd say it isn't being used," concluded Alpha Four.

"Fifty-seven is less than expected. We need to enter with caution, they're deceptive, that's about the only thing we know about them," started a concerned Alpha One. He observed the factory for a couple more seconds before adding, "All teams, move in."

***

Bravo One's team headed down the steep bank and swiftly moved to the side of the road. They took cover behind its high, concrete barriers and watched for any movement. When they were sure nothing was in sight, Bravo One started to move forwards. He vaulted the road's concrete side guard and approached the factory, with the other seven right behind. Within seconds, they were all pressed up tightly against the giant, metal shutters. Bravo Six stuck three strips of tape on one of the shutters, making a door-shaped border. Bravo Nine did the same on the other shutter, sticking two strips of tape up, parallel, and a third connecting the two at the top. Bravo One's team then split, so two were at either side of both shutters.

"Ready to breach," said Bravo One whilst Bravo Six and Nine each held a small detonator in their right hands.

***

The five remaining members of Alpha team and the four of Bravo team had already made it down the muddy bank and were halfway through the, almost empty, car park. Still with no one in sight, they wasted no time in approaching the factory, unhappy with the car park's lack of cover. Bravo Two's team quickly headed right and silently climbed the staircase, placing the same tape around the perimeter of the door they approached.

"Ready to breach," said Bravo Two, as the four of them took a couple of steps back.

"I still have no confirmation whether those inside are armed," added Alpha Four, frantically studying the images on his CAT.

"Copy. You know what to do, breach when ready," concluded Alpha One.

***

Bravo One nodded his head towards Bravo Six and said, "Ringing the bell in three... two... one."

Bravo Six, Nine, and Three all flicked the detonators at the same time. With their eyes averted, the tape didn't explode but instead ignited to a high enough temperature that it cut through the door. The door-shaped cut-outs fell inwards, and Bravo team flooded through after each. Bravo One's team found cover immediately, hiding behind oversized pieces of idle machinery and huge crates encased in bubble wrap. As Bravo One looked up, he saw Bravo Two's team spread out on a mezzanine. Bullets filled the factory. The few Night Vipers were quickly being overrun. They moved to the back of the factory, desperately trying to find cover. When they'd just about found some protection from Bravo team, both high and low, Alpha team came from behind. Within a minute, the Night Vipers' numbers had already been cut in half. It didn't take much longer though for Alpha and Bravo team's momentum to wear off.

"Twenty-one Vipers left," informed Alpha Four.

The Night Vipers continued to stay in cover, suppressed by Bravo Two's team above them. The remaining, dwindling numbers were huddled in the centre of the factory, surrounded by machines. They stayed silent and motionless. Then, together, they all jumped up and opened fire, spraying bullets in all directions. The sudden move was enough to make Bravo and Alpha team duck down into cover. Bravo Five fell back against the wall on the mezzanine after taking a shot to the chest.

"I'm good… it hit my vest," said Bravo Five, trying to focus on breathing.

The Night Vipers weren't concerned with preserving their bullets and, as soon as they were empty, Alpha and Bravo team applied a similar tactic back at them. They emerged from cover and opened fire. The Night Vipers fell shortly after.

"That was a pretty pointless last stand," said Alpha Three.

The comment cemented Alpha One's initial thoughts. For a security force trusted with guarding high-value targets, they wouldn't have done that without a good reason.

"One's heading out the back!" shouted Alpha Seven, as she gave chase, shortly followed by Alpha One and Five.

The Viper charged through the door and ran out towards the road. Before any of them could even exit the building, the Viper dropped to the floor.

"Target down," said Blindspot, his piercing blue eyes observing the motionless Viper through his scope.

Alpha Seven stood in the doorway, staring at the Viper. She knew what she'd done wasn't right.

"Alpha Seven…" started Alpha One, in a voice that was somehow both stern and tender.

"I know, I know…" she interrupted, "I shouldn't have just run after him, I should've waited for your orders."

"Well, yes," said Alpha One. As hard as he tried, he couldn't help but sound like a schoolteacher in those kinds of situations. "I take it you know why you should've waited." It was only six months ago that many members of Charlie team had lost their lives while Alpha One was too far away to help.

Alpha Seven nodded but still refused to turn around.

"Just make sure you give yourself time to think in future. But well done for spotting him, we could've easily missed him… in fact, we did easily miss him."

She gave half a smile. "I'll go and check on Bravo Five."

"We might have a problem," announced Alpha Five, as if just casually mentioning it in passing.

The comment brought a lot of attention, but it was only after he finished staring at a small screen on the wall that he clarified his statement.

"That Viper's just activated a silent alarm. More Vipers are on their way."

"Alright…" said Alpha One, gaining everyone's full attention, "the Vipers won't take long to arrive which means that we don't have long to obtain the intel we need. All the machines are off and look as though they have been for a while, so…"

"Wait, all the machines are off?" asked Alpha Four.

"Yeah," answered Alpha One, slightly confused.

"So, ALL of them are off?" asked Alpha Four.

"Yes, all of them."

"And you're definitely sure?" added Alpha Four.

Still confused, Alpha One asked, "Is there a point to this?"

"Well, according to the thermal scan, one of those machines is giving off a lot of heat. And I mean, more heat than you're giving off," answered Alpha Four, finally clearing up some confusion.

"Now you come to mention it, this machine is kind of warm," said Alpha Three, as he started touching the closest one.

"It's not that machine," said Alpha Four bluntly. "It's the machine set two rows back and one to your right."

Now back in the main room, it was Alpha One who moved over to the one in question and felt some of its components. With each part he touched, he got lower and lower to the floor, until he felt the floor itself.

"The heat's coming from under the ground," he said, still tracing the hottest parts with his hand. "Let's get this thing shifted," he added.

They swarmed around it, trying to take it apart bit by bit, leaving Alpha Seven and Bravo Five on the mezzanine. After a couple of minutes of being unsuccessful in moving a single part, Alpha One took a step back to look at it from a different angle. He looked around it, then up to the roof, then down to the floor. A patch of silver paint caught his eye. It was on the floor, to the right-hand side of the machine and was accompanied by scratches and scuff marks. He bent down and felt the marks. It seemed they were from repetitive contact with something metallic. He then looked up and noticed a pipe covered in scuff marks.

Standing side on, it was perfectly in line with the marks on the floor.

"It opens like a trapdoor. It's got to tilt up," announced Alpha One.

"Maybe you can open it back at the computer screen on the wall," suggested Alpha Two.

Alpha Five moved back over to it and started touching, pressing, and swiping the screen. All of a sudden, the machine started to move.

It levered up, revealing a small trapdoor underneath its solid, metal platform. The heat rushing out of the door was instantly felt by everyone in the factory, with the closest three members of Bravo team lifting their arms to cover their faces from it. The small gap seemed to be at the top of a long drop down, with only a metal ladder in sight.

"Alpha One, the drone in the sky is picking up four vehicles heading our way. I'm unable to get an internal scan on two, their sides are too thick," said Alpha Four.

"Hold your position. Bravo team, head outside and set up an ambush for those vehicles, but only engage if you need to, we don't want to go making enemies of everyone. Alpha Two and Seven, stay up here and search for anything of any interest, if Bravo team needs backing up, then back them up. Alpha Three and Five, you're with me heading to the earth's core," said Alpha One, before they all split up.

The three that were left standing by the hidden trapdoor, all stared down the hole, just about able to make out the bottom.

"Age before beauty, Sir," said Alpha Three, as he looked up at Alpha One.

"Sure, I'm not going to stand in your way," replied Alpha One, as he took a step back and gestured for Alpha Three to descend first.

Alpha Three looked towards Alpha Five for support, but it was misplaced as Alpha Five added, "I can't blame him. I know I wouldn't want you falling on me."

Alpha Three moved forwards, grabbed the ladder tightly with both hands, and got down on his knees.

"You know, you really need a catchphrase of some kind. One you use all the time," said Alpha Three, half trying to take his mind away from the ladder and what was a life-threatening drop in his mind. He slowly edged backwards until he was at the edge of the hole, before tentatively feeling for the ladder's rungs. Once his feet were securely on, he started to descend, closely followed by Alpha Five, then Alpha One. Despite their tactical gloves, the rungs of the ladder were almost too hot to touch.

"Something like, 'let's do this'," added Alpha Three.

"I am not shouting 'let's do this' every time we clear a building."

"How about, 'let's roll out'?"

"How about we just stay focussed?" concluded Alpha One.

"I don't think that's very good," mumbled Alpha Three.

The hole wasn't as deep as it first looked, and before long, Alpha Three had his feet firmly on solid ground. The heat hadn't got any worse; in fact, they had started to become more accustomed to it. They found themselves stood in a small, circular space, with mud walls, only one tight tunnel, and no door. Alpha One moved over to one of the walls and placed his right hand on it.

"It's clay," he said whilst rubbing some of it through his fingertips.

They slowly started to move down the tight passage, also with exposed clay lining the walls. Alpha One led them through the twisting tunnel, finding no alternate routes and meeting no resistance. The temperature stayed at the same, uncomfortable level throughout.

"This tunnel's going on forever. How big is it?" asked Alpha Three.

"It probably isn't that big. We've doubled back three times, so I don't think we're too far from the ladder, assuming you could run through walls," answered Alpha One, just before they came to an opening.

As they approached with caution, they kept their eyes and rifles fixed on the end of the tunnel. Their way had been lit by a few oil lamps scattered along the tunnel, but as soon as the clearing came into view, the extra light was a welcome change. Moving into the large room, they spread out, checking for any Night Vipers but still none were found. The giant space was full of green plants and heat lamps, explaining the harsh temperatures.

"They're drugs," announced Alpha One, staring at the plants.

"It's not that surprising, is it?" asked Alpha Three from the other side of the room. "It explains why they use oil lamps, they're using as little energy as possible so their drug operation doesn't get exposed."

"These are dying," added Alpha One.

"Okay, so they're not gardeners, but it explains the heat."

"Yeah, except the reason these plants are dying is because it's too hot down here," replied Alpha Five who had just checked the perimeter of the room and found no other way out.

"Which means?" questioned Alpha Three, as he started smelling the plants.

"It means they're hiding something," answered Alpha Five.

"We're under a factory, in an unknown, secret lair. Why would you hide anything behind something that's illegal?" asked Alpha Three.

Alpha One stuck his finger in the plants' soil and took a quick sniff. "If you wanted to hide something that's more illegal."

Alpha Three started to take pictures, whilst the other two started to look in and around the plants and the tables they sat on.

"I'm going to get a message to Bravo team, to see if they're alright," said Alpha Five, as he stood up and started to type a message on his CAT.

Alpha One continued looking around the tables. He grabbed hold of a pipe, which ran under the plants, and pulled it out of the tank it was connected to. Fresh water poured out and ran on to the clay floor.

"Bravo team are dealing with some pretty strong contact, but they're holding their own," said Alpha Five.

Without any warning, liquid started falling from the ceiling. Within the clay ceiling were small, unseen sprinklers. All three of them were covered in just a few seconds. It started to cool them down and would've been welcome if it wasn't for the smell.

"Does this water have a funny smell?" asked Alpha Three, a little concerned.

"It isn't water… it's fuel. We need to leave, now!" shouted Alpha One and before he could finish his command, they'd all started to head down the clay corridor.

They all ran back through the twisting tunnel, with fuel still pouring on them. Alpha Five was the first back and wasted no time in scurrying up the ladder. Alpha Three was next, and despite the imminent fire, he still placed each hand and foot on the rung of the ladder carefully, moving quicker than usual, but still not quick enough for Alpha One who shouted, "Move!" from just a couple of rungs below him. Almost at the top, they heard a loud '*POP*' and the tunnel below them turned bright blue, with flames trying to chase them up the ladder, but even they couldn't stretch that far. The added heat helped Alpha Three to move up the final few rungs of the ladder and roll out on to the surface, closely followed by Alpha One.

"Why didn't the flames make it to the surface?" asked Alpha Three, daring a look back down the tunnel.

Alpha One had thought the same, but the concern for Bravo team was more important.

"Is everyone good?"

***

*Six Minutes Earlier*

Bravo One watched as Alpha One, Three, and Five climbed down the ladder and disappeared into the dark hole. He then followed the rest of his team, including Bravo Five, outside to set up an ambush. Within a minute, all twelve of them were scattered amongst the wooden crates and concrete blocks in the car park and storage depot.

"The four vehicles are approaching the car park. The first and fourth are cars, the middle two are trucks. Four people in each of the cars, but I still can't get an internal reading of the two trucks, I've only got confirmation of three in each of the cabins," said Alpha Four, as he continued to watch the vehicles approach via the drone in the sky.

"Any confirmation on weapons?" asked Bravo One, lurking behind one of the wooden crates.

"Negative," answered Blindspot, focussing down his scope.

The vehicles pulled round and stopped in front of the single door Alpha team used when breaching. The eight people from the cars and the six from the two cabs all climbed out and started to head towards the door.

"They are armed and are Vipers," said Alpha Four.

"Let's do this quick and quiet," added Bravo One.

They all aimed from around their cover and opened fire, taking all fourteen Vipers down in just a few seconds.

"Night Vipers are down," said Bravo Two as he began to stand up.

"Hold!" shouted Alpha Four. "We still don't know what's inside those trucks."

Bravo Two crouched back behind the concrete block.

"Bravo Seven, go and investigate," said Bravo One, as they all kept their rifles fixed on the trucks.

Bravo Seven approached with caution, edging each foot in front of the other with his rifle held up. Suddenly, the top and two sides of the first truck flipped open revealing a giant, metal turret mounted on an equally large metal box. Bravo Seven wasted no time, as he dived in front of the truck's engine for cover. The second truck then revealed the same machine and, in unison, they both opened fire. The two machine guns started to chew their way through the concrete blocks. Bravo One and the others behind the wooden crates quickly shifted their positions to find more substantial cover.

"Switching to live rounds!" shouted Bravo One.

From the top of the hill, Blindspot also switched ammunition and focussed his fire on a single turret, hitting the exact same spot each and every time, but the turrets remained strong. One shifted its gaze up the hill and spat a few hundred bullets towards Alpha Four and Blindspot. They quickly threw themselves back, out of sight. Bravo team were unable to get more than a few shots on the turrets at one time before they turned to fire on them.

Bravo Seven was still in front of the first truck's engine when he removed a small pack of explosives from under his bulletproof vest. He then laid his rifle on the floor and started to crawl under the truck, sticking the charge directly under the closest turret. He quickly climbed out, grabbed his rifle, and ran inside the factory under Bravo team's covering fire. Once safe, he detonated the charge.

The truck was nothing more than charred metal and ash, but the turret was still operational... to some extent. It continued to spin around, facing each team member in turn, but was unable to fire since having lost connection to the box that once operated it. With the first turret unable to do any damage, they turned their fire on the second.

It demolished the wooden crate, which Bravo One had previously been using for cover, in seconds, sending splinters of wood flying in all directions. No matter how many bullets made contact, the second turret in effect brushed them aside as if they were nothing.

"I'm out of live rounds," said Bravo Three.

"Me too," added Bravo Seven.

"I think I've got something of use," announced Alpha Four, as he rolled over and started searching through his huge rucksack of gear.

"What is it?" asked Bravo One, shouting over the noise from the turret.

Alpha Four continued to search through his bag until finally retrieving a small cylinder.

"It acts like thermite, but it should be enough to cut through that armour," he said, as he retook control of the drone and flew it back towards himself.

After spending a couple of seconds attaching the device to the bottom of the drone, he flew it towards the turret. It was flown high, until it was directly above the turret, before quickly lowering itself. Once the drone was holding the device in front of its target, Alpha Four activated it. Bright blue flames roared from the device, as the drone's blades increased their speeds to keep the device steady. It burnt through the armour, melting it piece by piece, until part of the drone fell out of the sky. By the time the device stopped burning and had started to cool, the turret and the drone were misshapen and had welded parts of themselves together. Slowly, Bravo team started to approach the turrets. The first was still spinning around, almost in distress, as it failed to do anything.

"These things are connected to something, right?" asked Bravo One, as he approached the melted turret.

"That's right, see if you can find a computer of some sort," replied Alpha Four.

"Well, I think I've found it. It says, *'Detonation Successful'*," said Bravo One, looking at a screen on the turret's base.

"Detonation successful?" pondered Bravo Two, confused.

"Is everyone good?" asked Alpha One, suddenly back in radio contact.

"Yeah, Alpha Four suddenly remembered he was carrying a firework in his pocket. Like that wouldn't have been helpful from the start," replied Bravo One. "Don't suppose you've got any idea what could've been detonated, do you?"

"I might have an idea…" started Alpha One.

"If it's not urgent, I think you should come up to the office on the first floor," said Alpha Two, almost as if it was an order, not a request.

"I'll be right there," concluded Alpha One.

Without wasting a second, he headed up the only flight of metal stairs and entered the single room on the first floor. Inside, the walls were blue, with paint peeling off, the tables, running the entire perimeter of the room, were pressed up to the walls. Paper was everywhere, covering the floor, the tables, and the two chairs. There were a couple of empty noticeboards to the left, where Alpha Seven was standing, with the pins still stuck in them holding tiny scraps of paper where the full sheets had been ripped off earlier. Alpha Two was stood in the right-hand corner, holding a single sheet of A4 paper.

"Take a look at this," he said, passing the paper to Alpha One.

After scanning the document, he saw only a satellite's view of what looked like an industrial estate, with a pinpoint on it, accompanied by a collection of numbers in a grid format.

"Do you recognise the code?" asked Alpha Two.

"Yeah, it's a code we used when we were spies."

"We weren't spies," added Alpha Two in a low tone.

"What kind of a code?" asked Alpha Seven.

"It's pretty simple, but that's the genius of it, anyone can work it out with the right key," said Alpha One.

"Key?" questioned Alpha Seven.

Alpha Two started nodding, "It depended on the size of the message. If we wanted two words of up to four letters, like this one, then the coded message they sent us would be in a grid of four by four, and our key, which was always the date the message was received, would be in a two by four grid. So basically, the number of letters is denoted by the code and the number of words by the key."

Alpha Seven was clearly confused. She began to ask a question but was stopped before she had the chance.

Alpha One took note of the numbers in the four by four grid; '10, 6, 0, -4' in the top row; '7, -5, 4, 3' in the second row; '-10, -2, 0, -1' in the third row; and '0, 1, 1, 2' in the bottom row.

"In simple terms…" started Alpha One, aware there was nothing simple with what he was about to say, "the so-called 'key' is always the date the message was sent. So, for this message, if it really was meant for us, it would be today's date." Whilst trying to find a pen on the desk, Alpha One continued, "The parts of the date which should be included, the day, month, two-digit year, or four-digit year, all depend on the size on the final message."

"And how do you know the size of the final message?"

"Well, that depends where the coded message is located on the paper. For this one, it's four centimetres from the left and two centimetres below the image of the map, so the final message will be two words, up to four letters each," he continued, finally locating a pen.

"What do you do next?" she asked.

"It's a matrix, so you do the dot product."

Alpha Seven didn't need to ask anything, her face did all the questioning she needed.

"It's basically a fancy way of combining two things. Much like an addition combines two numbers, the dot product combines two matrices," added Alpha One.

Alpha Seven looked at the paper for a couple of seconds, released a huge lungful of air, and said, "Well, as you haven't even started explaining how to do this... 'dot product', I think I'll let you work it out and then just look amazed once you've finished." She then took a step back.

Alpha One put the date in a two by four grid, next to the coded message and drew a dot between them. One at a time, he started adding numbers to a third grid, two high, four wide. Within less than a minute, he had '10, 15, 9, 14' in the top row and '0, 13, 5, 0' in the bottom row.

"Wow!" added Alpha Seven, sarcastically.

"Next step, these numbers represent letters," started Alpha One.

"Let me guess, there's some different equation for each letter and number," said Alpha Seven, pretending she had little interest, despite her watching everything Alpha One did.

"Actually, the final step is relatively simple... genuinely, this time," said Alpha One, matching her sarcasm from earlier. "Each number represents a letter, and its position, in the alphabet. So, *A* would be one, *B* would be two, and so on." He quickly jotted down six letters, adding, "Oh, and zero obviously represents either no letter or a space, you just have to notice which one it is." The message simply read '*Join me*'.

All three of them stood around the message.

"Why didn't they just write, 'Join me'? It's not like it was top secret," said Alpha Seven.

"Whoever did it knows who we are, and who we were. They're making a statement and letting us know who they're after," replied Alpha One, concerned.

"Who are they after?" asked Alpha Seven.

"One of us," replied Alpha One.

"You think this is the location of the meeting?" asked Alpha Two.

Alpha One nodded. "Everything that's happened has been for us to read this message; the poisoned food, the murder of the factory owner, everything. Like it's a game for them."

Alpha Seven stayed quiet, unsure whether to involve herself or not.

"What are we going to do?" asked Alpha Two.

Alpha One folded up the piece of paper and put it into one of his pockets, answering, "We play their game, and we win."

# Chapter 5 – The Tale of the Shadows

10th September
18:45 BST
73 hrs 28 min. Until Deadline

Alpha team entered the Molehill by the rear entrance in a two-car convoy. Both cars were the 4x4s they usually took out when blending in. They were black on the outside, with heavily tinted rear windows, helping to maintain the secrecy of any high-value target they may be transporting. The number plates were able to cycle between four different combinations on a rolling plate, making it quicker than a vehicle change. Inside was warm, comfortable, and secure, with padded, white doors and seats, and just about a bulletproof everything.

Bravo team had already entered in their convoy of three cars twenty-five minutes earlier. The entrance was hidden, yet it wasn't blocked off. They turned down a narrow street, drove through an underground car park and moved under a low bridge, which led into a long tunnel. The tunnel was made with reinforced concrete, but for the first few hundred metres, graffiti covered most of it, helping it to blend in as a derelict site. All the way through the tunnel, tiny, unseen scanners covered the walls, identifying and mapping everything contained within. Everything down to a lone ant could, and would, be identified.

What looked like the end of the tunnel opened, as if it was a door, as soon as the scanners had cleared them for entry. They didn't stop as they moved through the doorway and drove down a steep ramp. After another long, twisting journey, they were finally within the giant hangar of the Molehill.

Alpha One was driving the first car, with Alpha Two in the passenger seat, and Alpha Seven sat in the middle seat at the back. With the other four in the second car, Alpha One took the opportunity to talk before they left the vehicle.

"What we found in the factory's office stays between the three of us. Understood?"

The other two nodded. Alpha Seven was clearly more confused by his statement than Alpha Two, but she still didn't see the need to say anything.

"I'll fill the rest of the team in when it's safe," concluded Alpha One, before the three of them exited their vehicle to join the other members of the team. They all headed straight for the meeting room, eager to debrief as soon as possible.

Everyone was in the meeting room except for Charlie One and Two, and they all fell silent when Alpha team entered, aware that anything they had would be time sensitive.

Scott didn't keep them in suspense.

"So far, we have very little to go on. The factory was indeed a Night Viper safe house, which has now been shut down, but unfortunately provided next to no actionable intelligence. There were a few addresses noted for drop-offs, which are being investigated as we speak. Should any become leads, we will obviously move in with immediate effect. Diana, I understand you had a little more luck in tailing the owner of the factories."

"Yes…" started Diana, as she stood up. "The owner's office had a lot of information, including the location of the Night Viper's safe house. There appear to be various…" she paused, trying to find the word, "assets, which are related to either Fellscient or the Night Vipers, however, nothing else directly ties to the poisoned food. The owner did say 'sixteen sixty-five' was to be used as a code to something, but what, well your guess is as good as mine. The best lead we have is an image of the man who killed the factory owner and attempted to prevent us from stealing the information in his office."

She then nodded her head towards VOICE, who instinctively pressed one of the keys on his laptop. An image appeared behind him on one of the five, huge computer monitors. The image showed the man in the flat cap, his face fully visible.

Diana then continued. "We've had no matches for facial recognition, but we are currently scanning and if any camera catches his face, we will know."

Scott took a closer look at the image, before glancing towards Daniel, who returned a look of nothing more than confusion.

"No need for facial recognition, I know who this is," announced Scott. "This is Kale."

Everyone in the room looked from Scott, to the image, and back to Scott.

"And you didn't think about mentioning this when the letter arrived?" questioned Bosse.

Scott usually supported the questions Bosse asked, but he couldn't help but think this one had no purpose other than to irritate him.

"I'm afraid I hadn't made the connection when the letter arrived," he said dryly, before addressing the room as a whole. "Frederick 'Kale' Bridge gave himself the title of captain within his group of men. They called themselves everything from mercenaries to revolutionists. Personally, I think they were nothing more than a group who liked killing. Back in my old…" He paused, unsure whether 'life' or 'job' fitted better, "life, he, and his group, were one of the many I was tasked with stopping. I'd infiltrated his group, earned his trust, and gave him the location of a small village, located in the middle of nowhere, as a hideout for someone of interest to him. We'd arranged for two teams to ambush them when they arrived, but fifteen minutes before the arranged meet, we lost contact with both teams. I wasn't stationed too far away, so I took the final team and headed to the village. When we arrived, all the villagers had been executed." He paused again, recalling the sight of the destroyed village. "Both our two teams, along with Kale and his men were all missing. Up until a few moments ago, their whereabouts have all remained unknown."

"You think he's trying to take revenge on you?" asked Bravo One, before clarifying. "For setting him up, I mean."

"I don't know, Liath. I don't know," answered Scott, shrugging his shoulders.

"How would he know who you are?" asked Kenny.

Scott shrugged his shoulders again, saying, "Although we never met, I had to get close to him. Everything from the village being real, and my own information being correct, made it even more authentic and helped to earn his trust. But how he knows about me here, I haven't a clue."

"This extra information may help us identify his whereabouts," concluded Bosse, as he picked up a stack of paper and knocked it on the table to straighten it up, making it clear the meeting had finished. They were all a little surprised by the premature end to the meeting but knew better than to argue.

Just before they left, Scott shouted, "Make sure you all get some rest. I don't know when you'll next get the chance." He then turned to Daniel and gave him a short glance.

Although there were no flaring nostrils or raised eyebrows, Daniel knew exactly what the look was for.

He approached and began whispering, "You want me to go to the location?"

Scott nodded. "Somehow, I just can't believe that Kale would've found me here."

"So why me?"

Scott glanced towards Bosse, who was staring at the pair just out of earshot. "The date and time this poison takes effect, the thirteenth of September, at eight thirteen p.m."

Daniel thought for a moment. "It could be a coincidence."

"I hope it is," concluded Scott. As he watched Daniel leave the room, he caught Bosse out of the corner of his eye.

"I think you'll want to hear this," Bosse said.

Scott then noticed VOICE stood a few paces back, eager to join in. Scott gestured for Bosse to continue.

"Do you remember your mission at the compound earlier this year?" he asked.

"You know I do," replied Scott.

"Well, after you captured Mr Wilson, and brought him back to base, you mentioned a potential leak within our organisation."

"That's right, they knew we were coming. They'd moved their security, the Night Vipers, to ambush us during our exfil, they knew exactly how we operated," answered Scott.

Bosse nodded and continued. "Well, you asked me to look into it, and I think we've found something."

"We?" asked Scott, more concerned with VOICE's potential involvement than the potential answers.

He'd also asked Diana to investigate the breach as well, but Bosse didn't know that. It also seemed a coincidence that the investigation had taken over six months and something just so happened to be found on the same day Kale's note arrived.

"Yes. VOICE has assisted me. He seemed an obvious choice, as he wasn't a part of our organisation when this supposed leak occurred," said Bosse.

Whilst Scott wasn't overly pleased with his involvement, Bosse was right; he did seem like an obvious choice to assist him.

"So?" questioned Scott.

"It seems you were right; a leak did occur..." started Bosse. "VOICE found a data trail accessing all our information. Whoever it was had a way in for almost a month before shutting down their own access."

"I thought this was supposed to be secure?" questioned Scott.

"Well, that's where it gets a little more interesting. They used an access code to get in."

"Whose?" asked Scott.

"It belonged to Adrian."

Scott fell silent. He was confused, and wanted to ask so many questions all at the same time, but was unable to even make a sound. As far as he was concerned, Adrian's access code died with him during the plane crash with Echo team.

"Whoever has been into our system somehow got Adrian's access code. One that only he knew," added Bosse.

"How?" asked Scott, finding it hard to add anything else.

Bosse merely shrugged his shoulders and stepped aside for VOICE to say what he'd been so eagerly waiting to.

"I cannot tell you how they obtained Adrian's access code, nor do I know who it is, but they first accessed our system just hours after the plane crash, when his code and those of Echo team should have all become non-existent. From there, they created a back door. Upon finding the leak, I have been through the entire system, searching for any more back doors, but have so far found nothing. However, the breach was not external. In my expert opinion, I surmise that someone within the Molehill has used Adrian's access code to cover up their own trail."

"Why weren't the codes blocked?" asked Scott.

"Well, as I was not here, I cannot say why. However, it appeared that the termination of just Adrian's code was marked as 'not urgent'. The others were all destroyed within the hour," added VOICE.

"So, we're no closer to finding the leak?" asked Scott.

The only thing he got back was a single shake of the head from Bosse.

"Perhaps Mr Wilson will be able to help. He helped to take down Crabble, and in your own words, you think we want the same thing; to dismantle Fellscient," said Bosse, offering what seemed to be the only potential way forwards. "I know this must be hard for you, bringing the plane crash back to the surface, but Echo One's death must have hit you harder than anyone else, and I still recommend talking about it. It can do no harm, after all."

Scott ignored Bosse's last comment, no matter how right it was, and left the meeting room, making his way to the interrogation room. He knew there was no need to get Mr Wilson moved; Bosse would arrange it whilst he was on his way.

A few minutes later, Alpha One entered the interrogation room. Mr Wilson was already sat in his chair, with the cold, metal table pushed up against his stomach, keeping him tight against the wall behind. Alpha One immediately took a seat.

"I've only just got here myself. Last time I had a little time to relax, I take it this one's a pretty urgent chat," said Mr Wilson in his Los Angeles accent.

He looked similar to Bosse in his age, height, and short grey hair, both on his head and sprouting from his nostrils and ears. Although Alpha One had only had the pleasure of speaking to Mr Wilson a couple of times, it was painfully apparent that his love of riddles, and his need to play the long game, being more moves ahead than anyone could even think of, made any questioning difficult. That did make him predictable, however, one characteristic Alpha One would exploit, in time. The wall behind him, the only wall Alpha One faced, was a warm, cream colour, whereas the other three were white, cold, and almost hurt your eyes to look at. There was a fake, two-way mirror on the wall to Mr Wilson's left, its main purpose to pressure the one being interrogated, whilst the tiny cameras covering the walls picked up any micro expressions and recorded the entire conversation. Alpha One knew Bosse would likely be watching from his office, so already felt a little restricted with the questions he could ask.

"Who's leaking our information?" asked Alpha One.

Mr Wilson smiled. "I could tell you, but that would be no fun at all. One thing I will say, though, is it's sure to surprise you."

"Fine. Tell me about Kale."

"Well, I believe you already know him..." started Mr Wilson. Alpha One didn't entertain his sarcasm, he merely sat back and stayed silent. "In terms of Fellscient, which I assume is what you are asking me about, Kale is Grenham's right-hand man."

"Grenham?" questioned Alpha One.

"Yes, Grenham... Oh! You don't know who he is, do you? Sorry, I forgot. Well, Grenham is of the same level as Crabble. Well, the level Crabble held before Alpha Six blew his head off. You see..." Mr Wilson could see everything was new information to Alpha One, which he liked. "Would you allow me to tell you a story?"

"If it's related to Fellscient," said Alpha One, aware Mr Wilson's lust for proving his knowledge was helpful for both sides of the table.

"Well, a long time ago, in this very galaxy..." he started, "there was a fool, or court jester, to the king. He didn't like his assumed title but knew that great power could come of it. So, he decided to form his own consortium. Obviously, not many people wanted to do business with a fool, until he told them of all the riches he could steal from the king. They were blinded by those riches and agreed to join him. Contrary to his title, the fool was the most intelligent of them all and put in a few safety measures to ensure he could never be overthrown. One of those was called the 'Five Limbs of the Beast'."

"Did you make that last bit up?" asked Alpha One.

"I can assure you, I most certainly did not," he replied, surprisingly annoyed at the interruption. "Anyway, the 'Five Limbs of the Beast' dictates that only five people can be close to the top of the food chain, the fool in this case, and only they can know the fool's identity. What's more, when one of the limbs is cut off, only a direct descendant or their next in command can take over, or of course, the one who killed the limb. Over time, they became the 'Four Faithful'. Then, when the five had become just three, they became known as the 'Trio of Truth', ironic on so many levels. When you killed Crabble, there were no descendants, and no next in command, so his 'limb' has now been removed for good, unless Anthony wishes to take over, in which case he has exactly one year from the murder to do so. Nothing can ever replace it because that would directly violate the first of the age-old rules, which means the Fellscient beast has but two limbs remaining, assuming Anthony doesn't take over. It is considered wounded, but a wounded animal is all the more dangerous. Now, if we return to their origins, this consortium enjoyed living off the king's wealth, until he caught wind of their presence, that is. They had nothing to fear, however, because the fool had already acquired many allies who wanted to take back from the king. One of those allies was an apothecary who supplied the fool with both a poison, and an antidote. The fool slipped the poison into the king's food and took the antidote. When he was made to try the food, he was unharmed. The same could not be said for the king. I seem to recall you telling me a very similar thing last time we sat in this room."

"Do you think you could move this story on a bit? I'm sure you know I'm against the clock," added Alpha One, knowing full well he had previously mentioned a fool poisoning a king.

"I apologise. This consortium continued throughout history, playing a lead role in some of history's most famous events, but as for today? Well, the two rulers, whom you haven't yet uncovered, are both descendants of the original fool. Grenham is one of just two remaining 'Limbs', and Kale very much wants to take that position. He was a little on the disappointed side when Crabble died without reappointing a successor."

Silence descended in the room.

"Was that it?" asked Alpha One.

"You did say you were in a hurry. I'll make a deal with you. Sort out this poison thing with Kale, then return here and I'll tell you the entire story. I'll also tell you who leaked your data. It makes for an interesting listen. As for helping you, well, I think you'll figure it out for yourself. But a little bit of friendly advice for the road; Kale wants to take over Fellscient, and he's going to need a team he can trust behind him, so watch your back out there."

Alpha One stood up and moved back towards the door, as he twisted the handle, he paused for a moment, confident Mr Wilson would add something at the last possible moment. And he was right.

As the handle twisted, Mr Wilson added, "And please remember, these walls have ears as well as eyes. So, just be careful, okay?"

Alpha One left the room and shut the door behind him.

He knew he couldn't just rely on Daniel for a lead, it could take days or even months to get anywhere, and that wasn't time they had. But first, he needed to rest. He walked to his bedroom, located almost in the centre of the Molehill, and removed his black trousers and tight, black T-shirt, before lying straight down on his bed.

Only a few hours later, he woke. After getting dressed, in a clean set of identical clothes, he left his bedroom, which was nothing more than a grey-painted room with a single bed in it. After hearing the door shut, he pushed against slightly and tried the handle, ensuring its self-locking mechanism was working. He then headed straight to Bosse's office.

Once there, he gave a couple of short knocks on the door, before entering.

"Usually, people who knock wait until they're told they can enter," said Bosse, who was sat at his desk on his laptop.

"Well… I knocked to tell you I was coming in," replied Scott, as he strolled over to the chair on the opposite side of Bosse's desk. As he started to sit down, he added, "I'm just going to sit," before swiftly lowering himself so he was completely down.

"I expected you here over three hours ago," said Bosse, pretending to pay more attention to his laptop than their conversation.

"I had more important things to do."

"More important than saving the lives of those innocent people?"

As frustrated as he was, he knew Bosse was right, again.

"Annoying, isn't it, when I'm always right?"

After swallowing hard, Scott moved the conversation along. "Have you had any time to analyse what Mr Wilson said?"

Bosse didn't comment, he kept his gaze fixed on his laptop and shook his head.

"So, still no leads?" asked Scott.

"No, still no leads," answered Bosse. He left it a couple of seconds before adding, "I hope you haven't forgotten about the security mission you agreed to last month."

"Is this really the time?" asked an exasperated Scott.

"I believe it is. We are at a dead end with this case and more people require our services. They deserve our help just as much as everyone else. May I also remind you, that without the paying clients, we would not be here."

"I'll get Anthony to do it. I just hope he isn't needed elsewhere," said Scott.

"Well, I believe that depends on Daniel's ability. Doesn't it?" added Bosse, so calmly it was almost as if he should've known about it.

"How'd you find out?"

"It is best you don't keep secrets from me in the future, I have my ways of uncovering them."

"We'll see…" started Scott, as he leant on the desk to stand up. "Daniel should be there about now. He's done this many times before. He's good at it, too. I just hope things don't get complicated." Scott then moved towards the door and opened it.

"As do I," muttered Bosse.

Just as Scott was heading out of the door, he turned and added, "I'd like you to set me up an identity to see Emma's family. I heard her body was finally released and the family didn't buy the story."

"Emma?" questioned Bosse. "You mean the woman who died in your arms at the Swiss compound?"

"No…" said Scott dryly. "I mean the woman who died before I even got to her. The one who died scared, and alone. The one I promised to protect but failed to do so."

"It's only taken this long to release her body because we've had to create a tissue of lies to explain her death, by your own orders, I might add. And as the family didn't seem to believe them, it seemed a complete waste of time."

"As I think you know, the family has requested several private investigators to meet the family at their private residency. When there, I can find out why they didn't buy her death. There's more to this than meets the eye."

"Are you sure this is really the right time?"

"You tell me," replied Scott, as he left Bosse's office.

# Chapter 6 – The Life of the Lie

10<sup>th</sup> September
22:31 BST
69 hrs 42 min. Until Deadline

Daniel was sat at the back of a blue, single-decker bus. He was directly in front of the back row of five seats and was positioned on an aisle chair. He didn't travel by bus too often, but if necessary, this was always the seat he took, able to watch everyone entering and exiting the bus, with a slim chance of someone sitting next to him. The bus was relatively empty, with only four other passengers, and a fifth who joined at the following stop, and of course the large bus driver, locked away at the front.

The passenger closest to Daniel was sat one row in front, on the opposite side, pressed up against the window. She looked to be in her early forties and had her head buried in a book. Whilst Daniel couldn't make out the title, the few sketched images and the relatively low number of pages gave him the impression the book was aimed at a young adult reader. Not once did she raise her head. The only time Daniel did get a look at her was on his way in; she gave him half a glance as he walked down the aisle. She had shoulder-length, brown hair, a full face of make-up, and wore a tan-coloured raincoat. Daniel also noticed a small, dark brown handbag stuffed in the corner, down by her feet.

Towards the front of the bus, there was a boy and a girl, no more than twenty years of age, who were so close to each other they were almost sat on the same seat. She wore a short, black skirt, an equally short crop top, and had long, brown hair tied back in a ponytail. He, on the other hand, wore a pair of ripped, pale, denim shorts, so tight everything in his pockets were bulging through. His white T-shirt appeared to be in a children's size and looked as if it could at any minute burst. Finally, his sliders and long, white socks, pulled up as far as they would go, really completed the picture.

There was also someone sat two seats behind the couple. It was hard for Daniel to tell anything about this person, given their dark, grey hoodie and matching jogging bottoms covering most of them. With the hood pulled up, a phone concealing their eyes, and a pair of earphones, connected to the phone, disappearing under the hood, Daniel only had their hands to work with. Their hands seemed smooth and wrinkle-free, with relatively tight skin. There were no hairs on the back of their hands and none on the short, but skinny, fingers attached to them. When Daniel first got on the bus, he'd kicked the side of the seat in front of the mysterious figure and pretended to trip, hoping to get them to raise their head, but no such thing happened, their face remained a mystery.

Finally, the only person who got on after Daniel was an elderly gentleman who sat on the aisle seat at the very front. As he walked to his seat, he kept his hands on anything, trying to support himself. He had very thin, short, grey hair and wore oversized, beige trousers and a large, brown raincoat. Whilst his trousers and raincoat were a similar colour, they clearly didn't match and clashed with his smart, polished, black shoes.

After the elderly man had settled, they stopped at no more bus stops. Daniel had already planned the entire route and had chosen that specific one because of its low number of stops, making it more likely to be empty. Despite this, the journey still wasn't short, with a planned time of almost an hour. During his time in the hot, sweaty bus, Daniel had little to do but focus his mind and prepare himself for every eventuality. When he used to do this, he would always have a character he would assume and a clear objective in mind. But going in as himself, knowing they know that he's working against them, was something completely new. He found it hard to focus, given the constant interruption from the giggling near the front. The woman nearest to Daniel looked up from her book and appeared to snarl a couple of times, but the mysterious person kept their head down, and the elderly man kept his gaze fixed out of the closest window, watching as the buildings, the occasional tree, and the people all went past the window in a blur.

As the bus approached Daniel's stop, which was also the final stop on the route, located next to the bus depot, he started moving in his seat, ready to leave the bus. The woman to his right marked the page she was on, by folding down the top corner, and packed her book into her squashed handbag. The bus slowed down and came to a stop. Before the handbrake came on, the mysterious person leapt up and walked to the doors. As soon as they were open, they left at speed and disappeared into the unlit surrounds of the bus stop.

Daniel allowed the woman off before himself, not so much out of kindness, but because he preferred to be the one behind, able to watch everything they did. That being said, he certainly didn't refuse the "Thank you" she gave him, returning a smile. Allowing her to go first also helped Daniel to build a bigger picture, now he'd heard her Welsh accent.

Both passed the driver, both saying "Thank you" as they left.

Outside was still hot, but the freshness was certainly better than the bus. As Daniel paused for a moment, pretending to get his bearings, he saw the elderly gentleman pull himself up from his seat and leave, shortly followed by the final two.

The four passengers, who were still visible, all headed to the left, towards the large housing estate on the outskirts of the even larger industrial estate. With a hiss, the bus slowly moved off towards the bus depot, just around the corner. The housing estate was the only thing that provided any light and was enough to slightly illuminate the dark industrial estate, which had been shut down for the night. Daniel broke away from the rest of the pack and headed towards the darkness. He knew exactly where he was going, but that didn't make it any easier to find amongst the warren of tight turns and identical looking passageways. Of course, the lack of light and the seemingly randomly placed buildings didn't help either, but eventually, Daniel found the right place, in the exact spot marked by the GPS coordinates he'd found in the factory.

As he looked at the building, he wasn't sure what he was expecting to see, but that certainly wasn't it. It looked much like the others with its industrial style, limited windows, and maximised surface area. Even in the dark, Daniel could see it was crammed in between a DIY store and a bedding store, equally trying to push the boundaries of the land they owned. Daniel cautiously approached the door of the building, unsure what tricks and traps could await him. As he got closer, a sign on the door came into view. *'Come in. We've been expecting you'*, it read. The door looked like a fire escape that had been put in backwards, with a long metal bar on the outside. Daniel pushed the bar, pressing himself against the door as he did. The door swung in, and Daniel followed it inside.

Stood directly in front of him was Kale. He smiled.

"I'm glad you could make it. Now if you don't mind, we'll get straight on. I'm sure we both have things we need to be getting on with."

Before Daniel had a chance to respond, Kale gestured with his hand for him to follow and turned to walk away from him. He followed Kale a few paces behind, but the initial trust Kale had shown, turning his back on Daniel, was surprising. Although Daniel expected hundreds of eyes and half the number of guns to be trained on him, he didn't feel it, nor did he see them. As they walked through the empty reception area, complete with an empty desk, stained, light oak flooring, and dirty, cream walls, splattered with a disturbing red mist, Daniel somehow felt at ease. He'd been trying to keep himself calm before entering, unsure what he'd find, but now in, he felt like himself, something he hadn't felt in a long time.

Kale didn't check behind to see if Daniel was still following, he just pushed open the two heavy-looking doors that blocked his path. Light instantly filled the dingy reception area and Daniel wasted no time in moving through the doorway, whilst Kale held the doors open for him. The next room was massive. Although they were sealed inside a small, glass corridor, everything looked open-plan. There were several large rooms, which were also separated by glass walls, again making those large rooms appear to be one giant room. Most of the rooms were filled with lines of desks, each packed full of computer monitors, and people entirely focussed on whatever streams of data they were looking at. A couple of the rooms were empty, one of which had a giant table, similar to that at the Molehill. They then passed two adjoining rooms, which appeared to be where the… higher paid members worked. They also seemed entirely focussed on whatever their computer screens displayed, but whereas other rooms had up to twenty people, these slightly more special rooms had just five people, arranged so that each workstation was spaced out. Monitors took up most of the space on their desks, with the odd piece of paper lying around on some.

"These are our agents. They go out into the field and… Well, they basically do what you do. Whereas the people in the slightly more cramped rooms are solely based here, and do what you used to do," said Kale, as he stopped by the glass wall. "This is where you'll be working, shortly. I'm sure you've only come to betray us, but that's now, and that desk there…" he added, pointing to the only empty desk in the room, "is the future."

Daniel blocked the comment from his mind. Whatever tricks Kale was playing, he'd make sure they were used only to his own advantage.

Just as Daniel went to move on, he caught sight of one member in particular. Her desk was located next to the empty one. He hadn't seen that face in a very long time. She had the face of someone he'd worked with in his previous life.

"Yes, that's Yue, but you already know that, don't you?" asked Kale.

***

*26th August 2013, Over Twelve Years Ago*

Daniel was sat in his office chair, behind his desk, in the middle of the shared workspace, as he always was. His usual ham and mustard sandwiches were tightly fastened in the Tupperware box to his left. The ham and white bread were the cheapest in the supermarket, and there was only a trace amount of mustard on just one slice of bread, the same as always. The empty, tea-stained mug to his right was ready to be refilled for the third time that day, and had been for a few minutes. He'd hoped one of his colleagues would head to the tiny kitchen area at the back, but everyone knew they'd be inundated with empty cups and mugs and likely had the same idea as Daniel. It wasn't like his work was time sensitive, it just seemed too much effort to even make his own, let alone everyone else's tea.

He let another fifteen minutes pass, with still no movement towards the kitchen area. Eventually, he decided to bite the bullet and head to the kitchen. He'd barely risen to his feet before cups and mugs were raised in the air. Reluctantly, he collected them and moved to the back of the office. After filling up the kettle, the first of what would likely be four times, he flicked the switch and turned to view the office whilst he waited. To his left, tucked in the corner, was the back of an unfamiliar head. He couldn't see their face but was sure he hadn't met them before. With a not-so-subtle glance over at their workspace, Daniel saw little but a computer monitor, keyboard, computer, laptop, and a newspaper. There was no mug for tea or coffee, no sign of any lunch, and certainly nothing personal decorating the desk, like every other agent in the room.

"Daniel," came from a deep, jovial voice to his left.

It was his boss, wandering towards him. He was greying, in his late forties, with a thick, grey moustache covering his top lip.

"I'm glad I caught you. How are those reports on the unregistered oil rigs coming along?"

"They're almost complete. You should have them by the end of the day. It seems the oil rigs are genuine and they are drilling for oil, but as expected, they're a front for the terror organisation we've been tracking for the past few weeks. I've found nothing about why they need these rigs, but shutting them down should halt their plans," replied Daniel.

"Good. I just thought I'd check as… you know who has been on my back all morning."

"Yeah, I understand Richard," added Daniel, only half paying attention to what his boss was saying.

"Well… I'll leave you to it," concluded Richard, aware his words were getting lost somewhere.

Just as he was about to wander back to his office as if he had all the time in the world, Daniel grabbed his arm.

"Who is that?" he mouthed, and unintentionally whispered at the same time, whilst tilting his head towards the unknown agent.

Richard looked over towards them and raised his thin, greying eyebrows. "That's Ying Yue, but she goes by 'Yue'. She's come from upstairs to work with us. The orders came from well above my head, but she's got a decent enough track record, so I saw no reason to complain. Why?"

"Just curious," replied Daniel, as he released his grip on Richard's hairy arm.

By this point, the kettle was rumbling and shaking. He made the four batches of tea and coffee and delivered them, before making his way over to Yue. She had straight, long, black hair and sat with a very upright posture.

"Can I get you anything?" asked Daniel.

She looked up at him and simply said, "No, thank you," before returning her eyes back to her monitor.

"Okay, well, let me know if you change your mind."

She didn't give him another glance but just nodded her head a few times and started delicately touching the keys in front of her. Just as Daniel turned away, he saw the newspaper on her desk again. It was pressed up against the computer and was raised up. To Daniel, it looked like there was a hard drive or memory stick plugged into the USB port, which wasn't unusual. They were often downloading information both for and from their various assets and informants, but hiding it under a newspaper seemed a little strange. Daniel returned to his desk and continued his work as quickly as he could, wanting to proceed with his next self-assigned case as soon as possible.

***

"Shall we move on? There's lots to be getting on with," said Kale, bringing Daniel firmly back to the present.

Daniel nodded once, broke his gaze from Yue, and followed Kale through the door at the end of the corridor. Kale opened only one of the two doors and held it open for Daniel to take it. Daniel was surprised by the door's weight, as it caught him off guard and almost pushed him back into the corridor. There weren't any more rooms, just a wide, open space, with pristine, white walls and a spiral staircase. The flooring also remained constant, even on the stairs. They ascended, each footstep echoing in the unfurnished space. The staircase led to a single door, at which they both stopped. Kale gave four firm knocks on the door and waited.

"Enter," came from a regal-sounding voice inside the room. Cautiously, Daniel followed Kale inside.

The room was relatively dark, with most of the furniture made from wood. It was clear the room was used as one person's office, with an oversized desk in the centre, and other pieces of furniture scattered around the vast room. There were a few double sofas, an unmanned bar to one side, a drinks cabinet closer to the desk, and a few odd decorations, none of which Daniel understood. There were eight armed guards stood around the room. They were more like statues, barely even moving to breathe. They each wore identical, black tactical gear and had black masks obscuring their faces.

Sat behind the desk, with his chair turned to face out of the wide window behind the desk, was a man. He swung his chair round to face the two guests, as he let a smile creep across his face. It was a face Daniel recognised immediately. The man's face appeared identical to Richard's but over a decade older.

"Daniel, I'm glad you could make it. It is lovely to finally meet you, in the flesh," he said in the same regal voice. Daniel said nothing, prompting the man in the chair to beckon Daniel to come closer, saying, "Come."

Daniel moved forwards and stopped in front of the desk.

"That will be all, Kale," he added.

Kale nodded and replied, "As you wish, Grenham." He then left the room, closing the door behind him.

"So, that's what you're called now, is it? Grenham? What happened to Carl?" asked Daniel.

"As I was saying, I'm glad you're here. I trust the clue wasn't too difficult for you to find?" asked Grenham, ignoring Daniel's question. "Well, obviously you didn't find it too difficult as you're here. Now, do you mind if we get straight on with business?"

"I certainly have no objections," answered Daniel, eager to obtain information as quickly as possible.

"Very well. I know Kale has given you the tour of the facility. That office space and this room up here is all there is."

Grenham then beckoned Daniel even closer to look out of the window behind him. The window overlooked all the office spaces below, with every desk visible. It was clearly tinted, but Daniel didn't remember seeing it as he walked along the corridor.

"I want to start by saying that we are on your side. I'm not saying we don't have a vendetta against your organisation, but we certainly don't have one against you. You are free to come and go as you please. You won't be searched on your exit and you can do what you feel is best with the data that your access code allows. We trust you to do the right thing. After all, trust is what we base ourselves on."

"That's good to hear," said Daniel, as he stared out of the tinted window. "But what exactly am I here for?"

"That depends on who you ask," started Grenham. "You're here to gather any information you can on the poisoned food… from your perspective. From ours, however, you're here to join us. We both know how much of an asset you'll be."

Daniel was about to speak but was instantly cut off.

"I know you have no intention of betraying your team, and we don't want you to. We want what's best for the world, just like you and your team, so why can't we work together?"

"You want to help the world?" asked Daniel, slightly exasperated. "You poisoned food which was consumed by hundreds of thousands of innocent people."

"Innocent?" questioned Grenham. "Oh no, they weren't innocent. I really am surprised you didn't do your homework. The people who consumed that product were targeted by us and were either a corrupt government worker, a corrupt public sector worker, or an unconvicted criminal, the list just goes on. In fact, a couple of them came on to our radar and were planning the mass extinction of the entire population. Of course, there were many innocent people who did also consume the food, I admit, but there must always be sacrifices for the greater good."

"People who planned the mass extinction of the Earth? It takes one to know one," added Daniel.

"Oof, that hurts," said Grenham. "What we do here is in the best interest of humanity. I know you'll need time to come to that realisation, and that's why you'll be working here… so you can see what we really do, free of any prior assumptions, or misconceptions. As I said, you are free to come and go, but please just give us a chance, we're not the villains."

"So, what? I just pop in whenever I feel like it? Access your data files?"

"That is pretty much it, yes. In time, I believe you will learn to trust us."

Grenham then pressed a button on his desk. A couple of seconds later, a different door opened and a woman emerged; the same woman that was on the bus.

"This is my secretary, Tria," said Grenham. "Tria, this is Daniel. He will be working with us."

"It is very nice to meet you," she said.

"Likewise," replied Daniel, a little unsure whether Grenham knew about their recent encounter.

"Tria will help you to settle in. Anything you need, just send her an email or ring her on extension eight," added Grenham before looking towards Tria and concluding, "If you could show Daniel to his workspace, he can get straight on with his work."

Tria nodded and led Daniel out of the door he had entered through. He was led back to the office with more space and was shown to the empty desk.

"This is where you'll be working," she started.

Daniel noticed the other workers fail to even acknowledge the presence of a stranger, they all simply continued with their tasks.

"Your first assignment is to track down those who stole one of Van Gogh's paintings housed in a private collection. I know it didn't make headline news, for obvious reasons, but one of our analysts has tracked this theft back to a known group of mercenaries. You can find any information on them under the file name *Code Name Delta*. I know you'll want to settle in, so by all means take some time to… get used to our systems."

"Thank you," replied Daniel.

He instantly noticed Yue's head rise, as she stopped touching the keys on her keyboard.

"I hope you enjoy working here. And a piece of friendly advice, don't uncover anything that doesn't want to be uncovered. You'll find it useful in the long run," she concluded before leaving the room.

***

*9th September 2013*

Daniel was stood in the security office with his boss, Richard, and the security guard, Kris. The room was cramped, with barely enough room for one person to sit amongst the hundreds of TVs displaying various rooms around their complex. Kris was pressing away at the keys on his keyboard, causing one of the TV screens to flick, in reverse, from image to image at four times speed.

"What exactly are we looking for?" asked Kris.

Daniel didn't answer, he just waited until he saw what he wanted to on the TV screen.

"There!" he shouted.

The central monitor showed Yue walking along the corridor.

"The timestamp shows this was two minutes and… thirty-one seconds before the breach," said Kris.

"Follow her," demanded Daniel, as they watched her walk out of the camera shot.

Kris brought up the feeds of several cameras along Yue's path until she finally entered a room. A couple of seconds later, Kris brought up another image, this time of Yue inside the room she had just entered.

"What room is she in?" asked Richard.

Kris hesitated slightly, before saying, "That's the… maintenance room."

"Why would she be in there?" asked Richard, as he started looking through the file containing her whereabouts during the system breach.

They then watched as she retrieved a roll of blue paper towels and some kind of disinfectant. She then left the room, prompting Kris to move the camera feed to back outside the room. The feed then went black.

"That's when we had the breach. The cameras didn't start recording until I'd rebooted them about half an hour later," said Kris.

"I'm sorry to say, but it looks like Yue's in the clear," added Richard.

"No," protested Daniel. "You are forced to bring her into the office, and then eleven days later, we have an entire system breach. Over fifty per cent of employees and assets, including you and I, have been compromised. It has to be her."

"Daniel, the orders to bring her into the office were above my head, but they were still from people who could've been included in the breach. Yue passed all of our investigations. She's in the clear for this," added Richard.

"Seventy-two hours, and we're still no closer to finding who breached our system," said Daniel.

"I know," started Richard, "but a newspaper covering a thumb drive and collecting cleaning supplies to wipe a spillage, which agrees with the account she gave during her interview, isn't even grounds for an investigation, and is certainly not enough to ruin her reputation over. Leave this investigation to the experts, as we're not even meant to be here since getting compromised."

***

Daniel had spent the past three hours searching through piles and piles of data on *'Operation Delta'*. During that time, Yue hadn't made eye contact or said a single word to him, but he did notice her work seemed slower than the others, everything from her typing speed to the time she took to read files. His presence was clearly having an effect on her. Of course, Daniel had taken a quick look at various files to test his access codes but found little was accessible, despite the 'we trust you' part of Grenham's speech.

It seemed, from Daniel's limited access, that Code Name Delta was more of a team than a group. They wanted to uncover something called 'The Treasure of Five'. What exactly that was Daniel was still unsure, but how it related to the stolen Van Gogh painting was where he did have a few ideas. The team had been involved in several robberies in the last six months, all of which related to artefacts, art pieces, or books from the nineteenth century. So, whatever The Treasure of Five was, it must've been created, or buried, during the nineteenth century. It wasn't all that much to boast about after three hours' work, but it yielded the strongest lead Grenham's team had come up with to date.

"What're you working on?" asked Yue out of the blue, as she swung her chair to face Daniel.

"You been working up the courage to speak to me?" he replied.

"Why would I need to work up the courage? It was YOU who accused ME of spying. If anything, I was waiting for an apology before I said anything, but I guess I should've known better."

"Why should I apologise? I still know it was you," added Daniel.

"After all this time, you still haven't let it go."

"It cost so many people their lives. I lost my family, I was meant to die, because of you!" shouted Daniel.

The other staff members in the room carried on with their work, as if nothing was happening around them.

"If we're going to work together, you need to let this go," she concluded, before turning her chair back to face her desk.

***

*12<sup>th</sup> September 2013*

Daniel had spent the past few days digging up everything he could find on Yue. It wasn't like he had much else to do whilst being away from the office. His home desk was covered in paper, empty cans of sugary drinks, empty bottles of equally sugary drinks, and a couple of shredded fast-food wrappers, all jumbled up like somebody had tipped a rubbish bin upside down. In all that time, he'd found nothing to suggest that Yue was the spy responsible for their data breach. The breach itself was sophisticated… and internal but, however it was done, it was likely during the power outage. It would've given Yue enough time to go from the office, down to the server room and download everything on file. Except, she wasn't in the office when the power went down, she was a further three minutes away, two if she ran, and that wouldn't allow enough time to slip into the server room and still remain unseen based on other accounts. It didn't seem to matter how many dead ends he had to hit, Yue was still his prime suspect, all because of something so trivial as a newspaper covering a thumb drive, not that he even knew there was one. He knew everyone else would dismiss it, had dismissed it, but if he could find enough evidence, if he could find any evidence, Richard would help; he'd helped before and he'd do it again.

Without warning, as they usually do, his phone started ringing. Sleep-deprived, it took Daniel a few rings before picking it up. The screen showed *DAD*. Daniel exhaled slightly, both welcoming and irritated by the distraction.

"Hello," he said after answering. "Oh, you know, a bit of this, a bit of that..." He then listened to his dad, before exhaling again. "Yes, I am. How did you know?" He listened again. "No, I hadn't forgotten you were in this line of work before me. And there's no need to say anything even remotely like, 'It was much harder back in my day'." He then stayed silent while his dad continued. He was the one who had got him into the job. He was also one of the agency's best and left shoes that couldn't even partially be filled. Whatever Daniel thought it was he was going through, the chances were his dad went through worse. "Yes, I guess so. Why is it that you need me to take you both? You can still drive you know..."

"Yes, I'll be there tomorrow...

"Yes, I'll leave it to internal affairs, even if it means they'll be barking up the wrong tree...

"Alright, see you then. Yep, bye... Yep... Yep, bye... Bye... No, okay, you're still talking... You know when people say 'bye', it's usually because they want to put the phone down... Bye... You sure you've finished this time? Alright. Bye then. Yep, bye."

Daniel let out yet another lungful of air, this time almost in relief, as he placed his phone back on his desk.

Whilst closing his laptop down and getting some rest, as had just been recommended, sounded like a good idea, he couldn't rest until he'd proven himself right. It wasn't so much wanting to find out who was responsible for the breach any more, he'd been burned and nothing was going to change that, but he had to prove that he was right, for himself.

It might have taken another five hours of trawling through the surveillance feeds, but eventually he saw a glimmer of hope that proved maybe he was right. Daniel instantly reached for his phone and called Richard, unaware it was two o'clock in the morning. Daniel let the phone ring… and ring. After several rings, a clearly frustrated, but also quite mumbly, Richard answered the phone.

"It's two o'clock in the morning. What do you want?" asked Richard.

"I've found it," answered Daniel.

"Look, I… I don't know what you've just said. It was like you've just thrown a few words at me," replied Richard.

"Right, okay. I've found evidence proving that I was right," added Daniel, triumphantly. There was only silence that followed. "Richard!"

"Oh, sorry. Er… I was listening."

"So, what do think?" asked Daniel.

"Do you think you could just run through the basics of what you said?"

"I said, 'I was right', about Yue. I've got evidence to prove it this time," he repeated.

"I'll be round yours in about an hour. Assuming I don't fall asleep in the meantime," said Richard, before ending the call.

***

Daniel had hoped to wrap up his first case before extracting any information on the poisoned food but, after a further seven hours of work and no traction in the case, he knew no one had enough time to wait. Two of the other agents had left the office during that time and Daniel's hope for an empty office whilst he conducted his research seemed as unlikely as finding Code Name Delta before sunset, not that he could actually see the sun, but that was something he'd become used to. He stood up to get some coffee and, to his surprise, was joined by Yue. She stayed a few paces behind him and said nothing until they were alone in the kitchen room behind their office space.

"Why do you still think it was me?" she asked, ensuring the door was closed.

Daniel grabbed a paper cup and placed it in the coffee machine. The machine had a simple on/off switch, the 'on' made the coffee pour, and the 'off' stopped it, obviously.

"I thought we had to let this go," he replied.

"How can you still think it was me? Have you not seen who runs this whole thing?"

"It's not him."

"Really!" she exploded. "Because it sure looks like Grenham is Richard. They've got the same face, voice, and everything!"

"It's his twin brother, Carl. You want to know how I know that? Because Richard died, because of you."

"No, he didn't. Do you want to know why I was sent down to your office? It was to investigate Richard. He was the one who was responsible for the breach," she added.

Daniel stopped moving. The coffee started overflowing and running down the side of the paper cup.

"But..." Nothing else came out. He'd been so sure, for so many years, that she was the one responsible, but in just a few words, he suddenly believed the complete opposite, because he'd finally heard something that fitted with all the pieces.

***

*13th September 2013*

Two and a quarter hours had passed, with still no sign of Richard. It was then that he got the message. His phone pinged and his screen lit up. The message was from Richard, reading, *'I'm not going to make it. Upload the evidence to a secure server and make sure that if anything happens to you, the evidence is sent everywhere. Now go about your normal routine, they're watching everything. Pick up your parents and proceed with whatever you'd already planned.'* Daniel read the message and wasted no time in uploading the evidence he'd gathered to a secure server.

He then followed the rest of the instructions. It wasn't easy going about his normal routine, but that was exactly what he'd been trained to do, act the part of a normal person. But his act didn't save him, or his family, from the events that followed. Friday the 13th of September 2013 was to be the lowest day in Daniel's life.

***

"It can't be," said Daniel, desperately trying to hold on to the thing that made the least sense.

"Didn't you think it was odd that someone on the brink of being killed was able to send a perfectly punctuated text message, basically telling you to do the thing that got you and your parents killed, as far as the world was concerned, anyway? And how exactly did he know that you were going to pick up your parents?" asked Yue.

Daniel paused for a moment. "How did you know?"

"Know what?" she asked.

"How did you know what was in that text message?" he clarified.

Yue swallowed hard and took a couple of moments' pause as she thought. "Because that man up there is Richard. He showed me. Most of the time, he brags about it. Carl never existed; it was always only Richard."

"So, how come you're working for him?"

"Because you uploaded that so-called 'evidence', I lost everything, well almost everything. My employer, the one who tasked me with investigating Richard in the first place, saw an opportunity to get even closer to him, so I pretended to crawl back to Richard, or Grenham, or whatever name he goes by, and ask for a job. I've been gathering evidence against him ever since."

"Uploading that evidence still cost me everything. So why should I suddenly believe that it wasn't your fault? Whether you were responsible for the attack, or the cause of it, it was still your fault."

"He isn't dead!" erupted Yue.

She then switched the coffee machine off and left the room, leaving Daniel alone with the countless thoughts running through his head. He knew it was going to take time to untangle the twisted accounts, unsure who, if anyone, was telling the truth, but that was time he didn't have. No matter how hard it was, he had to bottle up yet another bout of emotions, and questions, and proceed with what he was really there for.

A few minutes later, he too left the room to enter the office. As he opened the door, Kale was standing directly in front of him. Daniel noticed Yue had already taken her seat and her head was buried deep in her work.

"Can I have a word?" Kale asked, quietly.

# Chapter 7 – The Enemy of the Enemy

11<sup>th</sup> September
13:20 BST
54 hrs 53 min. Until Deadline

A few hundred metres up in the sky, a highly agile attack helicopter was dancing between various bullets and rockets whizzing past.

"This is as close as I can get you!" shouted the only pilot, as he looked behind to see nothing but an empty compartment.

Just moments earlier, Miss Cadlow had jumped from the back, already aware she was as close to the ground as possible.

From the ground, the guards on patrol had scattered themselves out and into cover, as their surface-to-air missiles attempted to take down the fleeing helicopter. They were guarding a giant estate, with a modern, and huge, villa in the centre of its grounds. It had a lovely view, overlooking the ocean from high above the rocky cliff face. Unfortunately, today, the view was that of scrambling guards, flares, roaring missiles, and gunfire. Just as they thought they'd won, seeing the helicopter fly off into the distance, they caught sight of a lone parachute descending at speed. In an instant, they turned fire on the owner of the parachute, but their training was much like the number of days they had off, limited. No matter how many bullets they sent in the general direction of the parachutist, none were on target.

However, the parachutist seemed just as inexperienced, as she headed towards the only tree in the grounds at what seemed like the speed of a car. Her chute got caught in the branches and she disappeared behind the huge trunk, still strapped to the parachute. The guards approached cautiously, aiming at the tree. Only a few hung back, as the rest continued to close in. They moved around the tree… and saw nothing but an empty parachute, dangling in a few of the branches. *Was there even somebody in there?* many of them thought. It didn't take long for them to get an answer.

A figure dropped down from the branches above, embedding a long blade into the closest guard. All in the same movement, she drew the blade back up, slicing another, before thrusting it into a third's chest. Within the tight group of ten guards, not one of them had the room, or the time, to get a clean shot off, but she was formidable with her blade. After what felt like only a couple of seconds, she had sliced her way through all the closest guards and had taken cover behind the huge tree, as the next bombardment of bullets came from the few who'd stayed further back. The tree was hundreds, maybe even thousands of years old, but it was able to absorb the impact of each bullet with ease, sacrificing only a few splinters each time.

"Whenever you're ready," said Miss Cadlow sarcastically, as she started to lose a little patience behind the tree.

"I thought you were dealing with them."

"Just take them down."

Miss Cadlow waited until the noise of the gunfire subsided, gun by gun. She hadn't heard gunfire actually become confused before, but as the guards were taken down, it seemed they were just as clueless.

Miss Cadlow then strolled out, her blade, a katana, clasped firmly in her right hand and her brown hair blowing in the wind. She seemed in no hurry, nor did she have any concern over the armed guards she casually approached. They were preoccupied and were felled one by one. It didn't take long before reinforcements arrived, but they didn't seem any more trained. Charging out like a stampede of animals, they too were taken down. The order they were eliminated in was easy to miss, but Miss Cadlow noticed. It was as the guards became a threat, and aimed in her general direction, that they were downed. It was almost a relief when they ran for cover, giving Miss Cadlow a chance to move up, in her same casual manner, in little danger.

By the time she'd finished strolling up the garden path, most of the guards were sprawled out over the precisely cut, pristine grass. After approaching the white wall of the villa, she pressed her back up against it and waited next to a small side door. The guards, now in much smaller numbers, were still charging out in dribs and drabs from the main, glass, sliding doors which covered most of the wall facing the bloodbath.

The door Miss Cadlow was waiting by, to the side of the giant, glass doors, was a side entrance and would open into a tighter space, where the corridors and rooms were less open-plan than the huge kitchen, lounge, diner, kind of observation room, and unusually placed bedroom monster room that the glass doors led to. The tighter turns and shorter sight lines would allow Miss Cadlow to use her trusted katana to the best of its ability. Unfortunately, that door was locked.

She checked her digital watch, fastened to her left wrist with a rubber strap. The screen displayed a timer ticking down. There were just ten seconds left. Sure enough, as the timer displayed eight zeros, the door made a *CLONK*, and a strange buzz, as it started to open outwards. One guard flew out. Miss Cadlow swung her blade round and thrust it behind her, into the building. It had caught a second guard in the torso. She drew the blade back out and cut it down the entire length of the first guard's back, leaving them both on the floor.

Before moving in, she turned and gave a very relaxed salute towards a completely out of place collection of rocks at the edge of the grass, bordering the cliff face.

"She's heading inside," said the person who had been providing cover from in amongst the collection of rocks with a marksman rifle.

He was dressed in a long, black coat and had a hood pulled up over his head. From between the rocks, only the barrel of his gun could be seen, and from above, only the long coat and two prosthetic legs.

Miss Cadlow only got a few steps into the building before the speakers, situated throughout the villa, started crackling. After the crackling stopped, a voice came through all of them, like a tannoy message, but at full volume.

"Ladies and gentlemen, boys and girls…" bellowed through the speakers, stopping all the remaining guards in their tracks. "Introducing to you, for one night only, the one… the only… Miss Cadloooowwww!"

She had no idea the announcement was going to be made, but that made her smile all the more. The guards remained frozen, allowing her enough time to approach. Inside the villa was cold where the air conditioning had been turned to the lowest temperature possible. She stayed out of the huge room whilst cutting down their numbers, letting a few guards get a shot or two off, to lure in more. Her blade found every guard who came through the doorway, as she sliced through as many as possible, as efficiently as possible. The bodies pilling up helped her even more, slowing down the guards' entry and spreading them out. Eventually, the guards did start to make it through, as they neglected to use their weapons and instead opted to just push through. Miss Cadlow was slowly pushed back into another room behind her, a bedroom, just a bedroom. A few guards followed her through, one of whom raised his rifle to fire. She dug her blade into the closest guard and twisted him round so he took the entire magazine of bullets. Once empty, she pushed the impaled guard back and struck the remaining two. Another was about to run through the doorway, but Miss Cadlow slammed the door shut, dazing the guard as it was stopped only by their nose. The door started to roll back and Miss Cadlow delivered a single, fatal, blow to the guard.

With no more guards flooding in, she strolled out of the room and into the giant, open-plan room where more commotion had broken out. She wandered around the corner to see the hooded figure, who'd been covering her, kneeling on the floor with a gloved hand pushing down on a guard's chest.

"I didn't think you were coming," she said as if striking up a conversation.

"Time is short, you were taking too long," he snapped back, before standing up and continuing through the quiet villa. His marksman rifle was now strapped to his back and he carried no weapon in his hands, but he didn't need to. His hands were the weapons.

As they made their way through the villa, only a few guards remained. One tried to catch them by surprise, as he leapt out from behind an ornamental pillar with a kitchen knife. The hooded figure merely raised his left arm to direct the knife away from him and threw his right fist into the guard's chest. With a final splutter of air ejected from his lungs, the guard fell to the floor.

"I'll get the SAMs, you get the target," he said, moving up the stairs to their right.

"You got it."

The hooded figure climbed the stairs and moved straight outside, on to the balcony. From there, he headed around the corner and up another set of stairs which led to the roof. As he moved up, he removed the glove on his right hand, revealing a prosthetic one, whilst taking a small, cylindrical object, shaped a little like a vial, from his pocket, placing it inside the sleeve of his right arm. After just sticking his head up above a conveniently placed air conditioning unit, a cluster of bullets clanged into it. He counted five guards, all making a final stand. As soon as they stopped, he jumped up, pointed his arm towards one of the guards and let the small object fire from up his sleeve, close to the speed of a bullet, before diving back into cover. The object made contact with one of the guards. It sent hundreds of volts surging through his body, causing him to firmly pull his rifle's trigger and release the remaining bullets in its magazine. The other guards dived for cover, as bullets sprayed everywhere. Even after the magazine was empty, the guards remained in cover, aware the hooded figure likely had them pinned down. As they sat there, contemplating their next move, a hand came from above one of them and grabbed him, heaving him out of sight. The guard who sat next to him turned to open fire, but failed to release a single bullet, as a prosthetic hand flew towards him and grabbed his throat. Its grip was relentless.

The guard who'd been electrocuted was still shaking under the voltage passing through his body, which left just two. They were sat together, next to the surface-to-air missile launcher. They'd obviously agreed a plan, and together, they stood up and opened fire. However, they didn't see the figure, they just saw one of the other guards flying towards them. He clattered into one, sending them falling off the roof. The other guard caught sight of movement to his right, but before he could react, his feet were lifted a metre from the ground. His body froze. Slowly, he was lowered to face the hooded figure. The last thing the guard saw was something few ever had, the figure's piercing, almost hypnotic, blue eyes.

The figure moved to the SAM turret and tore out several wires, before peering over the side of the roof. The two guards, who'd fallen, lay motionless on the floor, but someone else had just run out of the villa at speed. He was running for his life.

***

*Two Minutes Earlier*

Miss Cadlow didn't need to watch the hooded figure move up the stairs, she was focussed on what was in front of her. She also knew where the target would hide.

"Open the safe room," she said, as she approached a solid, steel door. It looked more like a giant vault door and was certainly not discreet.

"The door's opening now," said the same person who'd spoken through all the speakers.

Miss Cadlow could hear all the bolts and locks shift back and, after spinning the vault-style, circular handle ninety degrees clockwise, the door swung out. Inside, another door blocked her path. This one was a simple, wooden door. She approached it and gave six tuneful knocks. Seconds later, a crossbow bolt half emerged through the door. She saw this as almost an invitation to enter.

Twisting the handle, she stuck her head around the door and said, "That's not the way to treat your guests now, is it?"

Inside the small, bare room were two men. One was the target, a tall, skinny businessman, in a dark blue, pinstriped suit, with a gaunt expression. The other was a guard, who was dressed in the same black, tactical clothing as the other guards but had a red, chequered wild rag, or neckerchief as it was probably labelled in the shop, hanging around his neck. It wasn't much to separate him from the other guards, but it was enough for Miss Cadlow to notice.

It was the guard who had the crossbow in his hands, but he dropped it on the floor, knowing all too well that he wouldn't have the time to load another bolt. He stretched his hand behind his back and reached for a blade, lying on the only table behind him. The blade was a cutlass, a curved blade often seen in pirate films. Miss Cadlow instinctively knew the guard had some kind of training, as he adopted a duelling stance similar to the one she found herself in. But no matter what stance he took, or how much training he'd had, it was the curved blade that would let him down. Miss Cadlow knew it. The guard knew it. Even the target was slowly edging for the door. The blade was purely for display purposes, it would be sharp, but nothing compared to her own blade. Maintaining their distance, they started circling around the room. As soon as the target saw a clear path to the door, he was gone.

So long as the guard made the first move, she would win. Her green eyes focussed on the guard. She twitched. It wasn't big, but it was enough. The guard charged forwards and swung his blade. Miss Cadlow manoeuvred her body to the side and raised her blade. It looked like they had just passed each other, like a couple jousting who had missed, but as she maintained her slightly crouched stance, her back still to the guard, he fell. The blade had caught him.

As calmly as she'd entered, she left, in pursuit of the target. As she left the safe room and entered the giant, open-plan space, the hooded figure walked towards her, dragging the target inside by his right ankle.

"What've you found?" she asked.

"It seems you dropped something."

Their target was kicking and punching the air, trying to break free, but it was hopeless. Without any effort, the target was thrown into a dining chair.

"What is it you want? Money? I can get that," pleaded the target.

Silence descended in the room, as the other two maintained an emotionless stare towards him. All that made a noise was the target's heavy breathing.

"What do you want!" he screamed.

The hooded figure bent down, lent forwards, and slowly placed his gloved index finger on the target's lips.

"Shh. We are thinking," he said, softly. The target fell silent. "Now…" started the hooded figure, as if he was about to tell a fairy tale. "There will be some people popping by in a few minutes to find you. Your name was given… Well, that doesn't matter. What does matter is what you know."

"I'll tell you everything," the target said.

"Good."

"But not for you," Miss Cadlow added quietly.

"Now correct me if I'm wrong, but your company designed the poison, and antidote, which has infected certain people," the hooded figure said. The target nodded. "I understand you are keeping the antidote in a vault in your very own bank. Correct?" The target nodded again. "Good. And the, so-called, recipe for the antidote is no longer in your possession. Correct?" At this stage, the target had taken to nodding at every word that was said. "I see. Now the big problem here is what do you know of Fellscient?"

The target started to stutter and stumble over his words as he said, "They are the ones who wanted the poison. They have the recipe for the antidote and allowed me to keep one vial of it should I ever need it."

"And who have you been doing business with?"

"Three people. One of them I never met, the one in charge, Grenham I think they said his name was. But the two I did do business with were Kale and some secretary… er, Tria, I think. Although Kale was taking orders, he took charge of everything. There seemed very few things that were fed back to Grenham; it was Kale who oversaw the entire thing."

"I see," said the hooded figure, standing up. "Now, you've put me in very a difficult position because you've been very helpful, but that's the problem. I can't have you feeding this back to the people who are on their way. We were very fortunate to arrive first, and I'm afraid we can't waste that."

Fear filled the target. "Please," he said.

The hooded figure looked towards Miss Cadlow, who instinctively stood up and started to head out of the room.

"We're ready for our pickup," she said over the radio.

"Copy. I'm one mike out. There's a convoy of three cars approaching from the road, probably three mikes out," replied the pilot, as the helicopter started heading back towards the villa.

"I'll give you one last chance," started the hooded figure.

"Mr P," interrupted Miss Cadlow. The hooded figure turned to meet her glance. "We've got less than three minutes until they arrive."

"I understand," he said, before readdressing the target, crouching down towards him again. "Answer my next question in a way that I like and promise to not divulge any information you have on Fellscient, and you can live. When they arrive, tell them you know nothing of Fellscient, only the poison. You were hired anonymously and never met anyone. Okay?"

The target nodded eagerly.

"This secretary you met with. I want you to tell me everything you know of her. And I mean everything."

# Chapter 8 – The Clouding of the Truth

11th September
13:32 BST
54 hrs 41 min. Until Deadline

Travelling in a three-car convoy, Alpha team were driving up a long, twisting road. Alpha Two wasn't with them; he was still on his way back to the Molehill. They were heading to a villa owned by the man thought to have created the poison used. They were anticipating heavy resistance and didn't expect to have the element of surprise, as a helicopter had flown over their position one minute earlier. The road finally led to a gated entrance. They parked their cars just around the corner and decided to approach on foot.

"I've got no visual on any guards," said Blindspot.

Moving closer to the gate, still no guards came into view. Even at the gate, there were no guards.

"Where are they?" asked Alpha Three. He got no reply.

Alpha Five immediately got on with unlocking the gate by tugging the cover off a silver box and pulling out three of the eight wires inside. The gate opened, its wheels crunching on the loose gravel.

"Let's move," said Alpha One, as they all followed him through the gate.

Apart from the snaking, gravel path, there was just grass, perfectly cut and a vibrant green. It had been a few weeks since they'd seen grass that green, but that wasn't what they'd come for. The villa was just a few hundred metres up the path, but it was right inside the gate that they found the first guard. In fact, along the inside wall, next to the gate, were twelve guards. They were all dead. Alpha Seven confirmed it, as she checked their pulses.

"A single shot, each of them," Blindspot noted.

They continued up the path. At that moment, a helicopter could be heard. They knew they'd already been seen and, due to the lack of cover, they crouched down and prepared themselves to open fire. The helicopter came into view but seemed to have no intention of engaging. It was tilted down and was clearly prioritising speed. The helicopter flew over them and into the distance.

Hastily, they stood up and continued, even quicker now. It wasn't until the villa came into view that the remainder of the guards could be found. They were covering the grass, like a scrapyard for bodies. Alpha Seven checked a few of them, but it didn't look like any had survived.

"We've got knife wounds. Well, sword wounds," said Alpha Seven, as she inspected the bodies by the giant tree.

"These were all hit with a marksman's rifle," added Blindspot. He then checked his surroundings and locked his eyes on to a collection of rocks a little further back down the grounds. "There was a sniper in those rocks."

"Wait, just one person took this lot down?" asked Alpha Four.

"Either the sniper had a blade, or there were two," said Alpha One. "You really think one sniper could do this and protect someone who had a blade?"

"I could," replied Blindspot.

"Go and check where you think the sniper was," said Alpha One to Blindspot. "Alpha Three, stay out here and check the remainder of the guards. If any survived, we need to know what they saw, if anything. They rest of you, we're heading inside."

Blindspot made his way over to the rocks. It didn't look like anything was there, but as soon as he arrived he knew that was the place. He bent down to find something, anything, on who they were. He then lay prone, as if he was the sniper, and looked at the kind of angles he'd have. As he looked through a gap between the rocks, he found something. He reached forwards and grabbed whatever was in the hole between the rocks and pulled it out. It was a bullet casing. It was also the only one. It was possible that the sniper had collected them all and just missed one, but it wasn't possible for it to end up between the rocks like that by accident. He inspected the casing. On its side, there was something scratched into it, like a mark or a pattern. It was hard to work out what it was, as it seemed almost smudged, or like a child had drawn it. Blindspot tucked the bullet casing into one of his many pockets, zipped it up, and continued with his observations.

Inside the villa, the number of bodies hadn't reduced. If anything, there were more than outside. Blood soaked the carpets, rugs, and furniture. Then, Alpha One caught sight of their target. He moved over cautiously to him, sat in a chair. He checked his pulse.

"He's dead." The other three continued through the villa.

"Hey, what do you think this means?" asked Alpha Four from the kitchen area of a giant room containing a lounge, kitchen, dining area, and an observation point overlooking the sea, along with other out-of-place pieces of furniture, such as a bed. There was even a toilet and sink behind a piece of smoked glass, which some could argue was a separate room.

Alpha One moved over to Alpha Four and looked at the wall. There was a small piece of paper pinned to it by a knife, with even smaller writing on it. He read the note.

*He has one vial of the antidote in his private vault, inside his vault. This can of course be mass-produced.* The note was then signed, *Yours Sincerely, Mr P.*

Alpha Five then approached, holding a small tablet. "They erased all CCTV footage, except for this one, single image."

He then turned the tablet round and showed Alpha One the image. It was a still shot of a hooded figure. Whoever it was wore a long coat, with a hood pulled up over their head.

"This is definitely the one I saw outside the nightclub," said Alpha One in thought.

"It seems a little more than a coincidence that this one image remained on the footage. In fact, it's harder to keep this one image than it is to erase everything."

"Are the cameras still running?" asked Alpha One.

Alpha Five shook his head. "No, the feed was cut, and then erased. Both could have been done remotely, but they definitely don't have access to the cameras now."

"Alright," started Alpha One with a sigh. "Let's finish up here. We'll send in a clean-up crew. Whilst we're heading back to the Molehill, I'll get Bosse to dig a little deeper into this vault inside a vault thing."

***

Just a few hours later, they were back at the Molehill. With time, and leads, running even shorter, they went straight to the meeting room. Daniel had joined them and Bosse was already in his seat, ready to start immediately.

"If I may have your attention," said Bosse, as he rose to his feet like he was about to give a speech. Everyone in the room was already silent, so Bosse continued. "Firstly, as some of you may know, Alpha team arrived at the home of the man who created the poison. He was found dead. We believe this figure is the one responsible for his death." Bosse then slowly swung his podgy index finger round and pointed at the image of the hooded figure on the TV screen behind him. "Alpha One has also informed us that this is the same figure he saw when leaving the nightclub, the first Night Viper hideout we took down, earlier this year. Unfortunately, all attempts to identify this person have failed. Although our target died, we do believe this hooded figure gave us a lead on the antidote. There was a note left at the scene suggesting one vial of the antidote is being held inside the target's private vault. We've looked into this and have found the target owns a bank. It is located here."

He then pointed to the next image which popped up on the screen. This one was of a bank, although, it was no ordinary bank. The note was certainly more accurate, referring to it as a vault. It was located between two mountains and had little access apart from the four helicopter landing pads. The image was also accompanied by a couple of blueprints, showing the internal layout of the bank.

"The bank is not open to members of the public but can be accessed by the rich. After all, this is where many stash their money. One of our benefactors has kindly given us a way in, but this will only be available for one person. I leave it up to Scott to plan accordingly." Bosse then took his seat and allowed Scott to take over.

"Before I start, what did this…" he paused for a moment, pretending to recall Bosse's words, "…benefactor want in return?" Bosse looked puzzled. "They all want something, what did this one want?" Scott persisted.

"Nothing, it just so happens that it is the one to whom we've already agreed to provide a security escort. So long as that goes ahead, I see no reason why he would back out." Bosse spoke with a smug expression, like he was one move away from saying 'checkmate'.

"Very well," said Scott. "We're going to be better off limiting the numbers who go into the bank. Only Alpha Three, Four, Five, and Seven will be on this one. Anthony, you can head the security contract. I want Bravo and Delta team to remain here. If anything is found, we might need you to act quicker than we can." He paused whilst turning to Anthony. "Did you find anything useful on the sniper at the villa?"

Anthony shook his head. "No, but they were good... very good."

"And the blade?" asked Scott.

"Different people," he answered. "There were no bullet impacts where the sniper took cover, so there'd be no reason for the sniper to move out."

Anthony's hand moved into his pocket and grabbed the bullet casing. He wasn't sure why he hadn't mentioned it, it just felt like the right thing to do. After all, he'd realised on the way back to the Molehill what the symbol on the side of the bullet casing was, and he still couldn't make sense of it himself, let alone enough to explain it to the rest of the team.

"If that's all?" asked Scott to the whole room. Everyone looked to each other and casually nodded, as if they didn't have a ticking clock against them. "In which case, we'll plan the heist. The rest of you, you know what to do." They all left the room and went their separate ways.

***

Alpha team all went to their office space, to plan the heist, but on the way there, Scott had held Daniel back to have a quiet word.

"How did you get the information?" he asked.

"On what?"

"The maker of the poison."

"Kale gave it to me," he replied calmly and innocently.

"Willingly?"

"Yeah, he's playing a long game, I know that much, but he isn't winning. I've got to act naturally; he knows why I went there. It'd look a bit odd if I didn't pursue it."

Daniel had a point, but Kale had slipped through his fingers once and was clearly deceptive. He had to trust Daniel, but Kale's long game was a serious concern.

"So, they suspect nothing?"

"Nothing," Daniel concluded.

It didn't take much longer for them to arrive at the offices. Kenny had already spread printed versions of the bank's blueprints all over one of the tables.

"We've got four main access points; all helicopter landing pads. Three are for clients of the bank, the other is for deliveries and staff," started Mike.

"Well, we're only able to get one person in on the clients' helipad, so why don't we use the staff one for the rest of us?" suggested Samuel.

"It's best to hold some of our cards back," started Scott, as he bent down to lean over the blueprints. "The more spread out you are on entrance, the more of the bank you can cover. Plus, you might need to leave in separate ways as well."

"How about we dive off?" asked Samuel.

"No," said Mike. "I reckon they might suspect something's up if we walk around with parachutes on."

"We don't have to wear them, I could take them all and stash them," added Kenny.

"That's not very time effective," announced Scott. "It'd take too long to exit the mountain and get back here. It'd be much better if you went and returned by helicopter. It could drop you three off nearby and you could enter from outside, whilst the 'client' is taken in via the helipad."

"That should be better. It means we can enter in separate places," said Mike.

"But how can we leave through one of their helicopters? There might not be one for hours," added Samuel.

"You're being really negative today, aren't you?" said Mike. "But he does have a point."

"So, you don't leave by one of theirs. You leave in one of ours," suggested Scott.

"They've got several air defences, but if I could get to their control room, I can disable them," said Mike, still thinking the plan through in his head.

"Mike, I think you should be the client, you'll look more the part," said Samuel.

Mike wasn't really sure how to take the comment, whether it was a compliment or not, but before he could ask, Mia stepped in.

"If you tell me what to do, I can head to the control room and shut the turrets down."

Mike nodded, "Yeah, I can do that. It won't be too difficult."

"Good, Mike you'll enter as the client. Mia, you'll need to enter through the roof, there's an access panel, but the roof has an intermittent energy surge. From what we've gathered, every thirty seconds, a five-second surge is sent through, unless shut down if any guards are needed on the roof. You'll have to time your descent carefully, but also have a plan B just in case the panel can't be opened from the outside."

"Might that be the case?" asked Mia, a little more concerned.

At the same moment, Scott's phone buzzed in his pocket. He took it out and checked the message on the screen, before swiftly putting it back in his pocket and continuing.

"The information we have suggests it is accessible from the outside, but it's better to be over-prepared than under. There's an access point under the staff helipad, maybe one of you could climb down the mountainside and enter that way. We've also got another way to get one of you straight into their server room."

"I could do that," said Kenny.

"Okay. You'll somehow need to enter the rubbish chute. It runs throughout the entire bank, straight down the centre. If you can get up, one of the rooms it travels past is the server room. Once inside, both of you should be able to change into whatever clothes you need, likewise, Mia you might also be needed out of the control room, so be ready for anything. You'll all need to study the blueprints so you know where to go, but there'll be no communication once inside, so whatever plan you run with, it has to be yours and yours alone, and it must be stuck to, no exceptions. Once you've studied the blueprints, come up with a plan. I think those entrances are the best to spread you out throughout the bank, but if you want to change them, change them."

"You're not planning the rest?" asked Samuel.

"No, I'm needed elsewhere, but I know your plan'll work."

"How are we getting out?" asked Mia.

"Once the air defences are shut down, Hawk can fly in, pick you up, and leave before they realise what's going on. But you'll have to have perfect timing. Make sure you stick to the time in your plan. Or, if your cover remains intact, you might even be able to leave without the SAMs being shut down. As soon as they're deactivated, it'll likely trigger some kind of fail-safe, so maybe only do it if and when necessary," concluded Scott, as he stood up straight and directed Daniel to leave the room with him.

"What is it?" asked Daniel once they'd left the office space.

"I need you to go back to Kale." Scott let the words sink in a bit, but Daniel didn't seem in the least bit surprised.

"I'd planned to. If this antidote doesn't work, or if it isn't even there, we'll need something else to go on."

"We can't waste any time, it's already short," added Scott.

"No, I know. I also want to know what Kale wants out of this. It seems pretty clear that Grenham wants me to work for him, or with him, or however it was he put it. But Kale, something's not right with him. He's got another motive, a much stronger one than following orders, I just don't know what."

"Back on the island, before Crabble was killed, he said that Kale would likely take over from him. But from what Mr Wilson said when I last interrogated him, only someone who is a direct descendant, has been chosen by the person, or is the one who killed them can assume power. So, if Kale is intent on becoming one of these 'limbs', he might be prepared to kill for it."

"He's definitely prepared to kill," started Daniel. "But I think his motive runs even deeper than that. I've only witnessed it a couple of times, but the way he responds to Grenham, it's with pure hatred."

"Well, whatever it is, I'm sure you'll get to the bottom of it. Just make sure the poison is your priority," concluded Scott. He was about to walk away, but Daniel spoke again.

"What is it you're going to be doing?"

"Why?" asked Scott, finding it strange Daniel had asked such a question.

"Because it isn't like you to leave like that."

"I'm going to see Emma's family. There's something going on there and I need to make sure it isn't traced back to us. I've been fixed up with an identity as a private investigator," he answered.

"Emma?"

"You remember when I blew up the satellite earlier this year?"

"Oh, yes. Emma was the one who showed you around the Swiss compound, the ones who held the prototype which got you to space."

"Yes, except she didn't really work for them, she was only there because they'd threatened the lives of her family," Scott said, remembering what had happened.

"Do you still hold yourself responsible?" he asked.

"It's hard not to. I promised to get her out, but she died there." Scott turned and started to walk in the other direction.

"Don't get yourself killed!" shouted Daniel.

"Haven't done yet."

***

Daniel watched as Scott continued down the corridor and disappeared around the corner. Anthony left the offices just after and also walked off down the corridor. Daniel had one final place to go before he'd leave to go back to Kale.

A few minutes later, a giant, steel door was swung open on what seemed like hundreds of reinforced hinges. Daniel walked through and entered the holding cells. He was on floor two of five, in section A. He walked down the concrete aisle, with cells on either side, separated by steel bars and bulletproof, Perspex screens. Several of the cells were empty, but a few weren't. In one of them was Gold Viper, one of the three leaders of the Night Vipers who'd been captured during the siege on Crabble's island. In the cell opposite, was John Broady, the target from their previous case. But at the end of the row of cells was the man he had really come to see, Mr Wilson.

He was sat on his bed; his legs were crossed, and his eyes tightly shut. Daniel stood behind the screen and watched. Slowly, Mr Wilson opened his eyes and looked towards Daniel. He smiled.

"Please, do come in. Make sure you take your shoes off."

Daniel hadn't gone there to joke and didn't waste any time in small talk. "No, I've got questions, and you've got answers."

"Somebody got out on the wrong side of bed this morning."

Daniel's expression didn't budge.

"Very well. What would you like to talk about?" he asked.

"Can Kale be trusted?" asked Daniel.

Mr Wilson looked surprised by the question. "Well, that depends on what you have to offer."

"How do you mean?" questioned Daniel.

"I'll put it to you this way. If there's something you have that he wants, then yes, you can. He'll probably do anything for you, even tell the truth and give you his trust. If, however, you don't, then he'll let you know," said Mr Wilson.

"So, he will tell the truth?"

"What are you offering him?" asked Mr Wilson, more curious than ever.

"Everything," replied Daniel bluntly.

"Then yes, he probably will. But you do need to be careful. Just because he might tell you the truth, it doesn't mean the truth isn't clouded. I've had no contact with him, directly, anyway, but I do know that the questions you ask are what is most critical. After all, an answer to the wrong question could be interpreted in the wrong way."

Daniel had what he came for, the most straightforward answer he expected Mr Wilson to give. Even if his final comment seemed to bring them full circle, he knew what Mr Wilson was saying; at least he hoped he did. Daniel started to walk away, but Mr Wilson had one final thing to say.

"Giving him everything doesn't mean you can ask whatever you want. Answers have a price, and sometimes even everything isn't enough. If he thinks you're a loose end, he'll treat you like one without a second thought or hesitation. Do what he wants, be what he wants, and most of all, don't get in his way, nothing but a bullet can stop him."

Daniel left the cells and started making his way back out of the Molehill. As he approached the Molehill's hangar, he passed Diana on the way.

"Is everything okay?" she asked.

Daniel stopped dead in his tracks and swiftly answered, "Yes, everything's fine."

She could clearly see something was bothering him, like he had a lot on his mind, but accepted his answer and started to move off in the other direction.

"Actually," Daniel announced, causing Delta One to come closer.

"What is it?" she asked, unsure what he was going to say next.

"I need a favour."

# Chapter 9 – The Vault of the Vault
12<sup>th</sup> September
14:21 BST
29 hrs 52 min. Until Deadline

The wind was harsh and bitter amongst the mountains. Despite the humid temperatures elsewhere, the high altitudes allowed the snow to stay as a thick, white blanket, almost protecting the mountains from the cold winds. Even within the private helicopter, Alpha Five, or Michael Glut as he was about to become, could see the mountains almost shiver. His identity wasn't that of one of their benefactors, but rather a business associate of one, since the staff at the bank had met each and every person who owned one of the many vaults held within. It was unusual to allow anyone other than the owner to enter, but when a high-paying client asks for something, they didn't say no, they just watched that person like a hawk.

The helicopter had a long nose and a sleek interior, a loan from one of their other benefactors. From the back, Michael was unable to hear the pilot, but he knew the clearance codes had worked as they were still airborne. After circling the mountains for a few minutes, they were finally ready to make their approach. From the right window, Michael could see the bank, almost hanging off the side of one of the mountains.

They approached the landing pad at a steady pace. Once they were just a few hundred metres out, another helicopter passed them, heading away from the bank. It was a similar model to Michael's, with its equally overpriced design.

There was a soft rumble as they landed, almost as if the landing pad was a giant pillow. Michael was also unable to hear the blades slow down, but he didn't need to. The pilot came round and opened the door.

He leapt from the helicopter, dressed in a jet-black suit, with matching tie, belt, and shoes. He fastened the top button on his jacket and walked with a sense of power and dominance, almost as if he owned the place.

Michael moved over to the security checkpoint. It was still outside, which given the dark clouds covering the sun, and the biting winds, wasn't all that well thought through. One of the security guards, a giant guard who didn't exactly fit into his suit, thrust a plastic tray at him in which he was to place all his loose belongings. Knowing he might not be picking them back up, however, he'd taken nothing with him. With a quick shake of his head, he tried to move on to the next guard, but the first persisted with his tray, pushing it under Michael's nose.

"Phone," said the guard abruptly.

"No," replied Michael in an equally abrupt tone. As soon as he'd said it, he realised that mocking the guard had seemed like a better idea in his head, but it was far beyond that point now. A different guard went to block his path, as the rest became more on edge, almost waiting for an excuse to start a fight.

"Phone!" shouted the first guard.

"How dare you speak to me in that way," said Michael, somewhat on a knife-edge.

The raised voices had started to draw attention from outside the group of seven security guards. Another guard came over, this one seemingly with more authority, at least that was the way he walked and held himself.

"What seems to be the issue?" he asked.

"Not giving his phone," said the huge security guard.

"Not giving?" Michael questioned. "I don't have my phone. I left it on the helicopter because I don't want to leave it in your incapable hands."

"Why is that an issue?" asked the more important security guard to the rest of his men. They all shook their heads.

"He never told us that," said one of them.

"Well maybe that's because none of you actually asked. Do you know who I am?"

They all continued to shake their heads.

"I am the business partner of one of your richest clients, who stores over sixty per cent of our assets here. As such, I expect to be treated with respect, not like a common criminal," continued Michael, knowing that if he persisted, something good might come of it. Of course, he also knew it was a big risk, drawing so much attention to himself. For the time being, though, it was working. He was ushered through, briefly frisked, passed through a body scanner, and was out the other side.

"I haven't seen you before," said one of the security guards.

Michael froze. He knew he had to think quickly, and needed a lot of luck.

"That is because, on the rare occasions I visit, I arrive on landing pad two. I think in future I shall continue to do so," he said, knowing he had just come in on landing pad three.

"But that's where I usually am," added the guard.

"No, you're not," persisted Michael, buying himself a little more time to think.

"Yes, I am."

"I always come in on that landing pad…" said Michael, as he pointed to the landing pad to his right, knowing full well it was actually landing pad one. "And I have never seen you there before."

"That's landing pad one, Sir," said the guard.

"Excuse me!"

"That's landing pad one, Sir," repeated the guard.

"No, it isn't!" erupted Michael, still aware it was. "What kind of insubordinate guards do you employ here?"

"Why don't you come this way, Sir? Into the warm. We'll discuss this in my office," said the higher level security guard, as he directed Michael to the right.

He wasn't exactly sure whether he was in the clear or not, but either way, he knew the guard taking him to his office, alone, would only be used in his own favour. Plus, he'd also bypassed the metal detectors and not one of the guards was going to call him back. Although he didn't have anything on him which would set the alarms off, anyone watching via the security cameras would surely be focussed on him now. As they moved inside, Michael could hear his helicopter take off. He gave a quick glance behind and saw it move into the distance.

Michael was led past the oversized, glass doors leading to the bank's main foyer and was taken into a room next to it. The room had a desk, chair, paperwork, and computer, all the usual things you'd expect to see in an office space, along with two assault rifles and a shotgun hanging up on the wall.

"I cannot apologise enough, Sir," said the security guard.

Michael read the pyramid-shaped, wooden plaque on his desk which said *Chief Security Officer* but oddly didn't display his name.

"I must say, I am a little disappointed in your services, but I do understand that these things happen from time to time," replied Michael.

"I appreciate your understanding. If there is anything else you require, please don't hesitate to ask."

Michael wasn't really sure what to expect, but it wasn't being brought into the chief security officer's office for an apology. He at least expected to obtain something useful, whether it was physical or intel.

"Is that Burma?" asked Michael, as he pointed to a picture on the wall.

"Yes, that's right. Have you been there?" replied the chief security officer, as he turned around to face the picture.

"No, but a gentleman like myself is always on the lookout for business opportunities. This was one of the places myself and Mr Jenkins were contemplating investing in," replied Michael.

He actually recognised the picture because they'd been there in an episode of *Top Gear*, but that small bit of information didn't have to be included.

"Well, as I said, if you need anything, please just come and ask me," said the guard again, making it clear it was time for Michael to leave the office, so that's exactly what he did.

With half a nod, and an almost pained smile, Michael left, letting the door swing closed behind him.

He briefly glanced at his wristwatch. "A minute behind," he mumbled.

Without wasting any more time, he went straight through the oversized, smoked glass doors into where it was finally warm. The foyer was as equally oversized as the doors that led to it. There were some cashier-style desks in a line over to one side, and just empty floor everywhere else in the monstrous room. Michael walked over to one of the ten, manned desks, each with a thick, plastic screen separating them, just like in a bank. There was one other person, dressed similarly to Michael, being served at one of the desks, so he had plenty to choose from but went to the closest one.

"Can I help you, Sir?" said the cashier behind the desk.

They were all dressed the same, in a light blue suit and matching tie. This particular member of staff seemed to be in their thirties, had well-kempt, short, brown hair, without so much as a strand that had fallen out of place, and spoke with a very soft tone, as if he were playing the part of a servant to the demanding owner of an estate.

"I wish to check the contents of my partner's personal vault. I am, of course, a named visitor on his details," replied Michael.

"Certainly, if you could sign in," said the cashier, as he gestured towards a retinal scanner.

"I sure hope you're in," he mumbled.

He bent forwards and allowed his eyes to be scanned, seeing nothing but a red dot as it was happening. Suddenly, the red dot turned green and he was cleared.

"I'm afraid your clearance doesn't entitle you to visit the safe personally. Is it okay if we catalogue it for you?"

"No, it most certainly is not. I obtained clearance when the first deposit was made. A deposit which I'm sure still pays your wage to this day," replied Michael with a raised voice.

"I'm sorry, but our system doesn't agree."

"This always happens, why is no one here actually trained with how to use these things? I expect you hit the wrong button, didn't you? That's what always happens." Michael then put his hand into his inside jacket pocket and retrieved a folded up piece of paper. "This is the proof I received that I am allowed to enter the safe, so run your little computer again."

The piece of paper was opened and pressed up against the plastic screen. They'd seen the document from the benefactor who'd got them in and had made a copy with Michael's details.

"I shall run it again," answered the cashier after briefly inspecting the document.

Michael knew it would be tight for his information to be added but hoped his little outburst gave enough time for it to be done. He again leant forwards and allowed his eyes to be scanned.

"Oh," started the cashier. "I do apologise. You are entitled to enter the safe. I'm not sure what happened."

"Well, it's obvious isn't it? You don't know how to use your own system."

"If you would like to wait over there, a member of the security team will be along to escort you to the safe," concluded the cashier, ignoring Michael's final comment completely.

He made his way over to where the cashier had pointed, returning the document to his pocket as he went. Just around the corner, there was a small area with a couple of sofas and an armchair. He sat in the armchair and waited, briefly checking his watch, again.

***

*Six Minutes Earlier*

Before landing, the private helicopter circled the bank, and one by one, members of Alpha team were dropping into position. Alpha Seven was the first; she'd dropped on to the top of the mountain. The helicopter was flown low enough that it really was as simple as dropping a few metres into a bed of snow. Offloading the other two was a little trickier. The helicopter had to fly low, far lower than was allowed. Alarms and frantic messages bombarded the helicopter, warning them to raise their altitude or risk being taken down. Alpha Four leapt from the helicopter, just before it started to lift back up. There were a few metal bars running around the perimeter of the bank, used to attach harnesses to should any exterior work need to take place. He grabbed hold of one and managed to wrap his feet around it, which was just as well given the base of the mountain was out of sight. With all his strength, he held on and stayed as still as he could, ensuring he was secure. He turned to see the helicopter fly back up. He knew if he fell, there were no second chances.

He was dressed in a black, tactical suit, fitted with a harness and numerous pockets of all sizes. Alpha Four knew he'd only been allowed two minutes to climb the rubbish chute, so couldn't waste any more time. Slowly, he securely placed his feet and stretched up to the next metal bar, followed by the next, then the next, and then finally, he reached for the chute he would be climbing. There was a groove etched into it which would run the whole stretch. It was for a small machine, shaped a bit like a hammer, which would fly down to clear any blockage that had collected. Although this time, it was going to give Alpha Four a lifeline. He attached his harness to the groove with a specially adapted connector, designed specifically for this one mission, and started to climb.

Stretch after stretch, he edged his way up inside, using his boots and gloves, fitted with extra grips, to support his weight. He went as quickly as he could but ensured each hand and foot was placed securely before adding any weight to it. He'd got about halfway up, when he felt the chute start to rattle. It was the first stage in trying to clear a blockage. Alpha Four couldn't be sure whether the system had detected him as a blockage, or whether it had detected something else, but what he did know was he had seconds to get out. The inspection panel he was heading for was just a few metres above him, but the more the chute rattled, the harder it became to climb. He finally reached the panel and started to kick it in, but it wouldn't give.

The rattling chute made it difficult, but he had no time to think about that. Then the rattling stopped, and the next stage of clearing a blockage began. He could hear something coming, making the sound of a ski jumper sliding down a ramp. He continued to kick the panel, almost in desperation. He could let go at any moment, but he'd never climb back up in time, and the mission would fail. He couldn't let that happen, not even over his dead body. He continued to kick, and kick, then he saw the giant hammer fly towards him. He kept on kicking, the adrenaline making each kick more powerful, but it still wasn't enough. The hammer slid towards him. He closed his eyes and gave one final kick. Then, there was silence.

Slowly, he opened his eyes. He was still in the chute. The hammer was still above him, just inches away from his head. It was almost as if time had frozen. Then, it finally sank in. It wasn't time that had frozen, it was the hammer. He didn't wait to find answers, he just continued to kick the inspection panel, unsure how long the hammer would remain. After another ten kicks, the panel gave in and Alpha Four had his way out of the chute.

He unclipped his harness and climbed through into the next room. There was nobody in sight. He checked his watch.

"Two minutes behind," he said aloud.

Fortunately, the room he was in was exactly where he needed to be, the server room. It had to be located next to the rubbish chute because a cooling channel ran adjacent to it, keeping all the computers cool with the ice-cold water that ran through the pipes. He swiftly located the block of red terminals, which held the clients' details, and counted three in from the left, the one which specifically held the clients' security passes, such as their retinal scans, and those of any named visitors they had added. He found port forty-nine and removed a thick, white card which was inserted inside, replacing it with an identical-looking card. That would put Alpha Five's retinal scan in the system, but now he had to change his clearance.

There was a computer screen, and accompanying keyboard and mouse, to his right. He moved over to it and started it up. There was no lock on it because they didn't exactly expect anyone to be inside. Alpha Four scrolled down to port forty-nine and allowed the user personal access to Mr Jenkins' safe. He just hoped he was in time.

***

*Eight Minutes Earlier*

Alpha Seven dropped from the underside of the helicopter and fell a few metres into a bed of snow. She lay motionless for a few seconds, in her all-white tactical suit, until she was sure she was on stable ground. She had a white cloth snood covering her face, from the nose down, and goggles to protect her eyes from the snow and wind. Edging towards the face of the mountain, she almost had to swim through the deep snow. Once at the edge, she looked down to the bank, about twenty metres below her. A thick layer of cloud was just above, blocking the sun and making the windy mountains surprisingly cold for it being the end of summer. The wind was blowing a thin layer of snow from the mountains, making it hard to see down, but given her white clothes, it would help to obscure her.

There was nothing to anchor a rope into, so she had to make sure her descent was slow and steady. Placing one foot below the other, she crept down the side of the mountain. A lot of snow had been knocked off as she descended, so much that it had alerted the attention of the guards in the control room below. Even with the strong winds howling past her ears, she could still hear the inspection cover lift. Her hood was already up and she stayed motionless, holding on to a part of the mountain which protruded from the snow her legs were dug into. With the traces of snow blowing past in the wind, Alpha Seven was invisible.

The guard looked at the roof, seeing that it was snow that had landed on it, and moved back inside, all within thirty seconds. Alpha Seven still couldn't be sure whether the electric surges had been turned off or not. Now safe to move again, she continued down the mountain, knocking even more snow on to the bank's roof. The fact that the guard had seen it was snow they were a little more forgiving of any noises on the roof, but too many and she risked alerting them further.

Finally, she was within touching distance of the roof, but now faced the bigger problem. When were the electrical surges sent through the roof? Alpha Seven had been counting from the time the guard emerged from the hatch but still couldn't be sure it was safe. From under her white jacket, she retrieved a white pole, about one metre in length. It had an electricity tester on the end and Alpha Seven angled it down so it touched the roof. The rest of the pole didn't conduct electricity, so she'd be safe from that.

After twenty-four seconds of waiting, the tester picked up a strong electrical current, flashing red to show this. It continued to flash for five seconds, until the light went off. Alpha Seven moved immediately, dropping down on to the roof and running towards the inspection hatch. The pole condensed into a quarter of its size and was neatly tucked under her jacket, whilst she retrieved a small device, shaped like a phone. She bent down by the hatch and held the phone close to it. *Eighteen seconds*, she thought as the screen on the device showed a dial tick round. After another four seconds, the wheel was a third of the way round. After eight seconds, the wheel was two thirds round. Then, with just six seconds left, the wheel on the device's screen was finally back to the top and the hatch gave a clonk as the bolts securing it were released. She lifted the hatch, slid herself on to the ladder below and closed the hatch. *Just two seconds left*, she thought as a sigh of relief left her lungs.

Alpha Seven looked down below her feet and saw no guards. As far as she could tell, they were all still under the radar. After a quick check of her watch, showing that she was still on time for what had originally been planned, she placed the device back into her jacket, removed her goggles, and slowly moved down the ladder.

She could hear a couple of mumbled conversations in the room, again making her think that they were all in the clear. Alpha Seven silently placed her feet on the floor and took in her surroundings. There were four guards. They were armed, but their weapons were holstered. Three of them were in the corner having a conversation, the other was alone watching images from the surveillance cameras. Each of Alpha team knew they had to remain unseen, no trace of their presence could be found. That meant erasing all surveillance footage, ensuring no one would be able to identify them, and making sure nothing was left in the field that could be traced back to the Molehill, including their bullets. So, with no gun, Alpha Seven approached the lone guard to strike from behind. Although the room was over fifteen metres wide in each direction, and the single guard wasn't visible to the others, being encased within three walls of computer screens, Alpha Seven would still have to be quiet.

She had a chloroform-laced rag, which was retrieved from one of her many pockets, and wrapped it around the guard's face. He made a slight murmur, before going limp. The others hadn't heard. Taking the other three out in one go would be easy with a gas grenade. Alpha Seven even drew one from her suit but realised the time it took for the gas to clear wouldn't allow her enough time to stick to the schedule. Instead, she kept the chloroformed rag in her hand and moved over to the three guards. She wrapped it over the nearest one's mouth, who was knocked unconscious in an instant, before kicking another in the knee. The guard's knee bent back, and he yelled out, allowing Alpha Seven to focus on the next one. She kept her head down and her face obscured, despite the white snood still covering half of it.

The guard threw the first punch, blocked by Alpha Seven with little effort. The unconscious guard, sat in the chair between them, helped her to block, enabling her to pull the attacking guard closer and move him off balance. He toppled over the unconscious guard and landed at Alpha Seven's feet. She stretched over to retrieve the rag, still on the previous guard's face, and attempted to knock the final one out the same way. She'd got the rag within several inches of his face when he blocked it, using all his strength to push it back up. Veins and blood vessels swelled up on his taut face, as he struggled to hold the rag at such an uncomfortable angle. Alpha Seven used all her weight to push down, before finally knocking his elbow in, allowing the rag to crash down on to his face. It left just one conscious guard.

He was still holding his knee but had started to reach for his gun. Alpha Seven leapt towards him, sending them both to the floor, but she got the upper hand, staying on top of him and pushing her left arm down on his throat. Using her right hand to push down with even more force, it didn't take long before he too was lying on the floor, as still as a corpse.

Before she had a chance to start moving the bodies, a flashing, amber light caught her eye. Alpha Seven moved over to it. It was labelled, *'Rubbish Clearer'*. She instantly knew what it was. If Alpha Four was still in the chute, he'd need help. She started pounding the keys on the nearby keyboard. Mike had shown her how to shut down various systems, but this wasn't one of them. Fortunately, the ones she had learnt all had a very similar pattern to shutting them down. Find the system, access its commands, and then hit *'Shut down'*. She found the button and hit it, without any clue if it had worked. There were no cameras in the chute. *He has to be alive. He must be*, she thought, but Alpha Seven had no way of finding out. She still had a job to do, and that's what she did. After clearing away the bodies, and lacing them with a bit more chloroform, she started accessing the security cameras. There weren't any cameras in the server room, but Alpha Four was unable to leave until the ones outside the room had been shut down, ensuring his face wouldn't be picked up.

***

*Four Minutes Later*

Michael had been waiting for a couple of minutes, when a security guard approached him. This one wasn't dressed like the others; he wore a smart suit and a clear, curly cord connecting his earpiece to a small communications box sticking out from under his jacket. Michael could tell he was security, both by the way he walked, and the handgun holstered under his jacket. Michael saw it every time he moved his right leg forwards, exposing it as his jacket waved open.

"I understand you're waiting to be shown to your safe. Is that correct?" asked the guard with his strong, Scottish accent. His thick, greying beard and moustache covered most of his mouth, making it hard to see his lips move. He also wasn't small, at all. It looked like everything about him was made from muscle.

"Yes, that's right," answered Michael, rising to his feet.

"If you'd like to follow me, I'll show you to your safe. Can I get you anything, a drink perhaps?" asked the guard.

"No, I'm fine, just the safe."

The guard headed off through a wooden door, which blended in with the wooden-style walls, and Michael followed him through, just a few paces behind. The other side of the hidden door was much like the reception area, oversized, clean, and minimalist. Michael still didn't see any ornaments or decorations, and certainly no paintings. The walls were just as bare. The only small differences Michael noticed, between the two sides of the door, were the increases in comfort and affluence. It went from extremely expensive-looking furniture, flooring, paintwork, and so on, to flooring that had a little more spring in it, a slightly warmer shade of paint, and somehow a more overall expensive feel to it, almost like going from a five-star hotel to one that was so expensive, the star rating was beneath them. They approached a golden lift at the end of the wide corridor and the guard pressed the only available button on the panel. There was no way to know where the lift had been, as there were no numbers displayed at the top, nor a dial which would have been more fitting with its golden exterior. Within just a couple of seconds, the lift doors opened and they both stepped in. The interior was very different, being bright, white, and almost sterile looking. Michael also noticed the guard place a black key fob on a small panel inside the lift. No buttons were pressed, but the lift doors closed, and just a few seconds later, they opened again. They were on a different floor, but Michael had no way of knowing which one, with still no numbers displayed and the lack of feeling any kind of motion in the lift. The key fob was also going to be a previously unforeseen problem, as it appeared the fob had been loaded with the code to take them to that specific floor and nowhere else. Or possibly this guard was only allowed to enter this floor and a different guard would take the clients to different floors. He knew the safe was listed as being in section A, floor two, module F, but whether that actually correlated to floor numbers at the bank was anybody's guess.

Michael went to leave the lift, but the guard stood still. Their shoulders clashed as Michael walked into the back of him. Although he probably could've stood his ground, Michael had to feign a stumble over the collision. That's exactly what he did, completing his move with a filthy look, as if he'd just wiped the guard off the sole of his shoe. The guard then led Michael to the right and walked him to the second to last door down the corridor in silence. There were only doors on one side of the corridor, opposite the lift, which made Michael start to wonder what could be on the other side.

"This is yours," said the guard, sternly.

He then leant forwards, placed the same fob on the door, and watched as a retinal scanner emerged from the wall. Michael bent down and placed his eyes into it. The door promptly opened. It made a sound like an airlock, as the huge, steel door slowly opened inwards.

"Wait out here," Michael said, as he entered the safe. "Make sure no one comes in."

The room might've been called a safe, but its large area, steel walls, and controlled ventilation, with the option to remove all oxygen, made it more of a vault than the kind of wall safe that's slightly more common. Many of the safes were likely the same, all with valuable assets contained within. This safe, the one owned by Mr Jenkins, one of their benefactors, had a few ornaments in glass cases over to one side, a couple of paintings locked away behind glass on the other side, and a giant, four-metre cubed box of saffron. Michael was initially shocked by the saffron, not expecting to find it there, but the more thought he gave it, the more it actually made sense. It was more valuable than gold, per kilogram, so effectively made it easier to transport in and out of the safe and would raise a few less eyebrows than carrying that many diamonds around. Although Michael couldn't imagine anyone going into a supermarket and trying to sell what must've been about fifty thousand pounds worth of saffron. Yet for someone with as much money as Mr Jenkins, fifty thousand pounds seemed little more than small change, which was the one thing that didn't quite add up.

There was a sudden alarm that rang out throughout the room. The guard turned and was about to speak, but the alarm was silenced before he had the chance.

"False alarm," said the guard, turning to go back out of the room.

Whilst the saffron was a surprise, it wasn't what Michael was there for. In the centre of the room was a black briefcase. It was empty, but no one else knew that. Their benefactor always kept an empty briefcase in there for ease if he had to move any of his assets, or so he told them. Michael gave another glance at his watch.

"Three minutes early," he muttered.

He then spent the next four minutes wandering around the safe, looking at the paintings, trying to work out what the sculptures depicted, and letting the saffron run through his fingers.

"Stop right there," the Scottish guard shouted from outside the safe.

Michael could hear mumbling from another person.

"I said stop!" shouted the guard.

Crashing and banging followed shortly after as some kind of a fight seemed to break out. Michael stuck his head around the safe's door, with the briefcase clasped firmly in his hands. The Scottish guard was wrestling with another guard. It didn't take long for the Scottish guard to get on top, as he sent the other crashing into the wall before throwing a right hook that would've been capable of killing some people. The other guard fell to the floor.

"We need to move," said the Scottish guard, as he approached Michael.

"You must protect this briefcase at all costs," added Michael, as he closed the safe door and followed the guard.

"I'll take you back to reception. You can leave in your helicopter."

"No," said Michael. "You don't understand. My helicopter won't be back for another thirty minutes, and I doubt that was the only person here to steal this briefcase. You must protect me."

"I'll take you to a central room. You'll be safe there."

"I want to know how they got past your security. I thought nobody could get in here."

***

*Twenty Minutes Earlier*

Alpha Three clung on to the helicopter's railing as it suddenly raised its altitude. Alpha Four had only just jumped but was already out of sight. He knew his opening was close. He had to jump into the staff's helipad during their ascent, but the snow flying past, burning his eyes and cheeks, made it almost impossible to see. Their images of the bank had shown a narrow access ledge, running adjacent to the helipad, which was used for fastening winches if anything arrived that was too large to fly directly on to the helipad. There was a bright red, flashing light at the end which Alpha Three could make out intermittently. It was his only hope. He locked his eyes on to the light, obscured by layers of snow blowing past, and jumped towards it.

Next thing he knew, Alpha Three found himself clinging to a frozen, metal pole, hundreds of metres above a painful demise, with nothing more than a white tactical suit and a pair of white gloves with extra grips on them. From where Alpha Four had jumped, the wind seemed calmer, but Alpha Three found himself amongst a wind channel, making it seem like the middle of a blizzard. Slowly, he used his gloves to edge towards the staff helipad. There was a walkway a couple of metres above him, but staying lower helped him to stay hidden.

Eventually, he reached a wall and breathed a sigh of relief. After climbing up to the external door, he pressed a small device, shaped a little like a credit card, against a large, square box next to the door, which immediately sprung open, allowing Alpha Three inside.

He could feel the snow stuck to his face and how the coarse wind had set his cheeks alight. Without waiting to warm up, he removed his white tactical suit, along with his white boots and gloves, and stashed them behind a wooden crate in the open hangar-style helipad. He then headed through the door opposite which was, not by coincidence, the staff changing area. Staff switched over four times a day, but beyond that, there was no need for them to be in the changing room, so Alpha Three had plenty of time to find an outfit that fitted him. All the clothes and uniforms had to be hung up without being secured and couldn't be taken home, so they could be cleaned regularly by the cleaning crew. Whilst Alpha Three found a guard's uniform close to his size, he noticed there were no lockers, just a few shelves holding useless scraps of paper and empty sandwich wrappers. It seemed ironic for the staff guarding a vault to have nowhere to safely store any possessions whilst on duty, but then he realised it was unlikely any of them could take personal belongings in with them. Alpha Three slipped a guard's uniform on and checked his watch. He was three minutes behind, already.

His guard's uniform would allow him to walk around some parts of the bank above suspicion, and if their plan was still on track, Alpha Seven would have control of all cameras, preventing him from being picked up for not working in his 'usual' place. With purpose, he left the changing room and made his way along the narrow walkway above the hangar. The standard size boots where a little tight-fitting for his mammoth-sized feet, but it didn't stop him from striding over the clanging, metal grates of the walkway.

It didn't take long to leave the hangar and enter the even warmer interior of the bank. Their intel had highlighted a single route to reach his destination, but even assuming the route still conformed with the current layout, trying to remember the fifty-four right turns and the seventy-nine left turns would be by far the greatest ask.

Somehow, whether it be luck or an unusually good turn of memory, Alpha Three made it to his destination. He hid just around the corner from, assuming everyone else was still on track, the safe Alpha Five would be in. On his way there, he'd passed a few guards, none had even questioned his presence, but now he was in an area that was off limits to someone wearing his uniform. A couple of minutes had gone by, and there was still no sign of Alpha Five. He'd risked a couple of glances around the corner but still saw nothing. The thought that they might've got the wrong place even ran through his head, but even after the next few minutes, there was still no sign of them. Cautiously, he approached the lifts. Only his footsteps could be heard in the deathly silent corridor.

As he stared at the lift, he noticed the lift light flashing. It was Morse code. 'Wrong side', it read. He held his hand up to the flashing light to stop it, unsure where the actual camera was located.

"I'm definitely in the right place," he muttered.

The light then started flashing again. This time it read '46'. Alpha Three stood still for a moment, before another message came through, 'radio'. With a sudden moment of eureka, he understood the '46' message and tuned the radio, on his uniform, to channel forty-six.

"You're the wrong side of the lift," said Alpha Seven.

"But I followed the directions exactly. I can still remember them all."

"Well, none of these cameras are labelled, but Alpha Five got out of the lift and was seen on a CCTV camera, I'm looking at you through a different one."

"Did the lift have two doors, you know one where you get in one side and the door suddenly opens behind you. I mean they're always confusing me," replied Alpha Three.

"No, the lift's only got one door. So, Alpha Five entered on the east side and must've exited on the east side as well."

"But I'm on the east side," persisted Alpha Three.

"Well, you can't be."

Getting tired of the conversation, Alpha Three moved over to a fire alarm and pulled the lever down. The siren filled the corridor, before swiftly going silent.

"Why did you do that? I've got to reassure everyone it was a false alarm now," said Alpha Seven in annoyance.

"Which side did the alarm go off?" asked Alpha Three casually.

"The east side."

"Can you control the lift from up there?"

"I don't know, but I'll give it a go."

Then, the lift doors opened. Without so much as a first thought, Alpha Three entered the lift and let the doors close.

"Switch frequencies and break contact, they're going to be on high alert after that alarm," said Alpha Seven, as she broke away from the conversation.

Alpha Three also switched his radio to a different frequency and placed it back in its perfectly sized pocket on his belt. A few seconds later, the lift doors opened and Alpha Three entered what looked like the same corridor. The only difference being this one had a tall, stocky guard stood sentry outside one of the vaults.

"Stop right there!" shouted the guard, with a strong Scottish accent.

Alpha Three moved closer, finding that the nearer the guard was, the bigger he seemed to get.

"I said stop!" persisted the guard.

"It's now or never," muttered Alpha Three, as he threw himself at the guard.

He was never really ahead during the fight, and just staying alive seemed tough, but he suddenly found himself hurled towards the wall. The pain as his nose was crushed against the wall was bad, but the life-threatening punch that followed seemed like it was much worse, if it hadn't made everything go black.

The next thing he remembered was starting to open his eyes. His head was throbbing, and the bright, white strip lights were shining down. Opening his eyes was a struggle, and the only part that was open gave him a hazy outlook. He could feel someone tapping his face, trying to pull him up.

"We need to go!" shouted his supposed saviour. The noise erupted in his head.

By the time he'd been led into a room and sat on a chair, his senses had started to come back. Stood in front of him, was Alpha Four.

"What happened?" asked Alpha Three, remembering nothing after his fight with the Scottish guard.

"That guard hit you good," replied Alpha Four, with a sense of glee in his voice.

"Seriously? That one hit did all this to my head?"

"It sure did."

His vision had fully returned, but his head still felt like someone was crushing it in a vice.

"You shouldn't be here…"

"I know, but you seemed to need help. There are a group of guards on their way down to you. On the plus side, Alpha Five's part of the plan is going well," said Alpha Four.

"I'm thrilled for him."

***

Michael was in one of several secure locations around the bank. They weren't so much to keep their clients safe from any intruders, but it was a convenient way of getting them out of the way of the security who would no doubt be on their way to secure the vaults. Yet this was also to Michael's advantage. He'd been locked in a room with just two other guards. He could escape, but then he'd be a target for the security guards on patrol. However, that wasn't his plan.

"We have eyes on one suspect, heading towards the east quadrant, floor 2, section A," came from each of the guards' radios.

"That's towards us," one guard whispered. The other stayed silent and focussed on the door.

"I've lost sight of him," came over the radio. "Last seen, on floor 2, section A, module C."

Silence descended upon the room. A couple of minutes passed, and still nothing came over the radio. Then there was a knock at the door. The guards exchanged looks, trying to make the other open the door. Finally, one of them approached it, as if it was liable to bite. The guard entered a code on a panel beside the door, 'Two-four-two-eight'. The handle slowly twisted round.

Suddenly, the door burst in, startling the closest guard. The other raised his handgun but found himself in a battle of his own. The wire from one of the monitors in the room was wrapped around his neck. He hardly had time to work out what was happening but instinct kicked in. The gun was dropped to the floor and he started trying to pull the cord away, gasping for air, but Michael's element of surprise was enough. Before the guard could acknowledge what was happening, his body was starved of enough oxygen to shut down. Michael looked up to see Alpha Three stood over the other guard.

Alpha Four entered shortly after, also now dressed in a security outfit. Whilst he radioed through a message, the other two hid the body Michael had put on the floor, allowing Alpha Four to assume the now hidden man's identity, leaving the other guard unconscious on the floor.

"Target is in safe room twenty-nine, I repeat, he has entered safe room…" Alpha Four concluded the message by kicking his foot through one of the filing cabinets and letting out a cry of pain.

With the body cleared, all three of them got into character. Michael crouched down and cowered in the corner, whilst Alpha Three and Four started fighting each other. They could hear footsteps thundering down the corridor, like a stampede of antelope. This was the time. Alpha Four hit Alpha Three on the jaw, before throwing him to the floor. Security arrived just as he fell. Two of them leapt on Alpha Three and pinned his arms down.

The Scottish guard was there and bent down to look at Alpha Three.

"This is the guy," he announced, as several guards took him away. "Well done," he said to Alpha Four. "You can take the rest of your shift off."

Alpha Four wasn't sure what to do. He had to stay with Michael, but the Scottish guard clearly outranked him.

"I think not," announced Michael, as he stood up. "This man was the one to save my life. You just locked me in here, then ran away from the danger."

"I am in charge of this division, Sir," replied the guard.

"And I am a client, which means that I pay your salary and I pay his too. He is the only one who has proven himself, and as such, he is the only one I wish to accompany me. For all I know, you could be as useless as that pile on the floor." He then kicked the unconscious guard in disgust.

"Very well, Sir. As soon as the vault has been swept for any other intruders, you may both be on your way." The guard then gestured for Alpha Four to follow him. They moved to the corner of the room. "I'll get the surveillance team to guide you back to his room. Listen to what they say, do not deviate from their path, and do not disobey any orders given to you. Is that understood?"

Alpha Four nodded.

Then one of the guards from the control room spoke. "We've completed a sweep of the vault on every surveillance camera. That was the one and only intruder. We've traced his access point back to the staff helicopter; it appears that is how he entered. He then made his way to the security changing area and took one of the uniforms."

The Scottish guard reached behind him and retrieved a box. He handed it to Alpha Four. Inside was a spare set of earphones.

"Use these to communicate with the control room." The Scottish guard then moved over to one of the walls and placed his hand on it. A section of wall opened and revealed a small armoury. "Take this one."

Alpha Four was then handed a rifle. The guard's uniform he was wearing was only fitted with a walkie-talkie and a handgun, and clearly was only allowed on this floor in exceptional circumstances, but it had at least given him direct contact with the control room. The Scottish guard then left and headed in the same direction that Alpha Three was being taken.

Alpha Four looked towards Michael and smiled. "Sir, if you'd care to follow me, I'll take you back to your vault."

***

Of course, the only conscious person in the control room was Alpha Seven, but trying to act as a force of four was proving difficult. After the security breach, she'd been inundated with potential sightings, having to personally listen to each and every one. She'd already deleted the security footage but still had the cameras active, allowing her to follow Alpha Three and guide the others to their main prize. There were parts of the bank that even the control room didn't have access to, but because of their secrecy, they stood out on all the floor plans, as a great, empty space. The secret area was on three different floors, but all in the same location, stacked up like a three-storey house. With the rest of the floor plan now obtained through various files, many of them protected by weak restrictions, she planned out the quickest route for Michael and Alpha Four that would help them to avoid any guards.

"Head along the corridor until you reach the lift, don't press anything on the lift, I'll call it for you."

As there was still too much of a risk using the walkie-talkies, Alpha Four had placed the security earphones into his ears and was in constant contact with Alpha Seven.

"Control room, do you read me, over?"

Alpha Seven had been ignoring some of the calls since the security crisis had been avoided, but this one guard, with a heavy, Scottish accent, seemed persistent.

"Yes, we copy you, over."

"I want you to track the guard you're directing to the safe. He's only someone who keeps the other staff members in check and shouldn't even be on this floor. Make sure there's a unit stationed no less than one module away at all times. If anything happens, he'll be useless."

"Copy, I'm still following them on the cameras. I'll divert teams now." The line then went dead.

All of the security's earphones had tracking devices in them, which meant Alpha Seven could use the huge screen, displaying each level's floor plan, with hundreds of flashing blue lights, each one a guard. The guards dressed in Alpha Four's uniform weren't tracked, but they would no longer be on any of those levels.

Alpha Four's blue dot reached the lift. Calling it turned out to be relatively straightforward from the control room.

"I'm taking you down to floor twelve. Both thirteen and fourteen are restricted, and the lift can't go down that far, but part of our target should be on twelve."

"Should?" asked Alpha Four, as the lift doors closed.

"There's only one way to find out."

The lift took them down to level '*Twelve*', and Alpha Seven watched the blue dot leave but on the wrong side of the bank.

"The other side," said Alpha Seven.

"What do you mean?"

"You need to get out the same side you got in."

"We did," said Alpha Four.

"I'm watching your tracker. You're now on the opposite side."

"But we got out of the same door we entered th… Hang on." There was then just a faint whisper. "He says, are both sides identical?"

"Yes," replied Alpha Seven.

"Apparently, yes." There was another pause. "He's asking whether there's an option of section A and B for each floor.

Alpha Seven looked at every option available for the lift. "According to this, the bank is split into section A and B. Section B is the default for the lift and is used for the 'less wealthy' clients… Er, whilst section A requires a pass."

"Yes, but the side we want needs a pass…"

"Do you think he could get a bit closer to your earphones so I can actually hear him?" asked Alpha Seven.

"He's refusing to get any closer to me. This uniform's got a bit of a dominant smell of fried onions. I've got to admit, it's making me feel a little queasy." More silence followed. "It's the key fob that overrides it… Oh, where did you get that? It's alright, he stole one from the Scottish guy."

They then got back into the lift, this time scanning the fob. They were expecting the opposite doors to open, but instead, the lift moved up two floors, then back down to floor twelve. The same doors opened.

"How does that work?" asked Alpha Four. "Really, so the lift actually rotates as it moves? So they put the lift in some kind of spherical case and let it move on runners. Changing them would just be like changing train tracks?"

Alpha Seven desperately tried to listen to the other side of the conversation, but it was hopeless now they were out of the lift.

"When have you seen one? If you don't want to talk about it, why say it in the first place? I am focussed." Their conversation went silent once again, as they waited for Alpha Seven's instructions.

"Turn right, then keep on walking. The corridor should curve round to the left. After the sixteenth door, I run out of floor plan, that's where you're heading. There are no guards on this level, I'll tell you if that changes, but remember, I've got no camera feeds in that zone. In the meantime, I've got to help Alpha Three." Alpha Seven had done all she could. Now, they were on their own.

***

Michael and Alpha Four made it to the end of the corridor. They weren't sure what to expect, but a plain, white door certainly wasn't at the top of their list. It looked more like a maintenance door, one that simply locked with a standard key.

"Are we sure this is it?" asked Alpha Four.

"There's nowhere else. This is the end of the corridor," replied Michael, sharing similar concerns.

"What now?"

Michael then leant forwards and attempted to move the handle. It didn't budge.

"Worth a try," he admitted. He then pulled a pen and a paper clip from inside one of his suit's pockets.

"Where did they come from?" asked Alpha Four.

"The head of security's office. I took them from his desk whilst he was looking at a framed picture of Burma."

The pen had a small clip on it, which Michael tore off. He placed the pen back into his pocket and forced the pen clip into the round part of the lock. He then used the paper clip, half unfolded and bent into an unusual shape, and placed it just below the pen clip. Michael began twisting them both, trying to force the lock open. There was click. He tried the handle again, and the door opened.

"Are we sure this is definitely the place?" reiterated Alpha Four.

"No," said Michael, before entering the next room.

Inside was dark. He knew he was standing in another room and could just about make out its wall, but he didn't like his surroundings. His eyes would take time to adjust, the light still pouring in from the corridor made it even harder to focus. Whatever this room was, it must be part of the security for the main vault. There were likely infrared and thermal imaging cameras covering every inch of the room, but with Alpha Four still outside, Michael had a plan and stuck with it. There were small traces of light coming from the other side of the room. Michael made his way over there and found a small touchscreen panel. He hit the giant, green '*Open*' button and took a step back.

Hundreds of bright, white lights flicked on, lighting up the room like a sports field. Armed security flooded in from doors to the left and right of the room.

"On your knees!" one of them shouted.

Michael obeyed, and lowered himself, raising his hands in the process. More of the security forces left the room to take Alpha Four as well. He put up just as much of a fight.

"Identify yourself!" shouted the same guard. They all wore identical clothes. Their faces and bodies were obscured by black clothes, bulletproof vests, balaclavas. "Identify yourself!"

"My name is Captain Frederick Bridge, and I must say, I am appalled by your security."

The security guard knew the name, which was a huge relief to Michael given the number of rifles pointing at him.

"I need to see some identification."

"I'd hardly bring it with me. I am here to test the effectiveness of your security. My boss is storing something extremely valuable and we need to know it is secure. If you would contact the owner of this establishment, he will corroborate this, given his agreement in the test."

Michael would've had his fingers crossed if they weren't high up in the air. He knew the owner of the bank was dead and would be unable to back him up even if it was agreed. It was enough of a risk that the security guards had never seen Kale in the flesh but still knew of his name.

Another guard entered the room and took charge.

"Stand up!" he demanded.

They were both dragged to their feet and marched through into another room. The first they came to was a wide area, full of computer screens, enough weapons to form an army, a 3D model of the bank, and the images and bios of every member of staff in the building, pinned to one of the walls. The second room they were taken to was less pleasant. It was a small room, with cold, metal walls, and a concrete floor. There was nothing other than one single spotlight built into the ceiling. They were both led in and left with a single guard.

"Whilst we confirm your story, I want to take some time to get one or two things straight. If you have lied to me, you will both die a very slow and painful death. I will get the answers I require, and I will know how many of you attempted to breach the main vault," stated the guard.

"That's three things," said Michael with confidence.

The guard said nothing. Michael tried to imagine what he looked like under the mask. His voice sounded old. His accent was South African, but only traces of it remained. Still, the guard said nothing.

"There are three of us, but I think you already know that," said Michael.

"Yes, I have been tracking you since you failed to go through the metal detector, a very talented feat. I've sent a team to collect your friend. Apparently, they've given nothing away under basic interrogation, but I am yet to have a go, assuming you're lying, that is, which is something I always assume."

A few minutes went by. The guard hadn't spoken another word, he had just stood there, his arms folded, and his body taut. Alpha Three was then brought in. He had blood running from both nostrils and a swollen left eye. The team that the security guard had sent only comprised of four people, assuming it was the same number who escorted Alpha Three into the room.

Seconds later, the guard's attention was diverted. His head twisted to the right slightly as he listened to a message through his earpiece.

"It seems your account has been backed up. You may now leave and you can inform your boss that our security measures are sufficient for your needs."

"Are they though?" asked Michael, not at all sure how their story had been confirmed, or more to the point, who had confirmed it.

The guard froze. Michael's face showed confidence; the smirk slowly creeping along his face made it all the more prominent. It seemed impossible for the intruders to have got past all their security measures, but as the person who controlled his fate had authorised the test, he couldn't take the risk. He turned to the four who had brought Alpha Three in.

"Check on the vault. Check for any signs of a breach and check on the asset in section four."

The four guards left the room.

"Can we still go?" asked Michael. "I've got to debrief my boss on your disappointing results."

"As soon as we have searched you from top to bottom."

The guard wasn't lying. All three of them were searched thoroughly, far more thoroughly than any of them had expected, but nothing more than a pen was found. The guard had done his job. There was nothing more he could do. They had nothing on them. At that moment, he received another message.

"Impossible!" he shouted. "Put the bank on high alert. Nobody leaves without my say-so. Every member of staff is under suspicion."

"Something the matter?" asked Michael.

"Get these three out of my way!" he screamed, becoming more and more irate with every word. "Whoever you are working with will no doubt require your assistance to escape with the vial, so I'm going to ruin your little plan.

It will never make it out of this bank, I will win!" He then opened the door and gestured to some of the guards outside. "Team Two and Three, escort our guests to the helicopter and ensure they leave. If their helicopter is seen within our airspace longer than twenty seconds, shoot it down. If anyone even attempts to get close whilst you're escorting them out, shoot them all!"

They were escorted by eight of the security guards. They were led through a different door and into a private lift which took them straight to the surface, labelled *'Level 0'*. They were then led through the bank's reception area and through the entrance doors. No one was in sight, not even the guards at the security checkpoint were seen. There was a painfully piercing alarm ringing throughout the bank, informing all members of staff they were under suspicion. Michael's helicopter was already waiting on landing pad three but was guarded by no one. They climbed in, shutting the door behind them. The blades picked up speed, and before long, they were in the air. Hawk, their pilot, took them away from the helipad as quickly as he could.

"Did we get it?" asked Alpha Five.

In the co-pilot's seat, Alpha Seven twisted round and held up a small, cylindrical vial. It contained a green liquid, with a high viscosity.

"We sure did."

***

*Twenty-Seven Minutes Earlier*

Alpha Seven left the control room with haste. Although her tactical clothes were still on, she'd put one of the guard's outfits over the top. Given the several layers of clothing, the uniform fitted surprisingly well. Alpha Three was being held in one of the storage rooms, at least that's how it was labelled on the floor plan, but there was no quick way to get to it from the control room. In fact, there was no quick way to get anywhere from the control room.

The whole bank was still on a semi-high alert, despite the reassurance Alpha Seven had tried to give. Any more clients who arrived would have to be held outside the bank until a full sweep had been completed. Security always took priority, but it was only in the event of a code red, no client could be held at the bank any longer than they wished. It was one of the many directives Alpha Seven had read during her time in the control room and was one that could be of use.

A large team of guards had been sent down to the staff entrance to both secure it and gather any staff who could be conspiring against them. Despite this, Alpha Seven passed many guards, all suspicious of each other. She walked past them with purpose. Not one eyebrow was raised.

With just as much purpose and confidence, Alpha Seven entered the storage room. There were nine guards already in the room, eight around the perimeter of the room, and one in the centre, his face less than an inch from Alpha Three's.

"I'm going to give you three choices," started the Scottish guard, now stood behind Alpha Three, breathing down his neck. "You can answer all of my questions honestly, at the first time of asking, and then you can choose your own death. Or, you can put up a fight, before eventually giving up and still truthfully answering my questions, in which case, I'll choose the way you die. Or finally, you can live a life you will only wish was over, sat in that chair, but keep your lips tightly sealed. Now…"

"Sergeant McCoy," announced Alpha Seven.

The Scottish guard turned to look at the person who'd interrupted him. "Can I help you?"

"I've been instructed to transfer the prisoner to detention block C."

"Why?" questioned McCoy, both irritated and suspicious of the intruder.

"I haven't been told, Sir. I've received the orders from well above both our pay grades."

"The Shadows."

"Sir?" questioned Alpha Seven.

"The Shadow warriors, the ones who really run the security here. None of us have ever seen them, just shadows out of the corner of our eyes. There are days when a member of staff simply vanishes, never to be seen again. It is believed they are recruited into the Shadows. If it's really them, then I'll escort the prisoner, alone."

"But I'm not sure…"

"I don't care. This is my moment. I could become one of the Shadows, finally." The guard then looked towards Alpha Three. "And you're going to help me to become one."

Alpha Three was led out of the room. The door slammed shut behind them, and Alpha Seven was left to make another plan. She couldn't just follow him straight out of the room, he'd see, but at least she knew exactly where they were heading.

A few minutes had passed before Alpha Seven decided it was safe to leave. Suddenly, the door burst open and four armed figures flooded in. Their rifles were up and aimed at everyone in the room. They wore dark clothes and had balaclavas covering their faces.

"On your knees!" shouted one of them.

Nobody in the room hesitated.

"Where is the prisoner?"

"Sergeant McCoy took him," said Alpha Seven, ensuring she spoke first.

"Where?"

"I'll show you," said Alpha Seven, as she was about to stand.

"You will stay where you are!" demanded the Shadow warrior.

Alpha Seven did as they asked.

"Where did he take the prisoner?" They were clearly losing their patience and Alpha Seven couldn't risk having a bullet in her head.

"He should be heading to detention block C."

The Shadows immediately left the room. Alpha Seven waited just a few moments, then headed out herself.

The corridor was clear, and so with haste, Alpha Seven made her way to detention block C, but she didn't need to make it there. Cautiously turning every corner, Alpha Seven had almost made it to her destination when she heard a commotion coming from up ahead. She slowly edged her head around the corner and watched as the Shadows had Alpha Three and Sergeant McCoy pinned to the floor.

"I'm on your side!" screamed McCoy. "I want to be one of you!"

They were both lifted up and dragged away. Just before they left Alpha Seven's vision, one of the Shadows turned in her direction. She darted back behind the wall and stayed silent. Unsure whether to run, hide, or make a stand, she risked another look. They were all gone. She breathed a sigh of relief, *They didn't see me*. But they had.

Alpha Seven waited until only silence remained in the corridor before slowly peering around the corner for a third time. One of the Shadows was stood there, less than three inches from her face. The Shadow lashed out first, trying to catch her off guard, but her instincts were too good, as she dodged back. This wasn't anything that could be taught, it was just a natural ability, one of the many reasons she was chosen by Bosse. The Shadow then drew a baton and readied himself for combat. *A baton?* she thought. *Either they want me alive, or they're toying with me.* Whichever it was, Alpha Seven didn't care. The Shadow went to strike a blow, Alpha Seven dodged. The Shadow tried again, Alpha Seven blocked. The Shadow tried a third time, overstretching his reach. This time, Alpha Seven countered him. With a combination of multiple martial arts techniques, she disarmed him, flinging the baton away with one hand, balancing with the other, before delivering a powerful blow to his torso with her left boot.

The Shadow curled up in pain, but he wasn't done yet. With a growl, he pushed the pain to the back of his mind. Alpha Seven had moved several paces back, putting some distance between them. The Shadow started to charge, fuelled by anger and pain, but that had stopped him from thinking clearly. When Alpha Seven had removed the baton from his hand, she had also retrieved one of his three sidearms. She raised the handgun, and fired.

The Shadow stood motionless in the corridor. Alpha Seven had spared his life, firing just to his right, not out of kindness, but because she knew the uniform could have no blood on it if the next part of her plan was to work. However, the Shadow didn't know that and it was for the best that it stayed that way.

"You could've shot me the moment I peered around the corner, but you decided to bring me in alive. Now I'm repaying that act."

The Shadow was all the more confused. He hadn't spared her life, he was confident he could defeat her with his bare hands, but Alpha Seven had still spared his life. If he wasn't so sure she'd have no way out of the bank, he'd have put up more of fight. He'd been trained to see failure as no option, no matter what, but he also saw no need to waste his life needlessly.

"Thank you," he accepted.

"Now, I need just one more thing from you," said Alpha Seven, still with the gun pointed at his head. "I'm going to need your clothes."

Just five minutes later, the Shadow was bound and gagged in one of the toilets' cubicles, and Alpha Seven, disguised as a Shadow, was heading to the vault as quickly as she could. Just before the vault, Alpha Seven managed to catch up with the other three Shadows, still dragging

McCoy and Alpha Three along. Not one of them asked her, or as they still thought, him, how she'd got on. One thing was pretty clear though, the Shadows only ever spoke when it was absolutely necessary. If she'd come back empty-handed, it must've been because the intruder was dead. There was no margin, or even consideration, for defeat.

They escorted McCoy and Alpha Three straight through into what was labelled '*The Shadow Zone*' and into what appeared to be the main reception area.

"Take him to interrogation room two. Someone'll be by in a day or so to interrogate him," said the Shadow behind what looked like a doctor's reception room desk. The Shadow then looked at McCoy. "I hope you had a big breakfast, because we don't feed our guests down here. Well, maybe only to each other." McCoy was then dragged into a separate room and left alone, the huge steel door sealing him in the cold, dark room. "As for him, interrogation room one."

Alpha Seven followed the others as they escorted Alpha Three to interrogation room one. Alpha Four and Five were already inside, with another Shadow pacing the room, asserting his dominance.

The Shadow paused for a moment, listening to a message, a private message coming through his communication device alone.

"It seems your account has been backed up. You may now leave and you can inform your boss that our security measures are sufficient for your needs."

The whole thing seemed a little quick for Alpha Seven's liking, but then someone started to speak through her own earpiece and those around her.

"When they leave, we'll ensure they don't make it out of the valley. You're to plant a bomb on their helicopter. It has already been instructed to land and during your security checks, plant it and ensure no one can find it."

"Are they though?" asked Alpha Five.

His comment had clearly rattled the Shadow.

"Check on the vault. Check for any signs of a breach. And check on the asset in section four," he said, turning to the four of them.

It seemed planting the bomb would have to wait. Alpha Seven followed them out of the room and towards another set of doors. These were only unlocked after one of the Shadows had completed a retinal scan. In fact, the next three doors all had the same procedure. Alpha Seven was only thankful they didn't all have to scan their eyes. Eventually, they made it to a vault door. Part of its locking mechanism was released remotely, from someone back in the Shadows' command centre, whilst the rest of the mechanism had to be unlocked from the door itself. Each of the previous doors had all sealed shut in turn, leaving the four of them alone. One of the Shadows moved over to the vault door. There was a keypad on it. Not only did it require two separate codes, but whilst inputting them, the fingerprints and blood vessels within the fingers were all compared to those on record. If the Shadow typing in the code was nervous, the system would know and would put the whole bank on lockdown, which was not the kind of thing you'd want to do by accident.

With the slightly dramatic sound of the door's hydraulics shifting, the vault slowly opened, but inside, there weren't riches of gold, stacks of banknotes, or even hundreds of original paintings. Inside, there was a lift and nothing more. The lift door opened and they all entered, almost as if it was just an ordinary day's work.

"Entering the dead zone now," said one of the Shadows, as the lift door closed.

When they opened, two of the Shadows left. Alpha Seven didn't know which level the antidote would be on, she wasn't even sure what it would look like, but it appeared she was heading down to the lower level of the vault, as the doors once again closed. The lift descended one more level, before Alpha Seven and the last Shadow exited.

The design was what you'd expect from a multibillion-pound bank. The kind of thing depicted in heist movies, with a huge open expanse in the centre, and several smaller areas around the perimeter. Each of the areas was unlocked. Something that had perhaps been done remotely for inspection, because each area could have been secured with the vault-style door they had blocking the entrances. Alpha Seven checked all the areas on the left, one by one. They each had various artefacts, or pieces of artwork. Few had money, diamonds, or gold, but the vault probably cost more to secure than any raw material could be worth. It seemed only items that were priceless, one-of-a-kind things that would never be sold, were kept safe in the depths of the vault.

"Alright, all looks good," said the Shadow. "Let's check on section four."

Alpha Seven said nothing. She still couldn't be sure just how well they knew each other, but even an acquaintance could probably tell the difference between Alpha Seven's voice and that of the male Shadow. She'd been lucky enough that her height and build wasn't too dissimilar from the original guard's. They moved towards the far end of the vault. There was another door, again partially open. The Shadow opened it further.

Inside was almost empty, except for one large box, about the same size and shape as an old-fashioned suitcase. As the Shadow twisted a dial on the box, unlocking it, Alpha Seven knew this was the time she'd have even half a chance. As the Shadow started to lift the lid on the temperature controlled box, Alpha Seven spun round and aimed her sidearm into the main vault. The Shadow followed suit.

"Did you hear something?" he asked.

Alpha Seven said nothing. The Shadow's senses were picking up everything in the vault, but he was just imagining it, starting to hear things that weren't there, his mind playing tricks on him. Alpha Seven seized her chance, lifted the lid, grabbed the contents, and closed it again. She then started to move forwards, as if to check the vault again for intruders.

"It's gone," said the Shadow. "The box is empty."

Alpha Seven spun around in surprise.

She'd expected there to be certain procedures, something like searching the only two who had been in that part of the vault, but there weren't. It seemed the main priority was to shut down the whole facility. After all, if you can't escape, the Shadows would know how futile stealing something would be. They both entered the lift and climbed to the surface.

"We've lost the asset in section four, Sir," said the Shadow once back in radio contact.

"All Shadows, lock down the bank. No one leaves," came back through their earpieces.

Alpha Seven looked up and saw Alpha Three, Four, and Five all getting escorted out. Alpha Five had both hands by his side. His fist was clenched apart from his thumb and index finger. He didn't know where Alpha Seven was, but if she saw that signal, it was to tell her to get back to the helicopter, and that's exactly what she did.

Shadows had already started to fan out across the bank, securing every area, and it seemed as though she'd volunteered to secure one of the landing pads.

Just in time to watch Hawk land, Alpha Seven made it outside, welcoming the harsh, cold winds. There were two other Shadows already stood there, and as she readied herself to take them out with two well-placed bullets, they received another message through their earpieces.

"We are to proceed with the planting of the bomb in the helicopter currently at landing pad two. Make sure the bomb is set for a remote detonation, we don't want them in our airspace when it goes off."

It was perfect timing. Alpha Seven looked to the two Shadows and flicked her head to the side, telling them to get the bomb, whilst she prevented the helicopter from leaving. At least that's how they perceived it. Once out of sight, Alpha Seven removed the Shadow's uniform, revealing her white camouflage once again, and climbed into the helicopter, taking the co-pilot's chair.

The other three emerged shortly after, still with their escort.

"Bomb has been planted. A two-minute timer has been set," said Alpha Seven over the Shadow's radio.

"I said to set it for a remote detonation! Just get them out of our airspace!" came back.

With Alpha Three, Four, and Five all safely, and swiftly, inside, the helicopter was ushered away quickly. Hawk had clearance for take-off within just a couple of seconds and wasted no time in leaving.

"Did we get it?" asked Alpha Five.

Alpha Seven turned around and showed them the vial.

"We sure did."

She passed it back to Alpha Five, who examined the green liquid, before placing it in a box, no bigger than an A5 piece of paper, they'd kept on the helicopter.

"It was being stored in a temperature-controlled environment. I couldn't see what conditions or temperature it was at, but we need to get it back as quickly as possible," said Alpha Seven, as she climbed into the back.

"Agreed. Hawk, what's our ETA?" asked Alpha Five.

"Twenty-two minutes back to the runway."

"Okay, there's temperature-controlling facilities on our C4 Donkey. Let's just hope twenty-two minutes isn't too long."

"We might be a little longer than that," said Hawk, as he suddenly started taking evasive manoeuvres.

They all strapped themselves in, as Alpha Five looked out of the window. Some kind of missile was heading for them.

Hawk released a barrage of flares, deterring the missile, but then another was launched from the ground. Then another, and another. Hawk continued to take evasive manoeuvres, making some of the missiles pass straight by, whilst others became distracted by the flares, but before long, the final set of flares were fired. As the next projectile hurled itself through the air towards them, it seemed nothing could change its destiny.

# Chapter 10 – The Price of the Deed

12th September
11:01 BST
33 hrs 12 min. Until Deadline

Anthony was on his way to meet the client he'd be providing protection for. As always, his route had been chosen for him, avoiding the worst of the traffic but also taking the most open and exposed roads. No tunnels, no bridges, and no wrong turns. Whilst driving at a steady speed, blending in with the other vehicles around, he had an incoming call from Bosse flash up on the car's heads-up display. Reluctantly, he answered but said nothing.

"I can see you're only a couple of minutes out," started Bosse. "I thought this would be a good time to run through the job."

"Most people explain a job before sending someone on it."

"Well, I am not most people, and as you were going to accept no matter what it was, I didn't see the need." Bosse paused for a response, but he knew Anthony wouldn't reply. "You are to protect one of our clients, Mr Jenkins. He is to speak in court today and give evidence against his former business partner. His testimony is expected to be the final blow in the case and Mr Jenkins is concerned that he will become a target. His former business partner is well connected so do not treat this as a trivial job. I expect…"

Anthony ended the call.

Once at the location, which just so happened to be a thirty-storey high-rise building, he drove past it, took the next corner and descended into the building's garage, large enough to store over one hundred vehicles. There seemed to be minimal security, no more than two guards stood by the automated barrier, and a third sat in a tiny box just to the side. What Anthony hadn't noticed, however, was the hidden security system, comprising of concrete bollards, a wrought iron portcullis that could drop from the ceiling, and a set of blast-proof doors, the kind the Molehill used. Just in case that wasn't enough, there was also a small security force that could arrive in just twenty seconds.

He pulled into a space furthest into the garage and started heading towards the only set of lift doors he could see. Before Anthony made it halfway, they opened and a man in his late forties exited. His face was full of scars, his nose had been broken several times, and he had a cauliflower ear, the kind you mainly see in rugby players.

"You must be Ant," said the man. His voice matched his face, deep, loud, and something you wouldn't want to hear on a dark night.

Anthony put his right hand out to shake. The man put his left out, turned it upside down and shook.

"Lost all feeling in this one after an argument with a hippo," he said showing his slightly limp right hand. "But the hippo sure won't be doing it again. Shall we get on?" He led the way to the lift and pressed the button for the fifteenth floor. It was at this moment that Anthony realised the button for the thirteenth floor was missing.

"Are you superstitious?" Anthony asked.

"No, but I don't like crossing people on the stairs, and I also salute magpies."

Almost as soon as the lift doors closed, they opened again, this time on to floor fifteen, which just so happened to be the fourteenth floor. In front of them was a short corridor with a desk. Behind the desk sat a woman, likely Mr Jenkins' personal assistant. She looked up and smiled at them both.

"Mr Jenkins is expecting you. You can go straight in," she said, maintaining her smile.

At most, she was in her mid twenties, with long, blond hair and eyes that were a deep blue in colour. They both entered the room behind the door. As it turned out, floor fifteen was Mr Jenkins' living space, with the entire floor devoted to that one purpose. It was all open-plan, including the bathroom, and given the large expanse of windows spanning the full perimeter of the floor, Anthony couldn't help but feel sorry for whoever owned the building opposite.

"Welcome," said Mr Jenkins, with his arms spread out. He was sat on an uncomfortable-looking, brown, leather sofa, one of six which created a rectangular area for a lounge. "I'm glad you could make it, although we'll have to be quick, I'm expected in court within the hour."

His voice and appearance was almost that of a politician. He spoke as if everything around him was somehow beneath him. To him, Anthony was nothing more than a hired gun, and he was in control of everyone. First impressions are powerful, and the one Mr Jenkins left was that he thought himself as king of everything.

"Could you please supply him with a weapon," he said to the guard who had brought Anthony in.

"I have my own."

"Your boss was very clear. Nothing can be traced back to you, so we are to supply the firearms. Did he not tell you?"

"No."

Anthony handed his sidearm to the guard and grabbed the one passed to him. It didn't look a whole lot different, but to Anthony it was like the difference between a manual and an automatic car. He held it in his palm, the weight was different for a start, but it would have to do. He took the magazine out and examined the bullets. Real, just as he had suspected. It wasn't that Bosse didn't want them tracing anything back to the Molehill, it was more that he didn't want Mr Jenkins to find out about their bullets. Anthony's original handgun had a grip coded to the blood vessels in his hand, so only he could use it, and most importantly, nobody would be able to retrieve the magazine. Whilst most of Alpha team had their rifles, and each other's, coded to their palms and their sidearms without the coded grip, Anthony was the opposite, leaving his trusted rifle without the protection.

"I'm sorry that I haven't the time to show you around my humble abode, but I was expecting you here a little earlier."

"Unfortunately, I had other matters to attend to. Didn't my boss tell you?"

The room turned to ice in an instant.

Then, to Anthony's right, another figure emerged. A young boy, about fourteen years old, made his way over to Mr Jenkins. He was wearing jeans and a T-shirt, both with designer labels. The bright white trainers were the same, but he also wore a flat cap, one that looked tatty and worn.

"Are you ready to go?" he asked the boy.

"Yep, I've been waiting for hours," replied the boy.

"This is my son, Timothy," said Mr Jenkins, as if he should've known. "He'll be joining us today, to see what it's really like to beat your biggest rival."

"I wasn't informed," added Anthony.

"I have just informed you, and I know it won't be a problem. Shall we get going?"

"In the future, you need to consult with me first."

Mr Jenkins smiled and leant closer to Anthony. "When you have as much money as me, there is nothing that I need to do."

Anthony also leant closer. "I can put a bullet between your eyes from over one hundred metres away. Don't ever forget that."

Mr Jenkins took half a step back, and then led the way further into the apartment to a second lift.

"This is my personal lift and takes me down to my own vehicles."

Sure enough, the lift took them to a fleet of vehicles. There was every brand of high-end sports car from every corner of the globe. It was like a museum for brand-new cars.

"We'll go in the Ferrari, the Ferrari. It was the first sports car I ever purchased," said Mr Jenkins. "Anthony, you're with Timothy. He chooses the vehicle."

"Are they secure?" asked Anthony.

Mr Jenkins looked puzzled. "They don't need to be. They're fast."

That seemed to be the end of the conversation. Mr Jenkins and the guard entered one of two LaFerraris, the bright yellow one, and started the engine.

Timothy ran straight to one car in particular, a McLaren P1. The Mustangs would have been more to Anthony's taste, but he had his orders. They entered the car and followed Mr Jenkins out into the street. It purred as it crawled on to the road.

"Can we make sure we win?" asked Timothy.

Anthony frowned at him.

"My dad will race you to the courthouse. He always told me that if you don't win, there was no point in taking part."

"Did he?" muttered Anthony.

If Mr Jenkins was to put his foot down, Anthony would've raced him anyway, not because of what the boy said, but because he wanted to see how he'd react after losing. There was just one problem; they were caught in a queue of traffic, where even the pedestrians were moving quicker. Anthony watched everything, and everyone. If Mr Jenkins was truly in danger, this would be the perfect time to approach him. He watched the pedestrians; any that showed too much interest in the queue of traffic, or the car park they had just left. Or any who didn't show enough interest in the two sports cars. He watched all the cars and their passengers, whether any of them looked towards the two cars too many times. Anthony's job had been made a lot harder by the fact that he was driving a McLaren sports car with a blue and orange racing livery, and Mr Jenkins was in a bright yellow Ferrari that could probably be seen from a jumbo jet flying overhead.

"Is Anthony your real name?" asked Timothy.

"What do you mean by real?"

"Well, you know. Your real name, like, the… like the one you were given… when you were born."

"I don't know, then."

"You don't like talking much, do you?" he asked.

"No."

Although Anthony didn't care much for talking, it was because he was so focussed on watching everything around him. Perhaps there was a time when that was different, but it was a time Anthony had long tried to forget.

"My dad always tells me to talk more. Apparently, if I don't dominate conversations then I won't achieve anything."

"That doesn't surprise me."

Silence descended in the car, all except for the hum of the engine and occasional beeping of horns further back in the traffic.

"Have you ever killed anyone?" Timothy asked suddenly.

"Yes," he answered with some reluctance.

"My dad says the world is made of those who are paid to get their hands dirty, and those who pay to keep them clean."

"It sounds like someone needs to wire your dad's jaw shut."

If that hadn't ended the conversation, the sound of the Ferrari roaring, as Mr Jenkins bumped up a low part of the kerb, finished the job. Anthony followed, his higher ride height helping him to drive on to the pavement quicker. Pedestrians dived out of the way as the two cars swerved round lamp posts, benches, and everything else that got in their way. Anthony knew he couldn't beat Mr Jenkins as soon as they set off, his chance would come later. For now, he kept his bonnet as close to the yellow spoiler as he could.

At last, they cleared the obstruction; roadworks, with barriers and temporary traffic lights causing the blockage, with four workmen all leaning over a hole in the ground. Both cars found another sloped part of the pavement and descended back on to the road. Mr Jenkins put his foot down. The yellow Ferrari sprung to life as it squeezed between the traffic slowly backing up on the other side of the road, but with every turn, Anthony closed the distance. He was looking further into the distance, watching and predicting where each car would be as they approached.

Mr Jenkins turned a corner on to a stretch of road without any moving cars, and Anthony followed. He was now solely focussed on the car in front. If he hadn't been, he would have noticed the group of people further up the road before it was too late.

Just as Mr Jenkins approached them, they threw a stinger out on to the road; a long, thin tool full of metal, razor-sharp teeth that sits on the road, almost unseen, and bursts the tyres of anything that drives over it. Mr Jenkins did exactly that. His tyres burst instantly, sending him into an uncontrollable spin, as his car ploughed into the line of parked cars. Anthony could only watch, as he slowed down to stop before the stinger, but whoever had disabled Mr Jenkins' car had other ideas. Out of the corner of his eye, Anthony caught sight of an orange flash and, before he could react, a burst of flames erupted beside the car, tipping it over on to its roof. The next thing he knew, he was upside down, hanging from the roof of the car by his seat belt, watching helplessly as an armed group of six approached Mr Jenkins' car and dragged him out.

***

*Thirty Seconds Earlier*

"I have eyes on the two cars. Target is in the first."

"Copy."

Six men were all stood at the side of the road, watching two sports cars approach them at great speed. Five of them were wearing balaclavas; the sixth was clearly not a usual member of their team and found it hard to know who was talking.

"Ruben, is the stinger ready?"

"Aye."

"Are you sure this is the best way to go about this? This could kill them!" said the sixth man, his hands trembling in his jacket pockets.

"When the first car reaches the mark, throw it." One of them then touched their ear and spoke again. "Olive, you in position?"

"I need quiet," she replied. That was all he needed to hear.

The yellow car reached a speed limit signpost, displaying '30' in big red numbers. That was the marker. The stinger was thrown out and the car drove over it. Within a couple of seconds, it had already ploughed into a line of parked cars, but the other car was still approaching. They all knew better than to ask Olive for updates, but they all wanted to. The car started to slow, as it approached them, but it wouldn't make it. A rocket was fired from one of the rooftops and hit the road less than a metre from the second car. It was enough to roll the car over on to its roof as it clattered into other parked cars, coming to an abrupt halt.

"What are you doing? You could've killed them!" screamed the unmasked man.

"Ruben, watch the second car. Everyone else, with me."

They approached the yellow car. There was no sign of any movement, but with their suppressed handguns raised, they were taking no chances. They moved around the car. A bullet was fired from inside, as one of the masked assailants fell to the floor with a grunt. The others moved straight in, dragging two men from the car, one unconscious, the other trying to fight off his attackers.

"Christophe, you good?"

"I'm good," was said by the one lying on the floor, focussing on his breathing. The bullet had hit his vest, but that hadn't stopped it from hurting.

One of them carried their target in a fireman's lift to a white van parked at the side of the road. He was thrown in, like a rolled-up carpet that's no longer wanted. The other one from the car had had his hands tied behind his back and was now knelt on the road.

"I'm in a bit of a hurry, so I'll make this short. If you're going to hurt any of my men, make sure you kill us all, because I will not rest until I have levelled the score. Unfortunately for you, it will involve your death."

The man climbed to his feet and charged towards one of the masked men. He knew exactly which one was talking. The move had caught them all off guard, as he clattered into him, knocking them both to the ground. With a single move, he broke his plastic restraints and wrapped his left hand around the bottom of the balaclava. The others watched. They knew their boss would have it all under control.

The masked assailant drew a knife from his jacket and plunged it into the raging guard on top of him. The guard squeezed tighter, but it was already too late. Within a few seconds, he started to feel faint, after a few more, he could no longer hold his own body weight. The masked assailant breathed a sigh of relief, as he pushed the dead weight off himself and on to the ground. The knife had found a major artery.

"What have you done!" exclaimed the unmasked man. "Mr Klien explicitly told you no killing!"

"For the record," started the man getting off the floor. "I had no intention of killing him. He hurt Christophe, and simply shooting him whilst he was on knees would not have repaid the debt. Killing him was an unfortunate occurrence, but one that I'm sure Mr Klien will accept."

"I'm having nothing to do with this." The unmasked man turned and started walking away.

"I'm afraid you can't leave. You see, you refused to wear a mask and we can't afford to let the police catch up to you. Mr Klien gave express instructions to leave no trace of his involvement and, unless you reconsider, you will fall into that category."

He continued to walk. The masked assailant picked his suppressed handgun up from the floor, aimed it, and fired a single bullet. The man fell to floor.

He looked to one of the others. "You just can't reason with some people. Let's get to the other car before anyone else causes us any problems."

They all made their way to the second car, but they were too late. The car was empty. Sirens sounded in the distance. The emergency services weren't in sight, but it wouldn't be long before that changed. Just beside the car was an inspection hatch.

"They're in the sewers," one of them said.

"Ruben, Martin, follow them. The rest of you, we're leaving!"

They headed back to the van and climbed in, including Olive, who'd made it down from the roof, whilst the other two lifted the inspection cover and climbed down into the sewer.

***

In the darkness of the sewers running throughout the city, Anthony and Timothy were trying to get away from whoever had entered the sewers a couple of minutes after them. The start of their journey was quick, knowing full well that if they made it past a few junctions, their chances of being followed were low. Despite its darkness, Anthony felt the left-hand wall and followed it, taking every left turn that came.

"My head hurts," said Timothy.

"Good."

"Good? What's good about it?" he asked, his shoulder being clasped by Anthony.

"Pain means you're alive. It's if you stop feeling it that should worry you."

They continued to walk, their feet wading in water, the smell more of stagnant water than sewerage.

"Where are we?" asked Timothy.

"I haven't a clue. It's some sort of Victorian-style sewer."

"So, are we walking in poo?"

"It doesn't smell like it's used as that any more. I assume it's used as more of an overflow in excessive flooding."

The underground sewerage system was a vast array of twisting tunnels with drains allowing a small amount of light in from the world above. The noise of their boots splashing in the water echoed throughout the tunnels, but so did the noise of the ones following them. Anthony had already identified two sets of footsteps, but what he couldn't understand was how they were able to keep track of them. There was also something else eating away at him; how they knew that was going to be their route. Mr Jenkins had decided to take that turn on a spur-of-the-moment decision. It wasn't the prearranged route, and not even he knew they were going to take that road.

Anthony turned around and saw a faint light glistening off the water. The light wasn't close, but it soon would be. Timothy was pulled along at a quicker pace. They needed to leave the sewers quickly but also needed enough time to get out without being followed. Whilst their pace quickened, so did that of the two chasing them.

Anthony was left with little choice. The next inspection hatch he came to, he climbed up the ladder and lifted the metal, circular cover. He checked his surroundings, then pulled Timothy out after him. They were in a residential estate, a couple of streets away from where they were ambushed. Replacing the cover, they made their way down the street. Anthony looked at the letter boxes of each house, some built into the doors, others attached to the wall. He examined them all, until seeing one in particular. Letters and leaflets of unwanted information were poking out from one of them.

"This one," said Anthony, as they made their way towards the house.

"Why this one?"

"Look at the post sticking from the letter box. Either they're really popular, or no one's collected the post for at least a few days, and that means there's a good chance nobody's in."

Timothy smiled, as the simple act of looking at people's letter boxes had helped them to find an empty place to hide. They moved around to the back of the house, where Anthony bent down to pick the lock on the back door. He used two pins, jabbing them into the lock, and started trying to twist them.

"You're doing it wrong," said Timothy.

Anthony said nothing.

"You're meant to be gentle. You're unlocking it, not breaking it."

Anthony stood up and moved aside for Timothy to have a go. With a single movement, and just a couple of seconds, the door was unlocked and they were inside. Both headed upstairs to one of the windows at the front of the house. They stared down the road as the inspection cover was lifted and two masked assailants climbed out of the sewers. They stopped and looked around the street, before one of them pulled what looked like a phone out of his pocket. He looked at it for a few seconds, then looked up to the house they were in. Both Anthony and Timothy dived back from the window, but it wouldn't have mattered, they knew exactly where they were.

"Get to the bathroom and lie down flat in the bath," said Anthony, as he started making his way back downstairs.

He searched through as many kitchen drawers as he could in the time he had. He found corkscrews, spatulas, spoons, tongs, and enough cutlery for a family of fifty but nothing that was of major use.

"They haven't got a bath," said Timothy, starting to come down the stairs.

"Then find somewhere to hide and don't make a sound."

There was a drinks cabinet over to one side. Anthony took a half-finished bottle of brandy, removed the lid, rammed one of the kitchen tea towels in its neck, and tipped it upside down until the towel was fully soaked. There was a gas cooker, so he lit one of the rings on the stove, making it quicker to light the towel should he need to. He then found a cupboard full of glasses. A handful at a time, he scooped them out and threw them all over the floor. Finally, he picked up a knife block and folded his body into the cupboard under the sink. Then, all he could do was wait.

The front door was kicked in and two sets of footsteps approached.

"The boy's upstairs," whispered one of them.

They then split up, one clearing downstairs, the other about to head upstairs. His boots crunched on the glass. Anthony now knew exactly where he was. He counted the steps. Three… Four… Five. He'd now be past the cupboard Anthony was hiding in. Slowly, he opened it and checked his surroundings. The assailant was just about to leave the kitchen. Anthony silently drew one of the knives from the block and held the blade between his fingertips. Suddenly, more glass crunched from beside him. He turned and saw the other assailant emerge from the corner. Quicker than the man could raise his gun, Anthony threw the knife.

It caught his hand, almost cutting the handgun from his grip. It slid along the floor, but the other had heard. He spun round and trained his gun at Anthony, firing a few bullets. Anthony ducked behind the kitchen units.

"Get the boy, this one's mine!" yelled the unarmed man.

Anthony knew he had to reach the stairs first, and he had just one advantage, they didn't know where they were. The attacker had taken a wrong turn as he left the kitchen and would end up in the living room, but it would only buy Anthony a few more crucial seconds.

As the unarmed assailant drew a knife from his vest and started to charge towards Anthony, he grabbed the bottle of brandy, lit the towel over the cooker and ran for the stairs. The other attacker had already found them, so Anthony did the only thing he could. He threw the bottle at the assailant, but he dived back just in time.

As the glass shattered, it erupted in flames. The nearest assailant took two steps back as his hair almost caught alight. The stairs were blocked, but all Anthony had done was start a timer. The flames quickly caught the wooden banister and the carpet. Within seconds, the tops of the flames were already upstairs and out of sight.

"Martin, get in through one of the windows."

"You got it, Ruben."

The armed guard quickly left through the back door. He could've swiftly removed Anthony with a single shot, but this was clearly not what Ruben had wanted. He'd let them escape through the sewers, now he was going to make that right by bringing his boss Anthony's head.

Most of the knives in the block were already missing, but three still remained. Anthony threw one towards Ruben, who swiftly dodged.

"Missed."

But that was Anthony's plan. In the second it took to dodge the knife, he'd disappeared.

There was little point in running, or hiding, so Anthony waited just around the corner. There was a small blind spot where the wall jutted out to create an open archway. He was stood on a small, round table, poised with both knives. There was more crunching glass, slow and steady. As Ruben approached the corner, his steps got even slower, until finally stopping.

Anthony waited, his focus greater than ever. Ruben leapt round the corner. He caught sight of Anthony but his knife wasn't raised enough to catch him. Anthony almost stepped from the table and down on to Ruben, burying one knife into his right shoulder. The other two knives came crashing together, as they became locked in a battle of strength. Anthony twisted the knife in Ruben's shoulder, causing him to shriek in pain but tighten his grip on his own knife. The two of them continued to wrestle for any advantage. Eventually, Ruben shifted his stance to slice his knife across Anthony's chest, but his opponent was just as quick. The knives came together again, this time clattering to the other side of the room, free from their owners.

Anthony kicked out, separating the two of them for a moment. Ruben bent down and flicked a handful of glass in Anthony's face, distracting him for long enough to get close. Ruben tackled him, sending them both crashing through a glass coffee table. The fire had started to reach them, the smoke making visibility almost impossible. Ruben's hands found Anthony's neck and tightened their grip. Anthony reached around for anything beside him to help. His hand found a somehow intact vase that was once on the coffee table. He grabbed hold of it and smashed it over Ruben's head. It was enough for Anthony to push back, finding enough purchase to climb back to his feet.

Again, Ruben charged, like a bull that had somehow seen red amongst the thick smoke. They both went flying back through the window behind, crashing out into the garden. Both lay on the grass for a second, as smoke started pouring from the broken window. Anthony got to his feet and leant against the nearby shed. As Ruben started climbing to his feet, his eyes starting to burn from the smoke, Anthony swung the shed door open, catching Ruben square in the face. He fell back to the floor, this time without getting back up.

Anthony found a small phone lying on the grass, which had fallen out of Ruben's pocket as they'd crashed through the window. Out of the corner of his eye, he saw Timothy running down the street, with Martin just behind. He picked up a garden fork, lying just inside the shed, and chased after them. As he made it to the street, he saw Martin stop and aim his handgun at Timothy. He couldn't be sure whether Timothy was about to be wounded, threatened, or worse, but Anthony took no chances. With the garden fork weighed up in his hands, he threw it the ten metres it needed to go. Two of the three prongs dug into his back. He fell to his knees, dropped the gun, then let his face hit the hot ground.

Anthony could hear sirens approaching, so chased after Timothy.

"They're both down, we have to go!"

They headed back into the sewers, walked for another thirty minutes, then resurfaced. Anthony had checked the last few inspection covers, but all had led to busy roads. This one, however, seemed to be on a quiet street.

"We need a car," said Anthony, looking up and down the street at the long line parked on both sides.

"How about this one?" replied Timothy, pointing to the most expensive-looking one.

Anthony ignored him and made his way towards an older car, one purchased before the year 2000 according to its number plate.

"This can't be tracked." He opened the car door with ease and started its engine after simply touching two exposed wires he'd cut from under the steering wheel.

"I thought that only happened in films."

"Even films have to be based on reality," replied Anthony. "Before we leave, I need to know how they tracked us."

He pulled the small phone out of his pocket and examined it. It was tracking Timothy or something on him. Anthony held the phone towards him. The stronger the signal, the quicker the small, circular icon on the screen flashed. It was at its quickest near Timothy's head.

"Pass me the hat," he said, taking it from Timothy's head. He scanned it away from Timothy, then scanned him again whilst the hat was away from him. "This is how they were tracking us. Where did you get it?"

"My dad. It used to be his, but that's all he ever told me about it."

Anthony buried his head in the phone.

"What are you doing?" asked Timothy.

"Finding your dad."

Timothy leant over his shoulder, watching everything he did. A couple of minutes later, he put the phone down, flicked the radio to the local station, threw the hat out of the window, and drove.

Timothy looked down, as he started twiddling with his fingers. "Do you think my dad's still alive?" he asked.

"That's what I'm going to find out, as soon as I've dropped you off at a safe location."

"What? No, I'm coming with you."

Anthony kept his gaze fixed on the road, and said nothing.

"I'm coming with you, and I'm going to help get him back," he persisted.

"He might not be coming back," Anthony said, solemnly.

"I know that he is. I know that, and I am going to help you."

Anthony held his finger up, as silence descended upon the car. He turned the radio up and listened.

"And we've just had a statement through from the police, asking for public help. Just over half an hour ago, they were called to the scene of a house fire. Two armed suspects were apprehended at the scene, both of which are being treated for injuries, one is believed to be in critical condition. This crime has been linked to the murder of businessman Kenneth Roads, found with a single gunshot wound just twenty minutes prior to the house fire. The police are looking for another male, believed to be over six feet tall and in his early forties, and a young boy aged between fourteen and sixteen. The police believe this boy has been kidnapped and the third suspect is highly dangerous. If you see anything suspicious, report it immediately, and do not approach them… And in other news, a fifty-five-year-old man has been savagely attacked by a squirrel…"

Anthony turned the radio back down. "Early forties," he muttered, shaking his head.

***

The white van pulled through the security gates without an issue. They'd arrived at the nearby airport within the hour and were heading round to one of the many private hangars. The rear entrance to the airport had just as much security as the front, with high-tech vehicle scanners, several layers of retractable barriers, and enough armed guards to give any army a run for their money. However, if enough money was paid, most of these security measures could be overlooked.

Despite the large sum that had been transferred to the airport's head of security the day before, hundreds of cameras still followed the van as it travelled to hangar '147'. If it deviated from its prearranged path, even by a metre, there were over twenty cars ready to intercept it. They were not, however, needed. The van arrived without an issue and parked up in front of a white, private jet. The van's side door slid open and Mr Jenkins, with his hands bound in front of him, was escorted out by two of the masked assailants. They stopped in front of a smartly dressed gentleman, about forty years of age. He had dark-rimmed, round glasses and a very regal-looking posture.

"This way," he said, leading them up the steps of the private jet.

Inside was cool and welcoming after the sweaty climate in the back of the van. Mr Jenkins was shown to a chair, the smartly dressed man sat opposite. He directed one of the masked assailants to leave the plane with a simple flick of his hand. The other finally removed his mask.

"We are camera-free now, Sir," he said.

It wasn't all too surprising why he'd been wearing a mask, his face seemed misshapen, as if everything had been broken several times over, and his skin was greasy, pitted, and dirty.

Mr Jenkins held his hands up. "Thank you, Lucas."

The assailant leant forwards and cut the plastic that was keeping Mr Jenkins' wrists together.

"I trust there were no problems?" asked the smartly dressed man.

The other two fell silent.

"Unfortunately, my son got away," said Mr Jenkins.

"I see. And what is being done about it?"

At this point, the question was being directed to Lucas, seemingly in charge of the other masked assailants.

"Two of my men were unsuccessful. One is in the hospital, the other is in the morgue. The tracker placed on the boy has also been stationary for almost twenty minutes. We believe he lost the hat somehow."

"I am very sorry about your men, but I must ask. How was this possible? I was assured that every detail was planned down to the finest possible margin."

"The person protecting him," started Lucas. "He was not in our original plan."

The businessman shifted his focus back to Mr Jenkins.

"It was a necessary precaution. He is from a private institution which provides help with all aspects, from espionage, to counter-espionage, to security, to removing security. I thought it would help to sell my innocence a little better."

"I do hope covering your own back will not cost us."

"I can assure…"

The businessman held up his right index finger. "Do not talk over me, Mr Jenkins… Myself and my business partners have put a lot of money into this operation. If anything goes wrong, we will all hold you responsible. And we are very powerful, as you know. If the boy cannot be captured, then he must be killed."

Again, Mr Jenkins was about to speak but the same finger silenced him.

"Lucas, I'm sure you and your men can deal with just one man. If the boy is a potential problem, eliminate him. In the meantime, Mr Jenkins, I wish to know about this private institution you speak so highly of. Perhaps we can make a deal with them. Or perhaps they will be a problem for us."

Lucas put the mask back over his face and left the jet. The rest of the masked assailants were waiting outside.

"What's the call?" asked one of them.

"We're moving to phase three. The jet's being prepped for take-off," said Lucas.

"What about the boy? I thought they needed him?" asked another.

"The plan's changed. When he arrives here, we are to eliminate both of them. Is that understood?"

They all nodded in agreement.

"Good," said Lucas. "Whoever this bodyguard is, he's good. He'll no doubt have Ruben's phone on him, so we'll send him a message. If we get the kid, we'll pay him."

"You think he'll go through with it?"

"No, but he'll probably try and double-cross us some way, and that means that he'll have the kid with him and he'll bring him out into the open, even if it's only bait. That's all we need. Aly's got the ransom footage; we'll use that to convince him. Let's get this done for Ruben and Martin."

All four of them started pumping the air with their fists.

***

Anthony was just approaching the airport's main in road, when he suddenly indicated left, pulled into the closest lay-by at speed, and slammed his foot on the brake. The phone he'd taken from Ruben had started to buzz. A video had been sent through to it. Anthony blocked the camera on the front and back with his thumb and index finger, then hit play. He wasn't sure whether he was watching something live or recorded, but it was the context that was important. Mr Jenkins was sat in a dark space, with a flashlight shining in his face. The image was moving, as was Mr Jenkins, almost as if they were travelling in something like the van Anthony saw after the car crash.

Then someone started to speak. It was clearly disguised, using a standard AI voice scrambler.

"As you can see, we have Mr Jenkins firmly in our custody. This is not the kind of negotiation where we are prepared to hand over our prisoner. We are, however, prepared to offer you a deal. We want Mr Jenkins' boy and we are prepared to pay you the sum of a quarter of a million US dollars worth of Bitcoin. This will be transferred into an account of your choosing as soon as you hand him over. Please think this over carefully, because if we catch up to you before you accept, you will find yourself in a very similar situation to Mr Jenkins. Once you have decided to accept, you can find us at the nearest airport, in hangar one four seven. Use the code word 'Robin' at the airport and you will be escorted to us promptly. Please do not try to double-cross us, we will know, and you will regret it."

The video then ended. According to the tracker Anthony was using on Ruben's phone, there was a second tracking device set up, likely on Mr Jenkins' person. If this was the case, the tracker had been stationary in the airport during the entire video, making it pre-recorded. But how did they know they weren't going to get Timothy? Thoughts continued to run through his head, but he had just one thing to focus on, get Mr Jenkins back. Now all he needed was a plan. And twenty minutes later, it was already in motion.

***

Lucas watched as the white jet fired up its engines and moved just outside the hangar. He'd had the call from security informing him that someone had given the code word, 'Robin'. Security were on their way down and, if possible, the boy would be taken on to the jet and they would leave. Mr Jenkins had given them the new order, they were to try everything in their power to get his son back, but if that couldn't be done, they'd leave without him.

The airport itself seemed almost derelict. They were in the private section, which housed all the private hangars. The two runways were on the other side of the main airport building, and every ninety seconds, another plane lifted itself into view as it gained altitude. On the private side of the airport, only a few vehicles were driving across the taxiway, waiting for permission at every lane. A couple of luggage cars pulled into their maintenance hangar just up the taxiway. A fuel tanker lumbered past on its way to refill another thirsty plane. A cleaning crew arrived at hangar one four five to polish someone else's pride and joy.

A convoy of three cars arrived and stopped about fifty metres away from hangar one four seven. They were the instructions given by Lucas, and they were to be obeyed without exception. The left-hand side doors of the central car opened. Out of the back, an elderly man and a child exited the vehicle, along with a younger woman from the passenger seat, who'd pass as a bouncer for the worst kind of venue.

Lucas was too far away to get a positive ID on any of them.

"Olive, is that them?" he asked. There was only silence that followed. The three who had exited the vehicle remained stationary, waiting for instructions. "Olive, do you have confirmation?" Again, only silence followed. "Olive, do you read me? Olive, can you hear me? Oliveira?" Still nothing.

"What should we do?" asked Aly, resting his index finger over the trigger of his suppressed handgun.

"Hold here, with me. Christophe, get on the mini gun. This is Lucas, White Robin, you are cleared for take-off, we are about to go loud."

Christophe moved back inside the hangar and took hold of a dusty, blue, plastic tarpaulin. He flung it to the side, revealing a mini gun mounted on a few boxes full of sand.

***

*Nine Minutes Earlier*

Anthony entered the airport through one of the many side doors. He'd given Timothy his instructions. He was to walk through the main entrance, find the first member of airport security and say the word 'Robin'. Even if they didn't know what it meant, or why a fourteen-year-old boy had just randomly said it, one of the countless audio devices around the building and on each member of staff would pick the word up. Within a few seconds, that security guard would be given a message from one of their superiors. The message wouldn't make sense, but it would be followed to the letter. What's more, that was exactly what happened, but that gave Anthony just ten minutes at the most.

Bosse had kept good relations with all the nearby airports and airfields. Occasionally, he'd need to change a flight's take-off and landing location, diverting attention away from the Molehill. It was easy enough to get one of the airports to sign the necessary paperwork and add those planes to the take-off and landing schedules. Plus, anyone who decided to trace one of the flights leaving the Molehill would be led along a path of breadcrumbs. Of course, Bosse had to pay regular sums of money, provide armed personnel to assist with security, and give intel on anyone potentially of interest, but they were small prices to pay to stay under the radar. This was yet another situation where the good relationship had come in handy. Bosse had already been in contact with the head of security, and by the time Anthony had entered, he'd already been fitted up with a legitimate way of getting close to hangar one four seven.

Within just three minutes, he was in a change of clothes, inside an airport vehicle with three other security guards, and was armed with one of their assault rifles. The airport's chief of security had been informed of the plan, and just what was going on. She'd spoken to Bosse personally and delayed Timothy's escort to hangar one four seven as much as possible, without making it look suspicious. The cover she'd provided Anthony and the other three was that of a cleaning crew. It was a daily occurrence for the airport to provide a free-of-charge cleaning service for every private plane whenever required. In fact, just one day earlier, the airport had carried out that service for the white, private jet located in hangar one four seven.

As quickly as they could, the maintenance van took them to hangar one four five. Timothy's car was just two minutes out. Once inside hangar one four five and out of sight, the three security guards and Anthony retrieved their rifles and left the hangar out of its side door. They then approached the hangar in question, with the security guards waiting near the front, and Anthony heading to the back. There was a service ladder on the outside which he took to the roof. Each rung of the ladder was taken as quickly as possible, but as soon as his head surfaced on the roof, he saw someone set up in a sniper's position.

Timothy's car was less than a minute out, but the roof had no cover. If he was spotted before he got to the sniper, his and Timothy's fate would be sealed. He approached quickly and quietly. His rifle was fitted with a suppressor to prevent a national incident breaking out at the sound of gunfire at an airport. Anthony had it raised. Planes continued to take off, as if nothing was happening, just a few hundred metres away. The roar of their engines covered the noise of Anthony's footsteps, but the sniper still knew he was coming. Perhaps it was the vibrations on the roof, or the faint noise that did get past the other planes, or maybe it was just a sixth sense, the hairs standing up on the back of her neck. Her hand slipped from the fifty-calibre rifle her head was resting against and reached down for the handgun in its chest-level holster. She rolled over and drew the gun, but Anthony was wise to the move. He couldn't risk Timothy's life any more. Before she could release any bullets, Anthony found his mark and fired three times. The kidnapping of Mr Jenkins and his son had gone wrong, and Oliveira was the next person to pay the price. Anthony picked up the sniper rifle and looked through the heavily magnified scope. He could see Timothy stood with more security.

Suddenly, the private jet just outside hangar one four seven started to move. Its engines had gone from a quiet rumble, to a loud howl. He noticed the sniper had a harness on, one that was attached to a cable at the edge of the roof. It would, by far, provide the quickest way down, one that would only be needed if they planned to leave in a hurry. The jet continued to crawl away. Time was not on anyone's side. Anthony unclipped the harness and slipped it over his own clothes. Then, without giving time for doubt, he leapt from the roof and descended like a spider on a single silk thread. He naturally swung into the hangar, as the harness fed through the line and lowered him quickly but smoothly.

In the few seconds of his descent, Anthony took in his surroundings. There were two armed assailants outside the hangar, and another crouching behind a mounted mini gun. Anthony released the harness and swung down on top of him. The landing wasn't graceful, but it had pushed him back from the mini gun. The other two turned around, their handguns raised, but before they could fire, suppressed gunfire came from the left. One of them dived for cover, the other stood their ground and got a couple of shots off, but unlike his, the returning fire was on target.

Anthony grabbed his rifle as the other assailant retrieved his sidearm. They both drew at the same time and were left in a stalemate, each aiming for the centre of mass of the person opposite.

"Drop it!" ordered Anthony, as the other three security guards entered the hangar, one covering him, the other two pinning the final assailant down, who was still hiding behind empty crates once used for smuggled cargo.

"Drop it!" repeated Anthony.

"Don't you dare!" shouted the final assailant. "Be the man I trained you to be. Take him out. He was the one who killed Martin. Now avenge him!"

The man was in two minds. He knew firing would result in his death, but he could still take Anthony down with him. He turned towards his boss and assessed his options. Two guns against one wouldn't work in his favour. He slowly placed the gun on the ground and held up his hands.

"Coward!" bellowed the final assailant, as he stood up and aimed towards Anthony.

He too had made his choice, but his resulted in just one death, his own. The two security guards each put multiple bullets into him.

"The plane," mumbled Anthony, as he ran out of the hangar.

Two of the security guards stayed back, whilst the other one followed him. The jet had already reached the end of the first taxiway and was turning to approach the final one; the one that would lead to the runway, the one that would lead to freedom.

Both cars escorting Timothy approached, barely stopping as the doors of one opened and Anthony, along with one of the security guards, jumped in. The car spat up mud and grass as it took the most direct route to the plane.

Just as the plane made it to the edge of the runway, the car swerved and blocked its path. Despite its weight, it wouldn't be able to push past. Anthony and the guard leapt from the car and moved towards the plane, Anthony's rifle covering all the tiny windows on the left-hand side. The door opened and swung down, but nobody came out to open fire. Anthony took point and moved up the steps. He covered every corner of the plane, seeing just the pilot and Mr Jenkins. Anthony approached slowly, watching for any traps, but there weren't any. The security guard cleared the cockpit, securing the pilot as he went. Anthony helped Mr Jenkins to his feet and cut the plastic ties from his wrists.

"Where's Timmy?" he asked.

"Outside."

He pushed past Anthony and ran down the steps to hug his son. It seemed the crisis was over, but Anthony couldn't help but think otherwise. Nothing seemed to add up. The plane had been cleaned the day before, but the inside told a different story. The kidnappers knew too much about Mr Jenkins and his son, details even Anthony wasn't privy to. The plane was prepared to take off with just one pilot to guard Mr Jenkins and deliver him to whoever paid. There was something he was missing, but he didn't know what.

Then his phone started to ring. "Yep," he said answering it.

"We need you back at the Molehill this instant," said Bosse on the other end of the call.

"Why? What about Mr Jenkins?" asked Anthony. Although he was reluctant to take on the job, he still had to see it through to the end.

"The courtroom has already been adjourned for today. In light of the kidnapping, they were generous enough to postpone Mr Jenkins giving evidence until a more convenient time for him. I've arranged for a police escort to pick them up and return them to his home. After all, I'm sure there will be countless press conferences and we can't be seen on any of them. You've done your job, and I'll ensure we get paid extra for this. Now get back here, there's a helicopter on standby at the airport to bring you back. We think we've got a lead we cannot ignore."

***

On the second runway, a few hundred metres away, an identical white, private jet was waiting for final permission to take off. A smartly dressed businessman was finishing his phone call before it started to pick up speed.

"It is with regret that I inform you of Mr Jenkins' failure. I can assure you that this situation will not be taken lightly. I suggest our best course of action is to release the files we have on him. This will destroy them both, I know, but I'm sure we can all live with that." He listened for a few seconds, nodding to what he heard. "Let us make sure we do not fail again." He put the phone down.

The jet had again started to move, this time with a great acceleration. Once at take-off speed, it lifted into the air effortlessly. Buildings flashed by, each of them getting smaller and smaller with every passing second, but the man wasn't looking out of the window. His full attention was focussed on his tablet displaying a still image taken at the airport. It was a picture of Anthony.

# Chapter 11 – The Conflict of the Lies

12th September

11:47 BST

32 hrs 26 min. Until Deadline

Daniel took the same bus, from the same stop, and got off at the same stop he'd used previously. Everything was as before, with one exception. This time, it was the middle of the day. It surprised him how much busier the industrial estate was at that time. There were still few pedestrians but what seemed like hundreds of cars. The roads running throughout the industrial estate were all blocked, with cars jostling to pull out of one car park, just to park in the opposite one. Builders picked up supplies, whilst others just wandered throughout various shops, but came out with nothing more than a handful of samples of various materials. Daniel knew exactly where he was going this time, but with the high volume of traffic, he opted for the back routes, squeezing down the tight alleyways between the shops and warehouses.

As he moved down the passageways, stepping over and between discarded takeaway wrappers and empty drinks bottles, Daniel saw a face that was all too familiar. Or rather, two faces. Tria, Grenham's secretary was stood in conversation with another person. Slowly, she turned to the right and Daniel saw her profile. It was all he needed to see.

"LoLa," he muttered.

Although he didn't know her real name, she was the woman he'd met in a bar. Unbeknownst to him at first, she was the one who'd provided the location of Crabble's island, where the natural disaster weapon was held. He hadn't seen her since, but now, with Tria, it all seemed too much of a coincidence.

Then he felt a silencer press up against his lower back.

"Forwards," was the only word he heard from behind.

Daniel did as he was told. Slowly raising his hands, he moved forwards. LoLa and Tria turned to him, neither surprised by his presence.

"Daniel, I'm glad you could join us," said LoLa. "But I would like to get one thing clear, from now on, you may call me Miss Cadlow. I think we're a little past acquaintances now, don't you?"

"Does it often result in guns being pointed at those acquaintances?" asked Daniel.

The silencer was removed from his back and the figure behind him slowly emerged in front. He had a large hood pulled over his head and a cloak covering much of his body. He was about 6'2", walked with a strong limp, and had at least one prosthetic hand, the other tucked into a large pocket in his cloak. Daniel could only assume there was still a suppressed handgun trained on him, only this time concealed within the figure's pocket. Although Daniel couldn't get much from him, one thing was perfectly clear, the figure was extremely relaxed, even Miss Cadlow and Tria weren't as relaxed as him. It was almost as if he knew nothing could hurt him.

"What am I doing here?"

The three of them shared glances at one another, but it was Miss Cadlow who spoke. "I am surprised that was your first question."

"There isn't much else to ask. You clearly know how I work and knew I'd use the alleyways. You're obviously not working with Grenham or Kale, as neither are here, nor were they aware of our previous encounter, Tria." Nobody reacted, meaning they all knew about Tria tailing him.

"You helped us with locating Crabble. I'm not interested in how you met, or who you're fighting, or even why you're doing it. So, the only question I currently have is 'what am I doing here?'"

"You think you know who infiltrated your offices, leaked all that data, killed Richard, killed your parents?" said Miss Cadlow. "Well, you know nothing. And when you go back into their office, Grenham will want to speak with you. He will tell you that Yue has gone rogue, that she was the one responsible. They will give you evidence of this, and then they will ask you to help track her down and kill her. And you will no doubt end up helping them, because most of the evidence they will give you will be true, but it will all be taken out of context. Whether you help them or not is entirely up to you, but there is one thing that you should know first. Your father isn't dead. But depending on the choices you make, he soon may well be."

Before Daniel could take anything in, he heard a few leaves crunch and a twig snap behind him, but it was too late, he was too distracted. He felt a small, stabbing pain in his neck, then nothing.

The next thing he knew, his eyes slowly let in light. Everything seemed a blur for a moment, but piece by piece, things came back to him. Daniel was lying on the ground, a few browned leaves clinging to his T-shirt. He climbed to his feet, and let all his senses come back. There was a sharp pain in his neck. He felt the tiny, raised area of skin around its location, then checked the time on his phone. Whatever he'd been injected with had rendered him unconscious for less than half an hour. So many thoughts ran through his head, but he tried to block them all. He'd find out more when he spoke to Grenham. Daniel knew that the first person to dictate a story controls the narrative, and he wasn't going to let that cloud his judgement.

By the time he'd reached Grenham's building, he'd cleaned up his appearance and straightened his mind.

If he heard anything in there, he had to act as if it was new information. Daniel pushed the bar on the door and entered. Just inside the door, six of the masked guards were waiting. At first, Daniel thought they were waiting for him, but then two more appeared with Grenham.

"Finally. We expected you here over half an hour ago. Where have you been?" asked Grenham.

"I, I got held up."

"Well that doesn't matter, we've got to get moving."

Grenham followed the eight guards through a side door and into a small garage. From the outside, it should've been a part of the neighbouring building but was just one of its many illusions. Inside the garage was a single vehicle, a heavily armoured van, the kind that looked like any other white delivery van but was built like the best kind of SWAT vehicles. Three guards climbed into the cab, the rest got into the back.

"Where are we going?" asked Daniel.

"One of our own has turned against us."

He was almost too afraid to ask. "Who?"

"Yue. I can hardly believe that she slipped through our net. Kale overheard the two of you talking, so we started to dig into what really happened." One of the guards then handed him a tablet, which he passed straight over to Daniel. "Hit play."

Daniel's index finger reluctantly touched the centre of the screen. The image turned into a video. He knew immediately what it was. The camera was outside one of the buildings at a crossroads. A car approached a set of red traffic lights. Although the footage was in black and white, Daniel remembered the lights being red all too well as he came to stop at them. He didn't want to watch what happened next but forced himself to. It would be the first time he'd ever seen any footage of the incident since it happened. An oil tanker emerged into the picture, first swerving towards Daniel's car, then away from it. The truck hit a row of parked cars on the other side of the road almost as fast as it could go. The tanker came free from the truck and collided with an oncoming lorry. A giant flame erupted, engulfing everything. It was powerful enough to pick up Daniel's car and throw it through the window of the nearest shop. Then the camera feed cut out.

"Why did you show me this?" asked Daniel.

"Keep watching," said Grenham.

The screen flicked on to the next video, this one from the road opposite, and in colour. The video had clearly been magnified but showed the driver of the tanker before the crash. Before he'd even made it to the crossroads, he slumped forwards in his chair, dead.

"And just one more."

Again, the screen flicked to another video. This camera was a little further down the road. Daniel watched as his car moved past the camera and towards the crossroads. Then something caught his eye. In the block of flats opposite, on the third floor, something was hanging out of the window. The image was in perfect clarity, having clearly undergone heavy rendering processes to make the image cleaner. It was a sniper. A flash came from the muzzle of the gun. Moments later, a heat haze could be seen travelling past the camera as people started to run in all directions. The video played on, until someone exited the building, carrying a large duffel bag. That was the only person to not be running, or hiding. The image was frozen and zoomed in on the sniper's face. It was an unmistakable picture. It was Yue.

Daniel sat in silence for a moment.

"There is something else I need to tell you, before we catch up to Yue," said Grenham. "Your parents are still alive."

"Parents," mumbled Daniel.

His head was in a whirlwind of emotions, but he still noticed it. The first difference in the two stories he'd been told. Miss Cadlow had only mentioned his father being alive, now it was suddenly both his parents.

Twenty minutes went by, with nothing but the constant hum of the engine, as they headed out of town and towards the wide, open countryside.

"Where are we going?" asked Daniel, finally starting to quiet his mind.

"There's a conference centre about thirty miles further down the road. It's where Kale has tracked Yue to. We know it's a conference centre, but we think it's one used by Yue's employers. Whether or not they hired her to steal secrets, or whether she's been working with them on a longer term basis is irrelevant. She failed us, now she must be erased."

Daniel thought for a second. It was obvious he'd only been shown that footage to motivate him into taking Yue down, but the real question was why had she suddenly gone on the run?

"Where do I come into this?" he asked.

"The conference centre is impenetrable from any external attack. Its structure alone could withstand any missile. So we're going to level the building from the inside. You're going to plant a bomb which will cause a chain reaction and bring the entire place down," replied Grenham.

"Where is it being planted?"

"Craig knows the details," said Grenham, shifting his gaze towards one of the masked guards next to Daniel. "He'll be going in with you. You're going to be each other's cover, so you might as well get to know one another."

"Is he going to keep his mask on the whole time?" asked Daniel.

"No," said Craig.

"Craig will fit in well with his new role as a security guard. Not the ones you'll see around the perimeter, but the ones who handle all the interrogations." Grenham smiled. "Now, I suppose I'll talk you through the plan."

Everything was happening too quickly, even for Daniel, but he'd made his choice, he would see it through to the end, whatever the end would be. So, he listened to the plan, took in every detail, until he was ready to replicate it.

The only road leading to the conference centre was a long and winding one set between two steep hills. The nearest town was only a mile away as the crow flies, but three miles if that crow were to stick to public roads. The van pulled off the road and on to the grass verge. Daniel, Grenham, and most of the masked guards left the vehicle and joined Kale standing on the grass embankment. Craig and the driver continued down the road towards the conference centre.

"Daniel, I'm glad you're here," started Kale. "Come, I've already got your entrance sorted."

Daniel followed him, whilst the others made their way towards a second van, one that Kale had no doubt arrived in.

Kale lifted a patch of grass that had been freshly cut, revealing some kind of metal hatch.

"It's an inspection hatch. There are three of these placed at equal distances along the tunnel which runs underground. It was built in case an evacuation needed to happen, discreetly, but it makes for the perfect entrance as well."

"And what's your part?" asked Daniel.

"My part is done, for now, but I want you to know that I'm on your side. What Grenham told you might be true, but it's how you interpret the truth that matters. I've made a few slight alterations to Grenham's plan…" Daniel opened his mouth to speak. "Don't worry, you'll know what to do when the time comes, but you need to know what you're really going in there for. Grenham doesn't just want you to kill Yue, he also wants you to find your parents, and kill them. They're both in there. Now I've already said too much, so get in, plant the bomb, and get out. If you follow the plan to the letter, I'm sure you'll come across your parents. Now get going."

One thing was sure to Daniel, they didn't want him going in with a clear head. They wanted him full of emotions. They wanted him to be reckless, and relentless, but the reason why was still the mystery. He climbed down the ladder, beneath the already unfastened inspection hatch, and entered the darkness of the tunnel. It was a long way to the conference centre, and if he was stick to the plan, he'd have to run the entire way. And that was exactly what he did.

***

Kale moved away from the hatch and back towards the others.

"Did you tell him the rest?" asked Grenham.

Kale nodded, "He knows all he needs to."

"Good," concluded Grenham, as he climbed into the second van.

***

Eventually, Daniel made it to the end of the tunnel. The small flashlight in his right hand illuminated a door. It was a simple-looking door, with no reinforced joins, or a fancy keypad to enter a code. There was nothing, not even a handle. Daniel checked his watch, the only other thing he'd been allowed to take down with him.

"Six seconds," he muttered.

Then there was a loud clonk, and the door swung in. Everything had been timed to perfection, and this was no different. Nobody was near the door when he moved through it, but given again the lack of a door handle on the other side, it must've been opened electronically. Daniel noted a camera facing the door, the first of many he was sure he'd find.

Inside was a complete change from the tunnel, as he expected, but the sterile, white walls, automated doors, and state-of-the-art ventilation didn't exactly scream 'conference centre'. The room he'd entered into was more like a porch for a nuclear bunker, with lines of hazmat suits hung up along the walls, and various cubicles, resembling showers, over to one side.

Daniel continued through the door at the back, which promptly slid aside as he approached, and moved into a large corridor. This time, there were people, hundreds of them. Although Grenham had told him it was a corridor, it was more the size of King's Cross station. There were staircases leading in all different directions, smaller corridors and walkways, gangways and mezzanines, even several desks which could easily be mistaken for information desks. Of course, they weren't, it was just how the building was set out. Each office space and room was incorporated into the large expanse of walkway in the centre. Almost all the working spaces were there, some out in the open, others tucked out of sight, but this all helped Daniel to blend in. With hundreds of people moving from space to space, and all dressed in completely different attires, nobody would even notice his presence.

Without lingering, or making unnecessary eye contact, Daniel made his way up the nearest flight of stairs, across one of the gangways, then up another two flights of stairs. He was to meet with Craig near the very top of the building, being one of the more discreet locations. On his way up, he'd counted thirty-four cameras, all of which seemed to be pointed in his direction. He quickly made it to the final door and pushed it open.

Alarms filled the building, as all the stark, white lights turned a crimson red. Within seconds, Daniel had several rifles trained on him.

"Do not move!" shouted a guard holding one of them, in an unmistakeable and strong French accent.

If the building had had narrow corridors, plenty of rooms, and less cameras, he'd have fancied his chances of making a run for it, but in the open, he didn't stand a chance. Daniel fell to his knees and raised his hands. One guard approached, he was in his late thirties, early forties but clearly cared for his appearance. There were signs of plastic surgery, he had whitened teeth, and perfectly kempt hair, as if there wasn't a single strand that dared to be in the wrong place. The guard forced Daniel's wrists behind his back, fastened them together with a set of plastic cable ties, and then dragged him back to his feet. His watch was removed from his wrist.

Four of the guards escorted him along another gangway with iron-tight grips around his arms and shoulders, whilst another two held back and kept aim at him. Even if Daniel could break their grips and dispatch the four closest to him, he'd be gunned down before he got close to the two behind. However, as they approached the first set of stairs, the guard to his right got closer to him.

"Follow my lead, I've got a plan," she said.

Daniel couldn't recognise her behind the balaclava, one of the few who seemed to wear one, but Delta One's voice was unmistakable. They'd arranged a plan before he left for Kale. She was to follow him wherever they went and make video and audio recordings of any conversations. Of course, he'd planned to bug the offices but never got the chance, and when they headed into the conference centre, he'd assumed Delta One wouldn't be able to follow, let alone help him to escape. That was his first mistake, underestimating her, but now it was time to trust her. For the time being, at least, she was nothing more than another one of the guards.

He was escorted up a further three flights of stairs and through another doorway. The room on the other side must've been at the very top of the conference centre. Whilst the lower levels had no windows, this room had a full panoramic view of the surrounding area. The door closed behind him, cutting out the sound of the alarms. Either that or they switched off the second it closed.

The room was a large expanse of empty space, a few lone chairs, a table, and a desk at the far end. Sat at the desk, which Daniel was being led to, were two people. Two people he instantly recognised. One was Yue. The other was his father. Daniel was forced into a chair the opposite side of the desk, the watch was handed to his father, then the guards moved back to the door, Delta One clearly following the others' lead.

"Nice place you've got here," said Daniel, staring into the eyes of the man opposite.

"I think I owe you an explanation," said the grey-haired man in his seventies, as he put his watch back on his wrist for the first time that decade.

"Among other things," added Daniel.

"A part of me hoped you'd be happy to see me again, and I'm almost certain you are, but I also understand the hostilities. Now, I'm going to follow the assumption that Grenham has shown you the footage of that day." Daniel showed no emotion. "Well, the simple truth of the matter is Yue saved our lives. You see, that truck driver was trying to kill us. He swerved towards our car, Yue took him out and he swerved away."

"If that was true, why didn't she shoot the front left tyre? It would have stood a greater chance of pulling the truck away, shooting the driver was just luck he didn't still crash into us," added Daniel.

"I know, but Yue had to take that chance, shooting the tyre would've tipped the truck on to us, but I'm sure you already know that."

"Why?" asked Daniel.

"Because he was being blackmailed, it was his life or the lives of his family. Unfortunately, it cost him both."

"No, why did you disappear?"

"I've waited over a decade to tell you because I simply didn't know how to. That breach, which lost you your job, was us. It was me, it was Yue, and it was Richard."

Daniel again sat in silence. "Richard's brother was trying to uncover something that we couldn't let happen. A secret, if you like. So, the breach was just a cover. Whilst the systems were down, we erased all the files Grenham wanted. Unfortunately, he found out it was us. When word of Richard's death hit us, we had to take measures. Yue sent that message on his phone. We'd already planted the evidence to frame Yue, so that was her in the clear, Grenham would just think that we'd cut her loose. And so when that attack happened, it was the only chance I had to disappear."

"Why did you leave me?"

"Oh please, stop acting like a child, Daniel. You handled yourself just fine."

"Tell me why."

His father took in a deep breath through his large nostrils. "Because of what was on that file. And no, I won't tell you what it was, nor what was in it, but yes, the file was about you; you and several others. You're special Daniel, you always have been, and I will always protect you. That is why I had Yue try and convince you that Grenham was Richard, in an attempt to throw you off our scent, to keep you away from us and that file. I don't know whether you've ever even considered the question, but how exactly do think a group of people, half of whom had never even fired a gun in their lives, could turn into a team of highly skilled agents? A team who know each other inside and out. A team who act as if they are one. I know you've come here to destroy this place, to destroy us. I won't stop you. You need to earn their trust by any means necessary. That is why I can't tell you what was in that file. You need to be completely honest with him and you can't do that if you know the truth. I'm sure this isn't the reunion you expected, and I am sorry for that, but our time is brief and there are far more important things than bonding. Joining the Molehill and the rest of Alpha team was no coincidence, everything was meant to be." He nodded at the four guards standing over by the door.

Daniel heard them approach.

"You haven't said much," Daniel said to Yue. "Do you know what was in that file?"

She simply nodded and gave a smile. It was almost the same kind as one you'd give someone who'd just lost something or someone dear to them. Daniel felt a hand grip his arm and pull him out of his chair.

"Tell me what was in that file!" yelled Daniel, as they started to drag him towards the door.

"I'm sorry," said Yue, softly.

"This is all for your own good, Daniel. Now finish what you started," said his father, still as calm as when Daniel entered.

He shifted his gaze back to Yue, looking to her, almost pleading with her. Just as he was pulled through the doorway, he noticed her hands. She held up her index finger, then all four fingers, then clenched her fist tightly. That was to be the last time he'd see Yue ever again.

***

Mark watched as his son was dragged out of the room and the door closed.

"Thank you for coming, Yue. I know it couldn't have been easy, not after what I did to you."

"When we stopped that file from being stolen by Grenham, I really did think you were doing it for your son. It just shows how wrong I was," she said, staring at the closed door.

"Come now. Daniel never has to learn why we really did it, just as he will never learn what was on it. Richard should have known better. When I told him I'd made a deal with someone else, he understood."

"Is that what you say to everyone you work with?"

"Only when they have served their purpose, my dear."

Yue stood up and started to head for the door. About halfway there, she stopped, as if something had just jumped into her head.

"How did you know they would track me here?" she asked.

"They didn't, but I had to make it look believable for Daniel, didn't I?"

"So, how did they find us?"

"Isn't it obvious? Oh, I am sorry, my dear, I thought you'd worked that out by now. I still want Grenham dead, more than anything in the world, and I've found someone who can assist me in that. You see, I told Kale because, well, I'm afraid I've had to make a deal with someone else."

Before she could turn round, a gunshot echoed throughout the soundproof room. An instant later, she fell to the floor with a crippling pain in her stomach. Blood spread across the shiny floor, as she watched Mark approach. She smiled and started to laugh.

"What is it? You've finally realised what has happened? That you've lost and were always destined to?"

She shook her head slowly. "No. Because I no longer feel guilty for what I did."

"Well, there you go. Now you can rest easy. Although, you had nothing to feel guilty about, I explained at the time that it was for the greater good."

"Not guilty for that," she muttered. "I copied the file."

Mark didn't even have time to get angry. No sooner had the words left her lips, than the last traces of life slipped away.

He focussed on his breathing, trying to calm himself. He ran through several breathing exercises before he had finally composed himself. He checked his watch, the glass still cracked.

"Eight minutes. I'm sure I can get out of here in eight minutes. Even at my age."

He left the room, leaving Yue's body alone to be swallowed up by the earth, along with the building.

***

Daniel was led back down the stairs, to what must've been the ground floor. There were still four guards surrounding him, with a further two behind. He was marched past several employees, all sat at their desks. Not once did they take a second glance at him, almost as if it was a regular occurrence. They were approaching a door, one of the few Daniel had seen in the entire building. It slid open when they got to within a step of it. The other side was dark, almost absorbing the light from the rest of the building.

As Daniel was pushed in, one artificial bulb sprung to life, flickering as it woke up. The guards threw him on the floor, then left the room. The door closed behind them. Daniel had just about climbed back to his feet when he heard something. Someone else was in the room. In one of the dark corners a silhouette grew larger and larger. As its face emerged into the dim light, Daniel saw a crooked nose first, followed by a mouth with few teeth, scars stretching down beneath his T-shirt, and just one ear. He raised a small knife in his left hand, serrated one side, razor sharp the other.

"You are late," he said.

"Craig?"

"Now we must make up for the time you have cost us. Turn around."

Daniel turned around and let him cut his hands free. "Now I understand the mask."

Craig grabbed the light dangling on a thin cord and pulled it out of the ceiling. With a flash of electricity, the room was plunged back into darkness. Daniel couldn't be sure what Craig did next, but something caused yet another spark.

"That has short-circuited the door, they won't be able to get in now. At least, that's what I was told," he said.

"Nor us out," added Daniel.

Craig laughed. A laugh that would've been creepy enough in full daylight, let alone the darkness of the cold room. Daniel heard the table being scraped along the floor, then some kind of bolt being torn off. Then, with the creak of a trapdoor, light filled the room again.

"Age before beauty," said Craig.

Daniel jumped down. The room below was much like the one above, except instead of a bulb, the room was lit with powerful LED lights. Craig landed with a thud, then moved straight over to the door. He turned the handle, opened it ajar, and then listened.

"Stay close, the timing must be perfect," he said.

Two seconds later, they left, one after the other. Daniel stayed as close as he could, following Craig with every step he made. From time to time, he'd stop and check around corners, listen for anyone approaching, but they were clear. There were a lot less staff walking around than Daniel had seen earlier. Perhaps they were all upstairs trying to get the door open, or perhaps it had set off some kind of silent alarm and they were walking into an ambush.

"Where is everyone?" asked Daniel finally, in a quiet whisper.

"When I detached the bulb it sent out an emergency call, everything above ground went into lockdown, before I then shorted the door. When that happens, everyone below ground has to make their way to a safe room so security can sweep the entire building, but they'll all be too busy trying to get that door open for the time being." Craig smiled and chuckled to himself.

"Detaching the bulb is one way of putting it," Daniel mumbled. "How is it you know so much about this place?"

"Because Grenham told me."

"Not Kale?" asked Daniel.

"No, that's why I said Grenham. He doesn't allow us to speak with Kale."

Daniel followed Craig the rest of the way to the very base of the conference centre in silence. At the bottom, they passed Daniel's entrance point, and moved further down beyond the wide, open space. At the very back, outside the building's actual footprint, stood one final room. Craig pushed over a water cooler and a filing cabinet, revealing a door behind them. He rubbed his hands along the door's seal until he found what he was looking for. There was a small switch in the top, left-hand corner. He flicked it and the door released from the wall. They both went inside, Daniel checking his surroundings both in and outside the room.

The room itself was relatively small, but it was packed full of guns, ammunition, and explosives. There were boxes piled up to the ceiling around all four walls, along with six double-sided rows of the same. Every box seemed to be labelled with its contents, so it was no surprise Craig went straight for what he'd gone in there for. It was one of the larger boxes, its only label, however, a universal symbol for explosives.

"What is it?" asked Daniel, aware this seemed to be the only box without a name on its label.

"Something that will make a loud noise, that's all you need to know."

The box looked heavy, but Daniel thought better of asking whether he could help. Craig heaved the box up and on to his shoulder, then followed Daniel back out of the room.

"Why didn't we just set it off here? I'm no explosives expert, but I'm pretty sure igniting that room would remove any trace of everything, and everyone in this building," said Daniel.

"Because it isn't the plan, this is."

"What is?"

"You ask too many questions. It'll get you killed," said Craig, somewhat ending the conversation abruptly.

Craig took the lead back across the wide, open corridor and through a door beside one of the reception-looking areas. The room housed several maintenance coats, two large lockers, and several tools and pieces of maintenance equipment. Craig placed the box down over to one side, making it look as easy as if it had nothing more than a few stacks of paper in it. The lid was torn off and the box pushed so it touched the wall.

Daniel moved over to it and looked inside. There weren't packs of explosives, as he had expected, but just one large bomb. There was a cobweb of wires, of all different colours heading in all different directions, a small display on the top which wasn't lit, and a keypad, with all ten numbers, left, right, up, and down arrows, and several symbols.

Craig used one of the screwdrivers lying around to unscrew the cover for the ventilation shaft.

"This runs throughout the compound. When the bomb detonates, it will be like it's detonated in every room. The building will remain standing but everyone in it will die," said Craig, as he lifted the bomb up and placed it inside the shaft. "I will set the timer for five minutes."

"Are you okay with this?" asked Daniel.

"Of course, five minutes is plenty of time."

"No, I mean killing everyone in this building."

"Why wouldn't I be? It's our job and we will carry it out until it's finished."

Daniel watched as Craig tapped several of the keys, arming the bomb.

"Now, we must leave," he said.

They pushed one of the lockers over to the hatch and blocked it off.

"That will slow down anyone trying to disarm it."

Daniel opened the door of the maintenance room, but before he could even take a step outside, he felt a sharp pain in his chest. By the time his hands clasped around what felt like a dart, his eyelids became too heavy to lift and gravity started to become stronger. He never even felt the cold, hard floor.

Daniel's eyes opened to a bright light. By no means was this the second time he'd been unconscious, and it certainly wouldn't be the last. He was almost used to it. In fact, the first thought that ran through his head was how many more times he'd be knocked unconscious that day.

"He's back with us," came from a soft voice in the room.

Daniel saw figures, still murky, move around the room, then leave, all except for one. He was motionless, waiting for Daniel to see him. It was the same guard who had captured him before.

"So, we meet again," he said in his French accent. "How have you been keeping?"

Daniel stayed silent. He could hear Craig next to him, grunting and wriggling around in his chair. Both had their wrists fastened behind their backs, just as before.

"You may be interested to know that you've been unconscious for over half an hour, so yes, the bomb was disarmed. It was a shame you didn't set it for four minutes really, but then again, none of us would be here, would we?" said the guard.

"Let us go!" grunted Craig, still trying to break free.

"Let you go? Oh, no," replied the guard. "You see, your plan was almost watertight. You seemed to know everything about this place. I want to know how. I mean, how can a guard get the top job of interviewing a suspect on his first day? It's a betrayal waiting to happen, and I don't like betrayals. I also want to know what your exit strategy is, or rather, was."

"We don't have one," said Craig.

"I'm not sure I believe that. No one would have a plan so good but would omit an exit strategy. Plus, you would surely just have set the bomb off there and then, not for five minutes later. That being said, I'm afraid I also don't believe that you were the one to come up with the plan. You look more like the muscle." The guard shifted his attention to Daniel. "How about you?"

"We failed. Our exit strategy has expired. That's us done for," said Daniel bitterly.

The guard started to nod. "That does make sense. We found no vehicle within a two-mile radius. So, one more thing, who sent you?"

"No one," said Daniel.

The guard smiled. His smile then broke out into a laugh. Then he pulled out a handgun and fired it at Craig. He grunted in pain, trying not to show weakness. The bullet had entered his torso.

He leant towards Craig and whispered in his ear, "That looks painful." But then he froze. Something had caught his eye. "Where did you get that?" he asked. "The tattoo, where did you get it?"

Daniel looked over and saw a tattoo on Craig's right wrist. The tattoo was of a lion, roaring.

"I've always had it," said Craig.

The guard stood silent again, his mind clearly full of thoughts. He focussed on his breathing; Daniel counted the seconds of each inhale and exhale. The guard then seemed to focus elsewhere, as his index finger forced its way into Craig's injury.

Another guard entered the room. This time it was somebody Daniel was pleased to see. It was Delta One, now without a balaclava, surely there to get him out.

"Who sent you?" said the French guard.

Craig tried to ignore the pain, but he couldn't. "Grenham," he said finally.

"Grenham? Well, that sounds like a made-up name to me," replied the guard, as he pushed harder on the wound.

"It's true. I swear!" yelled Craig.

The guard backed off. "Very well." He then thought for a second. "Is he watching? Waiting for your return?"

Craig nodded.

"Good, then perhaps your exfil isn't quite over yet. It might've even been your plan all along, but it's worth a try," muttered the guard under his breath, almost thinking out loud. "How does a little field trip sound? Just the three of us and maybe a few extra guards." He checked his watch. "Come on."

He cut the cable tie from around Craig's legs, one Daniel didn't have, then pulled him to his feet. Daniel also stood up, and all four left the room, Delta One escorting Craig.

The guard then pulled Daniel closer. "If this was always your plan, it won't work. I'll be ready for anything you try, and I will kill you. I meant it when I say I hate betrayals; they are by far the lowest a man can get. Is that understood?"

Daniel said nothing.

They were both taken to the car park and thrown into the back of an armoured truck. Any attempt to escape would be futile with the number of armed guards nearby. Craig continued to groan in pain. As they waited in the truck, two of the cab doors opened, as the French guard and Delta One climbed in. Then two more guards entered the back of the armoured truck and slammed the doors shut behind them. Moments later, the vehicle sped out of the car park and on to the road. Within seconds, Daniel could see the conference centre become smaller and smaller out of the back windows.

Less than a minute later, the truck came to a screeching halt, closely followed by two gunshots, which echoed through the vehicle. The two guards in the back raised their rifles and kept them trained on the back door, but after a minute had gone by, without so much as a sound, they slowly opened them and stepped out. Another gunshot cracked, as one of the guards fell to the floor. The other turned to fire but was beaten to it, as yet another gunshot was fired and yet another guard fell. Daniel and Craig watched the open doors as a single set of footsteps approached.

The French guard emerged round the corner, no longer in a guard's uniform but in the uniform of one of Grenham's bodyguards.

"Would you like to watch the fireworks?" he asked.

The French guard turned to face the conference centre and held out his hand as if holding a detonator switch. His thumb pressed down on the imaginary device and, at the same time, the conference centre erupted in fire. A deafening boom hit them a split second later, as the conference centre was completely engulfed by the orange flame.

"Grenham sent two of us in?" asked Craig, struggling to sit up.

"He did, yes. At least I hope he only sent two of us in, otherwise I've just killed any extras. I was a contingency plan, in case you failed, which you did, by the way. I was to plant a second bomb in the armoury to level the building. Grenham only wanted the people killed, but this was his second choice. Or perhaps I was the main plan all along."

"You've never seen each other before?" asked Daniel, surprised they were acting like strangers.

"No," said the guard. "We have never been permitted to take our masks off in front of anyone, unless told to do so by Grenham. Odd really, because you do seem familiar."

He looked at Craig, whilst putting his own mask on. Craig did the same, taking one from his trouser pocket.

Clapping came from beside the van. "Très bien. Très bien." Grenham emerged, still clapping, with the rest of his men, Kale, and Delta One, with one of Grenham's guards pressing a handgun against her side. "What a show." He then averted his eyes from the inferno and looked at Craig. "But not all of you succeeded, did you?"

Daniel made sure he didn't break eye contact, but Craig was already looking down.

"Let me see if I've got this right. You failed. You're injured, and will take up valuable time and resources to get better. You needed rescuing, and you forced me into completing only my second-best plan. Is that all correct?"

Craig nodded slowly and mumbled something.

"You're sorry, is that what you said?" asked Grenham. "My, oh, my, you've become a real hindrance to the team, haven't you? And as you all know, we don't tolerate hindrances." Grenham slowly drew a handgun, aimed it at Craig, ensuring he had time to know what was going on, and pulled the trigger. The bullet tore straight through his mask. "But not to worry, you were always expendable."

One of Grenham's other men cut the plastic ties and freed Daniel.

"Before you all go," started Grenham. "There's just one last thing. How did you get compromised? I mean, how did Delta One here know where and when to attempt a rescue?"

The French guard leant forwards and spoke in Grenham's ear.

"A silent alarm? Now who could've set off a silent alarm?" he stared directly at Daniel. "I know it was hard for you, especially with your parents in there, but that is what you were told to do. As you can see, actions have consequences." He pointed to Craig. "And this is the consequence of your actions today." Grenham turned and started to walk away. "Clear this mess up quickly, we have our own conference to get to. Daniel can find his own way back."

"What about the girl?" asked the guard. Although his accent was still clearly French, it had changed, almost as if one of the accents was put on.

"Let her go. I hope Daniel's learnt his lesson for now."

Four of his bodyguards followed him whilst the others grabbed the body to move it further into the van. Daniel and Delta One also started to make their way back, heading to the hills on the left, with the nearest town just over the brow of the first.

The French guard climbed in and moved over to Craig. He lifted his sleeve and looked again at the tattoo. He then lifted his own sleeve up and looked at the exact same tattoo, a lion roaring. The other two guards had entered the front of the van, but Kale was still there. He saw it all. To the French guard, the tattoo was nothing but an unexplained coincidence, but to Kale, it was so much more. He unfastened Craig's jacket and pulled out a bright red scarf, one that he hadn't seen for many years.

He looked towards Grenham, climbing into the back of the truck he'd arrived in. Kale was filled with hatred, as suddenly everything started to click into place, but he couldn't act out of rage. He had to be smarter than the man who had gone from prey, to his biggest enemy in a matter of seconds.

Kale chased after Daniel. "Hold up."

"What do you want?"

"Can I have a word with Daniel, alone?" said Kale.

Delta One looked to Daniel. He nodded and she walked on a few more paces.

"Before the conference centre was destroyed, we got word from the team of Vipers stationed just outside the bank. Apparently, not everything went to plan."

Daniel stood silent, listening to every word that came out of his mouth, reading every expression on his face.

"You may no longer be in possession of the antidote. Now, Grenham is pleased about that, assuming they have lost it. He never wanted you to take it, but I think differently. We are far more alike than you realise, and perhaps more than you would like to be. I would like to work with you, with a more permanent, and equal, partnership."

"What's this got to do with the antidote?" asked Daniel, seeing nothing but the truth coming from Kale.

"We're heading to a meeting, as you heard. I'd like you to be there. Even if you arrive after we leave, just your presence at the location is enough for me. If you do come, I can give you the recipe for the antidote. It may be your last chance of saving those people."

"If we're really alike, why don't you just give it to me now?" asked Daniel.

"Because I don't have it on me, but I will. And if you turn up, it's all yours. That's all I'm asking for." Kale took out a scrap of paper and handed it to Daniel. "The coordinates. It's in Senegal. It'll take quite a few hours to get there, so don't leave it too long. I can't promise I'll still be there as I said, but if I turn on the news and hear all those people made a full recovery, then I'll know what choice you made." Kale then turned and headed back to the van. He hadn't made more than a few steps when he stopped and smiled. "The true victor isn't the one who wins the battle but the one who survives the war."

# Chapter 12 – The Test of the Elite



A few hundred metres offshore, Scott was piloting a small boat. Despite its yacht-like appearance, it was in fact the tender to a much larger superyacht he'd just arrived on. After a short flight to the Mediterranean coastline, he'd picked up the superyacht from one of the Molehill's generous sponsors and had sailed it the final few miles. Of course, those on shore weren't to know that. For all they knew, he'd been sailing throughout the Med for a month.

The superyacht wasn't exactly to Scott's personal taste, but it worked perfectly for Henry Bowls' taste, the character Scott would be portraying. He was a detective, a very unique detective, one that arrived on superyachts; one that worked privately. And one who investigated the most sensitive, and highly paid, of cases.

He was there to answer the call of Emma Smith's father, a supposedly innocent person who'd got caught up in Fellscient's illegal activities and had paid with her life. The Molehill had created a tissue of lies that explained her death as a simple accident, but it seemed her family were not satisfied. They'd hired several private investigators that could unravel any lie and rewrite it if necessary. Naturally, these private investigators weren't the kind to find missing cats, or even to solve thirty-year-old cold cases. They were kind who investigated high-profile murders, espionage, treason, and the kind of crimes that threatened anyone with large amounts of money, hence the rather affluent lifestyle.

Henry wasn't sure how many of these detectives had been called in, he wasn't even sure how many of them existed, but on his way over, he'd caught sight of two further superyachts moored in the previous cove. Once his tender had arrived at the jetty, full of fishing boats and tour boats, Henry hopped off and started walking towards the heart of the town just a few metres ahead. He was wearing a white polo shirt, with white shorts. His sunglasses cost more than most of the fishing boats, and the watch strapped to his right wrist likely cost more than all the fishing boats combined.

He knew exactly where he was heading, the other side of the town, but first he wanted to find out some more about his new clients. Henry approached the first restaurant and took a seat. It was almost midday local time, and he didn't need to arrive until midnight. There were a few others in the restaurant, a group of three, two of them eating eggs Benedict, the other just a croissant. Across the other side, another group were drinking iced coffees and attempting to eat pastries they'd bought from across the road. The lone waitress caught sight of them and exchanged a few words. The group swiftly returned the pastries to their wrappers and drank their iced coffees.

Henry called the waitress over, gesturing with his left hand. "I'll have a coffee, please," he said.

"Certainly, what sort would you like?" she replied.

"Just a plain coffee will be fine with some milk on the side."

"We have many kinds of plain coffee."

"Just whatever is coffee beans and hot water."

"I see, you wish for a 'create your own coffee'," she replied, before offering a menu. "Will you be having anything to eat?"

He couldn't deny, he was hungry, but there would be time to eat later. "No, thank you."

The waitress moved away with a smile.

The pavement was packed with tourists and residents all milling about, some with cameras, others with giant lilos. Two elderly gentlemen wandered past in nothing but Speedos, suddenly making Henry relieved he hadn't ordered anything to eat. Another couple walked in and just stopped in the shade, looking at the tables. If you hadn't seen someone with sunburn, you'd think they were from another planet, almost glowing red. They tested three different tables, and all the chairs around them before finally settling for one in the sun, which was just what they needed.

"Your coffee, Sir," announced the waitress. She approached with a tray but was more focussed on where to put it than anything else. The waitress kicked Henry in the foot, sending her stumbling forwards and the tray slamming on to the table. "I'm sorry," she said, catching her balance. Henry couldn't really hide the pain in his right big toe and grimaced as he looked at what was on the tray. The waitress then started moving the items to the table; an empty mug, a pot of boiling water, three espresso shots, a jug of warm milk, and four sachets of sugar; two white, and two brown. "Will there be anything else?"

"No, that's fine, thank you," replied Henry.

The waitress nodded and placed a small piece of paper on the table. Henry studied it, trying not to look like paying twenty euros for a coffee bothered him. He made his coffee, using all three shots of espresso so as to use everything he'd paid for, and filled the mug with hot water, leaving just enough room for the short pour of milk. Henry swivelled the mug around and lifted the handle with his left hand, blowing on the drink before taking a sip. Scott hated coffee, and this one was just as horrid, tasting of nothing more than bitter water, but Henry liked coffee, he started each day with a cup of it, and had two on the one day a week he had off, Tuesday.

He soldiered through the coffee, trying to enjoy every mouthful. Once finished, he took the bill and moved inside to pay. The waitress was inside with another gentleman, sat at the bar, looking through what looked like a takings book. Henry smiled at the waitress and handed her the bill with twenty-five euros in cash.

"Thank you," she replied, passing it to the man, who was yet to raise his eyes from the book.

"Just out if interest," Henry started. "You wouldn't happen to know anything about a 'Mr Smith', would you?"

Suddenly, the atmosphere turned very frosty, the supposed owner placed his pen down and answered a short "No" making it perfectly clear that was his one and only answer. The waitress had broken eye contact and started to move back outside to clear his table.

"Just thought I'd ask on the off chance," concluded Henry, as he turned to exit the building.

He left the restaurant and started to walk further into town, when he heard a distant, "Excuse me!"

He turned to see the waitress chase after him with a slip of paper.

"Sorry, but this is for you to keep," she said, handing him the bill.

She then left and returned to the restaurant. Henry looked at the piece of paper, noticing the writing scribbled on the back. *The Captain's Haven* is all it said. Henry screwed it up and threw it in the closest bin.

The town had been built on the side of a mountain and had shops and restaurants crammed into the tiniest of spaces. There was a set of steps leading up through the town, with shops on every other one. People were everywhere, many brushing past Henry. His hands stayed in his pockets, ensuring no one could pick them, and he never kept anything in his back pockets for the same reason. Henry spent most of the early afternoon wandering through all the shops. Most were the same, they either sold leather, clothes, ice cream, or memorabilia of the town, but once you'd seen each of the items for sale, you were sure to see them again, and again, and probably again. Although it was shaded, the heat lingered. Everyone climbing the steps were either bright red and trying to push through the pain, or stopping every third step for a break, leaning on their knees as they took each one slower than the last. It was at the summit of the steps that he caught sight of someone he really didn't want to see.

Stood in the doorway of one of the ice cream parlours was a short, dark-haired man, thirty-three years of age. His stomach appeared to be full of ice cream and the top three buttons of his shirt were undone, revealing a sweaty, hairy chest. Henry tried to sneak past, his head down, as he picked up pace, but it was hopeless.

"Mick!" exclaimed the man.

Henry hurried over to him and held a finger up to his lips. "My name is Henry, do you understand?"

The man nodded, becoming more and more excited by the second. "I can't believe I've seen you here."

"Nor can I," Henry muttered under his breath.

"Are you here on a secret mission?"

A single glance from Henry was enough to tell him to stop talking.

"Oh, I see. So who are you here for?"

Henry said nothing.

"So this is like, super top secret."

"I suggest you stop talking before I trap your tongue in the door of the ice cream shop," replied Henry before walking away. Much to his dismay, the man keenly followed.

"Is there anything I can do to help?"

"No."

"Oh, come on. There must be something," the man protested.

"Well, there isn't."

"Please. I never got the chance to thank you for saving my life." Suddenly, the man had become more serious, almost as if he was pleading with his life.

Henry knew it was a bad idea, but if Mr Smith had hired anyone to keep tabs on him, it would look more suspicious if he simply ignored the man who clearly knew him.

"Fine," answered Henry, reluctantly.

The man took a large mouthful of ice cream and continued after Henry.

"Look, Chris. If you really are going to help me, I need to make several things clear…"

"You remembered my name!" exclaimed Chris.

Henry ignored him and continued, "You call me Henry under all circumstances. We are old friends. I knew you through your younger brother, Mitchell. Is that clear?"

Chris nodded, still overly excited.

"Now, why are you here?" asked Henry.

"Well, I wanted to help people, just like you helped me."

Henry was clearly confused, but at least it hid his concern.

"So, I became a private investigator."

Henry's concern continued to increase.

"Did you know that mainland Europe has the highest crime rate in the world?"

"No, I didn't," answered Henry.

"Well, actually, I just made that up, but it could have. So I travel throughout Europe to dismantle crime organisations."

"And which crime organisation are you here to destroy this time?"

Chris hesitated. "Actually, this time I'm here to find someone's missing canary."

Henry couldn't help but snigger.

"You never know. I could be about to uncover a ruthless group of villains who steal canaries."

Chris knew how it sounded. He'd hoped the next time Henry, or Mick as he knew him, saw him it would be after he'd taken down someone on Interpol's most wanted list. They both climbed halfway up the mountainside and descended the other, towards the beach. Henry stopped at some of the shops, leaving Chris outside, and continued to ask about Mr Smith, but no matter who he asked, he got the same, cold response. It seemed whoever Mr Smith was, everyone in the town was in fear of him, or someone who was acquainted with him.

They made it to the beach by late afternoon. According to one of the locals, The Captain's Haven was a restaurant on the beach front, and that was where they were heading, even if Chris spent half his time looking in the sky.

"You know there's a good chance that it's flown home," said Henry.

"Unless it's been birdnapped."

They continued along the beach front, refusing several sunbeds on offer. Despite the high number of pedestrians, there were also a lot of cars muscling their way along the half road, half path at the back of the sandy beach. Two cars caught Henry's eye in particular. Aside from the suspicious nature of two identical Mercedes SUVs, painted jet black, with tinted windows, neither had number plates. They were both stationary outside a pedestrianised area, with the engines running. As Henry and Chris walked towards them, Henry looked through the front windscreen. His polarised lenses removed the bright reflections and allowed him to see four men in each vehicle. With the heat coming from them, it was a surprise they weren't just puddles of molten steel.

They both carried on past the two cars and along the road. Although there was only a short stretch between the two beachfront walkways, there were cars everywhere. Horns were blaring, and drivers were debating whether they could fit their sixteen-foot cars into a fifteen-foot space.

The impatient taxi drivers were swerving around cars and pedestrians, desperate to get as many runs in as possible before the sun set for the evening.

As suddenly as the road ended, so did the pavement, leaving just sand to walk along. Mr Smith's private residence was a few hundred metres further on, but he wasn't due there for another five hours. To their right was a restaurant. *The Captain's Haven* was written on the side of a huge banner, blowing in the wind above the building.

"Do you fancy grabbing something to eat?" suggested Henry.

"Um, well, sure. But I thought I was here to help you, not let you buy me dinner."

"Trust me, you are helping. I'm not going to tell you why I'm here, but your presence is helping to sell my cover. And don't worry, I'm not buying you dinner."

The few hours of walking had certainly taken their effect on Chris. His humorous comments had slowly subsided with each minute they'd spent in the beating sun. Only the promise of food had started to pick his spirits back up. Chris' constant requests to stop for beers and ice creams had been denied, which did little for keeping up his morale. Whilst he wanted to help someone who, in his eyes, must be a secret agent of some sort, he didn't think it would require him to lose half his body weight in sweat.

The restaurant was set on two floors. The bottom had a cocktail bar and was full of stools and small, round tables, whilst upstairs was laid out more like you'd expect to find a restaurant, with proper tables and chairs, and cutlery laid in individual pouches around every placing. A waiter led them to a table for two. Henry moved around the back and sat down to face the restaurant, whilst Chris had to make do with just a plain, white wall.

A waiter approached with two menus. He looked young, twenty at the oldest, and seemed as though he'd only been in the job for a day. He placed Chris' menu down on the table carefully, then moved around to Henry's side. His foot was slightly stuck out from under the table, giving him the quickest possible exit, should he need it. Unfortunately, the waiter didn't see it and kicked it with his left foot, before stumbling forwards towards the table. Henry instinctively leant back, as he winced with the pain, now in his left big toe. The menu was slammed down on to the table, followed by the waiter's hand as he just about managed to regain his balance without crashing to the floor.

He stood up straight, straightened his brand-new uniform and asked, "Can I get you anything to drink whilst you decide?"

"Two beers please," said Chris, almost pleading with the waiter.

With a cheery smile, the waiter left their table and moved into the kitchen. Within a few seconds, a different waiter brought over the two drinks, and also left. Chris took the glass closest to him and moved it even closer, before taking the other and starting to drink from it. "I don't know what you want to drink."

Henry took the time to take in his surroundings. There were eight groups in the restaurant. The majority were just out for a meal, talking amongst themselves and paying no interest to Henry. One of them was the family he'd seen in the cafe that morning. They'd met up with two more people, both older. The coincidence was in the back of Henry's mind, but none of them seemed to be raising any alarm bells. Nevertheless, he couldn't take any chances. He'd already put some of the pieces together. There was a husband and wife, with what looked like their son, maybe late teens. The two older people who had joined them were the right age to be one of their parents. He looked further, their positioning, who each person was facing, who controlled each conversation. The three men all wore a shirt and shorts, all varying colours of blue, whilst the two women wore shorts, a blouse, and matching sandals. Henry took all this in. Then, he casually approached.

They clearly hadn't eaten their meal, but Henry could think of no other opener. "What would you recommend?"

The husband, who either didn't hear the question, or pretended as such, was swiftly prompted to turn around by his wife's elbow digging in his side. He looked towards her in confusion.

"He's just asked you a question," she said under her breath.

"I'm sorry?" he asked, looking towards Henry.

"Is there anything you'd recommend?" he repeated.

"Well, I've gone for the steak," answered the gentleman.

"Is it any good?" asked Henry, trying to ascertain how many times they'd eaten there.

The waitress from this morning could've given the restaurant's name for any reason, one of which could be for someone who'd regularly dined there. It was a long shot, but as he had another few hours before the meeting, it was better to be thorough.

"I don't know, we've never been here before, but I did have a very nice one in the town."

*Not exactly much help here then, is it*, thought Henry. If they hadn't eaten there before, the chances were that they weren't of interest.

"We ate here last night," said the older woman, as she turned to Henry. It was suddenly clear she was the husband's mother.

"What did you have?" asked Henry, trying to be as polite as possible.

"Oh, just a… chicken breast," she replied, pulling a face anyone would find hard to replicate.

They still weren't the people he was hoping for. Henry needed someone who'd dined there regularly, someone who could know the reason for the waitress' message, or even better, someone who was the reason themselves, but he was there to keep a low profile, and as much as he wanted to just walk away, he had to keep up appearances and appear polite.

"Was it nice?"

"Yes, it was, it was quite nice. I wouldn't have it again. It was a bit dry, but the sauce was OK. He ate most of it," the mother concluded, pointing to the elderly gentleman beside her.

"And did you have the same?" asked Henry to the man, really wishing he hadn't approached the table at all.

The man looked up at Henry. "Pardon?"

"What did you have?" repeated Henry.

"The pork," he said.

"He asked you, 'what did you have?' " shouted his wife.

"I've just told him!" replied the man, with equal volume and a sigh.

"Oh, I thought you said 'pardon'," replied the mother, looking to the others for support.

"And, was that nice?" asked Henry.

"Well, he moaned about it," said the mother, "but I thought it was okay. I told him not to have a whole sandwich for lunch." She turned to her husband. "Didn't I?"

Henry slowly backed away from the table, as the restaurant descended into silence. His plan to keep a low profile wasn't exactly going to plan.

"Well, thanks for your help," said Henry with a small wave. He moved back into his seat and picked up the menu.

There were now two empty pint glasses on the table and a further one only about a quarter full. If Henry was to find out whether every guest had dined at the restaurant before, a far better approach was needed.

As it so happened, however, a better approach wasn't needed after all. Just a few minutes after ordering their food, three men arrived. They all wore black suits, with dark sunglasses. Maybe during the day, and in cooler temperatures, this wouldn't have looked suspicious, but for them all to be wearing sunglasses an hour after the sun had set, whoever they were, they weren't going for inconspicuous. They weren't led to a table but sat down at one in the corner, the only one that had been untouched the entire time Henry had been there. *They must be why I'm here*, he thought, but for the next two and a half hours, Henry got no answers. He'd asked the waiters, but they had pretended not to understand him. None of the other guests had even acknowledged their presence. They were at the far side of the restaurant and couldn't be approached without raising any suspicion.

"Do you want to help me further?" asked Henry.

"Sure, anything," replied Chris, who'd managed to polish off a loaf of bread, accompanied by oil and balsamic vinegar, a prawn cocktail, an entire mackerel, with chips, and both a baklava and a huge bowl of Greek yoghurt with honey and nuts. Of course, that wasn't including the alcohol, which was enough to give Henry concern that he wouldn't be able to stand, let alone help with the only plan he'd come up with.

"This is where we part ways, but I need one final favour," started Henry.

Chris leant forwards, his head starting to lollop on his shoulders. "What can I do?" he slurred.

"I need a distraction. A big distraction. Can you manage that?"

Chris nodded eagerly. He went to stand but was stopped by Henry.

"Not yet. I'm going to go to the bathroom. It's downstairs, so as soon as I disappear down those stairs there." He then pointed out the ones they'd used to enter the restaurant. "As soon as I've gone, I need you to start the distraction, okay?"

Chris nodded again. Henry could see the number of ideas running through his mind, but all of his plans would fail, that much Henry was sure of. However, that in itself would cause enough of a distraction.

Henry stood up, walked over to a waiter and whispered in his ear. He was then directed down the stairs and started to move out of sight. Now was the time for Chris to move.

He stood up, full of energy. Leaning on the table, he pushed his chair back three times, and then made his way towards the stairs, but to no one's surprise, he never made it that far. Catching his leg on another guest's chair, Chris began to stumble, picking up speed as he hurtled towards a group of diners. With a final stumble over one of the restaurant's resident cats, Chris landed on the table, flattening it. He then lay motionless on the floor, with tzatziki on his shorts and spaghetti carbonara around his face.

From just down the stairs, Henry watched the entire thing. He had to admit just how effective it was, even if it wasn't Chris' plan. The three men all stood up, along with everyone else in the restaurant. They'd felt safe with everyone sitting down, giving them enough time to act to any dangers, but now, they were on edge. There was a short exchange of words between them, before one started to head in Henry's direction. He sat at the bar and let the man pass him, leaving the restaurant. Henry followed him.

The man walked towards the same two black SUVs he'd seen earlier and went into the boot. By this point, Henry was casually leaning against one of the beach huts. The man pulled out two guns, tranquiliser guns from what Henry could see of the shape. The man then passed him again and returned to the restaurant, but this time, Henry approached the cars. When the boot was opened by the guard, the internal lights had all come on, showing the car was empty; at least, one of the cars was empty. Henry crouched down by the boot. It wasn't the kind of lock he could pick. It was an electric lock, the kind that could only be opened with the key. Fortunately, VOICE had fitted everyone's phones with an app capable of unlocking that kind of car. He scanned the number plate, then let the app bounce the key's signal to the car, unlocking it in the process, at least that's what he picked up from the nine-page booklet VOICE had given them explaining how it all worked. Henry opened the boot and actually found himself gasping at its contents. Inside were two people. They were both breathing, but neither moved. Perhaps he was distracted by the two people, but even that wasn't an excuse for letting his guard down. Before he could even think about what he was seeing, he felt a sharp prick in his neck, like a needle had just gone in. Henry knew instantly what had happened, he'd been hit by a tranquiliser dart. Within a second, his legs started to tire, and his eyelids became like solid iron gates, impossible to hold open. He never even remembered hitting the ground.

***

Henry regained consciousness slowly. His head felt like it had been through several cycles of a washing machine and his vision was blurry.

"It's alright, your vision'll return. I think. At least, mine did."

Henry couldn't really place the voice. He thought it was coming from his right, but he wasn't even sure if he was upside down or not.

"When did they get you?"

Henry recalled everything he could; the car, and the two people in the boot.

"I was hit with a tranquiliser dart."

"Same here. I was so distracted by that guy you dined with. You know, the one who passed out in someone's carbonara; such a waste of food."

"You were there?" asked Henry, now surer of his surroundings.

The person talking to him was on his right, and he was the right way up. He strained to get his vision back.

"Yeah, of course I was. You really don't know who I am, do you?"

Henry continued to strain. He could see enough to recognise the person. The youngest from the family of five he'd spoken to at the restaurant, and the ones he'd seen at the cafe that morning. Assuming it was still the same day.

"You see me yet?" he asked.

"Just about."

"Well, I guess it would take longer for you. You're not as young and fit as me."

"Exactly how old do you think I am?" asked Henry.

"Thirties, give or take."

Henry took in his surroundings. They were sat in a huge function room, with high ceilings, a round table big enough to make any dinner host jealous, and another ten people, also sat in chairs identical to the one Henry was in.

"What's going on?"

"Well, if I had to guess, I'd say we've all arrived at our destination. I take it you got the letter too?"

"The one inviting the best private detectives here?" asked Henry, fully aware that he hadn't received the letter but had more forced himself an invite.

"No, the one inviting you to your first free hearing test… Yes, of course the letter inviting you here. From what I've gathered, whoever's running this thing doesn't want us to know how to get in and out of this place. I mean, we all know where it is, so it's not like they've got any other reason to drug us."

"Are they other private investigators?" asked Henry.

"Yes. I recognise a couple of them. Well, most of them. Although, I doubt most could solve a basic case, so I'm really not sure why they're here. You see, they're only interested in high-profile cases, they get all the credit and money for solving them, but they actually hire other investigators to work those cases. I really am surprised they were even allowed in, someone as well prepared as whoever organised this must know what they're like."

Henry looked at the others around the room. "I saw those two in the boot of a car."

They both looked in their late thirties, both had long, black hair, both looked very similar, in fact, they both dressed the same as well.

"Two sisters, Mary and Ann. Their parents were born and raised in China but moved to the south of France before having their daughters. Mary and Ann were the names they changed to at the age of eighteen. Nobody knows what they were called before, other than them… and their parents. They rose to fame after solving the Thousand Island case."

Henry frowned; it was a case he'd never heard of.

"You must've heard of it. Everyone who is everyone wanted to solve it. It was a serial killer, one who always used Thousand Island dressing as a calling card."

"Why?" he asked.

"I doubt anyone really knows. He sometimes even used the dressing to kill the victim, whether by adding something they were allergic to, or even using it to suffocate the victim. Pretty nasty way to go."

Another one of the investigators started to wake.

"What of the others?" asked Henry, keen to find out as much as possible before they woke.

"That's Dustin," he pointed to a short, but very wide, man in a blue suit. "He spends most of his earnings on food, and girls, and food for girls. Over there, we have Mr C. There isn't really much to say about him, he'd probably struggle to solve his own murder even if he saw the killer. Then there's the Triple Shot. Two brothers, there used to be three, obviously, but the smartest of them got too close to solving one of their cases and the killer wasn't all too keen on that happening. They haven't actually solved a case since, but now they just get others to do their work for them. They own their own detective agency in Texas, where they've always lived. The more money they earn, the bigger their ranch gets. It's like a castle now," he mumbled.

"And the others?" asked Henry, still trying to at least get names for everyone.

"The tall, skinny bloke, Tick, presumably short for something, went into this line of work because he got bored making money on the stock market. I think the definition of too much money springs to mind. As for the other three, I can't say I recognise them."

"You think maybe they're here as decoys? Not actually investigators but just here almost undercover."

"Maybe." It was the first time he seemed unsure of something since Henry had met him.

"And yourself?"

"Well, all five of us work together. You know, the other four from the restaurant. As far as our clients are concerned, there's only one of us, hence why it's only me who's been kidnapped. When I was younger, there was a murder somewhere I was staying. I helped the detective, and after the case was solved, he kind of took me under his wing. I then passed on what I learnt to my family, and we went into business together. Beyond that, there isn't much more I can say other than we're good at what we do. If you're asking for my name though, I don't think we're quite at that level of friendship just yet, but if you have to call me something, you can call me John. Not sure why, but that's just the first name that came to mind." He then paused for a moment. "I'm not sure there's much point in asking your name."

There was a grandfather clock over to one side, showing a time of one twenty-eight, in the morning presumably. There was a card in front of him, as there was in front of everyone, each with their own names on. Inside, there was a message, it was short and sweet. *Leave your chair before it's permitted and you will not make it out of here alive.*

Throughout the next half an hour, all of the guests woke. When the clock struck two, the only door, a huge expanse of handcrafted oak, was opened. Four waiters entered, each with three glasses of champagne on a tray. One drink was left to the right of each person, before the waiters left and another person entered. He was dressed in a three-piece, tailored suit. It looked somehow more expensive than anything branded, almost like sewing a name in would decrease the price of it. According to the intel Henry was given, this fifty-nine-year-old was Mr Smith, Emma's father. He had a greying, thick beard, much like the hair on his head. He also walked with a slight limp in his left leg, something he tried to hide.

"Thank you all for coming," he started in an upper-class tone. "As I doubt you know, my dearest daughter, Emma, was murdered back in February of this year. There has been a cover-up of this matter, and you are here to give me closure. She was my everything, and I want those who are truly responsible to be held accountable." Mr Smith had been carrying another glass of champagne but, at this moment, placed it in the centre of the round table. "However, before you begin to investigate, I need to test just how effective you can be. For starters, I will make one thing perfectly clear. If you disobey me, you will be killed. Take the letter in front of you, for instance. Does anyone think it's a bluff?"

Everyone around the table glanced at one another. They probably did think it was a bluff but, at the same time, was it really worth taking that risk?

"Anyone?" pressed Mr Smith.

One of the three people John didn't recognise looked towards Mr Smith. "I think it's a bluff."

Mr Smith gestured for him to continue.

"Well, any one of us could have stood up before you entered. It's not like our chairs are rigged to blow, or poisoned darts are going to fly out of the walls. You're a very rich person in need of a detective, and I am the best. You see, I think this is the first test, being prepared to challenge anything, even in the face of death. We all have very high profiles and it would be impossible for you cover up our deaths." He then stood up.

"You are quite correct," started Mr Smith. "There are no explosives or poisoned darts. They would put everyone else at too much risk. But I also need to know that my orders can be followed. So, if you disobeyed me, standing up when you were not permitted so to do, for example, I would approach that person, retrieve the handgun in my right pocket, aim it between that person's eyes… and pull the trigger." Mr Smith then pulled a handgun out of his pocket and aimed at the investigator. "Are you still calling my bluff?"

The investigator shook his head frantically.

"Are you accepting that you got it wrong?"

The investigator started nodding frantically.

"Well, I can't have anyone making mistakes." Mr Smith pulled the trigger. The investigator's lifeless body fell to the floor.

"So much for them being decoys," whispered John.

"I would like you all to toast Mr Johnson's unnecessarily short life," said Mr Smith.

The remaining eleven investigators raised their glasses and said, "To Mr Johnson," in unison, before drinking their champagne, all with shaking hands.

"Good. At least now I know you can all follow orders. However, the tests are not yet over. One of you in this room has just been poisoned. When the clock hits five past two… one of you will die, unless of course, you take the antidote." He then pointed to the champagne he'd brought in with him. "There is only one antidote and you will need to take the entire drink, but I should add, if you take the antidote and you haven't been poisoned, then the antidote will kill you. I suggest you choose who to give the antidote to wisely, for I chose whom to poison wisely. Time's ticking." Mr Smith then stood to the side of the room and observed.

They sat in silence for almost the full five minutes. Eventually, someone did speak.

"Are we sure someone's even been poisoned?" asked John.

"Well, look at him. It's clear we can't call his bluff again," said Ann.

"If only one person's been poisoned, then that's just a one in twelve chance that it's each of us, because for all we know, Mr what's-his-name could've been the poisoned one," added Tick.

"No, he couldn't. He never took his drink," added Dustin.

"But the poison could still be sat in his glass," said Tick.

"We've only got ten seconds," said Ann.

"I don't think one of us has been poisoned," reassured John.

Henry kept quiet, watching Mr Smith, as the second hand clonked round to *XII*.

Five past two came and went. Nothing happened.

"See, I told you," said Tick.

Dustin's head hit the table.

"Maybe you spoke too soon," added John.

Then another head hit the table, one of the other ones John didn't recognise.

"This is perhaps a good time to mention that whilst I demand complete obedience, I may be lying to you," said Mr Smith, as he moved back towards the table. "Can we have three body bags in here please," he added, as if talking to the door itself.

"I've had enough of this. You've poisoned us all, haven't you?" blurted out the final one John didn't recognise. She reached forwards, grabbed the antidote and drained the entire glass.

"Could you make that four body bags, please?" said Mr Smith. "I'd sit down if I were you, the antidote acts far quicker than the…"

She fell to the floor.

"…poison," concluded Mr Smith. "Now, I must say, I'm not particularly disappointed with the outcome. They were all people I was going to kill at some point. I mean, none of them are actually any good, just armchair detectives if you will. And make no mistake, I am perfectly capable of covering up any of your deaths."

Eight more people entered the room; each pair swiftly wrapped one of the bodies up and took them out of the room. It was like they'd done it too many times before.

"Well done to you, Mr Pressure," Mr Smith said looking towards John. "You did make a correct statement. When you said I hadn't poisoned one person, you were correct. Now if you'd follow me, I'll show you to the next test."

Several gunshots could be heard. They weren't close, likely echoing throughout the house's surrounding woods, assuming that's where they were.

"That will be my son, he hunts anything that moves in the woods," said Mr Smith without needing to be asked.

"Animals, or people?" asked Henry.

"Animals," reassured Mr Smith. "Then again, people are animals." He left the room without another word.

Everyone was cautious, but seeing what would happen if they didn't follow, it wasn't like they had much choice. They left the room in single file, Henry leaving the room last. The corridor, and indeed every room they passed along the corridor, was exactly what Henry expected it to be after seeing the function room. The whole place was like a cross between a modernised castle, a country estate, and a movie set. They followed Mr Smith until he stopped outside one of the many rooms.

"As private investigators at the top of your game, you should find this next challenge relatively simple, but first I would like you all to draw sticks. The person who draws the shortest will enter a different room. Again, if you really are as good as you say, I'd like to think you can all avoid the shortest stick, all except the person to draw last that is." He looked straight towards Tick.

They each drew a stick from Mr Smith's hand. He obviously hid one end and made sure the other end of the sticks were all level with each other. A couple of them,

John included, looked like they knew exactly which to choose. Henry wasn't so sure, but at least he didn't choose the shortest. In fact, the shortest did go to Tick, as it so happened.

"If you'll please go through that door, you'll find a few members of my staff who will help you get ready for the next test. As for the rest of you, this way please."

They followed Mr Smith through another door, the opposite way to Tick, and into another oversized room, this one a giant drawing room.

"Does anybody know why it is called a drawing room?" asked Mr Smith.

"Because people used to withdraw to this room of an evening," said Henry.

"That is indeed the accepted reason behind its name, yes, but I'm not so sure anyone will ever know with one hundred per cent certainty whether that is true or not."

The room, although large, was somehow cosy. There was an open fireplace as the centrepiece on one wall, a few sofas, all soft and warm, a drinks cabinet was over to one side, and a giant bearskin rug covered most of the floor.

"Your fellow investigator is having his role in this next test explained to him, and once he is ready, we can begin. You will be tasked with solving a murder. It will be a mock-up of a murder that took place in this very room, over one hundred years ago. Your fellow investigator will be able to help you in the best way possible, but I should warn you that failure to solve the case will result in another loss of life."

Just as Mr Smith finished talking, as if it was as well rehearsed as a stage show, there was a knock on the furthest wall. He smiled and moved over to it. Henry didn't notice it at first, but it was the only wall with nothing on it and nothing in front of it. Mr Smith twisted a painting of the surrounding scenery, long before tourism, and the wall split in two. Moving apart, it revealed a second half to the room, and inside, sat in a huge armchair, with a headrest bigger than his head, Tick was slumped over to one side, dead.

"Off you go," said Mr Smith.

The two Triple Shot brothers stepped up first. They observed the body for about fifteen minutes, trying to find every little sign there was. One of them made notes on a few scraps of creased paper, and the other did most of the talking.

"I think you've had long enough. You two, up you come," said Mr Smith.

The brothers were replaced by Ann and Mary. They also both observed the body, making notes in a far more organised A5 notepad. Mary focussed more on the body, the way he was positioned, any distinctive marks or defensive wounds, whilst Ann seemed far more focussed on the knife, sticking out from the top of Tick's right shoulder. With about twenty minutes gone this time, the final three approached. Mr C held back and watched from afar, it was perfectly clear to everyone that he was well out of his depth and survival was the only thing on his mind. John made preliminary notes before anyone spoke.

*Signs of sweat in hairline, face bone dry.*
*Less blood than expected around knife wound, inflicted post death?*
*Tie tied leaning to right, suggesting right-handed. Jacket unfastened, contrary to earlier.*
*Shirt gathered and folded beneath trousers, shirt tucked in after belt put on.*
*Shirt cuff damp.*
*Fingers clean of blood.*
*Watch strapped to left wrist, as before, however earlier drink was lifted with left hand, suggesting left-handed.*
*Belt tied with spare hanging to right, suggesting left-handed.*
*Scuff mark on right shoe.*
*Shoelaces tied in manner accustomed to left-handed people.*

"And now, I wish to hear your opinions," said Mr Smith.

It seemed clear that he didn't want them conferring. Henry had made his own conclusions, not too far from John's, but Mr C couldn't quite say the same.

The Triple Shot brothers stepped up first, flicking through each scrap of paper.

"It seems clear the cause of death was the knife wound to the neck. The angle of the wound makes it clear that either the victim was sitting down, or the murderer was over seven-feet tall. Assuming the victim was sat down, it wasn't in this chair. You can see that by the lack of blood marks on it. Wherever he was murdered, it wasn't here. As for who it was, it's impossible to say without testing the knife for fingerprints and finding the actual crime scene."

They performed their whole explanation like they were presenting a show. One did the talking, the other pointed out the relevant places of interest.

"Aside from the fact that over one hundred years ago, they could not dust for fingerprints, if I were to tell you that the only person whose fingerprints were on the knife was our chef?" asked Mr Smith.

The two brothers briefly conferred with each other. "Then your chef would become our prime suspect. However, the knife is clearly not a kitchen knife."

"I see. And you three? Do you agree?" asked Mr Smith.

"No," said John, backed up by Henry's shaking head.

"And you, Mr C?"

He continued to stay quiet.

"Would you like to leave this place? You would of course be off the case, but…"

"Yes," blurted out Mr C.

"Very well." Mr Smith then cleared his throat. Two armed guards entered and escorted Mr C out of the room, almost as if they'd planned for it all along. "I doubt you'll all be seeing him for a while. Please, continue with your thoughts."

John spoke again, "The knife wound did not kill Tick. There is far too little blood and must've been inflicted post death." Henry saw the two sisters nodding their heads. "We believe he was poisoned."

Mr Smith was curious by the belief. "Go on."

"Shortly after leaving us, he began to feel unwell, perhaps symptoms of dizziness or nausea. He went to the bathroom. I imagine he started to feel worse, so untied his tie and loosened his collar. He would have splashed his face with water, hence making his shirt cuffs wet. His shirt came untucked and his jacket unfastened."

Henry then stepped in and took over. "At some point, Tick succumbed to the poison, which is when his appearance was altered. Other signs, such as his shoelaces, belt and the hand in which he used to both raise his champagne glass and choose the shortest stick, all suggest he was left-handed. However, the person who reset his appearance tied his tie as a right-handed person, with the knot leaning to the right. His face was dried, but signs of both water and perspiration remained in his hairline. He was placed in the chair, with the knife in his shoulder for us to find."

"And who did it?" asked Mr Smith.

"You," said Henry.

"It seems the only viable time to inflict the poison would have been in the champagne," continued John. "Of course, you weren't the one to set the scene, you were with us, but you were the one to ensure Tick took the shortest stick."

"And the two of you?" asked Mr Smith.

"We agree," they said in unison.

"The four of you are correct," he concluded. He then turned his attention to the two brothers. "I'm afraid your assumptions were wrong. You will now by escorted from this place." His words were cold.

Eight armed guards then entered, obviously a little more concerned that the brothers might fight their way out.

But they went quietly; the hope of being let free was just too tempting.

"I have decided that the four of you will investigate the case. I have chosen you, not because of your assumptions, nor because of your accuracy, but instead because I feel you are the four who are best suited to this case. Please enjoy the rest of the night here, or by all means, leave. I will be in contact with each of you personally in the coming weeks with instructions on how to proceed. Thank you once again for taking on this case." He then turned to John. "And excellent powers of deduction, I must say."

"Induction," replied John, regretting it almost instantly.

Mr Smith started nodding, as a slight smile broke out, before he left the room. Henry could've sworn the room got warmer as he left, but silence had also fallen. No one was really sure whether they were allowed to leave or whether it was another test.

Ann and Mary were the first to brave it out. They left the room and started to explore the house. Henry and John, however, decided the leave altogether. They just walked out of the front gates. Over to the side, several guards were digging holes, eight holes, but the guards weren't concerned by the two leaving. The gates themselves were like something from a post-apocalyptic world, designed to keep out hordes of the undead. Once outside, there were two paths, one leading up a steep hill, the other down into the woods. John went down, closely followed by Henry. The events of that night were beyond what either of them had experienced before, yet neither were fazed. It was almost as if what had just happened had in fact happened many times before.

"Where did you learn to do all that?" asked Henry.

"My master taught me."

"Your master?"

"Yeah, only don't tell him I called him that, he hates it. I told you about the detective teaching me everything.

Well, a few years ago, I took a part-time job at his business, 'Pressure Investigations' it was called. I thought I was just going to handle some paperwork, answer the phone, that kind of stuff, but the owner had other ideas. He taught me to be almost as good as him, then, he told me the final part of my training was to go out on my own and pass on what I'd learnt. So, I started a more family-orientated private investigator service, taught my family what I'd learnt, and well, here I am."

"But they don't actually take the lead?" asked Henry.

"Normally, we have so many cases that we all work our own. Well, not all of us, some are more suited to a more office-based life of filing and making the tea, but this one was different."

"And your master?" asked Henry.

"He still works cases, though slightly more low profile these days. He'll only work cases for people he knows, or the ones that really interest him."

"And this one didn't interest him?"

"Actually, it did, but he gave his invitation to me. He said, and I quote, 'It'll be good for you to learn'," said John, putting on a bad French accent to mimic his master.

They emerged from the woods a few minutes later to a small harbour. It was mainly full of tenders for the larger yachts out in the cove. A bird launched itself from one of the boats, as its silhouette moved into the trees. John held his right hand up to his forehead and mumbled something under his breath.

"You hopping on?" John then asked, as he approached one of the smaller boats.

As John likely knew where Henry's tender was, it seemed pointless to refuse. "Sure."

They both climbed aboard a small dinghy and set on their way.

"What about you? I somehow doubt you got an invitation," shouted John over the noise of the engine.

"I made an invitation. Wanted to come here, find out what it was all about."

"Why?"

Henry still couldn't tell him the truth. No matter how much he trusted him, it was still too risky. "Maybe you'll find out next time we meet."

"I look forward to it. Do you mind if I ask you something?"

"Fire away," shouted Henry.

The dinghy had now started to bounce up and down on the waves. The further out to sea they got, the bigger the waves became. It was a relatively short journey around the cove to the neighbouring one, where Henry's tender was being kept, but there was still more time for talking than Henry wanted.

"Who do you work for?"

The question surprised Henry. He hesitated a little, before answering, "I work for myself."

"Then why do you keep checking the time?"

He wasn't even aware that he had kept checking the time.

"You've checked your watch fifty-two times since you woke up," added John, as Henry's tender came into sight.

"I had to leave my team behind. We're working a pretty crucial case, and I've left them to do it alone whilst I pursue my own vendetta." It was by far the most truth he'd spoken all night.

"And those murders, they didn't faze you at all?"

"No," said Henry. "That wasn't like anything I've experienced before, yet it didn't seem all that different to what I do every day. Did that make sense?"

John laughed. "In a weird kind of a way, yeah, it did. Oddly, I feel the same."

John seemed to accept Henry's answer, as the rest of their journey was in silence. The dinghy pulled up alongside Henry's tender and he hopped aboard.

"For the past few months, since Pressure told me to go it alone," started John, "it took me a while to realise that, at some point, you've got to let the ones you care for use their own wings. It's the only way they'll know if they can fly by themselves. If you've trained them, then I'm sure they're just fine."

"You know, you're very wise for someone so much younger than me," said Henry.

With a smile, John turned the dinghy around.

"They'll be fine," he reiterated, and headed back towards the other cove. Henry thought about what he'd said for a moment.

"I'm sure they will be too," he muttered.

# Chapter 13 – The Biting of the Past
12th September
18:28 BST
25 hrs 45 min. Until Deadline

The bright orange spark flew towards them, leaving a plume of thick smoke in its wake. Flares popped from each side of the helicopter, but it wasn't enough. The missile slapped the right side of the tail, sending them into a dangerous spin. Whilst Hawk wrestled with the cyclic, the others just tried to hang on, clutching whatever was close to their seats. Alpha Five and Seven wrapped their fingers through some netting, whilst Alpha Three and Four held on to the helicopter's structural roll cage.

There was nothing Hawk could do to regain control, they were heading for the ground and nothing would change that. Still amongst the mountains, stretching high above them on all sides, crashing on level ground was difficult enough. He manoeuvred the cyclic around, flicking switches and heaving up levers, desperately trying to slow their descent. Warning lights flashed, all predicting the inevitable demise of the helicopter.

It crashed down surprisingly softly on a slope, landing on a thick blanket of snow, but continued to spin as it slid downwards. Hawk's work still wasn't complete, as he caught sight of the end of the rocky slope. With no idea how far down the drop was going to be, staying in the helicopter seemed like a bad idea.

"Everyone out!" bellowed Hawk, as the others noticed the drop.

As they were still spinning, they had to time their jump so they wouldn't end up under the helicopter. Alpha Five and Seven were the first to leap out, disappearing amongst the snow as they came to a stop. The helicopter had already slowed down, but as the next two went to jump, it hit a large rock, sending both Alpha Three and Four to the other side. As everyone lay without moving, the helicopter seemed to be safe. That was, until there was a sound of cracking beneath where they had come to rest.

They had to move slowly, to prevent speeding up the cliff edge's inevitable crumble, but quickly enough to get out in time. Alpha Four moved over to Hawk, who was already climbing to the other side of the cockpit to carefully exit. Even with the ominous sound of the crumbling cliff face, the helicopter didn't budge and it seemed as though they still had time to move, but they were wrong. As they waited for Hawk to reach the door, the once sturdy platform turned to dust and boulders, as the helicopter looked to be eaten by the mountains.

Alpha Five and Seven rushed to the new edge, flicking a few stones over. They looked down, hoping by some miracle that something had saved them. About twenty metres down, there was a wide ledge, with all three of them lying there.

"Are you alright?" shouted Alpha Five, able to see the three people-shaped imprints in the deep snow.

"Ask me in a month or so," muttered Alpha Three, as he climbed out of the hole he'd made.

"Yeah, we're all good," added Alpha Four, loud enough for them all to hear.

"You speak for yourselves," groaned Hawk, as he rolled on to his knees, clutching his chest.

He was taking short, shallow breaths, as Alpha Four bent down to take a look. Part of the helicopter's internal structure was lodged in his side.

"You've got a couple of broken ribs, you'll live," assured Alpha Four, brushing over the two-foot metal pole protruding from him.

"Oh good, for a minute I thought I was just making a fuss."

Alpha Three looked down to where the helicopter had fallen to the very base of the mountain. The ledge they were standing on was originally more the size of the landing pad back at the bank but, since a huge helicopter-shaped bite had been taken out of it, only a small platform remained.

"I reckon we've used this year's allowance of luck today."

"I don't feel all that lucky," muttered Hawk, climbing to his feet.

Back on top of the cliff edge, Alpha Five checked on the vial. He retrieved the box from inside his jacket and opened it up. The vial was still intact.

"It's all good," said Alpha Five with a sense of relief. "How are you going to get back up to us?"

"We're not," said Alpha Four. "There's no way we can climb back up with Hawk. There was a small village about a kilometre east of here. I'm pretty sure that's where the missile came from. If it's some kind of outpost for the bank, then they should have a radio we can use to contact the Molehill."

"Yeah, I bet they have got a radio, as well as a whole army that are probably on their way to look for us," added Alpha Five.

"That's why we're going to split up. The two of you need to call for help as soon as possible. If the helicopter sent out a distress signal on impact, like it's meant to, then any help will be walking into the same trap we did. If contacting them isn't possible, then you'll need to disable whatever missiles or rockets they have before we can exfil. The sun'll be setting in about an hour, so we'll have to move quickly."

"What about you?" asked Alpha Five.

"The ledge leads down to the base of the mountain. We'll head down and see what we can salvage from the wreckage."

"Best of luck!" shouted Alpha Five, as they both moved away from the edge.

Without a word to each other, they headed towards a narrow section of trees so they could move around the closest mountain and up to the village to the east. They moved into the small, wooded area, stepping between the roots, half buried in the snow, still in silence. They walked a little faster than an amble, for them, although it would probably be considered a swift route march for anyone else.

"Do you mind if I ask you something?" asked Alpha Seven.

The question had come as a bit of a shock, not because he didn't think either of them would speak, but because it was a complete contrast to the whistling wind and scraping tree branches.

"Sure," he said casually.

"Does that mean you do mind, or you don't?"

"What's the question?"

"Well… Well, I was just going to ask, and you don't have to answer, but I just wondered… Well, what happened between you and the team?"

"Why?" said Alpha Five, still trying to be as casual as possible.

"The team obviously still trusts you, and it's not like they treat you any differently, but it's clear there's some tension."

"I'm surprised you haven't been told."

"No, and I didn't think it was my place to ask," said Alpha Seven.

"Well, if it's all the same to you, I'd really rather not bring those memories back."

"Oh, of course. I was just curious, that's all."

The rest of their journey throughout the woods was frosty, not just because of the freezing temperatures, but because of the silence. The longer it went on, the worse it got. No matter how hard he tried, Alpha Seven's question had brought back several memories he'd tried to suppress.

The threat from whoever had shot them down was high. Although it made their journey a little longer, they'd been covering their tracks as they went. Whether or not their foe was a part of the bank, they'd want some kind of confirmation of death. It wasn't until about twenty minutes into the two Alphas' journey that they finally saw their opposition. The duo had left the woods and had made their way around the mountain to a small clearing, with a few boulders scattered around the edge. They both laid prone behind one of them. Alpha Seven's white camouflage helped her to blend in perfectly, but Alpha Five had to press himself as close to the rocks as possible. Their enemy was at the other end of the clearing and was moving slowly, checking every inch of land.

"How were you recruited?" asked Alpha Five, striking up the conversation at what appeared to be an odd time.

"I thought you all knew."

"No, we never find out how someone was recruited, just that they have, and whatever information from their past is necessary."

Alpha Seven paused for a moment. It wasn't really something she wanted to say, not because it was secret, just because she didn't want to say it.

"I was a first responder for a few years, and then I went into emergency A & E. After something happened, I… Well, I left and went freelance. Anyway, I got myself into a spot of bother and, just like a guardian angel, Bosse turned up and offered me a way out."

"Bosse is no guardian angel," muttered Alpha Five. Getting a quizzical look in return, he continued, "No matter what he promises you, it will always benefit him more."

"Is there a problem with that?"

Alpha Five gave an equally quizzical look back.

"Well, so what if it benefits him more?" added Alpha Seven. "At the end of the day, someone's got to benefit more. So long as you get something out of it, I don't see the problem."

The words hit surprisingly hard. It wasn't ever his way of thinking, but maybe, just maybe, Alpha Seven was on to something.

"Heads down, they're getting close," he whispered, whilst brushing snow over himself. Alpha Seven buried her head in the snow and let her clothing do the rest.

The patrol closed to within a few feet of them, still moving slowly, but methodically. They stood out against the snow, wearing dark-coloured tactical clothes. They also all had enormous builds, like one of the entry requirements was to look like you were made from bricks and mortar. Alpha Seven was holding a small, circular disc with a switch on it. When the patrol was almost on top of them, she flicked the switch. The sound of gunfire could be heard a few hundred metres away. The patrol looked towards the noise, and after a few head nods, hastily headed towards it.

Whilst travelling through the woods, Alpha Seven had stuck a speaker, although only the size of a thumbnail, on one of the trees. It was something she'd taken with her to the bank, but it was serving its purpose just as well out in the mountains.

With the patrol a safe distance away, Alpha Five and Seven continued on their way to the village. The closer they got, the thicker the snow became, now enough to cover their knees with every step. Hard work didn't come close to the effort they were putting in. The only noise was from their panting, each breath of the icy air made them want to cough, but they simply didn't have the energy. Their fingers had gone numb, their noses bright red and frozen, and they couldn't even be sure their feet were still with them, but finally, the snow started to get shallower.

The heat from the village could be felt long before they set eyes on it.

As they approached, they continued to feel warmer, speeding up like they'd caught sight of an oasis in the desert. Gradually, the snow continued to get shallower, until finally, there was no more than a light dusting on the floor. The village, or encampment, was set inside what looked to be a small crater. At the very top of the, now snow-free, crater edge, they could see the entire village. For the amount of heat that seemed to be coming from the area, there weren't that many fires that were lit. Nor were there any guards patrolling the outside of the crater. However, what seemed most surprising, as they turned to see where they had come from, was the fact that their tracks were still perfectly visible, but the patrols' were nowhere to be seen. After they'd crossed paths, they'd followed the patrol's tracks for about one hundred metres, until they'd suddenly run out. Alpha Five and Seven had had to stop covering their tracks when the snow got so bad, and it seemed almost impossible that a group so big could successfully cover their own tracks in snow that deep.

They carefully moved down the crater's wall and towards a patch of long grasses, stopping just short. They were in what looked like a large, raised bed which sat about a metre off the ground. Whilst there were no guards around the perimeter of the village, there were more than enough to deal with inside it. Timing their move perfectly, they climbed in amongst the tall grasses and lay prone.

At the edge of the tall grasses, Alpha Five and Seven looked towards the main part of the village. It seemed to be where the majority of the guards patrolled and was where almost all the buildings and structures were. There were too many to sneak past, and they had too little firepower to engage them, so their only hope was to wait for the patrol to discover they'd been tricked in the woods and return to find the tracks leading to the village. If the alarm was raised, there would be a chance a lot of the guards would move away from the centre of the village and in doing so would allow Alpha Five and Seven a chance to slip in undetected.

"You want to tell me what happened between you and the team?" whispered Alpha Seven.

"No," he replied bluntly.

"I know you're lying."

"How?" he asked, before swiftly adding, "And if you say 'because your lips are moving', I will stand up and start yelling."

"Touché… Seriously though, you've got to tell me."

"Why? Because you're caring? Because you're nosey?"

"Maybe a bit of both," she joked, "but mainly because I've got something I want to get off my chest, and I think you're the only one who might actually get it."

They fell silent, as a guard wandered past. It had somewhat broken the moment, but it still gave Alpha Five a chance to think. He did want to tell her and wasn't really sure why. For whatever reason, he also thought that she would be the only one to get what he'd been through.

The guard moved away, but they both stayed silent for a moment longer.

"My father was the founder of a group of hitmen," Alpha Five said. "He started it long before I was born and, unsurprisingly, he brought me up to be a part of it. He always wanted me to be the best, take his creation to the next level, make it bigger and better, but all I wanted was to make him proud. So, with every hit I was given, I followed through with it, like a weapon." He paused at his choice of words. He'd always thought it, but actually saying the words made it all too real. "There was this one hit. It was just like all the others. I'd planned everything out, took the target out cleanly. Everything was going to plan, until I turned around. Hanging on the wall was a picture. It was a picture of the target, stood next to my father."

"Your father knew him?" asked Alpha Seven. It was a stupid question, she knew the moment her lips opened, but she just couldn't help herself.

"Somewhat. The person I'd killed… was my uncle. As it so happened, my uncle had founded a rival group of assassins." Alpha Five again stopped talking.

"You couldn't make this stuff up."

Alpha Five let out a little laugh. "No, you couldn't."

"Was that when you decided to leave?"

"No, but it wasn't long after. It kind of snowballed from there. My uncle's group wanted revenge. I found myself pitted against some of my family that I'd never met. All to protect my father, who'd lied to me. When I did get out, Bosse helped me to disappear. Part of that was joining his newly found team of special security agents, or SSA as he called it back then."

"I'd always seen SSA on some of the doors at the Molehill, but I never asked what it stood for."

"We don't call it that any more. Now we just work for an organisation without a name, but when I first joined, it was like a home from home; a group working in the shadows, and a leader that I rely on but can never trust."

"Scott?"

"Bosse."

Their conversation was cut short by a thundering sound towards the other side of the village. It got faster and faster. The other guards began to move with more speed and haste as they headed towards the perimeter of the crater. As the thundering noise continued to get quicker, it became all too familiar. Seconds later, an armoured helicopter appeared above the buildings.

"It's a HAHA," muttered Alpha Five.

"A what?"

"A heavily armoured helicopter attacker, and yes, I'm pretty sure they put the words in that strange order just so it spelt 'HAHA'," he replied.

A bright beam of light hit the ground and started smoothly rolling over the village. The HAHA's searchlight illuminated the entire area, almost too bright to look at. As the beam shone over the guards, now searching the surrounding area, they ducked their heads down and looked away from the blinding light. If it did catch an intruder in its powerful gaze, they'd likely be rooted to the spot.

Whilst the guards did a quick sweep of the inner part of the village, they seemed more concerned with making it to the perimeter of the crater.

"They don't think we're inside yet," whispered Alpha Seven.

"Unless it's a trap."

The guards in their way had had their numbers cut by more than half. It gave them the perfect opportunity to approach, but it also seemed a little too good to be true.

"I've got a plan, but you need to trust me," said Alpha Seven.

"My favourite kind of plans all start like that," mumbled Alpha Five.

***

At the base of the mountain, Alpha Three and Four had finally reached the crash site after aiding a wounded Hawk. Hawk's couple of broken ribs were causing him pain, but part of the way into their journey, he'd started to lose blood. The wound was from part of the support in his chair that had broken free and lodged itself just above his kidneys during the crash. The debris had been left in, but Alpha Four had managed to stem the bleeding, until then. Hawk had been left at the top of a steep drop, still within sight of their helicopter but about twenty metres above it.

As Alpha Three and Four approached the helicopter, smoke pouring from what was left, they heard talking to their right. Instinctively, they both dived behind the closest rocks. The smoke made it hard to see whoever was approaching, but that also meant it kept them in the shadows as well, against the fast-setting sun.

A patrol of six armed guards emerged from a path leading back up the mountain. They all seemed relaxed, as they spread themselves out over the crash site without caution. Their rifles weren't raised and their eyes seemed fixed on the debris. They didn't know anyone else was there. Whilst there were only six, the odds were against Alpha Three and Four, given their lack of weapons. They started making hand signals to each other, running through a plan in a very basic sign language.

An element of surprise could give them the upper hand, but that would lose them their greatest weapon, the shadows. With the patrol split up, and finding it hard to see each other, Alpha Three locked eyes on his target. He approached from behind, staying low and quiet, like a lion staking its prey. Then, when the time was right, he struck. Leaping forwards, Alpha Three wrapped his right arm around the guard's neck and his left around his waist, pinning both arms down. Alpha Four grabbed the gun, placing a finger behind the trigger to ensure the gun wouldn't go off. It seemed like Alpha Three had been squeezing for hours, with the struggling guard trying to wriggle free. Murmurs were the only thing able to leave his mouth, but they couldn't be heard over the whistling winds. Eventually, the guard had nothing left, and was dragged back into the shadows. The other five were still unaware of their chances of success slowly decreasing.

Alpha Four took the guard's rifle and moved past the rocks to reach the opposite side of the helicopter. The wind had picked up further. Now it wasn't the smoke that caused the reduced visibility, it was the snow getting blown past. Alpha Four could just about make out two figures. He aimed the rifle at one, pulled the trigger, and then quickly moved to the other. They both fell. The noise of the two shots echoed throughout the mountains, attracting the attention of the other three guards, but as the noise of the shots bounced around, they couldn't find the source.

A third figure became visible, but Alpha Four's part was done for now. He watched as another came in behind, but this one was different; he wasn't carrying a rifle but a long steel pipe from the helicopter. He swung the pipe into the back of the guard's knee, causing him to drop to the floor. With a second swing, this time at head height, the guard slumped back and didn't move. Another guard came from Alpha Four's left. Alpha Three saw him and moved closer, the pipe still clutched in his hand. He swung it down on the guard's rifle, lowering it as a short burst of bullets erupted from the barrel. Alpha Three then used all his strength to push the guard back into the wreckage. As they clattered into it, the guard was dazed for only second, but that was enough for Alpha Three to push his head forwards. Their two skulls cracked together like leather on willow. The guard slid down the side of the helicopter. Alpha Three could sense the final guard behind him. Without hesitation, he turned and threw the pipe, like a javelin, at the guard. It hit his chest and caused him to collapse to the floor on his knees, clutching his ribcage. The guard groaned, until Alpha Three approached and his weathered hand silenced him.

They had to move quickly. As soon as the patrol failed to check in, more would likely be sent. Both Alpha Three and Four began to search the wreckage, looking for anything of any use. They searched from the direction the wind was blowing, giving them the best chance of seeing anything through the thick screen of smoke. Most of the helicopter was unrecognisable, but a few flares with a flare gun and their Medipack was recovered from its bombproof case. The cockpit was much the same as the rear, with a cluster of shredded wires and smashed glass.

"There's no way we can cancel the distress call," announced Alpha Four, as he stared at the jumble of computer systems.

"What about sending a second message?"

"Does anything in here look capable of sending a message?"

Alpha Three didn't answer.

"We'll just have to hope that the other two are having more luck," concluded Alpha Four.

***

Still in the tall grasses, Alpha Five watched the guards slowly increase their perimeter. Most were no longer between him and the main village. He caught sight of a flash over to his right. It lasted less than a second, but he knew Alpha Seven, however she'd got a hold of a flashlight, had found a way in. The HAHA had also slowly moved out and was now circling the crater's perimeter.

He waited another few seconds, then sprinted towards the village's open gateway. He'd gone from prone to running almost as quickly as he ran into his next cover within the village. There were simply built buildings, mainly made from wood, with few places to hide. Alpha Five was only against one of these buildings, but moving from cover to cover, he slowly approached his target building. Standing taller than anything around, there was a brick house in the centre.

Only a couple of guards had walked into his line of vision, and neither saw the ghost that crept through their homes. As he went, Alpha Five checked every building he passed, but they were all identical; two double bunks, a square table, and four chairs. Not one had so much as a picture on the table or taped to their beds. It looked worse than a prison.

It had taken about fifteen minutes, but Alpha Five was finally within touching distance of the house. He peered through the window for just a second but saw all he needed. It was full of guards, patrolling every room. Although the house was set three storeys high and sat in a twenty-metre square area, each room appeared to have at least two guards at any given time. He quickly swept the perimeter. There were two doors on the ground floor, one leading down to a basement, and a total of thirty-nine windows, none of which were open.

Although whatever fired the missile wouldn't be in the house, some kind of radio probably was. By whatever means, he had to get inside.

One of the windows opened, Alpha Five froze.

"Alpha Five, I know you're out there." The voice bellowed from the central window on the top floor. It was a little more like a Juliet balcony, but the window didn't stretch all the way down to the floor. "I've got something that you want, and I know you've got something that I want."

Alpha Five slowly looked up to the window and saw Alpha Seven, bound and gagged, being clutched by a masked figure at the window.

"My guards will be preoccupied exterminating your other friends, so why don't you let yourself in and we'll have a little chat. I'm sure you can find your way up. After all, it must be like old times for you." The window closed and the surrounding area was plunged back into almost silence.

The other guards were nowhere to be heard around the crater, and the HAHA had moved even further out. Alpha Five thought quickly, hundreds of thoughts running through his mind like a computer on overdrive. *Who was he? It doesn't matter. How am I going to get in? A window? No, they're all shut. The door? But they'll be expecting that. How did he know who I was? Think about that later. How about a drainpipe? No, there's still no way in. It has to be the door, but how do I get past them? Think!* Thoughts continued to surge through his head until he saw the fuse box on the outside wall. A plan quickly came together.

Alpha Five spent a couple of crucial minutes heading away from the house, looking for one of the patrolling guards. Once he'd found his target, he approached and removed the guard as quickly as a coiled snake could strike. Now Alpha Five had a suppressed rifle to work with. He headed back to the house, opened the fuse box and fired five bullets into it. The house was submerged into a near blackness, only illuminated by the nearby fires. He then walked around the perimeter of the building, firing a single bullet into random windows, shattering the glass. If he couldn't apply stealth, then maybe he could inflict fear. The front door was bashed in, but he continued circling the building, shattering window after window. Once his final bullet had done its job, Alpha Five entered through the open door.

He had to be quick, the longer he took, the more the guards' eyes would adjust to the darkness. With purpose, he entered the house's corridor and climbed the first flight of stairs. Once on the first floor, Alpha Five had become one of the guards, moving around in the dark with the same fully-automatic rifle in hand. Even once their eyes had adjusted, all they could see of each other were silhouettes in the night. It took time, more precious time, but Alpha Five made it to the top floor. With his ear pressed up against what he was sure was the correct door, he listened for anything. There was a light shining from under the door. With confidence, he opened it and went in.

***

Alpha Three and Four made it back to Hawk's position and started to patch up his wounds with the medical supplies gathered from the wreckage. The debris hadn't ruptured any major organs and hadn't cut through any major veins or arteries, but it was the slow blood loss that was the greatest threat. After disinfecting the wound, and wrapping bandages around it, they stopped to consider their next move.

It was unlikely they'd be able to get Hawk back up the mountain, and knew they couldn't leave him. The next search party would have to arrive on foot, which at least gave them time to work on some kind of a shelter. Their worst enemy was the wind, able to inflict hypothermia quicker than the snow itself. Alpha Three dug a narrow trench in the snow, just wide enough for all three to fit snugly inside, whilst Alpha Four unravelled a large sheet of what looked like tinfoil. It was a part of their medical pack and was used to keep warm. All three lay down on the sheet in the trench, wrapped it over the top of them and covered it as best they could with snow. They were unable to disable the distress beacon, so help from the Molehill would be on its way, and if Alpha Five and Seven were unable to disable whatever took them down, their help would be in the same position as them.

They knew if anyone was coming, they'd take at least another twenty minutes to arrive, but to their surprise, and soon to be dismay, a helicopter could be heard approaching just a few minutes after going under the snow. The noise of its blades echoed between the mountains, making it sound more like a fleet of them were arriving. It continued to get closer and closer, all the time sounding as if it was already overhead. Cautiously, Alpha Four looked up and saw one of the last things he wanted to. The HAHA was circling the crash site.

"Is it one of ours?" asked Alpha Three, almost fearing the answer he was going to get back.

"No," replied Alpha Four. That was all he needed to say.

Now the sun had set, it was safe enough to look out of their trench without being seen. The HAHA shone a spotlight down on to the wreckage, picking out the guards lying on the floor. One of them had sat back up under the constant thud of the helicopter. The guard was clearly dazed, he could hardly hear anything aside from the HAHA and couldn't see anything through the snow being blown all around him. The HAHA then rose into the sky, tilted down, and released a bombardment of rockets on to the crash site. It was instantly lit up by a fiery orange, like a giant bonfire that had been lit with a pack of explosives. It was by some miracle that it hadn't caused an avalanche.

Whilst Alpha Three and Four had watched the events unfold on the ground, Hawk had been studying the helicopter. He knew of their previous encounters with the near indestructible beast, but he knew better than most that a chain is only as strong as its weakest link. He'd noticed two small flaps, one on each side, open intermittently. If the HAHA was really as indestructible as it looked, and had a completely sealed chassis, there had to be a way for it to intake air. Everything from the cockpit to the engines was sealed, but the two flaps must provide the clean air to keep it running. He couldn't see a pattern for when they opened and closed, so he studied them further.

Hawk retrieved the flare gun and loaded a single flare into its barrel. He took aim. He watched it time and time again, open… and close. Still, he couldn't predict it, but the more he watched, the more he just knew when they would open. It flapped up… Then down… Then up again… Then down… He fired.

The flare flew from the gun and was no more than a few centimetres away from the helicopter when the right flap opened again. The flare shot inside. At first, nothing happened, but then the engine started to make throaty noises, like someone gasping for air whilst coughing. Hawk knew what was happening. He imagined all the alerts going off inside the cockpit, flashing red lights telling the pilots how everything was overheating. The HAHA started losing height, and metre by metre it fell to the ground.

Hawk knew it wasn't going to erupt in a massive fireball, but that could be used to their advantage.

Almost gracefully, the HAHA landed on the snowy base of the mountain. Although the flare would've burnt out, the inside of the helicopter would be full of smoke. The side door opened and two pilots staggered out, gasping for air. They took in huge lungfuls of the freezing, smoky air, making them cough all the more. Before the pilots could recover, Alpha Four was stood over them, aiming his stolen rifle. One slowly raised his hands, still trying to get fresh air. The other collapsed to the floor, their face buried in the snow.

By the time Alpha Three had made it down with Hawk, the smoke had cleared and they went straight into the cockpit. Hawk sat in one of the two chairs. It was surprisingly spacious throughout, with enough room to carry around a dozen fully armed guards. Even the cockpit was larger than any Hawk had been in before, with two large, almost armchair-styled seats and a large enough control desk to make the instrument panel in a jumbo jet look insignificant. Hawk worked out how to use the radio and contacted the Molehill immediately, informing them of everything he knew.

****

*Eight Minutes Earlier*

Alpha Five stepped through the doorway and into the light. It took his eyes a few seconds to adjust, but he was relying on the masked figure wanting them alive for something.

"I'm glad you made it."

The voice was weak and every word was wheezy, like they were wearing some kind of breathing apparatus. When he shouted, it must've been through a megaphone of some description.

Alpha Five waited until he could see everything in the room. Alpha Seven was over to his left, tied to a lone chair. There were two guards, both pointing fully-automatic rifles at him, either side of the door he'd just entered through. Then there was the masked figure, directly ahead. The rest of the room was laid out like a bedroom, exactly as you'd find in a brochure advertising the house.

"Who are you?" asked Alpha Five.

"I can't say I'm surprised you don't recognise my voice. The last time we met, I was complete, but since your so-called 'Alpha One' fired a shot, removing half my face, I have changed a lot."

"Green Viper?"

"So, you do remember me," started the masked figure. "At least I used to be Green Viper, but when you killed Crabble, the Night Vipers were passed on to new ownership. Now, we are all used, like assets which are just expendable."

"Do you often talk to someone before killing them?" asked Alpha Five.

Even with a mask on, the figure still looked noticeably surprised. "I am not going to kill you. You are nothing more than bait. I want a bigger fish. I want Alpha One."

"Why don't you let me use your radio? I can call him for you,"

"No," replied Green Viper. "No, I have a plan of my own. You see, when your rescue party arrives, we'll shoot them down just as we did to you. Then, I shall take the vial you stole from the bank and take it back to Hailey, so that we can start over. The cure will fetch us more than enough to rebuild the Night Vipers, but once the Molehill hears of the rescue team's demise, they'll send everything, which will be met with destruction of equal measure; a bomb large enough to take down this entire mountain if we're getting specific."

Alpha Five knew about Hailey, the leader of the Night Vipers. It was hardly surprising that she wanted to break free of Fellscient, but there was one piece of the puzzle Alpha Five couldn't quite place.

"How did you know where we were?"

"Grenham's little lapdog sent me here to observe your next move. They knew the bank was the only location the antidote could be found, so he stationed me here a few weeks ago. My orders were to observe, nothing more, but I've decided to use my own initiative."

"So Grenham wanted us to leave with the vial?"

"No, it was Kale who told me not to engage. He told me that under no circumstances should you leave without the vial. You see, he wants his master's plan to fail, so he can just step into his shoes, but I'm only playing this game for myself." Green Viper's words were filled with hatred. Everything he did or said was purely out of spite. It was almost like he was spitting his words out.

Green Viper moved over to a small touchscreen panel on the wall and tapped in a few commands. The lights throughout the building sprung back on, as light once again poured into the dark streets around the house. He started nodding to himself, feeling his plan come together.

"When your rescuers are shot down, your friends will throw everything they have at me, but with the vial, I'll be safe from their wrath. That being said, I am willing to make you a peace offering. Give me the vial, and she can go free."

Alpha Five considered it for a moment.

"If you say yes soon enough, she might even be able to warn off the search and rescue," added Green Viper.

Throughout their conversation, Alpha Seven had stayed quiet. She hadn't had the gag around her mouth since Alpha Five had entered but had decided to take everything in instead. She saw the touch panel on the wall only activated with his finger. She also saw Alpha Five and the numerous plans running through his head, but staying quiet allowed Alpha Seven to complete one of her own.

She'd only told Alpha Five about getting in. Getting out was kept as a surprise.

"You know I told you how I got into a spot of bother when I went freelance?" asked Alpha Seven.

Green Viper was cautious about every word she was going to say, but intrigue got the better of him, so he turned to Alpha Five and waited for him to answer.

Alpha Five nodded.

"Well… I killed someone. Actually, I killed a lot of people."

"That's not where I thought your story was going," said Alpha Five.

Green Viper spun his head from left to right, as each person spoke, taking everything in; at least he thought he was.

"My sister was rushed into A & E with a drug overdose. It was all a bit of a panic and nobody asked any questions, so they didn't know we were related and I was assigned to help her, but there was nothing that could be done… She died."

"And what of the people you killed?" asked Alpha Five, as intrigued as Green Viper.

"When I went freelance, I dug a little deeper. It was no surprise she'd taken drugs, but the drug that had been pumped into her system wasn't one that she'd had access to. In fact, very few people had access to it, and only one lived in the area. He owned a palace, full of guards. One night, I snuck in and killed every single person with the help of a mix of drugs I stole from the hospital."

"I think you might be my new favourite person," started Green Viper, the anger in his voice had changed to admiration quicker than flicking a switch.

She ignored him and continued. "You see, it's easy enough to take someone out without even seeing them. I pumped a toxic gas into the ventilation. It was only weak but was enough for what I had to do."

Alpha Five had stopped asking questions, he knew there was a clue in what she was saying. It was then that he heard something, a hissing from outside. He knew he didn't have time to think, but he had to. *Has she put a gas in the vents? Where did she get it from?* Then, there was a '*POP*', the sound of an igniting flame. He charged forwards and leapt on to the chair to cover Alpha Seven as the door blew in, sending a ball of fire throughout the building and out of every window. The door was blown clean from its hinges and was thrust into Green Viper. The other two guards were too close to the explosion. They were shown the quickest way out of the building.

"What was that?" shouted Alpha Five, as he quickly untied Alpha Seven.

"I slipped a small canister of gas on to the roof. They thought they'd caught me trying to do something, when actually they'd caught me after I'd finished. Turning the backup generator on started a chain reaction," she replied.

"But how did you know I'd disable the power?"

"Because I know how you think."

"How are we still alive?" asked Alpha Five.

"It wasn't the most volatile of gases, that's why it took so long to ignite and why it burnt out almost instantly. The force you felt was from a compression of air, not the explosion."

"A compression of air?"

"I'll explain later, let's just disable the turrets," concluded Alpha Seven, as they left the building.

The guards that hadn't been blown from the building were staggering around it, but none of them were in a position to provide any resistance. On the way out, Alpha Five and Seven each collected a fully loaded rifle from the dazed guards.

"There's a control room just down the road, that's where we can disable the turrets," shouted Alpha Seven, as she led him down the road.

"Where did the compressed air come from?" shouted Alpha Five, as alarms cried out all around the crater.

"It's simple, when they powered up the generator, it ignited a small fuse I'd put in earlier, which in turn started a slow chain reaction, causing the canister to explode. The explosion was small, but it was enough to light the compressed air they use in their ventilation system, ironically used to extinguish any fires. Anyone within a metre of the air ducts on each floor took the brunt of the force, and anyone close to the ground felt next to nothing."

Alpha Five didn't reply, he was now focussed on the control room they were approaching. That, and how Alpha Seven knew so much about blowing a building up without harming them.

"Was any of that story the truth?" asked Alpha Five.

"You seriously want to do this now?" replied Alpha Seven, just as they approached the control room.

"Was it true?"

"No, none of it. I was just trying to tell you that the building was about to blow," she replied.

"Alpha One has always said that every lie has a grain of truth to it."

She ignored the comment and kicked the door down. They entered together, both rifles raised.

"Clear!" shouted Alpha Seven.

"Clear!" replied Alpha Five, slightly quieter. He sat down in the metal, foldable chair and started tapping the keys on the single keyboard, attached by a wire to a single computer screen. "It's done. They're shut down."

Alpha Five stood up, raised his rifle, and started smashing the computer screen and keyboard with the stock of his rifle. Reactivating the turrets from there would be impossible now.

As they left the control room, guards were everywhere. None of them seemed to know what they were doing, and were scattered, running in every direction like ants looking for food. They both headed to the outskirts of the crater, trying to gain height and cover for when their exfil arrived.

They'd almost made it to the crater's bank when they heard an approaching helicopter. Moments later, it rose up from behind the crater, hovering like a hornet; the HAHA.

Once it reached the top, it flared, and turned to face the crater, its two twin-mounted mini guns spooled. The side door opened, and Alpha Three's head popped out.

"Are you coming, or what?" he shouted over the noise of the blades.

Neither of them could hear him, but his face was clear enough to know it was friendly. They continued towards the HAHA.

Suddenly, they were thrown in the air, as what felt like a giant hand pushed them forwards. Alpha Seven was further up the crater's bank and rushed back to get Alpha Five on his feet. He looked down and saw a smouldering, black circle with an orange ring of fire around it just a few metres below him.

"Come on, it was an RPG," shouted Alpha Seven. At least it looked like she was shouting, but all he heard was a faint whisper.

"The vial," he muttered, reaching into his pocket and feeling for the case. It felt badly scuffed but hadn't been breached. He turned to see if any guards were in pursuit. They were a long way back but firing bullets towards them. It was at that moment that Alpha Five felt something hit his chest. It was so powerful it took his breath away and knocked him back to the ground. He was pulled to his feet yet again, and they continued towards the HAHA. He wasn't even sure what was going on, as he was pushed into the helicopter.

The HAHA opened fire, spitting thousands of bullets out in seconds. Buildings were turned to rubble just as quickly. There was smoke everywhere inside the helicopter.

"Hawk doesn't think we'll make it back to the airfield, so we've arranged for an exfil to pick us up a few miles away, assuming the engines don't overheat before we make it," shouted Alpha Three, as the noise from the wheezing engine also droned on.

"Leave the doors open, we won't make it otherwise," called Hawk from the cockpit. "Are we ready to leave?"

Alpha Five retrieved the case from under his jacket. There was a bullet hole in one side but just a dent in the other. The case had saved his life, but it may have cost thousands their own. Nobody needed to look inside, as a green gel oozed out of the hole.

"Yes, take us out of here," said Alpha Seven.

The helicopter spun around and headed away from the crater, carrying everyone in a deathly silence.

# Chapter 14 – The Deceit of the Deceptive

13th September

13:40 BST

6 hrs 33 min. Until Deadline

Grenham, Kale, and the remaining seven masked guards landed in a clearing, in a Senegalese jungle, in a two-helicopter convoy. In the first was Grenham, Kale, and two of the guards. Their journey was silent. Kale had considered throwing Grenham from the helicopter on numerous occasions but thought better of it. There were far better ways he could take his life, as callously as he had taken the life of one of Kale's own. Grenham had no value for life, Kale was sure he would show him the same regard. The helicopters had landed at the top of a short hill, standing just higher than the jungle itself. Down the hill was another clearing and a sawmill. The entire area had been cleared about ten years ago, with the sawmill placed at the same time. It was, as with most things owned by Fellscient, a front, hiding its true purpose as a safe house. Over the years, it had been used as a haven for those in trouble, with the surrounding, dense jungle providing ample protection. Although several times, much like this time, it was used to hold gatherings of the highest members of Fellscient.

Their walk down the hill was just as silent. There was a high presence of guards. They weren't usually there, but due to the highest ranking members of Fellscient turning up, their entire organisation could be wiped out in one attack. Nobody needed to check them in, or check any passes. There were hundreds of cameras throughout the clearing, all scanning their faces, the way they walked, even the blood vessels running within them, using cameras too small to see and an offsite server farm an acre big. From the outside, the sawmill looked exactly as any other. There were piles of logs stacked up as if they were ready to be taken away. Every piece of machinery was perfectly preserved, as if it was used and cared for every day. There were scratches and scuff marks on the main building, as if various tools had accidently marked them, and there was a thick layer of sawdust over much of the compound. Considering the fact the sawmill had never been used as one, the detail Fellscient had gone to, to make it look genuine, was beyond belief.

Inside the main sawmill building, there was a trapdoor hidden under another log pile. It was a combination of concrete and cast iron and needed a strong hydraulic system to lift it. Its vast weight meant that only by activating the hydraulics could the door be opened, so there was no need for any lock. Once lifted, all nine of Grenham's party descended the staircase that had been revealed. Inside wasn't like a secret passage you'd expect to find in a hidden tomb, but it was more of a modern-styled bunker, one that could keep you alive for years to come. In fact, that's exactly what it was, the kind of safe house that could keep you safe for up to five years with its own source of food and water. They didn't need to be shown the way, they'd all been there before. The meeting had taken place in the same room for the last nine years. It was the only room that looked medieval, with bare, stone walls, and a large, thick, handcrafted, wooden table in the centre with six matching chairs. The room was lit by nothing more than candlelight, with one dark corner.

They were the first to arrive. The seven guards waited outside, whilst Grenham took one of the seats and Kale stood behind him. It was the way the organisation had worked for centuries, only the limbs of the beast could take a seat, but Kale was counting down the minutes until he would take his own. They both waited in silence until, fifteen minutes later, and dead on time for their meeting, another member of Fellscient entered, the only other limb. He was an elderly gentleman, who was in his late seventies at best. His hair was a cross between grey and white, but he had a lot of it, sprouting from his head, face, nose, and ears. He held a walking cane, one that was no doubt custom made out of a tree that no longer existed. His three-piece suit was likely hand made by one of the greatest tailors of all time. His shoes, well, they certainly weren't bought from a high-street retailer. Yet no matter how much his outfit had cost him, he never bragged about his apparel, or told anyone where any of it had come from, or even let slip who had made them. He wore the highest quality clothes, not to show his wealth and power but simply because they were the clothes he liked the most.

"Marko, it is good to see you," said Grenham with a smile.

"Likewise, friend," replied Marko. His voice was weak and frail, but his diction was perfect.

"How have you been keeping?"

"Busy," answered Marko. They both shared a laugh before he turned his attention to Kale. "And how about you, Kale? What have you been keeping yourself busy with?"

"Murder, mostly." Kale then patted Grenham on the shoulder and smiled.

Marko laughed again, this time causing himself to cough. "I have always liked you, Kale."

"And I you, Marko."

Kale then moved over to Marko and gently squeezed his shoulder, reassuring him.

Out of everyone in Fellscient, Marko looked the least likely to be there, but he was by far the most respected member. In his younger years, he'd climbed the ranks of

Fellscient quicker than anyone previously, but it was his methods that people respected him for. He'd killed many people over the last sixty or so years, but every single one had been given a choice, to step aside and allow Marko past, or to stand their ground and have Marko walk over their dead corpse. At first, people laughed in his face, but that was always their final laugh. Now, even in his current state, people always got out of his way.

"When do you think our great leaders will arrive?" asked Grenham.

"I think one might already be here," said Marko.

An instant later, in the darkest corner of the room, a match was struck. The tiny, orange flame illuminated a silhouette of someone sat in the corner. They lit a cigar and flicked the match on to the floor.

"Is your sister not joining us?" asked Grenham.

The figure in the corner held the cigar up to his face, and for a second, it glowed a bright orange. The door opened again. This time a smartly dressed woman entered and stood in the shadows with the figure. She wasn't his sister but was the siblings' secretary. Her duties weren't limited to paperwork. As in some cases, like this one, she would speak on behalf of the siblings when they didn't want to waste their own breath.

"She will not be attending today, as she has some rather important business to attend to," said the secretary. Her voice was calm and soft. In some situations it was soothing, and somewhat relaxing, but in others it came across patronising and could infuriate whoever she was talking to.

"I'm sure we all have things to do that are important, but I thought these annual meetings were compulsory," said Grenham.

The secretary bent down so the figure in the corner could whisper in her ear.

"For you, yes," she said. The figure lifted the cigar back to his face, again causing it glow.

"Then let us get on," said Marko.

The secretary was the first to speak. "As I'm sure you're aware, this is the first meeting with just two limbs remaining. How likely are we to revive the third limb?"

"Crabble failed to appoint a successor," started Grenham, "so I believe only Anthony Mars can take over."

"Go on," prompted the secretary.

Grenham then gave the lead to Kale.

"Anthony Mars, known simply as Anthony, is a highly trained marksman. In his early years, he was trained by someone called Westbrook. Crabble was believed to have killed Westbrook, although no body was ever discovered."

"And the likelihood of this Westbrook still being alive is?" asked the secretary.

"Small but possible. He was at the top of a twenty-storey block of flats when it was destroyed, so survival does seem to be on the unlikely side of things. That being said, he was always a ghost, we have never been sure who Westbrook was, nor whether that was his real name." Kale then paused and brought the subject back to Anthony. "As far as Mr Mars is concerned however, Westbrook is most certainly dead. After a few years honing his already impressive skill set, he was recruited into Quentin Bosse's team. From there, he continued to improve his combat skills. As for now, I don't think anyone is capable of besting him in certain combat situations. His mind, however, might just provide the opening we require to get him to join us."

"But what if he doesn't join us?" asked Grenham. "Can we really operate while we are so low on numbers?"

Again, the secretary lowered herself to listen before relaying the message. "It is not the quantity of the members, but rather the quality."

"Am I right in saying that if someone kills Anthony before the twelve months is up, then they will be entitled to the seat?" asked Grenham.

The secretary nodded. "You are."

"Then why not decide who will take the seat, and then send them to kill Anthony as a test. Or better still, send multiple people in to kill him and the first one to do so gets the seat."

"What are your thoughts, Kale?" asked Marko.

"I am certainly dubious over Mr Mars' mental ability," admitted Kale. "Even if he were to join us, I would always be concerned of his intentions. I have, however, found a suitable candidate to take the seat. He isn't ready yet, but I am confident he will be before the twelve-month deadline."

"I'm surprised you haven't put your own name forwards," said Grenham.

"He has no need," said Marko.

The room fell silent.

A few moments later, the secretary spoke again. "As that conversation has run its course, how have your individual assignments been going?"

Marko spoke first this time. "Projects Stardom and Magic Wand are still going as planned and should be in operation by the end of next year. As for Project Charlie, I know it is over budget and two years past the deadline, but I am pleased to announce we are ready to begin the final stages."

"Everything is also going as planned at my end," said Grenham. "Project Cav… The ongoing operation is in order. Our captives have been prepared and are now ready for brainwashing. Our spy division continues to work tirelessly to put eyes and ears everywhere, whilst removing the enemies'. I have, however, pulled funding from Project Sixteen Sixty-Five. I know Hailey is unpleased, but the additional funding will be well spent on my project. As for Crabble's Project Fibonacci, I am pleased to say that it is still on track. With regards to my other project, Alchemy, Alpha team have been unsuccessful in obtaining the antidote, and their time is running short. Before long, their time will have run out completely and they will have failed, and with any political rivals removed, we will have a golden opportunity to seize power worldwide. I wonder just how long Daniel will want to stay on the losing side?"

"And you're sure this Daniel person is worth the effort?" asked the secretary.

"Well, Kale certainly thinks so. I trust that is who you alluded to regarding taking Crabble's seat?" asked Grenham.

Kale said nothing.

***

Outside, guards covered the sawmill and its surrounding area. Every inch was patrolled every minute. It was quite a change from the empty sawmill that could usually be seen. Whilst some guards were constantly on the move, others remained stationary, in cover, watching the surrounding area. Two of them, Adewayle and Antilles were positioned in the undergrowth, just a few metres into the jungle.

"Have you ever seen the boss?" asked Antilles.

"No."

"No, me neither. Why do you think we've been assigned to his personal escort? I mean, it's all a bit sudden, we've only just found out. Do you think it's for security reasons?"

"Nah. Rumour has it his last escort was found unsuitable. Apparently they spoke to him, that's a big no-no."

"They've probably been assigned duties like cleaning the toilets from now on," added Antilles.

"Yeah, assuming the toilets are at the bottom of the nearby canyon."

"Wait, you mean?"

"That's the rumour," said Adewayle.

They sat in silence for a few moments, watching the twisting labyrinth of the trees ahead.

"What do we do if we see someone out there?" asked Antilles.

"Shoot."

"What if they're friendly?"

"Our combat engagement booklet never mentioned if they were friendly. Anyway, how do you still not know what to do?"

"I've never been given anything more than cleaning the helicopters."

"You're lucky," started Adewayle, "I'm only allowed to clean the muddy trucks."

"And to think, we were the only two in the class to complete our training."

"Were you in my class?"

"Yes," said Antilles. "You must remember. We were with Frank, the one who used to sleepwalk."

"Oh yes, he ended up walking into the training officer's quarters and just sort of stopped, standing over the training officer whilst he slept. They say he was never the same… has to sleep with the light on now."

"Who, Frank?"

"No, the training officer. No, Frank was kicked out the following day and was picked up by the Night Vipers. I think he was on Crabble's island when it was under siege."

"How come he got kicked out and has seen more action than the two who made it through?"

"According to rumour…"

"Don't you know anything first-hand?" asked Antilles.

"According to rumour, the Night Vipers are made up entirely of those who failed to make the cut."

"No wonder they couldn't keep the island."

"Well, apparently the Night Vipers are just test subjects. Taini found a document detailing something about some drug that enhances your senses, strength, speed, the lot. They plan to test it on the Vipers because they're expendable."

"Didn't Taini find out any more?"

"I don't know, nobody's seen him since he told me and a few of the others."

"Romeo Three, Romeo Four, the boss is ready to move out. Head to the landing pad and secure it," came through their earpieces.

"Copy, check."

"Copy, check."

They both pushed the camouflaged netting away from them, wrapped it up and headed to the landing pad as quickly as they could. Neither of them wanted to find themselves at the bottom of a canyon.

***

Back underground, they'd discussed and updated each other on what had happened over the course of the last year. At this point, the one sat in the corner had finished his cigar, the indication to them all that their annual meeting was over. They'd travelled thousands of miles to discuss as much as they could in the time it took one of their leaders to finish his cigar. It was an odd custom, but one that had stood for many decades now.

However, this time things were slightly different. Usually once the cigar was finished, that was it, but this time he called the secretary down to whisper again in her ear.

"Kale, I believe you have one final point to add," she said.

They all turned to Kale.

"Indeed," he started. "As you all know, I joined this organisation many years ago, when I was rescued by you. I spent many, many months at the hands of those who took me, and I swore that I would not let one of them outlive me, but my search for them turned up no results."

Grenham spoke up. "We are all very sorry for…" but the figure in the corner simply raised his hand out of the shadows, his fingers outstretched, and silenced Grenham as if hitting his pause button.

Kale continued, "A couple of years ago, I had a conversation with our fine leader, and he was able to fill in a few gaps. You see, as I assume you already know, I was held captive just a few miles away from here, but I wasn't captured by an unknown group of mercenaries. I was captured by Fellscient, the ones who also saved me. And, if we're being specific, it was you Grenham who oversaw the entire operation."

"Now look," started Grenham, "I was only acting on orders. And it's not like I was actually there, torturing your men."

Kale nodded. "I'm glad you mentioned my men. What I also found out was that nobody was ever tortured there. The sounds were just recordings. The smell was just a concoction of chemicals. When I heard this, I really didn't know whether to squeeze the life out of the person telling me, or to ask why. Then it struck me. If no one was tortured, what happened to my men?"

"Okay, I think we've all heard…" again, Grenham was silenced by an outstretched hand.

"To my amazement, they all survived. However, the methods used on them were slightly different to me. They were brainwashed and have been administered with steady doses of various drugs every day since; the memories of their lives before blocked out completely. They were then assessed for loyalty, armed and dressed in all black clothes, complete with balaclavas, and finally, they were assigned to your personal protection where they remained to this day."

Grenham knew better than to speak, but instead slowly reached for the handgun in his holster.

"Now, I really didn't know how to feel when I saw the tattoo. I suddenly knew my men were alive, and that was the point that I realised they'd been under my nose this entire time. You hadn't even gone to the effort of removing my team's mark. Part of me wanted to kill every single person in this room. After all, I wasn't informed of their survival when I spoke to our leader those two years ago. But, as I realised when speaking to our leader just a few hours ago, that would achieve nothing, I was reminded of all the good I had done since joining Fellscient, and, although it took some time, I realised that not everyone is as evil as you. After all, I'd known for the last two years that you were the one who had me tortured. It was when I started to get suspicious about you that I dug into your past. For those two years I've known what you did, I've known it was Gold Viper who tortured me. How you removed him, when staging my rescue, so as to not waste a valuable asset. Yet I kept calm then, I kept calm every day since, and I am calm now, because I believe revenge is much like whisky. It might burn, but it's worth it, and the longer it ages, the better it gets. Finding out about my men, well that's when I decided enough was enough. When I reached out to our great leader once again, he helped me get back what was mine. For a brainwashing technique so effective and sophisticated, it was surprising that everything could be undone in just three minutes. It was all done whilst you sat in the warm embrace of your helicopter, before we took off to come here. A simple string of sounds, a short film of moving symbols and patterns, and one final word, the name of your operation, one almost mocking my own, 'Cavolo'."

Kale had stayed behind Grenham the entire time and could see how on edge he was.

Grenham's hand wrapped itself around the handgun, and the safety was flicked off, but suddenly, he felt a tight grip around his throat. Kale had wrapped the scarf he'd taken from Craig's dead body around his neck, and he pulled it tight.

"I'm afraid it is you who has become the hindrance," whispered Kale in his ear, "but it's alright, because you have always been expendable."

Grenham pulled the gun and fired it at each of the three people in front of him, but the gun did nothing more than click. Grenham was both confused and wriggling for his life. The figure in the corner again stretched his hand out into the light. He slowly let eight bullets roll off his hand and fall to the ground, before holding it back in the position to silence Grenham. As if it was the figure itself that caused it, Grenham stopped wriggling and sat silently in his chair, but Kale made sure the job was finished.

"Set the scene for Alpha team. They will be here within the hour," said the secretary.

"And my men?" asked Kale.

"They are quite okay. Everything Grenham did to them has now been undone, and they are once again your men."

"I am only sorry I did not find out sooner. Perhaps then none of this would have happened."

"We are sorry for your loss, Kale, but please be assured, it was Grenham's decision, not ours. We were also kept in the dark about them, which is one of the reasons we wanted to support you," said the secretary.

Kale knew it was a lie, but even he understood it was a necessary one.

One by one, the other three left the room and returned to their own helicopters. Kale was the last to leave, setting the scene, before finally taking one last look at the man who had given him so much but had taken away so much more.

As soon as he opened the door to leave, the remaining seven guards blocked his path.

"It is good to be back, Sir!" said one of them, before giving him an unusual sort of salute. The others then matched the salute.

Kale did nothing but smile.

# Chapter 15 – The Cost of the Cure
13th September
07:51 BST
12 hrs 22 min. Until Deadline

The platform lowered the BH4 helicopter to the base of the Molehill's hangar. Several medics were standing beside it and before the platform had even locked in place, they'd helped Hawk on to a stretcher and were carrying him away. He was still conscious, with bandages holding him together and painkillers dulling the pain, but now he needed surgery, and rest.

Samuel, Kenny, Mike, and Mia all followed him out, but their intentions of going with him were quickly altered. Bosse, accompanied by Daniel and Anthony, was waiting for them just a few paces away.

"I'm afraid you'll have to make do with rest on the plane. You've got a long flight ahead of you and time is of the essence. Scott will meet you there," said Bosse.

"Meet us where?" asked Mike.

"I'll explain everything en route. For now, though, you should have been in the air over an hour ago. Please do not waste any more time."

Bosse then turned and left the hangar. It was always hard to know whether he wanted someone to follow him or not, but Daniel and Anthony headed towards one of their C-8 Donkeys used for long-distance equipment and personnel transportation. The others followed without question. Their equipment had already been loaded, and within just five minutes, they were in the air, only sure of one thing, the clock had almost struck zero. Wherever they were heading was their final hope.

****

The flight was to take over six hours, giving them just six to find the cure and get it mass-produced. Giving them as much rest as possible, Bosse had allowed them the first four hours. The C-8 Donkey was spacious, especially with the limited equipment they were taking with them. They each had space to sleep and change. They then made their way towards the front of the plane, housing a separate room. That was where they'd meet with Bosse.

He was already waiting when Samuel, the last to arrive, closed the door. Bosse's face filled the huge 55" TV screen. Scott was on the TV to the side, with a slightly smaller 50" screen.

"You have less than two hours before you are due at your drop zone," started Bosse. "Daniel's latest encounter with Grenham and Kale gave us one final chance of finding the antidote before it is too late."

Nobody in the room made a sound.

"I know you might be apprehensive about this information, but as I said, this is our one and only chance of getting what we want. With the vial destroyed, the lives of all those people, innocent or otherwise, rests on your shoulders."

"What exactly was this information?" asked Mike.

"Kale provided the location of the recipe for this antidote."

"Are we sure the antidote even exists?" questioned Kenny. "It seems a bit of a coincidence that for every lead we've had, we've been one step behind. Now, all of a sudden, Kale is just giving us this cure; a cure for the poison that he released."

"I know it seems odd, and yes, this could very well be a trap, but you are better than the best of the best. There is no trap which can beat you. So, if there's only the slightest chance that this could pay off, then we are taking it," said Bosse.

"We?" questioned Anthony. "It seems like you made the decision for us."

"Time was short!" snapped Bosse. "I know that it may seem like we're running in blind, and yes, you will be going in alone. With Delta team on another assignment and Bravo team staying here until the heat on a conference centre that blew up a mere twenty miles from here dies down a bit. This is non-negotiable."

Again, the room fell silent.

"Where is this recipe?" asked Scott.

"In the middle of a jungle. The trees are too dense to get any kind of recon drone near enough without alerting the enemy. Hopefully we'll get satellite images, but they won't show much more than we already know. The plan is yours to come up with, but I expect perfect execution. There will be no second chances," said Bosse.

"And what happens if we find a recipe? We won't know whether it's actually the cure or whether it'll make things worse," added Mike.

"Daniel?" said Bosse. "What do you think?"

Daniel looked around the room. "I can't guaranty this isn't a trap, or that the antidote will work, or even that the antidote is there in the first place, but it's been Grenham trying to prevent us from getting it, and I think that Kale may just be the enemy of our enemy at the moment. I really do think it's in his best interest to help us. If we are walking into a trap, if we don't save those people, then I hope it isn't because we backed out or refused to follow a lead. We've got a chance of saving everyone, and that's all we've ever needed in the past."

Nobody could find the words to agree with Daniel, but they knew everything he'd said was true.

"I believe that settles it, then," said Bosse. "No matter how this goes, expect heavy resistance, and given your location, and the pressing time, I am authorising the use of real bullets. You'll find they've been packed along with those sedative rounds."

Bosse leant forwards, and then the screen turned black. Yet again, the only noise was that of the four humming engines outside.

Everyone turned to Alpha One.

"What's the plan?" asked Mike.

Scott sat silent for a moment longer. "The plan can wait. First, we need to discuss how this information came about."

"As you all know, I've been working undercover for Grenham, attempting to find the antidote," started Daniel without hesitation. "The first piece of intel that Kale gave me was the identity of the man who created both the poison and the antidote. We all know how that ended. So I went back, this time with Diana as back up, and I ended up getting a lot more than I'd bargained for." He paused. "I met my father. As some of you know, I joined Alpha team when I was involved in a car accident with my parents. I understood them to be dead, until yesterday. Now, I don't know how much Kale knows, or what he really wants out of this, but it seems like everything we have done has led us here, on purpose. I don't know why, but one thing my father said was that I was always meant to be here, and I've got a feeling he meant that literally."

"There's also something I should tell you," said Anthony. "When I killed Crabble, I mentioned a promise I'd made. It was a promise I made to myself. It was a promise to avenge Westbrook, my mentor, and I thought that killing Crabble would fulfil it. But when we were at the villa and I checked the sniper's position, I did find something." Anthony took out the shell casing he'd found.

Kenny leant over and looked at the marking on the side. "What is that?"

Samuel then took a closer look.

"It's meant to be a pigeon," said Anthony, "the code name that Westbrook used on our last mission together. It's the same as the shell casing I received in the post just a few days after his death. Somebody is messing with me and I want to know who, but I know it's got something to do with that hooded figure."

"As we're all confessing something," started Mia, "there's one thing you don't know about how my sister died." She took a deep breath before continuing. "I told Mike how she was rushed into A & E and how I tried to save her whilst I was working there. But what I didn't mention was that I was the one who discovered her and called it in. I was off duty at the time but still counted as the first responder. And on the wall she was propped up against was a symbol, almost a mural. It was of a beast, a mythical beast."

"A mngwa?" asked Scott.

Mia nodded. "I've seen the reports of the same tattoo on Mr Wilson, and on Gert, the Dutchman at the nightclub, but for whatever reason, it was left out of all the reports relating to my sister."

"Somebody's been manipulating us for a very long time," said Scott. "And we may not be able to undo the past, but we can stop whoever this is from controlling us further. I don't know what will happen tomorrow, or next week, or in a decade's time, but for now, I think Kale might be on our side and might be our only chance of saving those people. I can't promise we'll find our own answers in the middle of the jungle, but we've been brought here for a reason. I won't drag any of you along if you don't want to come, but I think it's about time we found out why."

Daniel stood up. "I agree, and I will join you. Even if we are no closer to finding out why we're here, at least we finally know we're heading in the right direction."

"I'm happy if we just find a cure for those people," added Mia.

One by one, the others stood up.

Scott smiled. "Good. Now before we start, has anyone else got anything they need to get off their chest?"

Everyone turned to Mike.

He raised his hands and shook his head. "Don't look at me!"

***

"Thirty seconds!" shouted Alpha Two as the Donkey's cargo door opened. The six members of Alpha team had a parachute strapped to their backs, a rifle strapped to their fronts, and wore jungle camouflage. Of course, Alpha Four had a whole rucksack over his chest. The C-8 Donkey was flying at the lowest altitude it dared over the endless trees below, all passing in a blur.

"Now!"

Alpha Two was the first to jump, pulling his chute as soon as he was clear of the plane. The others followed him out almost instantly, and within just a few seconds, the plane had all but vanished as they headed below the tallest trees. Before long, they'd formed a line in the air, all following Alpha Two as he drew towards the river winding through the jungle.

They were out in the open and drifting down softly when Alpha Two spotted a red spark just above the water. The red torch burned brighter the closer they got, even reflecting off the murky, green river. Alpha Two approached the light, pulling down hard on his chute and lifting his legs as he skimmed above a patch of long grasses on the bank. As soon as his legs hit the ground, they started running, trying to reduce their speed. Before Alpha Two had even stopped, the parachute was being gathered up so it didn't catch a freak gust of wind. As he turned to see the rest of the team do the same, he looked back towards the red light. Alpha One threw the red flare into the river. The green quickly covered the vibrant red as it sank to the bottom.

Alpha One climbed into the boat that was half over the riverbank. "Pleasant flight?"

"We've had worse," said Alpha Two, as he and the rest of Alpha team climbed in.

Alpha Three was last to enter, pushing the boat fully into the water before leaping in. The motor was started, and they were heading upstream.

"Where did you get the boat from?" asked Alpha Five.

"There's a village just downstream. I haven't a clue how they got it, but they seemed willing to lend it to me; for the right price, anyway. Fortunately, I know a lot of the tribe, not that they were willing to give me a discount on the boat," replied Alpha One over the noise of the motor behind them.

"I thought it would smell worse," shouted Alpha Three.

"It's a river, not the Everglades," replied Alpha Four.

Their journey may have been little more than a mile as the crow flies, but heading through the twisting river, it was more like five. Even if they were in a boat that seemed intent on skimming along the water like a flat stone, it took a lot longer than any of them wanted.

Eventually they reached their destination, or as near as the boat could take them. Rounding the final bend, they were faced with a waterfall. They'd grounded the boat about fifty metres back, but the noise of the torrent pouring over the edge of the cliff was already deafening. There was a narrow section of trees on a small bank, with more water running perpendicular on the other side. The only way through was to continue down the short stretch of water on foot. It was shallow, allowing them to wade in it for the entire two hundred metres. The trees closed in on both sides, making it impossible to see if anything lurked at the water's edge, let alone under the green water itself.

"How come we haven't seen any alligators?" shouted Alpha Three.

"Because they don't live here," replied Alpha Four.

Eventually, they made it to the end of the second river, where the path started to go up. The noise of the waterfall was surprisingly dulled by the thick layers of trees and foliage. Their CAT devices had made a nearby scan of the jungle's elevation changes. It had found them the shallowest gradient to climb the hill but couldn't account for the foliage blocking their path.

"What about crocodiles?" asked Alpha Three.

"Asleep. You've got more chance of seeing dolphins."

"Dolphins?" scoffed Alpha Three.

"He's right, you know. River dolphins do tend to live in rivers," added Alpha Five.

"River dolphins are a thing?" asked Alpha Three.

They headed through the jungle in single file, Alpha Two cutting through any branches or bushes with a long machete Alpha One had picked up from the village. They cut their way through the thinnest parts, all the while heading up and around the monstrous waterfall. Their target was a sawmill, half a kilometre to the east. According to the satellite images, there was a clearing near the location which had had a large presence of helicopters just an hour prior. Whilst the sawmill itself wasn't visible from above, previous images had shown its inactivity for over ten years.

Security around the sawmill would be high, but not high enough. The density of the jungle, and the dangers within it, would make any guard sceptical about how they could be found. After all, it wasn't uncommon for training exercises to take place nearby. As far as they were concerned, if they heard a plane flying overhead it was just another training exercise, which had gone slightly off course, with no risk of their location becoming compromised. It would be like stumbling across a needle in a mile-long haystack, except Alpha team were looking for it with a magnet.

"What about snakes?" asked Alpha Three.

"They'll mainly be in the trees, which is surprising for a species that tends to dislike falling. Then again, they have been known to drop down on to their prey," said Alpha Four.

Alpha Three's head slowly lowered into his jacket, his neck vanishing altogether. "Do I even want to ask about spiders?"

"Somehow, I doubt it."

Eventually, the first signs of the location came into view. There were two watchtowers, built into the largest trees, which stood sentry near the perimeter of a clearing.

"Is this the place?" asked Alpha Two in a low whisper.

"Must be," replied Alpha One. "Look at the clearing. It's only the ground that's open. The trees still overhang it, which must be what conceals it from above. There's probably enough room to fly a helicopter in for transport, but that's about it."

"Two on each watchtower," said Blindspot. "They're using standard camouflage." He was looking through his infrared scope. "Are we taking them out or trying to slip past?"

"We take them out."

"Are you sure you want to use the sedative rounds? Bosse seemed pretty adamant with the order he gave us," questioned Alpha Two.

"I'm sure. It's my decision and it stands. Now everyone to your positions," replied Alpha One, crouching down.

Blindspot found his first target and fired his suppressed weapon. He steadied the muzzle, and then fired again.

"Two on the left are down." His rifle swung to the right. He fired another two shots in quick succession. "We're clear."

They all advanced towards the watchtowers. It was only when they got to them that they could see the sawmill, and that was exactly what it was, a sawmill. It was a huge building made from wood, with tools and machinery scattered everywhere. There were several piles of logs stacked up in various places. If you'd just so happened to walk through, you'd think it was a working sawmill. The machinery was old but cared for. The logs seemed freshly cut. The building was covered in a thick layer of dead leaves, but the one thing that looked out of place, was the floor. There wasn't so much as a leaf or twig in sight. It had recently been cleared.

"You all know the plan. Let's get on with it," said Alpha One.

Blindspot climbed up on to one of the watchtowers. From the ground, it looked just like an ordinary tree, but there were reinforced, man-made branches at convenient places to climb the trunk and reach a kind of platform that was made in a similar way to a giant bird's nest. Twigs, branches, and sticks were all intertwined to make the platform secure, but also invisible.

"Hold," said Blindspot.

Everybody did as he said, freezing in their tracks. They'd already started to split up, with Alpha One and Two heading to the left, and Alpha Four and Seven heading to the right where they could check the second clearing for enemy activity.

"There are three pairs of armed guards lying in the undergrowth around the perimeter of the clearing. They're wearing more camouflage," said Blindspot, every word clear and concise. He aimed his rifle towards the first couple and fired twice. He then moved on to the next and fired another two times, and then the same with the third couple. "All targets down."

They continued to move closer, but it wasn't to be for long. As Alpha Two's feet rustled through the leaves, which were all a dull shade of brown, he failed to notice two small boxes. They were coloured to blend in with the ground and the thin, red line between them was impossible to see with the naked eye. As his leg passed between the two boxes and the red light lost contact with the other box, a silent alarm was sent to the control centre at the sawmill. Usually, the room would be unmanned, but they were expecting visitors and this had confirmed it. Within just a few seconds, the two guards inside the control room had viewed all the camera feeds around the sawmill, displaying standard, thermal, and infrared images. It had taken them only another five seconds to spot the armed operatives moving closer. After the large, red button was depressed into the table, an alarm rang out within the sawmill. Every guard still stationed there sprang to life, throwing on bulletproof vests and gathering their rifles and ammunition. Just under thirty seconds after the red light had broken its contact with the second box, several doors of the sawmill swung open and the jungle was filled with the noise of gunfire.

Alpha Two leapt into a ditch a few feet in front of him. Bullets had already started flying everywhere, hitting trees, the ground, and disappearing out of sight. Alpha One had crouched and taken cover behind one of the trees, but he knew they had to move.

"On three!" he shouted to Alpha Two, but no counting followed, out loud anyway.

Alpha One pulled a grenade from under his vest and threw it towards the edge of the jungle's border. Just as smoke started pouring from it, both Alpha One and Two had counted to three in their heads. Simultaneously, they rose to their feet and headed for the ever-increasing area of fog. With bullets hitting only their shadows, they both made it to the smoke, but they were no safer, as shots were fired randomly. Neither slowed down, they knew where they were heading, and nothing was going to change that.

Outside the smoke, a guard had pulled the pin out of his own grenade. He was ready to throw it, but before he had the chance, everything went blank. Blindspot had seen him and fired a single shot to his chest, but that hadn't stopped the grenade rolling out of his hand as he dropped to the floor. Just as Alpha One and Two emerged from the smoke, the grenade blew, throwing shrapnel everywhere and ripping a hole in the side of the sawmill. As they covered their faces, Alpha Two saw just what damage it had done. The hatch they were heading for had been blown clean off its hinges, giving them a much easier way in.

Most of the guards were concentrating their fire on the rest of the team, and the few that were trying to stop Alpha One and Two were not enough, especially not with Blindspot providing assistance. Just as they were heading down the steps that had been revealed by the missing cellar trapdoor, a bullet finally found its mark. It punched its way into Alpha One's vest, sending him stumbling down the steps. On reaching the floor at the bottom, he took just a few seconds to check for any wounds, but the bullet had been stopped by the vest.

"It didn't go through," confirmed Alpha Two as he took a look.

"It doesn't stop it from hurting though," replied Alpha One, getting helped back to his feet.

There had been very little communication between each of them once the shooting had started, speaking only when necessary, so when they heard, "RPG!", they knew it was serious. Both started running further down the dark corridor they found themselves in, until, just a couple of seconds later, the ground threw them off their feet. Dust and mud rained down from the tunnel's bare ceiling. Then, the ceiling itself started to crumble. Almost as if it was melting, it slowly came down. They had enough time to leave and head back to the surface, but that wasn't where they were needed. The ceiling near the entrance made contact with the floor, and the tunnel was sealed in from the outside. There had been dim lights running along the ceiling, but they had swiftly gone out in the collapse. With all light from the outside also cut off, they clicked on their flashlights, on the ends of their rifles, and began to move deeper underground. The only way, was forwards.

***

Alpha Four and Seven were focussing their fire on the guards taking cover inside the sawmill. They'd seen the tunnel collapse to their left, leaving a narrow gully in its wake, but they couldn't think about that. Their target was the clearing to their right. Satellite images had shown there were still helicopters there, and whoever got to them first would be in control.

"We're both okay," said Alpha One over a crackly line. "We're heading further underground, so may lose radio contact. Best of luck."

"We've got to get up that hill!" shouted Alpha Seven, as she ducked down behind a rock.

"Agreed."

"We can head back towards the jungle behind us, then up the hill, but we'll have to be quick," she added.

Alpha Four nodded in agreement, and they both kept their heads low and backed away from the sawmill clearing. There was a small bank behind them which they slid down, taking them out of the line of fire, for the time being. They moved along the bank and further into the jungle. Travelling as quickly as they could, hurdling any roots and low branches, ducking under any higher ones, they kept the clearing just in sight, but the guards would only have a short dash up the hill. Blindspot would no doubt be taking out as many as he could, but there were too many even for him.

Alpha Four and Seven climbed up a steep bank, their boots slipping on the loose mud, their hands clawing at the dead leaves. At the top, they saw the clearing again, only a few metres ahead, and they'd made it before the enemy, but as Alpha Four looked down the hill, it was obvious neither would make it to any of the six helicopters before they were fired upon.

"Let's stay in cover, we've got the advantage. We'll let them come close, then open fire," said Alpha Four.

"Have you got anything in your rucksack that might useful?" asked Alpha Seven.

He smiled. "Always."

***

As soon as the final guards heading up to the helicopters had disappeared from Blindspot's line of sight, he reloaded his rifle, then sat still and silent in the trees. Alpha Three and Five had slowly started to retreat further into the jungle. As soon as they were out of the guards' sight, they split up and took cover amongst the foliage. The dead leaves and fallen branches wouldn't protect them from incoming bullets, but they would help to keep them hidden.

Blindspot counted, as twenty-one guards approached their last known location. More had stayed back around the sawmill, whilst what must have been the last few headed back inside, no doubt trying to find Alpha One and Two.

"We're activating a jammer," said Alpha Four. "It'll knock out our comms and CATs until I switch it off."

Without waiting for a reply, the jammer was activated and they were on their own. But so were the guards. Of the twenty-one guards, two of them stayed near where Alpha Three and Five had been. They'd separated themselves from the rest of the group, which saved Blindspot the job, but their worst mistake was still being out of sight from those who stayed back at the sawmill.

Blindspot grabbed a branch from the tree he was in and threw it down a few metres away from the guards. They both turned in its direction, one turning his back on the other. Blindspot lined up a shot on the one at the back and fired. As the other guard turned to see what the noise right behind him was, the noise of the guard hitting the ground, he too found himself hit with a sedative-laced bullet and hit the ground.

"Nineteen left," muttered Blindspot, as he looked further down the slope the other guards were on. They had also split up, deciding their two targets were hiding rather than running. Blindspot watched them all through his thermal scope. One had ventured too far from the group and could no longer be seen by them. Blindspot took the shot. Then, there were eighteen.

Alpha Five watched as two approached him. They were less than a metre away, but they still couldn't see him. They took a step closer.

"One more," he whispered.

As if they'd heard him themselves, they both moved another step in his direction. There was a snap from behind, where one of Blindspot's bullets had hit a branch, causing them both to turn their backs on Alpha Five. He leant up and grabbed one of the guards, kicking his knees and pulling him to the ground. He fired a single shot at the other, allowing him to fall by himself. Another guard had seen all this happen, but Blindspot made sure he didn't tell anyone. Alpha Five covered the guard's mouth and fired another shot. The guard was still in an instant.

Others had heard all the movement, but they arrived to only see one guard lying on the ground, the others already concealed by the jungle's floor. Another guard found themself away from the group, and as with the others, unconscious. Alpha Three saw the next one, just a few metres in front. He drew his handgun and fired. The guards turned to see another fall. Then Alpha Five had the same idea, so the guards turned in yet another direction. Blindspot delivered another shot, leaving just eleven. To the guards, they were just dropping for no reason. It didn't matter which direction they turned, they only ever saw one of their own.

They tried to radio through to get reinforcements, but no message got there. Two guards decided to head back to try and get some help. Blindspot knew they were too close to the others. If he shot, his position would be compromised. He looked towards the others in the group and found another target. This one wasn't out of sight, but would provide the perfect distraction. As the two guards approached, Blindspot shot the one he'd lined up. The others looked towards that falling guard, as Blindspot leapt from the trees. He landed on one of his targets, bringing him down with his rifle, before swinging it round and knocking the feet from under the other. As swiftly as he dropped on to them, Blindspot drew a handgun and shot both guards in the temple. He then dived into cover, rustling the leaves as he went.

The eight remaining guards were torn between firing randomly and shouting for backup. Alpha Three saw the first go to shoot at the trees but managed to fire a bullet faster, taking him down, but compromising his own position in the process. Another two took aim and went to fire, but Alpha Five shot one in the side of the head and charged into the other. He too was spotted. Alpha Three fired at another, but missed as the guard took cover.

One emerged from the trees on Alpha Three's right but fell to the floor before he could line up a shot. Blindspot was still using his infrared scope, highlighting each guard through the trees. The one who had taken cover from Alpha Three started to crawl through the undergrowth to reposition, but Blindspot identified him and fired. He laid motionless on the ground. The final three were all further down the hill and were running to get back to where the commotion had broken out, but Blindspot took them down, one after the other, with three consecutive shots. He stood up and joined Alpha Three. They looked towards Alpha Five, ensuring the guard he'd tackled was down, but as they turned to him, Alpha Five's gun was raised. He fired four shots past them with his handgun. They both turned and saw two more guards fall forwards, both with two green smudges at centre of mass.

"We need to get moving," said Alpha Five. "They came down because the others hadn't reported back. When they don't return, we can expect a lot more."

"Maybe that could work in our favour," said Alpha Three with a grin.

***

*Two Minutes Earlier*

"How far down do you think this tunnel goes?" asked Alpha Two.

"I haven't a clue, but it seems odd to even have it," replied Alpha One.

"How do you mean?"

"Well, if you had armed personnel waiting inside the sawmill, why would you have a secret passageway on the outside? If it was inside, we still wouldn't be through."

"Maybe this is just a dead end," suggested Alpha Two.

"Maybe, but there's no turning back now."

They slowly continued down the tunnel, sloping at a constant sixty-degree angle, with their rifles held high.

"Do you mind if I ask you something?" asked Alpha Two.

"Of course not, so long as this is the right time."

"Well, it isn't the wrong time."

Alpha One stopped for a moment, almost more out of hesitation. *What does that mean?* he thought. The hesitation wasn't big, but the torch fixed to his rifle lowered for a second, and Alpha Two noticed.

"Is what we do really helping?" he asked.

"How do you mean?" replied Alpha One, fully aware what he meant.

"When we help people, nine times out of ten, it's a job requested by the elite, someone who has enough money to invest in us. Then what happens, assuming it's actually a credible threat, which it mostly isn't, what happens then?"

"That's up to the client, not us," said Alpha One, "and one case out of ten is better than none. We're only here because of the people who give us that money. Without them, everyone who's been poisoned wouldn't even have a chance of surviving."

"But what happens to all the people here? All of our enemies that we've taken down?" Alpha One wasn't given the time to respond. "I'll tell you what happens, exactly the same as the ones we took down on Crabble's island. We handed them over to local law enforcement and within just a few months, they were all released. How many of them do you think have just been shooting at us?"

"I know it isn't ideal, but we don't have the resources to keep all of them locked up forever."

"All of them? We barely have the resources to keep some of them locked up. What about John Broady? Have we heard anything from our client since handing over the confession?"

"What exactly are you getting at here?" asked Alpha One.

"What we're doing isn't working. Something needs to change. All we do is take people down, and then just watch them get right back up again. You take everything one step at a time, instead of looking at the future."

"I'd rather focus on getting the antidote before planning how to administer it, if that's what you mean."

Alpha Two began to speak, but Alpha One's clenched fist was held in the air.

"Lights out."

Both turned their flashlights off and were plunged into darkness, all except for the dim, cosy light gently glowing at the end of the tunnel. Whispered voices then filled the passage, and both Alpha One and Two approached the light slowly, and silently.

The whispered voices continued to grow louder.

"Have we got radio contact back with the group upstairs yet?"

"No, they must be using some kind of jammer on the surface."

"You think we're in danger down here?"

"Probably, but even if we are, no one is going to get past us."

"Supposing they did?"

"At least I'd know that I went out fighting."

Alpha One and Two continued to close in, still a part of the darkness. Even though they couldn't see each other, they knew instinctively when to move in. Together, their rifles emerged from the shadows. The two guards inside the dimly lit room were facing the other way but turned to see the two menacing figures loom over them. Both guards held their hands up slowly, their own rifles out of reach on the table a few metres to their left.

"Please don't hurt us, we surrender."

Both Alpha One and Two fired a single shot, rendering both guards unconscious. The room they found themselves in was lit only by a fire, burning softly in one corner. The walls, floor and ceiling were all still made of mud. It was an odd room to find at the end of a tunnel, but it was the solid, steel door which was more what they expected.

Also to their surprise, the door opened by simply pulling the handle.

"It's just unlocked," said Alpha Two, the handle still clasped in his hands.

"I assume this is used as a means of escape, in case someone breaches the other entrance, although I doubt we're still that near to the sawmill itself. We should enter with caution, it may be unlocked because someone wants us inside."

A small rumble could be felt in the room they were in, with more mud raining down as a fine mist.

"You think that was Alpha Three?" asked Alpha Two.

"I'd put money on it."

***

*Two Minutes Earlier*

With the jammer in place, and the guards unable to call for help, Alpha Four and Seven watched them approach the six helicopters. The guards were cautious, but quick. They circled the helicopters, checking in and around them for anyone, before climbing in to five of them. A few formed a perimeter, as the helicopters' blades started spinning.

With the flick of a switch, Alpha Four had primed an odd-looking grenade in his hand. A second later, he stood up and threw it towards the helicopters. Although its detonation was silent and invisible, the blades on the helicopters started to slow down. The pilots began flicking switches and pressing buttons repeatedly. Then, Alpha Four's rifle made the sound of an electric toothbrush being switched off. He looked down to see the small green light above the magazine had gone out. He pulled the rifle's trigger, but the only thing it could do was 'click'.

"Okay, so note to self. EMP effects a slightly larger area than expected," he said out loud.

The guards had started walking around the helicopters again, throwing their arms up in the air, gesticulating to each other. Alpha Four looked over to Alpha Seven. She was about ten metres away, holding a green box about the size of a toolbox. With a nod from Alpha Four, she twisted the dial on one side and held the opposite side towards the clearing. Again, nothing could be seen from the device, but the guards in front of it seemed to feel its effect. Some held their heads as if they were about to explode, others clutched their stomachs as they were overcome with an immense feeling of nausea.

Alpha Seven didn't know how the machine worked, but it was clear just what it was doing to the guards. From the corner of her eye, she saw Alpha Four stand up with his handgun and fire at each of them. As far as they were aware, he was shooting to kill them all, but they couldn't do anything, even their minds started to go numb with the anguish running through their bodies.

Two of the helicopters' cargo doors were sealed shut, and the pilots inside seemed unaffected by the device. To start with, they seemed even unaware of what was going on around them, but eventually, they swung the doors open and before their feet touched the ground, they were both curled up, holding their stomachs.

The guards didn't feel the rumbling ground, nor did they notice the orange flame glimmering through the trees, but Alpha Seven did. As soon as each of the guards had been taken down, she switched the dial back down to its original position and placed it on the ground.

"Do you think they're okay?" she shouted to Alpha Four.

He turned to where the explosion had taken place and scoffed. "Of course, it would've been Alpha Three, that's all."

Seemingly without any need for concern, Alpha Four checked around all the helicopters, ensuring he hadn't missed anyone, whilst Alpha Seven split the device into three parts, two smaller boxes, which in turn flattened to the size of a laptop, and a circular drum-shaped object with wires hanging out everywhere. That too folded down, much like a spyglass would, and before long, the large box was plenty small enough to fit in Alpha Four's rucksack.

"How did you know you would need that? I mean, I can't imagine there's much room for anything else in there," said Alpha Seven.

"You'd be surprised just how much I can fit in here," he replied, packing the device and the EMP grenade into his bag. "But no, I didn't know I'd need it. This was just one of the many things I packed to test in the field, much like the EMP, although that has knocked out all electronics within a one-mile radius. You see, setting 'one' is actually the strongest, and setting 'nine' is the weakest, for some reason."

"Do you think they need any help?"

"Probably, but they've got their mission, we've got ours," he replied.

***

*Two Minutes Earlier*

Alpha Five and Blindspot had just finished dragging all the bodies into the bushes and low-growing shrubs, concealing them, when they heard more guards approaching from the sawmill. They both got into cover themselves and were shortly joined by Alpha Three, holding a stick of dynamite.

"What's wrong with just a detonator?" asked Alpha Five.

"It won't pair, I think someone's set off an EMP."

Alpha Five inspected his rifle. "Rifle's down too, we need to switch to our secondary, they're completely analogue." Both Alpha Three and Five placed their rifles behind their backs and drew their handguns. Blindspot didn't. His rifle was still firmly in his hands. "It won't work," said Alpha Five.

Blindspot waited for the noise of the guards to get louder before aiming his rifle into the trees. He fired a single shot, which tore through a branch, bringing it crashing to the ground.

"I don't have handprint recognition on mine," he said, removing the scope, which could no longer display a thermal image, from the top of his rifle. "That branch is over the grenades, it'll stop them at the right time."

Sure enough, the guards did stop at the fallen branch, blocking the already overgrown path leading down the hill. Alpha Three struck a match, on a patch of flint sewn into his trousers, and lit the fuse on the dynamite. When it'd almost completely burnt away, he threw the stick so it landed a couple of metres in front of the fallen branch. A second later, it exploded, igniting with it two packs of explosives. The guards fell backwards, covering their faces as an orange ball of fire rolled into the air. In turn, the shock wave made its own small clearing, blowing any loose trunks or branches out of the way, along with the closest guards. One of the branches that was removed had been attached to a row of gas grenades half buried under the surface. Some were pulled clear from the ground and were flung somewhere into the jungle, others did what they were meant to. Only the pins were pulled out with the branch, and they started leaking a green smoke.

Before the guards could pick themselves up from the floor, they were engulfed by the green fog, but it wasn't anything to impair their senses, or to occupy them long enough for the others to slip by. This smoke was designed to put anyone within its grasp to sleep, and that's exactly what it did.

Bypassing the smoke altogether, Alpha Three and Five approached the clearing, with only their handguns and Blindspot to protect them from however many remained at the sawmill.

They sat in the line of trees bordering the opening. Several guards rushed towards the explosion. Blindspot took them all down, one by one. Before the last guard had even hit the floor, Alpha Three and Five emerged from the trees, their handguns raised. The clearing was without guards, for now, at least. The door of the sawmill was wide open, with no one in sight. The sound of their heavy boots, however, told a different story. Alpha Five listened carefully to any noises coming from the building. He heard their boots stomping on hollow, wooden planks, no doubt putting people on some kind of mezzanine. He heard magazines pulled from rifles and inspected. He heard the pounding of computer keys, and the groan of some kind of hydraulic piston. Then, the sawmill became quieter still. Only heavy breathing remained.

"They're waiting for us," whispered Alpha Five. If he could hear them, they could no doubt hear him. "Plan twenty-two."

With that, they split. Alpha Five climbed on to a low stack of logs, then leapt up to the lower part of a ledge jutting out from the first floor. He pulled himself up to stand on the ledge, his toes hanging off the edge. Shimmying around the building, Alpha Five made it across, or rather over, the open doorway. He'd brushed some of the sawdust and mud, which had settled on the ledge, down to the ground. It had made them all the more tense but hadn't raised any suspicions. Once around the corner, he jumped down, bending his knees and allowing his hands to take just as much of the impact as his legs. He walked on another eight feet before approaching a side door. It was ajar enough for Alpha Five to have a quick look at his soon-to-be surroundings. Guards were scattered everywhere, high and low, most using pieces of timber for cover, but they were mainly obscured from the front door. Now all he had to do was wait.

Alpha Three seized his chance to move the second he'd lost sight of Alpha Five. He counted to thirty, then retrieved a smoke grenade from his vest. After pulling the pin out, he threw it into the sawmill, followed by another, then another. The smoke created a wall which eyes couldn't penetrate, but bullets could. He aimed his handgun round the corner and emptied the entire magazine. Bullets flew back, pounding the wooden doors and being absorbed by the jungle beyond them. Alpha Three continued firing whole magazines at a time until the smoke started to clear.

To the guards inside, all they could see through the dispersing fog was one final enemy, desperately firing a handgun. As the guards targeted the lone shooter, he turned and ran. They were winning, they had him on the run, but one thing they couldn't do was let him escape. If that happened, he'd be back.

The guards gave chase, their rifles aimed to take out the final enemy, but he'd already disappeared into the jungle. As they headed towards his last known location, some of them started to fall. There were flashes coming from between the trees. Then the enemy reappeared from the left, also returning fire. The guards took their own cover, but it was nothing compared to what they had in the sawmill. They could hear something behind them. One of their helicopters had started to make a noise. Some of the guards had obviously made it through to the airfield. The advantage was back in their favour. All they had to do was hold off the sniper.

The helicopter gained altitude and approached, swinging round to face the clearing side-on. There was nothing even the sniper could do to take cover from it. There was someone sat at one of the helicopter's side-mounted mini guns, ready to fire. If they'd been more focussed on them, they would've noticed the gunner was wearing jungle camouflage, the same as the enemy they'd chased away. As the mini gun spooled up, the unthinkable happened, not just for the guards on the ground, but also for the helicopter. A rocket emerged from the sawmill, making impact with the helicopter before the pilot could even react.

Alarms rang out in the cockpit, as smoke and fire engulfed the spinning helicopter. The guards in the sawmill had seen who was occupying their vehicle. They'd fired the rocket to take it down, but their actions didn't help. The helicopter continued to spin uncontrollably, unable to pick up altitude. Its rotor blade caught one of the trees, ripping it clean off. With nothing keeping it up, the helicopter tilted to its side and headed for the ground. The blades tried to chew the mud, but they were almost filed down by it. The last of the blades dragged the helicopter across the clearing until it finally stopped. The gunner was on the side facing up and leapt to the ground. Alpha Three quickly came to her aid. The pilot climbed up shortly after, rolling over the side and down. The guards had wanted to destroy the helicopter, and they'd succeeded, but the only things left in the clearing were the three assailants and a crumpled mess of a helicopter. Everyone else, who'd been there before, was now scattered across the floor of the clearing and the jungle.

It wasn't the planned signal for Alpha Five to move in, but it would have to do. As the remaining guards left the sawmill to finish off any survivors, Alpha Five pushed the door in and raised his handgun. The guards were without cover from his position and were easy pickings. He fired relentlessly, reloading his magazine with every twelve guards he brought down. A few were still on the mezzanine of the sawmill, but from their great vantage point, they could only see the others fall. By the time they knew what was happening, it was too late, and they were too few. A grenade was thrown up to the mezzanine, exploding and bringing it crashing down to the floor. A few guards rolled out of the way of the platform, but they were easy pickings for Alpha Five. In the space of just two minutes, a room full of guards went from having the advantage, to lying on the ground, either unconscious, or worse.

"We're clear!" shouted Alpha Five, after giving the building a final check for anyone who could've avoided him.

Alpha Three was the first to enter.

"Are they okay?"

"Yeah, Alpha Seven is tending to Four's wounds, and her own," said Alpha Three, "so the feigned retreat thing worked."

"Well, it worked for the Normans, even if it was an accident. Then again, they didn't have a helicopter crashing on to the field." Alpha Five moved over to a computer tucked in the corner.

"What is it?" asked Alpha Three.

"It's a computer," said Alpha Five.

"You know what I mean."

"Before we entered, someone was on this. I heard what sounded like a reinforced door close, and if I had to guess I'd say it's got something to do with that log pile. Bullets have been fired at it, grenades have exploded near it, and an entire upper floor has landed on it, and there isn't even a scratch to be seen."

Alpha Three moved over to it and tapped it with the butt of his gun. It sounded just like metal hitting metal.

With a couple of minutes of Alpha Five vigorously hitting the keyboard, the entire log pile lifted up. There was a trapdoor hidden under it.

"Is it just me, or is there a trapdoor everywhere we seem to go?" asked Alpha Three. "I mean, how many do you think we've missed?"

Alpha Five ignored him, "Are you three going to be okay?"

The sound of gunfire echoed through the hidden passage.

Blindspot had also arrived, but it was Alpha Seven who held her thumb up, with a bandage running between her other hand and her teeth, trying to wrap it around her upper arm.

Alpha Three and Five made their way down the steps under the fake log pile. "How do you think the others are getting on?"

***

*Nine Minutes Earlier*

Alpha One and Two hadn't made it more than a minute beyond the door when they started to inspect their rifles. The light might've been stronger on the other side of the door, but they didn't need it to know something was wrong.

"Is your rifle still working?" asked Alpha Two.

"No, some kind of EMP must've knocked out the palm print. They'll be locked for everyone now."

They both switched to their sidearms and continued. There were tight tunnels and wider corridors all mixed together but very few rooms. It was almost as if it was designed so any intruders would get lost. Although the ground was nothing more than mud, and the walls were lined with untreated wood, everything seemed clean and well looked after. The ground was as smooth as concrete, the walls free of any splinters. There didn't seem to be any dust or loose clumps of mud.

They opted to stay together, rather than split up. They'd covered many of the directions, with most splitting paths rejoining just a few metres on, but there hadn't been anything of interest. It wasn't until another five minutes had passed when they found a guarded room. There were only two guards stationed outside, stood sentry by its doors, but it was already their most promising lead. In unison, they both fired their handguns, and the guards slowly slid down the wall. Before they made it to the door, more guards came into earshot. The noise of them charging down the tunnels echoed throughout the system. They came into view, before either could find cover. Alpha One raised his handgun and fired, running forwards to the closest tunnel intersection. Alpha Two moved back to the tunnel they'd come from.

"We need more firepower!" shouted Alpha Two. "I'm going to go and get one of the rifles!"

The other guards opened fire, drowning out Alpha One, shouting to call him back. He didn't have long to see the guards, but he estimated about a dozen had come down the tunnels, and he'd only taken out one.

As the bullets flew, Alpha One removed the suppressor on his handgun. He knew Alpha Two would be able to pick out that specific noise amongst the other firearms, and if it stopped firing, he'd know to approach as if the guards had won.

Alpha One fired blindly around the next corner, emptying his entire magazine. He heard a guard fall, but only one. They continued to close in, the noise of gunfire still echoing throughout the tunnel. But if he was going to win, seemingly on his own, he'd need them to get closer, a lot closer.

Soon, even the guards ceased firing, hoping one of them might've got a lucky shot. Their boots slowly crept closer, approaching Alpha One who, unbeknownst to them, was waiting. A rifle emerged round the corner, swinging to face him. Alpha One caught it with his left hand and fired a single shot with his right. He then pushed the guard out and used him for cover against the next wave of bullets. He continued to fire at the guards, taking out any who moved from cover, but they were too spaced out for him to remove them all, not in the tunnel at least. The room he was heading for was only a couple of metres away. It was the next place with any kind of protection. He pushed the guard on, now firing to suppress the others, allowing him to move further up. The doorway was close enough and he pushed the dead guard forwards to move through it, but as he pushed the guard down, another moved out of cover to fire.

Alpha One dispatched him with the last bullet in his gun, but not before the guard got a shot off. It was a lucky shot, no doubt, but it found its mark. The bullet slipped between the dead guard's right arm and waist and managed to embed itself in Alpha One's lower right wrist. He dropped his handgun as he fell into the room. It was lying on the floor, but before he could reach to grab it, another bullet blew it even further away.

The pain in his wrist might've been a concern, but the greater one was how he was going to remove the rest of the guards. He counted another seven were left. His best chance was to hold them off until Alpha Two arrived.

Another guard came around the corner. Alpha One did the same as before, holding the rifle away from himself. He raised his knee to catch the guard's torso. The guard lost his grip on the rifle as they both fell further into the room. A second guard emerged in the doorway, aiming towards Alpha One. Alpha One locked himself together with the nearest guard, making it almost impossible to shoot one without hitting the other, but he couldn't take advantage of the fight; if it ever looked like he was winning, the guard in the doorway would surely fire at them both.

He allowed the closest guard to take control of the fight, as the man climbed on top of him and clamped his hands down on Alpha One's neck. He watched the door, waiting for Alpha Two, and just as the last of the air in his lungs was used up, the guard in the doorway turned away, taking several bullets in the chest straight after. This was all Alpha One needed. He raised his legs and pushed the guard up, stretching his grip. Kicking his legs out, they became untangled. Alpha One gasped for air, as the guard went to make another move, but he saw Alpha Two move into the doorway, still firing at the others and still aware of what was happening in the room. He threw his own handgun inside. Alpha One rolled out of the way, as the guard charged forwards to make a tackle. He caught the gun with his left hand, rolled over on to his right side and fired every bullet in the clip at the guard. All the bullets hit the guard at the centre of mass.

Alpha One lay on the ground for a few more seconds, catching his breath, until Alpha Two came further into the room. The gunfire was over. He helped Alpha One to his feet, as they both moved over to the table taking up most of the room.

"Upstairs is clear," said Alpha Five, as both he and Alpha Three joined them from the other side.

There were six chairs surrounding the table, and in one, at the head of the table, a body was sat slumped over. His head hung over his chest, and his chest leant towards the table. Alpha Two moved over to him and pushed him back, so he sat upright.

"It's Grenham. He's dead," said Alpha Two. He pulled down the collar of the dead man's T-shirt and saw a thick rim of blue bruises around his neck. "It looks like there's been a change of leadership."

Alpha One saw a scrap of paper in the centre of the table. He picked it up and examined it. The paper was full of zeros and ones.

"It's binary," said Alpha Five over his shoulder.

"Is it the antidote?" asked Alpha Three.

They turned to Alpha Five. He raised his shoulders. "There's no way of finding out until they test it, but if we get it to the surface, I can upload it and at least see what it says."

"Alright, I'll go with you. You two, secure the tunnel," said Alpha One, holding his wrist.

They left the room.

"Head further down the tunnel, I'll wrap up here," said Alpha Two. Then, he was alone.

He'd let no more than a minute pass until stretching down to Grenham's hand. It was clasped around a tape recorder. At first, Alpha Two thought maybe it was recording them, but it wasn't recording anything.

Daniel listened for any footsteps approaching, then hit play.

"Daniel, I'll keep this as brief as possible, but will start by saying this is probably best listened to alone." The voice was Kale's. "I usually prefer pen and paper, but sometimes you have to move with the times. I'm extremely glad you decided to come, assuming you're not listening to this ten years in the future. Unless you're listening not for the first time, I mean, maybe you're listening to me in a time I no longer reside in. Does that mean I'm eternal? Sorry, I know I said I'd keep this brief, but I'm going to go on the assumption that you're listening to me for the first time, before anyone has died or made a full recovery from the poison, but I'm sure you are, because you and I really aren't that dissimilar. I'm also going to assume the others have taken the binary note upstairs, a little touch I'm very pleased with. I take it you've found my predecessor? It was unfortunate… Actually, no it wasn't. I took great pleasure in what I did and I can honestly say that the world is a safer place because of it. Together, we will do good in this world, by any means necessary… I've got to admit, I'm finding all this modern technology a bit of a hindrance. I mean, if this was paper, I'd just throw this message away and write, *I look forward to working with you further*. But in all seriousness, I'm glad you're here, and I think you should know, I've put my whole reputation on the line for you. Please don't disappoint." The recording ended with a click.

Daniel took in a deep breath, closed his eyes, and exhaled. He let the recording device slip from his hand and stamped his boot down on it. Then, Daniel simply left the room.

***

Alpha One and Five climbed the stairs and entered the sawmill. Alpha Five moved straight over to the computer with the note in hand. The keys were almost pushed down into the computer itself he was typing so quickly.

"It's a list of chemicals, drugs, quantities. I mean, we've got penicillin, magnesium, glucagon, the list goes on," said Alpha Five. "I'd say it looks genuine, but whether it'll work, there's no way of knowing, until they administer it, anyway. They'll know the kind of poison so should at least know whether this is likely to work. I can send it to every hospital in the world, with clear instructions for what it is. I can't promise they'll use it, but given the tight timeline, I'd say they probably will."

"But if it doesn't work, it'll be too late," added Alpha One.

Alpha Five nodded his head. "What's the call?"

Alpha One looked around at his team. He then looked down to his watch, showing just eight minutes to three.

"How long will it take to mass-produce?"

"Looking at the list, I'd say most hospitals would already have the drugs and chemicals stored, but to produce enough for everyone? You're probably looking at five hours at least," said Alpha Five.

Alpha One let a lungful of air leave his chest.

"I don't think we have a choice."

# Epilogue – The Echo of the Beginning

13th September

17:52 BST

2 hrs 21 min. Until Deadline


Kale's helicopter soared over the top of a green and dense rainforest. It was a perfectly normal model, if you take normal to have a luxury interior with a minibar and even a bed which could fold down from the wall. However, it had no armoured modifications, it was just one of the most high-end helicopters on the market. The rain poured down on to the highest trees, to then fall from their leaves to drip on to the next layer, and on to the next, and the next to finally make its way to the forest floor. It rained most days, just as Kale remembered, unlikely to be dry for more than a fortnight over the whole year. Yet, this was the first time it had rained in over three weeks. It had come out of nowhere, being sunny just half an hour prior.

His helicopter was heading for a tiny opening in the trees. It was angled, almost like a tunnel, so it was invisible to any drone or satellite images. In fact, if you flew past it, you'd just think that was the way the trees had grown there. The helicopter squeezed through the perfectly maintained gap and followed it to the ground. From inside, the sound was that of the classical music Kale was listening to through the various speakers, but from the outside, there was enough noise to make animals within a one-mile radius turn their heads. Of course, if anyone did hear them, they'd have no idea where the sound came from after echoing throughout the jungle.

The helicopter gently touched the ground and brought its blades to a stop. Kale waited until that particular piece of music had concluded. There were no guards patrolling the grounds or checking in the new arrival, the trees and nearby animals were all the protection they needed to keep out any unwelcome guests.

Kale gracefully stepped down from the helicopter and made his way over to the hidden trapdoor. Much like the forest floor, it was covered in a thick blanket of brown leaves, fallen branches, and the tiniest of trees pushing out from the ground, but Kale knew better than to put his hands amongst what would no doubt be a living forest floor. He raised his hand to the pilot. Seconds later, the trapdoor started to rise from the ground, revealing a set of steps underneath it. Kale entered the dimly lit staircase, and the door was sealed shut behind him.

The staircase went down about ten metres, but the smell hit Kale instantly. The smell he remembered all too well the last time he was there, the smell of death. But as he'd found out, the smell was nothing more than a mix of chemicals pumped around the ventilation system, a technique he couldn't deny was effective. He doubted whether anyone had actually died in the place, but he knew for the prisoners there, that wouldn't be what they thought.

As he reached the bottom, the long corridors of the prison came into view. The entire place wasn't any more than thirty metres square, but the hive of corridors and tight turns made it seem much bigger, and helped to disorientate the prisoners whilst they were being moved. Kale approached one of the scientists working there. He was holding a clipboard, wore a long, white coat, and was clean-shaven with pristinely kept grey hair on his head. He turned and saw Kale.

"Welcome back." He fell silent. "Or… Or… Welcome for the first time, Sir." He smiled a little, but Kale kept a blank expression. "I understand you've taken over this facility from Grenham, so allow me to give you a tour. Well, I suppose you know the layout already... Because you, obviously, would have read up on it before coming here and would know it for no other reason that I can think of," he shouted, making his attempts to backtrack obvious. "I would just like to say that when you were kept here, which was appalling by the way, I wasn't working here."

"The prisoners," said Kale, still showing no emotion.

"Yes, the prisoners. Well, all four arrived about six months ago. Grenham wished for us to use similar tactics as were used on you and your men, but we had decided to do some preparation work first. We've used sedatives to disorientate them, before we will start working on their minds. They don't know who they're sat next to. However, as of yet, we haven't moved past the preliminary stage, so is there anything you would like us to do differently?"

"That method never effectively worked on me, or my men, and weakening their minds beforehand won't make enough of a difference. This must be permanent. It's time for a new approach." Kale then held up a small vial. "I've had this developed from numerous scientists, specialising in every aspect. There are more on the way, but as I'm here, I wish to see the first test with my own eyes."

The scientist took the vial and handed it to another person, dressed as an armed guard, and whispered something in his ear.

"If you'd like to follow me," he said, directing Kale down one of the many corridors. "May I ask, why is Grenham no longer working here?"

"Because his services were no longer required," answered Kale, deliberately keeping his answer short.

The scientist swallowed hard and asked, "What will this drug do?"

"We will both have the answer to that question after this test, but it should alter the chemicals released by the brain.

Among many other things, it will increase the fear they are currently in. We will leave them in a state of fear until we are ready to proceed. Then all we need to do is coincide the reduction in fear with setting eyes on me, resulting in a natural instinct of trusting me."

"You make it sound far simpler than it actually is. We don't even know if it'll work," said the scientist.

"Well, that is the purpose of tests, is it not? To test what works and what doesn't, then to refine your work. It won't be long before we can alter the allegiances of anyone. Much of our research was obtained from The Vesper after his death, but it will be me who finishes his work. There will be no more moles, no more unfaithfulness, and no more failure. We are all counting on you, so don't waste your usefulness; for your sake, and for Fellscient's. But don't misunderstand me, this is a test and mistakes are acceptable. What I want most from these prisoners isn't just for their allegiances to change. If it doesn't work this time, there is always another chance. No, what I want most from them, is for them to be rescued."

***

He wasn't sure how long he'd been there, nor where 'here' was. He didn't know who was with him, and he didn't even know how he got there. The last thing he remembered was crashing, he died, or at least should have. The plane exploded with him in, but he was never there. Maybe he was dead, at least that explained his memory before being dragged to the chair he'd been fastened to twenty-three hours of every day since. There was a bag over his head, and a gag across his mouth. There were three other people in the room, but they couldn't communicate either. In fact, the other three were taken away regularly, but it seemed to do them no good, they came back unable to walk most of the time.

However, today was different for two reasons. One of them, he would never know, the other was that for the first time, it was him who was taken, not one of the other three. His wrists were cut free and he was pulled to his feet. Thanks to the hour's daily exercise, his legs still worked, but they lagged behind the guards escorting him. Being dragged half the way, he was taken to an isolated room where the bag over his head was removed. Although it was dark and dingy, the light racing into his eyes almost burnt.

He could just about see one the guards approaching with something in his hand. Then, he felt a sharp stab in his neck. At first, nothing happened, but eventually, something did change. He could feel his heart rate increase, pounding the inside of his chest. Since he'd been taken, he'd been confused, filled with a range of emotions, and had plenty of time to work on numerous plans to escape, but all of a sudden, he started to feel scared. The plans he'd made were instantly brushed aside, sure to fail. The guard stood in front of him looked more menacing than any he'd ever seen, but as quickly as it came, the feeling drifted away. He was again filled with confusion, more so than before. Now, he couldn't understand why he'd felt that way. Things that felt so trivial now were like nightmares only seconds ago.

***

"Was that everything you hoped for?" asked the scientist stood with Kale behind a two-way mirror.

They'd been watching the test from there and had seen streams of data on the numerous laptops. It had all been obtained with the sensors that had been placed all over his body when he'd first arrived.

"No, but as I said, this is how we will refine it. It'll be stronger and last for longer. It will work. For now, though, I wish for you to use the entirety of the M-K-1 batch that'll arrive tomorrow. Use it on all four of them and see who it affects the most. A chain is only as strong as its weakest link and that will be how we find it. Carry on, doctor," concluded Kale, as he turned and left the room.

Waiting in the corridor, just outside the room, was Green Viper. His mask still covered what was left of his face.

"Thank you, for your work outside the bank and streamlining the guards at this compound. I take it you told Alpha team everything you were suppose to?" asked Kale.

Green Viper nodded. "Yes, they think you wanted them to leave with the antidote."

"Good." Kale started to leave. "And I must congratulate you on that remarkable shot. When I saw the footage, I could hardly believe my eyes."

"And what of our arrangement?"

"It still stands. I know Grenham mistreated you, but rest assured, I will not. And you can tell Hailey that she will have whatever resources are required for project one-six-six-five, as well as my eternal respect, so long as I continue to get the same in return."

Kale didn't wait for a reply, as he continued down the corridor.

Before he was even outside, he started to make a call. As the phone was dialling, he pressed a large, red button on the wall, halfway up the staircase. The trapdoor once again opened and Kale emerged back into the jungle. The phone went through four ring cycles before it was answered.

"Has it been done?" asked the person on the other end.

"It has. The results showed some promise. By the end of the year, I expect we will be able to roll it out," replied Kale.

"Good. As you have some free time, I have another job for you."

"Name it," said Kale, stepping back into his helicopter.

"Grenham's secretary. I have become suspicious of her. Grenham was far too short-sighted to see it, but I am sure you will not be. Keep an eye on her. I would like to know everyone she is in contact with and who all of her associates are. Some may even be in the rest of Grenham's… or your, spy network."

Kale looked down to a second phone in his hand, this one showing a news headline. It read *'First patients on road to recovery, but where did the cure come from?'*.

"Very well, I may even ask Daniel if he will assist me." He signalled for the pilot to take off by pressing a small, green button on a console panel to his right.

"I hope bringing Daniel into our family will not cause any problems."

"It won't, you have my word."

The call was ended by the person on the other end. Kale didn't need to tell the pilot where to go, as soon as the helicopter was clear of the jungle, it would fly South to the nearest runway. From there, he would head back to Grenham's old office and move in, before starting his investigation on Tria.

As the helicopter left through the same narrow passage between the trees, Kale sat back and made the most of his own thoughts. Classical music started playing through the speakers again. He was as calm as he'd ever been. Kale closed his eyes and allowed his mind to wander along with the gentle music.

*Thank you. Thank you for getting to the end and thank you for giving this book a go in the first place. At the time of publishing this novel, the first had sold copies in the hundreds, which is far beyond what I'd expected. Hopefully you've just read a book that you loved and wished hadn't ended. Hopefully you've had as much fun reading it, as I've had writing it, because if I'm being honest, there were moments in this story that even I didn't see coming.*

*But I do have one more favour to ask. I'd love to hear what you thought of it. I'd love to know what you liked, what you didn't. Because it isn't just going to help the next reader in deciding whether or not to pick this book up, but it'll help me to hopefully make the next one better, maybe even to the dizzy heights of a coveted five-star review. And if you're eager to read more, why not check out the first in this series, if you haven't already.*

*Carol and Charles' adventure continues
in the next Silent Codename spinoff.*

**COMING SOON**

www.ingramcontent.com/pod-product-compliance
Lightning Source LLC
Chambersburg PA
CBHW051119190726
48290CB00006B/1606